American Daughters

American Daughters

A NOVEL

PIPER HUGULEY

WILLIAM MORROW
An Imprint of HarperCollins*Publishers*

AMERICAN DAUGHTERS. Copyright © 2024 by Piper Huguley. All rights reserved. Printed in the United States of America. No part of this book may be used or reproduced in any manner whatsoever without written permission except in the case of brief quotations embodied in critical articles and reviews. For information, address HarperCollins Publishers, 195 Broadway, New York, NY 10007.

HarperCollins books may be purchased for educational, business, or sales promotional use. For information, please email the Special Markets Department at SPsales@harpercollins.com.

FIRST EDITION

Designed by Diahann Sturge

Library of Congress Cataloging-in-Publication Data has been applied for.

ISBN 978-0-06-327370-2

24 25 26 27 28 LBC 5 4 3 2 1

*To the women who are at the point of making change
in their lives, but are still hesitating: Do it.*

Good Daughters

Portia

The egg I had for breakfast this morning didn't taste rotten, but these days, it was not always easy to know about the state of the food one ate because of the many ways merchants could mask spoiled food. *Dear God, please don't let me be bilious in public.* I swallowed hard, harder, not wanting to draw attention or suffer the humiliation of being ill in public. I could not leave the hotel mezzanine and miss Father as he greeted the president. I sat next to some large potted palms, enjoying, for once, the feeling of invisibility, of not being seen or noticed. Of not being in the spotlight as Booker T. Washington's only daughter.

My plain clothing helped me, just a plain white shirtwaist and a long dove-gray skirt. My only embellishment was my bandbox hat, which had a black-and-white stripe around the crown. It remained firmly perched upon my head, despite my nervous state, as I folded my hands, looking down into the lobby of the student union building, watching the activity below as if I were in a nickelodeon, anticipating seeing my father after his speech in the nearby auditorium.

Ever since the Atlanta Exposition six years before, Father had gotten more and more invitations to speak about the condition of the Negro in the United States to the point where he was viewed as the leader of our people and had been consulted by many elected officials regarding the position of the Negro in their towns. Father's latest conquest had been the new president of the United States, Mr. Theodore Roosevelt, who had just come into the office after poor President McKinley had been shot by a crazy man. To show his growing influence, Mr. Roosevelt had invited Father to dinner at the White House, the first Negro to come through the front door as an invited guest.

One week ago, that invite made me, a special student at Wellesley College, so happy. One week ago, I was so proud. My dear father was friends with the president, almost an equal to him.

Except.

I took in a ragged breath at the memory and my current ill situation. Would that I could close my eyes to the news, but that had never been possible for me. I had always insisted on being fully informed. Unfortunately.

America—or better said, white America—was not yet ready, more than thirty years after the emancipation of enslaved people, to have a Negro dine openly at the White House with the president. No one, not even the horrified press, could be soothed that Father, with those gray eyes of his, had half-white heritage. His father, my grandfather, whoever he was, was whispered to have been a member of the legendary First Families of Virginia, the FFV, those white people who had settled the Virginia wilderness in the wake of Jamestown in 1619. After all, Father's middle name was Taliaferro—an FFV name.

The problem came from his other half, from the bloodline of the Negro cook and washerwoman known simply as Janey, my dearly beloved and adoring grandmother whom I had never met. She would have never dreamed her son would reach the heights of sitting down to dinner with the president of the United States.

I shut my mind's eye to the portrayals of him in the newspapers. So many ugly cartoons. Those hateful portrayals didn't even look like my father but showed him committing all kinds of acts of indecency of theft, of improper decorum, of rude behavior, with a caricature of him, the nationally known, stately, happily married educator trying to have his way with Roosevelt's oldest daughter. My father, the epitome of a Victorian gentleman, could never, would never, commit such an unspeakable act. I slowed my breath, breathing out of my mouth, just under a whistle, since whistling would have been rude.

So now, it was wonderful happenstance that the schedules of these two famous men would overlap just one week later here at Yale. I leaned forward, staring down at my father fretting with the rim of his top hat, circling it in his hands, waiting, waiting, waiting on his new friend, the president of the United States, who was due to come through there on his way to the auditorium for his speech.

Then, the whirlwind better known as President Theodore Roosevelt walked into the lobby, surrounded by a cadre of other white men, who all had very stern looks on their faces. Father stepped out toward his friend, hand extended, and . . .

And . . .

And?

And.

The president passed my father right by without any kind of look, acknowledgment, or awareness of him as a human being.

I blinked. As if that would help me clear my eyes from what I had just seen. I couldn't let it register in my mind that Father, my father, the most famous man of the race in the world, had been treated in such a way by the president of the United States.

What could it all have meant? A wave of shame washed over me and I chewed on a fingertip of my glove. I thought I might have enjoyed meeting the new president with his young family after the presidency of the sad, staid McKinleys came to such a shocking end.

A strange sour taste seeped into my mouth. I recognized the taste as the precursor to illness. It was too late for the bathroom. I turned to the palm tree next to me and all the sick went right onto the poor plant's roots.

"Hello?"

A voice, slightly husky but friendly, reached through the palm

leaves from the other side, which were sharp so she carefully parted
them. When she did, I could see the speaker, a beautiful young
woman who wore an outrageous, even for 1901, lavender hat with
a curious-looking lavender bird peeping through netting, tilt her
head toward me.

"Me?" I swallowed my gorge, not wanting to be sick again in front
of a strange white woman.

"Yes. Are you Portia Washington?"

"I've done nothing wrong." My words came quickly, lest this
young woman tell me that I had no business being there. Yes, we
were in the North in New England, not back home in the South
where, as a Negro woman, I might have been more harshly questioned for being in such a fancy building. I closed my eyes.

"Oh no. I didn't think you had. I was told to keep a look out for
you, and now here you are, ill. Are you all right?"

"Yes." Even though I was not. Who was this woman? Why
wouldn't she leave me alone in my distress? I had a right to be
here.

"What did the poor palm plant ever do to deserve that fate, Miss
Washington?" Her impossibly blue eyes were merry, but I gulped.
The poor plant certainly did not deserve that fate. She covered her
mouth with a gloved hand, laughing a little, and produced a delicate
hankie, holding it out to me. I did not want to take it—it did not look
as if it were purposeful—but I took it anyway, dabbing at my mouth.

She stared at me, then made a beckoning gesture. "Come with me.
I'll take you to my room. You need to recover from your episode."

I shook my head no. "I'll be fine. Thank you, anyway." I looked
down at the hankie in my hand inscribed with the initials ALR. *ALR?*

She shook her head too. "No, you don't understand. Father told
me to come look for you. I'm Alice. Alice Roosevelt. Your father told
my father about you and I came to find you. Come on."

This . . . young woman was the president's daughter.

"Come away from that poor plant. You don't want to be around when it keels over and dies."

In spite of myself, I laughed and she did too. I stood to follow her, the president's daughter. I held out the hankie and she waved a hand. "I have many others."

"Alice? I thought the president's daughter was named Ethel." I came around from the far side of the potted plants and she came around on the other and met me in the front of the forest.

"There." Alice straightened. "She is. Ethel is my younger sister. I mean. All the bunnies are my younger siblings. But I came first. From Father's first marriage. Which is why people forget to mention me. I'm the unwelcome extra."

I turned to her and in that instant, a web of connection knit itself between us. I knew what that was like, as a fellow unwelcome extra. "As did I. I came first from my father's first marriage too."

"Well, isn't that something. I bet you've never heard of me because..."

"My father didn't mention you to me."

"I wasn't at the White House when your father was there. No matter what those horrid cartoonists drew. I've been with my other family ... sort of on a vacation."

Alice knew what had happened. She must keep up with the news, which was really intriguing. Women didn't, or we weren't supposed to, care about such things. Still, something about what she said made me wonder, because it was October. "Didn't the First Family move into the President's House just last month?"

Her shoulders slumped. "Oh, okay. I admit it. I was banished."

"You were?"

"Yes. Edith, my darling stepmother, didn't want me to come to the President's House. Can you imagine? I have just as much right to be there as anyone else, but they are afraid that I'll misbehave."

I eyed the lovely young woman. "Misbehave? How old are you? Eighteen? Like me?"

She raised an eyebrow. "I'm seventeen, I'll be eighteen in February. I know how to behave, and yet I'm treated like a pariah. I objected. So I made sure to come out when Father came up here to New England and I'll go back to DC with him. She cannot keep me from living with my father."

The instant connection I felt with her, another first daughter, meant I was rooting for her already. "Now that you mention it, I think I do remember hearing of you when your father was vice president."

"That's better, yes. And you do look like him." She inclined her head toward the space in the lobby where my father had been.

I narrowed my eyes and looked for Theodore Roosevelt in the face of Alice. She shook her head.

"No. I don't look like Papa. No point in looking. I'm a walking ghost for all anyone knows. My mother died practically on the day that I was born."

"Oh dear. I'm sorry."

"Now you are apologizing. Why?"

That cord of connection connecting the two of us strengthened "I also know what it's like to be a walking ghost. I was a few months old when my mother died." I stepped backward after I told her the information that I was so used to keeping to myself. Information that I did not share with just anyone. "Then I lost the only other mother I had ever known from that point when I was six."

"Two ghost mothers? I didn't think anyone could have bested my poor story, but I think you just have. We'll have tea in my suite to help your stomach and compare ghost stories."

I would like that, except: "I'm not sure of what to do. I need to meet up with my father."

"We can get a messenger to tell him where you are. I usually love to hear the speeches, but you aren't feeling well and I've never met anyone who has bested me in the ghost department. I've heard my father lots of times anyway, haven't you?"

True. Resting somewhere close by, away from the foul smell of my sickness, sounded wonderful.

"Just stay with me. We'll go back to my suite. Don't worry." Alice lifted a hand, as if she were summoning someone. "They'll think you are my maid and won't bother you."

No doubt that this was also true.

I followed her quick pace, gripping at my stomach with my hand. I wanted to come with her, this new person whom I already shared a tie with. Yet something held me back.

Why did Alice's words sting with the same hurt as my witness of my father's humiliation?

Alice

October 1901

When your father is one of the greatest big-game hunters of all time, he tells a certain kind of bedtime story, the adventurous bold kind, whether you like them or not. I never got bedtime stories from him when I was small but got them instead once the bunnies, my brothers and sister, came along. When they did, this is what he would say:

When a male lion comes upon a pride, he fights the male lions who protect that pride so that he may take over that group of fetching females. But it is the females only he wants. Any cubs, any of them that are not his, he murders. Thus, now that the cubs are now dead, this sets about a change in the lionesses so that they welcome the advances of the new male lion, who, as the primary male lion, will not stop mating with her until she is full of his seed.

Oh, what a jolly time my father had telling this story to his children when they were young. The bunnies would squirm and squeal with delight at these horrible exploits of the terrible fierce lions. My brothers would set about, growling and pacing on the ground with delight, while little Ethel would cozy up to her mother, not willing to play lioness.

Who could blame her? I surely did not.

I would stand apart from it all and watch, not a bunny, not a beloved, just a mere observer with no real role in this happy little family scene, and wonder to myself:

Is there no story for when those lionesses die? The males have no

*one to create a new pride with. The cubs must be left behind to starve,
silently, slowly, to thin away and die. Who takes care of them?*

No one.

Certainly not the male lion. He's off on a new adventure, always in
search of that pride that has the female he wants and desires. Those
cubs are not a thought to him. Whether they are his or not.

That's who I am. The lone cub, with no mother, and no real father.
Left behind.

So why shouldn't I do whatever the hell I want?

MOST OF WHAT I remember about my father is him rushing, running, rising to go somewhere. Away from me. Always in the opposite
direction. Which is a natural reaction one would have, I suppose, to
a ghost.

For that is what I am. A ghost of my mother. Even our names are
the same. Alice Lee Roosevelt. Which is one reason why I am eager
to marry to change it.

Every single person in my circle has sought to try to make up to
me that I'm a ghost. Well. All except Father. And his wife. My stepmother. Well, my mother now, Edith. She's the only mother I'm ever
going to know so I might as well claim her.

Except that I look like my mother, the one who died giving birth
to me, the woman who managed to hook Papa away from "dear
mother" while he was off attending Harvard and broke them up. So
her initial reactions to me have always been to, well, replace me in
his imagination.

She finally succeeded in giving him a girl, my little sister, Ethel,
who is really blameless in all this. But I know what Edith's motive
was. And, to be honest, it pretty much worked.

So ever since Ethel was born, my sole motive in life is to make
Papa see that I exist. That I'm not a ghost. I'm me. I'm as far away
from Mother Alice as anyone can ever be.

Sometimes it works.

Other times. It does not.

Only once I saw Portia did it ever occur to me that there were other things in life that I could be doing that would be better than playing my game of "Father, look at me."

She was royal in her appearance, something I had never seen in anyone else. Especially not a Negro. Everything in life said that Negroes were as far from royalty as anyone could be, but not Portia. The way she held her head was so polished, so balanced. It was clear that this was someone who had never, not once, hung her head in slavery, so different from her father in the way he looked after my father had given him the cut direct. It was the look, the thing my Southern grandmother told my aunt was referred to as Negroes knowing their place. So after we spoke, I couldn't help but invite her to come to my suite. "We can speak in private there. I can have tea brought to us."

Her large eyes looked around us, unsure of what to do. "My papa. He'll be looking for me."

I made a gesture and Father's secretary came to my side. "Please send Mr. Washington a note. Let him know that I have taken his daughter, Portia, to my suite to entertain her and will ensure her safe return to their hotel for dinner."

Mr. Jackson withdrew from my side quickly, and I was happy to see it. Finally someone was beginning to understand my new position as first daughter. A qualm of sadness washed over me. Well, there was Ethel but she was too young to enjoy any position of influence. The recently departed McKinleys had two daughters but they died.

Girls born for their fathers are born for good luck.

Why was there so much death involved in the climb to the presidency?

I knew whenever Papa would look at me, he thought of death. There was no better way to lift that from his shoulders than to live,

live loud, live large, live as though no one could control you, but just live. He did it, going to lead those Rough Riders or to ranch after the first Alice died. But he didn't think I was entitled to live. So instead, he would look at me, or over me, push up his pince-nez, as he wondered aloud: "Why can you not behave?"

With no name. Since he could not say the A word.

I would mimic him, even though I had no problem seeing him, for I had not ruined my eyesight reading as he had as a child. "Papa. If you could tell me the point in behaving, then I'll better understand what you wish me to do."

His comments were always code for sending me away. So he would not have to look at me and see ghost Alice. He would turn around and let Mother know that I needed to make yet another lengthy visit to Aunt Bye or to my Lee family. To prevent embarrassment. Or to forget me. It was always hard to tell which one.

Now, it was easy to lead this young woman to the hotel where we were staying, up the elevator to my suite, and to sweep in past the Irish maid who waited there. I gestured widely to a chair in the corner and Portia went to it, but she stopped and looked at it. I motioned again. "Please. Have a seat. The tea will be here shortly."

I turned to the maid and gave her one of my looks.

She opened her mouth, just a fraction, and I narrowed my eyes more. She closed it and went out of the room.

Portia sat on the edge of the chair. I sat in another, across the room and across the wide table from her, and collapsed.

"Is it not a curse being a woman?" I spoke aloud to her.

"I suppose I've never given it a moment's thought."

"Well, I have. I have thought about it a lot and decided that I've been cursed. I would have much rather been a man."

"Because?" Her gray eyes fixed me with a quizzical look.

I sat up and gave her one right back. "Do you think being born a boy would have made your father happier with you?"

"Oh no. He's much pleased with me as I am."

Well, not all of us can say that.

"I imagine. If I had been born a boy, though, my father would have taken me ranching with him."

The door swung wide open and the maid came in, bearing a large silver tray with a hot pot of tea and a platter of food balanced on it. She placed it on the large oak table between us. Picking up a cup and saucer, she poured for me, putting in my usual slash of milk and a squeeze of lemon. She handed it off to me and, with a saucy curtsy, turned and walked out. "And where might you be going?"

"I'll not pour for that one." She inclined her head toward Portia whose eyes barely changed, but I noticed blinked in quick double time at this slight.

"How dare you?" I set down my saucer on the table.

"Ma'am. I know the rules and you do as well."

"Well, blast the rules." I leaned forward with my hands on my knees.

The maid's eyes went wide at my swear, but this was just the re-action I was aiming for.

"Get out, you. I'll pour."

Portia stood, but I gestured to her to sit. The maid retreated and I stood, reaching for the teacup. "What would you like?"

"A lump of sugar and a squeeze of lemon." I fixed the tea for her and held out the cup. "Sip it slowly. Something sweet might help you. There are some nice little cakes and tea cookies." My hand itched to reach for one, but I knew it was not wise for me to have one, lest my figure balloon outward. I sighed and had a cucumber sandwich instead.

Portia took her tea and came forward, selecting one cake. She went back to her chair and sat down more comfortably.

I nodded at her comfort. That was better. Then I shook my head.

"I'm sorry for my swearing but I wanted her to know that I meant business."

"I don't want you to get into trouble."

"Getting into trouble is what I do best. Don't worry. Please. Eat."

The sounds of us drinking our tea filled the room, but it was a companionable noise, not at all uncomfortable.

Portia had the fine art of not making a sound when she sipped her tea, something that had always been hard for me. So difficult not to slurp.

She now asked me, "Why do you think your father would have taken you if you were a boy?"

"He would have made a papoose of me. Raised me up to be a ranch hand. I do not understand why he didn't anyway. I could have done well enough to be a girl ranch hand."

"Well, I wish you could come to Alabama with me. Father believes in women knowing how to do it all. I've done my share of working in the model farm and it gives me no pleasure. Still, I'm glad that he did it, for it gave me great insight into his struggles when he was a boy."

"Oh yes. As a young slave. He would have had quite a struggle then."

Portia gave me a slight smile, one that stopped right at the corners of her mouth. "I'm always grateful that his journey to prominence has meant that my own life and those of many others in my race have been made so much easier. So I seek to always make him proud. And to make his heart easy."

I almost spit out my tea, for being slightly too hot and at the very thought. "My father? An easy heart? From me? Dear me. I'm only coming to Washington, DC, now because he's been afraid I'll make a show of myself in the great White House. He forgets that I was there twice before, once when we visited Harrison and the other time with the McKinleys."

"Well, would you?"

"Would I what?"

"Make a show of yourself?"

I shook my head and went at my tea again. "Not on purpose. But there are times when I feel I cannot help it."

"What could you possibly do to get him to see you differently?"

"Do? What do you mean what could I do?"

"I am in school." Portia sipped without sound again. "Not that it is a pleasing time, but I am studying. I have been through the program already at Tuskegee and it was too easy a program. So I've been sent to Wellesley to get more learning. It's been hard. Hard enough, that I feel as if I need a break."

"A break?" Apparently I'm not the only one capable of being exiled.

"Self-imposed. It's not easy since there aren't many who look like me there."

I held up a hand. "I can only imagine. Those horrible bluestockings are probably jealous that you're smart and pretty too."

"Thank you. In spite of my current difficulty in school, I am hoping to become a teacher."

"That's splendid. Imagine that. Having an occupation. I have no occupation. I'm meant to be an ornament."

Portia's winglike eyebrows met in her forehead. "Is that something that someone aspires to be?"

"Excuse me?"

"I mean, when you were little, that's what you wanted to be?"

"Of course not. I wanted to be a ranch hand. I wanted to go with my father to the Wild West and be with him in the Rough Riders."

She swallowed her bite of cake. "Oh."

"Yes. Oh. Exactly. So, since I cannot have what I want, I'll be an ornament."

"It seems as if there ought to be another choice."

"Not for me. Not for the single upper-class daughter of a rich prominent man like my father."

"It really gives me something to think about. From the cradle, I was taught—no, made—to think of my life as one of purpose. That I had to select something to do and make sure to uplift the race. For the most part, that is education or medicine."

"A doctor? Or even better, maybe you'll take the reins of Tuskegee from your father when he is no longer able to run it." *Imagine that!* No, actually I couldn't, but that sounded grand to me.

Portia coughed a bit, retrieving a fresh hankie from her reticule. "My goodness."

I could see her point. The thought of Portia in such a way made me blink my own eyes of China blue. "I should be proud to know a woman doctor or a principal."

"I could never do such a thing, even though we have had a woman doctor on our campus. Father hired Dr. Dillon, I mean, Dr. Johnson, who was my doctor as a child."

"See there! What an example to our sex! Why not?" And once again. Here I am. Asking why not.

"I don't like the sight of blood. Not even my own." Portia coughed delicately. I knew what she meant.

"It brings to mind that dear Dr. Johnson passed away earlier this year. In childbirth." She quieted and I could completely understand. The bond that we shared of women passing away in their prime from childbed loomed large in our lives.

"So instead, I need more training to be a different kind of teacher than what Tuskegee produces. A music teacher."

"Oh dear. That doesn't sound very exciting." It didn't have to be a doctor, but a boring music teacher? But then I was not musically inclined myself, so it would not excite me in the least.

"It is to me. No one in my family has ever been a music teacher before."

I waved my hand. "No. I mean, it's not an occupation that will, well, ruffle or upset anyone."

Portia nodded. "Precisely. I don't want to upset anyone. I look forward to teaching others the joy and pleasure of musicianship until I have a husband and children of my own."

"Well, don't rush it. We are only eighteen and seventeen." Was that Sword of Damocles hanging over my head? Marriage? Husband? I intended to enjoy these years of being an ornament in my father's care. "Well, it means you know music and there is a piano in the next room." I put down my tea and rubbed my hands together. "I do like a good coon song. Will you sing some?"

Portia stopped sipping at her tea and put down her teacup with a clatter. Her gray eyes, once calm and placid, were now stormy and strange. Well, at least things were about to get more exciting.

Just as I liked it.

Portia

October 1901

I've had this question before. But it always came when I was prepared for it. I was not prepared for this question in the middle of finishing off one of the best cakes I had ever had. They were much better than the ones at school. The rich fondant practically stuck to my teeth. I took a sip of the hot tea to melt it off and to help me think of what to say to the daughter of the president of the United States.

Think.

Think.

Think.

I'm not a coon so I don't play coon songs.

How dare you?

Do I look as if I play in brothels to you, Alice?

"That one by Ernest Hogan is great. What's it called?"

As if I would know. But looking at her, in her blue eyes, with the smooth porcelain skin we are all supposed to desire, with the face and features of the textbook perfect Gibson girl, she did not mean to offend. She wanted to know.

So here was my chance.

"I'm trained in classical music. I don't have any familiarity with *those* kinds of songs." I made sure to put my emphasis where it belonged so that she understood.

All Negroes are not coons. Sigh.

Her shoulders, set so high, went down by the merest fraction. "Oh. The boring stuff."

I put the teacup down so that I didn't smash it. "I don't think of the greats as boring."

"I didn't mean to offend you. I just was putting it forward that the music, I mean the real music of today, is so much . . ." She moved back and forth a little bit. "Peppier."

"I can do peppy."

We both stood and she extended her arm. "This way then."

I entered the next room and there, in the corner, was a pianoforte. I lifted the lid and blew a bit of the dust off it. I tested a few notes and it took all that was within me not to cringe. I lifted the top lid and reached in to tune it, making it better and more endurable, for my sake, not for hers.

"I should ask Father if they have one of those player pianos at the White House. Have you ever seen one?"

I nodded. They were awful, intended to put piano players out of work, but this was not a time to say that.

"They almost always play coon songs. And ragtime."

I kept up my tuning, with my tongue clenched firmly between my teeth, an old childhood habit I never broke whenever things got too tough for me.

There.

I lowered the lid and brushed a little of the dust off me. "Now." I sat down at the stool in front of it and ran a few scales before I launched into "Moonlight Sonata."

Beethoven was my favorite great and this piece, albeit one of his gloomier songs, was one of my best pieces. I longed to go to Bonn, where he was born and raised, to study in his homeland. I never put my words into a form that my father would readily agree to. I knew he was much consumed with the school and keeping it afloat. I would never dare to bother him with my requests. What was the point of educating a Negro woman in such a way? It was a move that was set up to disappointment. At least, that's what my mother, whom I think of as Margaret in my mind, had said to me once when I mentioned in an offhand way that I wanted to study in Germany.

"What is wrong with you, Portia?" she had said in her pinched voice. " Your selfishness knows no bounds."

"I don't see why it is selfish."

"You don't? Look at how your father's shoulders slump at the end of the day when he comes back to the Oaks and tell me it isn't selfish. He carries the entire race upon his shoulders and you want to flit off to Germany."

I tried not to think of it, but it was true. There was no reason for me to say anything. And yet . . .

I found my fingers moving to a different medley, one that might be more pleasing to Alice. Not a coon song, not ragtime, but still, the music, the amazing music of my people. The spiritual.

This song was the one that I had soothed myself with for so many times when I was young, especially after Margaret scolded me about something.

Sometimes I feel like a motherless child
Sometimes I feel like a motherless child
Sometimes I feel like a motherless child
A long ways from home
A long ways from home
True believer
A long ways from home
A long ways from home
Sometimes I feel like I'm almos' gone
Sometimes I feel like I'm almos' gone
Sometimes I feel like I'm almos' gone
Way up in de heab'nly land
Way up in de heab'nly land
True believer

Way up in de heab'nly land
Way up in de heab'nly land
Sometimes I feel like a motherless child
Sometimes I feel like a motherless child
Sometimes I feel like a motherless child
A long ways from home
There's praying everywhere

My fingers trailed off at the end. I placed them in my lap. There had been days when I would cry while I sang and played it, but it had comforted me so many times; it was rather like my little brother Ernest, whom we called Dave, and his comfort blankie. It soothed me.

I twirled on the stool and saw Alice sitting up on the small fainting couch across the room, staring at me.

"I'm sorry," I felt moved to say. "Sometimes, I get wrapped up in what I'm singing and I'm . . . transported."

"You have a lot of talent. I just never knew, or realized . . . My goodness."

"I like those better than coon songs, to be honest. The music of the Jubilees."

"I have seen the Jubilees performed before, in Boston with my aunt. With everyone crying. I never cried, though. Although, I will admit it, the music always made me think of my grandmother."

"Your grandmother?"

"Yes. She lived in Georgia and they say that she loved to hear the slaves singing such songs from the quarters. But she also died on the day that I was born. I never knew her. So I've a ghost mother and grandmother."

Twice over? Oh my. How terrible.

But one might look at my predicament and think the same. The death of my birth mother and my replacement mama within such a short span. How could it be endured? I blinked and her eyes seemed to show a different side. Something beyond being an ornament. A world-weary sorrow. And then, it occurred to me. If Alice carried this burden, then what of her father?

A loud knock at the door disturbed my reverie and made Alice jump up. "Only one person in the world knocks like that," she murmured under her breath and went to answer herself, and a wind swept in.

Or more accurately, a hurricane blustered in and I heard the voice boom from the parlor. "Well, at least you are in here, behaving yourself more appropriately."

"Father, the most wonderful music . . . Bedroom . . . Portia . . ."

Alice's voice, low compared to her father's, made me panic and I slammed the lid down on the keys and stood up.

Before I could exit the room, or hide in the closets, they were both there, instantly, before me. The president of the United States and his irrepressible daughter. "Hello there." His voice boomed out and he stepped forward. "You must be Portia."

I curtsied. They both laughed. Alice stood with her arm through her father's broad arm.

"Well, now. Alice says you play quite the piano. Isn't that wonderful?"

I looked between the both of them. "You don't mind me being here?"

"Of course not! How else is she to have music when she wants? As they say, 'Music hath charms to soothe the savage breast,' and no one needs more soothing than Alice here—who really can be a beast when she wants to be! I'm of a mind to hear some music myself! I love that coon song 'All Coons Look Alike to Me.'"

"That's the one I was trying to think of, Father."

"Yes." The president looked delighted with himself for remembering the horrid song title and here I was, back at square one again.

"Do you know that one?" Their eager faces made my heart sink.

I couldn't give the president of the United States the same response as I gave his daughter. What could I say?

I sat down again at the piano and ran a scale up and down the keys. Ready to play the offensive song. Of course I knew it. All the young people of my age did. But knowing it and playing it were two different things.

"Oh my, yes. I love that I'm about to hear some good music."

There was a knock at the door. Again. I breathed a sigh of relief. I took my hand from the keys to see the Roosevelts looking at each other. "Who could that be at your door, Alice? Have you already come up with a suitor here in New England? Some young man dying of love for you?"

"No, Father. I'm as mystified as you are."

"Well, then. I'll make use of myself to see who dares knock upon my daughter's door." The president stood and went into the other room once more.

I wiped my hands down my skirt. Maybe I had enough playing for today.

It was a male voice, and Alice and I looked at each other.

I stood and went back out to the outer room and there, in the doorway, was my father. This time, TR did not look displeased to see him, but instead, acted as if they were old friends.

"You tracked me down here, did you, Washington?"

My father, gentleman that he was, had the good grace to look uncomfortable. "I was told that my daughter was here in your daughter's rooms. Perhaps I should have sent someone else."

"Your daughter? What could you mean by that?"

I stepped forward to avoid a misunderstanding. "Mr. President. My name is Portia Washington. I'm the daughter of Booker T. Washington."

"You told me to look out for her, Father," Alice put in.

He looked between us, our gray eyes as much of a connection

between the two of us as his blue eyes were with Alice. "The piano player? Ah. Is your daughter?"

We both nodded. "I'll get my wrap, Father."

The president held up his hand. "Well, now wait. I was about to hear some good music. We can sit out here in the parlor and hear the music that your daughter will play. What of that, Washington? Do you like coon songs, too?"

My father saw me, as he often only did, bless him, give the slightest shake of my head and he turned full on to face the president. "Ah, sir. My daughter has been gently raised. Portia doesn't know much of that kind of music. But I know she will be able to play something that you'll like. Maybe some of the old home songs of the South, perhaps?"

Both gentlemen made their way into the parlor. My father sat down in the chair where I had been and the president sat across from him, reaching over his bulk for another one of the cakes.

"Father!" Alice exclaimed.

"Your mother isn't here. We won't tell her, eh?" His white teeth chomped down on the cake and took it all in one swallow.

Alice winked at him, and they both laughed. "Go ahead, Portia. Play us something," she suggested.

My father looked at me and nodded his head.

Alone, I went back to the piano and started to play some of the old spiritual music, songs that were sung to me in the cradle, one right after the other. When appropriate, I sang some of them. I didn't consider myself the best vocalist, but I could do well enough when called upon, as I was called upon now, playing and singing to entertain and soothe the savage breast of the president of the United States of America.

Or maybe he truly was a beast.

Alice

October 1901

That afternoon was the first time I acted as hostess for my father, with all my skills as an ornament come to the fore. I reordered fresh tea for Mr. Washington and my father as both men sat in my parlor, relaxed and calm, speaking of political matters and refreshing themselves after their speeches.

Of course, I could do this. My trip to Washington City, to start my crusade to find the right husband to be an ornament for, would work well. There was no need to be jealous of Portia and her goals, her skill, or her beauty. I could be happy for a new connection and still do what I needed to find myself a husband.

Within the hour, Portia came in, taking a break from her lovely playing, home songs, as Mr. Washington called them, and classical music of the Germans, something that she specialized in and was studying at school. When she came in the room, Mr. Washington stood, and his gray eyes, clearly of European heritage, glowed with warmth and pride. How fortunate Portia was to have made her father proud and for him to have seen her, really look at her with such appreciation. Mr. Washington boomed out, "We had better go. Thank you for the tea and the talk, Mr. President."

Now my father and I stood and he spoke for us. "An unexpected pleasure, Mr. Washington. Miss Washington. These times when I'm able to relax in such a way are few and far between these days. So thank you both."

I extended my arm to show them both toward the door. I pushed a small folded paper at Portia. "I hope you'll write," I whispered to her as our fathers said goodbye to each other.

"If you wish." Her hand shook a little as she took the paper, upon which I had foolishly written the address of the Executive Mansion. Who did not know it? Still, I didn't want her to think that I wasn't interested in continuing this connection. It would be most interesting to have a Negro friend, even as our fathers had been in such terrible trouble over their dinner last week.

Once they left my room, my father closed my door and faced me, his eyes certainly of a different nature than Mr. Washington's toward his daughter. I breathed in deeply. I should have known he was putting on.

"I told you to look out for the girl, but when did you get it in your mind to invite a young Negro girl to your rooms, Alice?"

"Today. Obviously, Papa."

He stomped back into my parlor, probably intent on having more of the cakes that Mama wouldn't let him have. I sat back in my appointed chair.

"Look. You have to be careful, Alice. You have no idea how the newspapers took stripes to me for having Mr. Washington in the mansion last week."

"I saw all that, Father. I love to keep up with politics in the papers."

"Well, maybe you didn't see the cartoonist who drew the panel that showed Mr. Washington with his hand up your dress?"

I shook my head. "Pure foolishness. I wasn't even there. I don't understand why people don't have anything else they can do."

"That's not the point. The point is that I don't want you to have to take such stripes as I did."

I stood and came next to him. "Portia is perfectly lovely, and her father is the epitome of a Victorian gentleman. Why should we not have a nice afternoon with them both? Even you admitted that my entertaining and hostessing was relaxing."

"For once," he grumbled, and I gave him a kiss on his red cheek, which then got even redder.

I pulled back from him and tilted my head. "I don't understand it. Why do we have to hide from the public that we can speak with Negroes as well as anyone else?"

"I don't know why, Alice, but we must. When you are in the White House, the name I came up with for our new home, the eye of the public will be intent upon you and you must act accordingly." He put a finger on my shoulder. "Be wary, Alice. That's all I'm asking. Take care. If she is to be your friend, you must keep it secret." He laid his finger on his lips.

I did the same.

"I know of your propensity to rebel, but in this, you must let me take the lead. I intend," he whispered, as if there were people in the room to actually hear us, "I intend to keep Mr. Washington as a contact. I am president of the Negroes as well as anyone else."

"And Negroes do vote, Father."

"Yes. Some of them do. They may not be in regular practice of it, but they do."

"And since they do, women should also, Father."

He jumped away from me, a little shocked. "Alice. Please."

I giggled a little. "I have to try since I have the ear of the president, Father. It was just a little joke."

"Thank the Lord." He straightened back up and adjusted his pince-nez. "Back to my suite of rooms I go. Please be ready early in the morning for our trip back on the train. And behave in the meantime."

"I will, Father." Maybe.

The maid came back in as my father left and, scowling, cleaned up the remains of the tea. Such a good day would be a good omen to my entrée into Washington, DC, society.

Oh, HOW WRONG I was. Father was determined to keep me on a short leash the next morning, as he and I boarded his special car to take the train back to the capital city, with an entire phalanx of reporters who greeted us as we went to the train station.

Thank goodness I had paid the right kind of attention to myself, fully corseted up in one of my light blue dresses with my bird hat on, ready to greet the day.

"What do you think about going to Washington, DC, Miss Roosevelt?"

I opened my mouth but Father was on top of it. "My Alice is happy to be coming home to the White House. She's eager to see her brothers and sister and mother."

"Will you attend school, Miss Roosevelt?" another asked.

I turned to the questioner, fixed him with a smile, opened my mouth, and . . .

My father said, "Alice is not concerned with academic study. She will be the first president's daughter to make her debut in the White House, once the period of mourning for President McKinley has come to an end."

Every single reporter made a note on that one, so happy that he gave them a tidbit of something, even though it stirred me just a bit. I'm not a political figure, so why should they care? Still, it did warm my heart a bit to hear that I would be making some kind of history in the White House and I hadn't even gotten there yet.

My father ushered me into the warm train car, where a spread of breakfast awaited us inside on a table. There was a desk fixed in the corner for my father to work, of course, and a davenport across from the table for me to sit and pester him to death as we traveled, no doubt. I did bring my book, so I would try to behave.

I fixed myself a plate, never one to be a shy eater, especially not of breakfast, and tucked into the warm plate of an egg over easy, ham, toast with jam, and a cup of tea. We ate in silence as the train jerked out of the station, not at all sick at the motion going over the tracks. Roosevelts were much hardier than that, for the most part.

I wiped my lips free of toast crumbs and jam. "Father. Perhaps you should let me speak to the reporters. I can do it, you know."

He stood, straightening his jacket, ready to get back to work, ringing the bell for them to come and clear the dirty dishes away. "I'm well aware of that. But remember what your mother wants."

I never got this kind of one-on-one time with him. So maybe I should ask. Maybe I should say the forbidden. Her name. So I did. Because I wanted to know something about her. "Alice Lee mother? Or Edith mother?"

At that exact moment, two men came into our compartment and cleaned away the dishes, quickly backing out of the atmosphere of tension that I had created. On purpose.

"I mean your mother. The one who is living."

I knew that's who he meant. I just wanted to see what he looked like when I mentioned her. "The other is my mother just as much," I whispered.

"Of course she is. But she . . . Well, she isn't here to want anything for you."

"What did she want for me, Father?"

He turned from me, moving to the desk, shuffling papers about. "What we want for you, both of us, is to keep your name clear from the papers."

"Ah. Mother Edith's edict of a woman's name only being in the papers upon birth, marriage, and death?"

"Yes."

"Well, didn't your little announcement destroy that a little bit?"

"No. A young woman's debut is the beginning of the marriage season. It's good that people know. After the holidays, in the new year, is when."

"Well, I certainly hope that I will have better apparel than at the inauguration. That dress was hideous. I might have been wearing a sign that said, 'I am young.'"

Father sat down in the chair provided for the desk, gripping his knees, a sure sign that I was trying his patience. "That's because you were young five years ago, Sister. And as the then vice president's daughter, it would not have done for you to show yourself as if you were ready for marriage. Now that's changed."

"Because you are the president? As I wished?"

"Sister." He lowered his head, looking at me, but he couldn't help a little smile playing around under his mustache.

I brought forth my book. "You cannot deny it, Father. It was all my doing. I cast my spells and changed your office." I lifted my hand, as if there was a wand in it, and made the sign of the cross in the air toward him. "You're welcome."

I gave him my most impish smile. Would he look at me? Through me?

"I mean, wasn't it something to show those ones who put you in to be vice president to keep you quiet? Ha! Look at you now. All because of me."

"Well, I suppose you'll do. Now, how about you cast your spell about Washington, DC, for a suitable husband, eh?"

He turned from me to his work on the desk, as I knew he would. No looks for me. Or the saying of my name. Our name. Well. I supposed I couldn't have expected it, not since I went to the place that was forbidden—mention of my mother. It would have been too much for him. And I shouldn't have put him in a vulnerable place now that he was the nation's leader. Still, there was that spot, deep within me, the place full of questions that wanted to know, the place that insisted on poking through the thick veil of secrets between us.

"I will, Father. I'm sure there will be someone out there rich enough who will be willing to take me off your hands for a fair price."

His chuckle resonated across the room to me as I cracked open my book, but I was being completely serious. He did not know that the book that I had brought with me to read on my trip was Mr. Washington's own book *Up from Slavery* that had gotten so much positive attention this year. They had obtained a copy for me at the front desk of the hotel when I requested it.

Another perk of being the president's daughter.

So many in New York had spoken well about how he depicted his life as a young man who had done much to lift himself from the peculiar institution that I knew I was bound to pick up a few tips from him regarding how someone might seek liberation.

Washington, DC, would be the place I would set myself free.

I couldn't wait.

Portia

November 1901

The options for a young woman of the race are not great.

There aren't many like me who go to college, especially one like Wellesley with those questionable cows who called me Marsh, short for my middle name of Marshall, instead of Portia. They insisted that no Negro should have ever been named after Shakespeare's most beautiful heroine. I needed to come away from that, so I went back to Alabama with my father for a little self-imposed break from the breathtaking horrors of being ignored and mistreated at the finest school for young ladies of quality in this country.

As I told Alice, the other choice was medicine, but I cannot stand the sight of blood, not even my own when I have my not-so-friendly visitor each month. I remember when the visitor came upon me and there was no one around, save for Margaret, the woman who had married my father when I was nine, to help me.

"Well, now," she had said. "It begins. Stay away from men if you want to avoid bringing shame to your father and to Tuskegee." And that was that.

The coming of my womanhood made me miss my mothers even more than I already had. How would they have ushered in this time for me? I liked to close my eyes and imagine a warm hug. A cup of tea. Soothing words with love in them. Things that I would have to learn to do for myself. Things Margaret would never do for me.

I could teach. Follow in Margaret's footsteps. Which did not sound appealing, but if I thought about it, my mothers were also teachers so I could follow in theirs instead. And learn the lesson of staying away from men—one of the handful of wise things Margaret ever said.

So I came home from Wellesley. While I was there, contemplating my next move, I resolved to do some good and organize a choir. Now that the hard work of establishing the school was in the past, Tuskegee was at the point where, in the cool of the evening, there could be some fun, like having music sings. The music sings would help me figure out who could sing the old soothing spiritual songs from our ancestral past, the ones my father loved and that I resolved would never be forgotten. While I was home, I would conduct sing-alongs, with an eye to forming a choir that might tour the country and sing spirituals to raise money for my father's ever impoverished school. Even I, as his oldest child and only daughter, understood—our all must go to Tuskegee.

The downside of coming home, defeated by Wellesley, meant staying in the Oaks where Margaret presided, I mean resided, with my father, but the bother of her was worth the journey. Besides, my brothers were also there and they provided a great buffer between the highly charged female energy of the two of us.

Since I was coming in during the term, I missed the hiring of new teachers, the entire phalanx of them who were eager to come to Tuskegee to serve under the auspices of my famous father. But now since I was one, on a temporary basis, I was required to attend teaching meetings. Since I loved my father, I didn't mind watching all the others fall all over him in awe. However, there was one of them who held himself off a little to the back, with a slight smile pulling at his lips, amused at the ceremony of the teachers fawning over my father.

His hair was parted and combed back into sleek submission on either side of his well-shaped head, and his mustache was also neatly waxed and tamed. His skin, smooth and supple looking, was a pleasant tan shade and his eyes, alert and sparkling, surveyed the carrying on with a little look of amusement.

And then, those light eyes met mine.

The amusement that had quirked about his lips disappeared and something else, something more alluring, more sinister, came about them. Why did I notice his lips were large, yes, Negro large, pleasingly plump, and slightly slick just below his waxed mustache?

Those are singing lips.

Yes, that's what it was. He looked as if he might be able to form the words to the Negro spirituals that I would teach the student choir. It would be beneficial to have another teacher to help with the students.

Calm down.

But a new feeling, one that stirred around in my loins, beckoned me like an age-old song, to make music with my body in a way that I had never imagined, told me something new.

You are a liar.

The gaze between us pulled like an invisible hook, and whatever force it was compelled me to cross the room to him, moving me to him, walking over to him to stand before him, so that I could inspect those lips up close and to see all of him.

Every part of him.

So he could see all of me.

There I stood, right in front of him in my usual white shirtwaist and dark skirt, wishing that I looked better, prettier, more attractive somehow.

Once I came closer to him, closer to his presence, I could see he was not as tall as I initially thought. But what he didn't have in height, he more than made up for in his broad shoulders and arms, those muscular arms that seemed to be fairly bursting from his suit.

Then he spoke and my body ceased functioning in that moment.

Well, not really, since I didn't die, but it was a kind of death. A death of one part of my life for another.

"Good day, Miss Portia."

Live the new life.

My eyelids fluttered rapidly, as if to cool the warm room in the August temperatures. "You know my name?"

He stepped one step closer to me to minimize the distance between us. "Who would not know the only daughter of the great Booker T. Washington? Why, you are the very image of him."

Girls born for their fathers are born for good luck.

The old saying resonated in my head. It was not the first time someone had said that to me, but it was the first time I was disappointed to hear it. As handsome as my father was, I did not want to be regarded by this man as handsome. "I am?"

"Yes. But of course, with appropriate female adjustment." Then his eyes, those intense eyes, made a casual sweep of my entire being. The new feeling grasped at my inner core and I quivered in a way I knew was unseemly.

Some training, I don't know if it came from my scattered youth or what, took control. "You have the advantage of me, sir. I do not know you and we have not been introduced."

He reached out and picked up my hand, which had been hanging in limp shock at my side, and pressed his lips, those lips, to the back of it. "I apologize. You're correct and I should not have been so bold as to speak to you until we were properly introduced to each other."

Lips.

"I'm Portia." What kind of fool was I for repeating my name, because hadn't he said it already? Oh dear.

He laughed a little bit, more amusement tumbling out of him as naturally as a scale.

"And I . . ." I started to say, but a familiar voice, the one my ear had been long attuned to, turned so naturally to, approached us. Saving me as he always did.

Father.

"Portia. Have you met William Pittman yet? I meant to make introductions, but of course other matters were more pressing."

As was always the case. "Thank you, Father," I said, feeling a little more at ease. Now I could speak to him. "I was just looking for someone to do so, so you came along at just the right time."

"I see," Father said. Mr. Pittman was still holding my hand from having kissed it. He let it go, and it slipped from his heated hold, bouncing against my skirt, as if it had no life.

"Mr. Pittman, this is my daughter and eldest child, Miss Portia Marshall Washington."

"How do you do?" Mr. Pittman smoothed his mustache ends down and I cleared my throat a little to calm myself since Father was there.

"Pleased to meet you, Mr. Pittman."

"Well, good," Father said. "Time to start the meeting. I'll see you in a few minutes, my dear."

And off he went. I never knew any part of my father so well as I knew the back of him.

It should have surprised me a bit that he so willingly relinquished me to Mr. Pittman's attention, but I was of the age when I should be thinking of marriage. My father, every inch the proper Victorian gentleman, just wanted to make sure things were set off on the right road but once they were, there was no need for him to supervise, I supposed.

"Do you sing, Mr. Pittman?"

"Sing?"

"Music. Songs."

"I've never given it any thought, to be perfectly honest."

My heart sank. Not think about music? Was there something

wrong with this handsome man? Was he going to not turn out to be a good connection in my life? What kind of gray world must he live in?

Unless . . . it was God's intent that *I* bring him music. Color. Happiness.

"Well. I've the charge of the sing-alongs this year."

"You? Are you sure you could do that?"

"It's what I've trained in, Mr. Pittman." I would not be distracted by his handsomeness. I had worked too hard and suffered from too many Wellesley girl insults to not stand up for my training.

He drew back a little. "I apologize. I did not mean to demean you. I'm just impressed."

I drew in a deep breath. That was better.

"Well, I invite you to audition. I'm here to make something of it and I need singers. Or if not, then another teacher to help organize the students."

"I would love to be of assistance to you, Miss Washington. In some way, even if singing is far away from my training as an architect, I'm willing to try."

This man, one of our race, was an architect?

Well.

I smoothed down my skirt with sweaty hands. "I appreciate that, Mr. Pittman." Out of the corner of my eye I could see my father preparing to take the dais that was set up at the end of the room. "Good day, sir."

"Wait. Let's sit together as we listen to your father's speech."

He spread out his arm to the seating area right up front of the entire assembly of new teachers.

He was an architect and he was not afraid to sit in front of everyone with Booker T. Washington's daughter.

My goodness. William Pittman was a different kind of man, for sure.

I followed where he pointed and I sat down to my father's left and Mr. Pittman sat next to me, with the other teachers prepared to hear my father's words of wisdom.

My mind wandered. After all, I had heard Father speak this opening many times before. This was a first time for all of them.

I was too acutely aware of the energy that fairly radiated from this man. How he had settled in the chair, comfortable in his skin, arms threatening to burst forth from his suit jacket sleeves and the way he would give me an occasional side glance.

And smile.

Reshaping those lips of his.

In that moment, it struck me. *This is what Mother Margaret wanted me to stay away from.* I understood her warnings, because I was drawn in as natural a way as a bee goes to pollen.

Stay away from men, she had said.

Why? My brothers were growing up as men and my father was a great man. Surely the acquaintance of someone like Mr. Pittman could mean me no harm.

This was so natural, how could it be dangerous? Still, now I saw what it was, the gray intensity that enticed my mother to my father. What had enticed my other mother to my father. What had enticed Margaret to my father, heaven forbid, even though I tried to stop that in every way my nine-year-old sensibility allowed.

Here I was, nearly ten years later and I still was as innocent as I was then.

That would have to change.

Immediately.

Portia

November 1901

Nothing was so suitable for an evening's entertainment back then as a sing-along. The other reason why I eagerly agreed to take them up was because of how deeply I believed in the need to carry on the songs of our people—the spiritual songs and not the cakewalk ones that people sang in mockery of the larger, lighter population. We had our own art. We did not need to mock theirs.

After dinner on Sundays was all mine. On the Sunday sing-along I held, I was a little stunned to realize that a good percentage of the student body deigned to show up at my little rehearsal at the chapel. There had to be a hundred students there.

My goodness.

When I went up front, I did my best to gather the attention of the young people, but clearly, by the way they arranged themselves, two by two like Noah's Ark, the similar energy of enticement conducted between myself and Mr. Pittman was present. The air was filled with the heady scent of . . . I didn't know what to call it, but I could not make heads or tails of whether or not it was very respectful to the ancestors whose creativity had crafted the songs we were about to sing.

"Excuse me!" I stood on my tiptoes and projected my voice outward, but I might as well have been speaking in the middle of a Boston city street.

A loud piercing whistle sounded out next to me and there he was: the source of the whistle. Mr. Pittman. Every young person in the room, dressed in the utterly bland, respectable uniform clothing as per Tuskegee rule, stilled and looked forward at us.

"Thank you." I smoothed down my skirt at the quiet. And at his nearby presence.

"You're welcome."

"I'm Miss Washington. I need for you all to rearrange yourself accordingly. This is not courtship mayhem time. We have to arrange ourselves by sound, not by someone you might have fond feelings for."

Most of them viewed me with skepticism, jaws dropped, mouths open, eyes narrowed as if in disbelief.

I stood in the midpoint of the church sanctuary. "Young ladies to my right, young men to my left."

Then protests really began in earnest. I shook my head. "If you want to come to sing-along, this is how it is."

Mr. Pittman, standing at my right, whistled again. "You all heard Miss Washington. Please rearrange yourselves accordingly or I will start handing out demerits."

None of them wanted those punishments, so after a minute or five of shuffling, the young people were appropriately sorted out.

I wanted to thank him again, but I did not want him to think that I could not handle my assignment. Word would get back to Father and then what? I arranged myself at the piano and began to play scales, directing them to follow. Mr. Pittman sat in a chair off to the side of the piano and just as I suspected, his voice sounded a fine baritone, and the deep, thrilling sound of it threatened to distract me.

I didn't let it because I had a job to do. By the time the session was over, and people rearranged themselves into Noah's Ark pairs to walk back to the dormitories, the time had been fruitful and I was pleased.

When the last ones left, I turned to Mr. Pittman and shut the cover on the piano. "Thank you so much for your help. I appreciated it."

"You're welcome. I'm happy to help every week if need be."

"Well, your voice would certainly be needed. The sound of it was quite pleasing."

"It is? Thank you very much, Miss Washington. I found singing quite relaxing after a busy week. Do you mind if I walk you back to the Oaks?"

"Oh, yes. That would be nice."

Fortunately, the Reverend Quincy hovered at the door, so I was free to leave as I knew he would close up the church building. He smiled at both of us, wishing us both a good evening, and our pairing ventured into the chill of the November evening.

"You have a lot of talent, Miss Washington."

"I'm hoping to obtain some additional training after I finish college."

"Training?"

I lowered my head. "Yes. I want to go to Germany to study with the masters."

"That's quite far."

"It is. Father doesn't want me to go so far alone. I need to figure out who would be my chaperone so that I can study and not worry about anyone approaching me for marriage just yet."

"Marriage?"

I turned to face him. "Well, I'm not yet nineteen. I wish for a husband and children but not quite yet." The examples of my mothers and Dr. Johnson loomed large before me. I did not want to be a ghost before my time, before I had a chance to, well, live. But I did not know this man that well, so I could not tell him my experience.

"Why not?"

Instead I said, "My father deeply believes that a woman should have a vocation and I need time to develop mine. If he didn't, why do you suppose he would spend so much time educating young women just as he educates the young men here at Tuskegee?"

"Good point. I was just of the mind that someone as pretty as you should have someone to take care of her."

I smiled, the first time I can recall doing such since I walked past this part of the campus. For the campus cemetery faced the chapel and my mothers were buried there. I had long felt comfort whenever I passed their graves, in the same row. Both of them, almost side by side, watching over me.

I spoke the words I knew they would want me to say. "Women of the race have much to do to help with the uplift of our people. It's just a question of what. I would not be my father's daughter if I were content to remain at home as some man's ornament."

He nodded. "I completely understand."

"I'm glad you do." *Whew.* I didn't want to have to rule him out as a future friend, or anything else, if he had the wrong understanding of what I needed to do with my life.

"You are more like your stepmother than you are different."

I whipped around to face him. "Too many say that, and it makes me feel as if I have a flaw that I must correct in myself to avoid the comparison."

He shook his head. "All I meant was that she is very busy here on the campus seeing to the correct administration of so much. She manages to be married to your father, helps caretake, teaches, and works in the community with wives and mothers."

I could see his point. But he did not know her as I did. It was best to remain silent on the subject, for now.

"All my mothers were women who had education and who worked."

"A plural usage?"

"Why, yes. My own mother who carried me in her womb died when I was nearly a year old. Then my father married again and the woman I remember as my mother, Olivia Davidson, passed away when I was but a child. They both were teachers and worked to bring Tuskegee to reality."

He nodded. "I see what you mean. Your father believed that of his own wives."

"Yes, he did. It makes sense that he would encourage it in me."

"How long is your vocation supposed to last, Miss Washington?"

I shrugged my shoulders. "I don't see why it needs to end upon marriage."

"Are you going to return here to teach after you are finished with your college and Germany?"

I blinked. "Honestly, I had not thought that far out in terms of my plans."

We walked up the hill with the Oaks in sight. "I think that you should. It would be a good idea to think about the future."

"I enjoy planning, Mr. Pittman, but isn't there a point when you need to be prepared for whatever comes your way? As a woman with a vocation and a purpose?"

"I think that's a wonderful idea. But what if you had someone who wanted you to be ready, really ready, for marriage? What then?"

I looked at my father's house, all alight in the November darkness, with the moon shining overhead. We had so many homes over the years. It was the goodness of Mr. Andrew Carnegie that permitted the commissioning of this house, for enlisting a Negro architect to have this house built, and for my father to be comfortable. "It's good that I have the leisure of time to consider these things."

"I am a few years older than you are and in a different position." His light eyes were intent on me in the darkness.

"Well then, Mr. Pittman. I beg you to think carefully about that difference in our ages and apply it to where you were at my age. Were you ready to take a wife then?"

"Good point well made."

I laughed a little. "I hope you are not offended, sir."

"I'm not." He reached over and grabbed my hand, bending over and kissing the back of it with those lips of his. They were soft, with just the right amount of wetness, thank goodness, and caressed my hand with a firm intent.

"Not at all, Miss Portia Washington. I completely understand your perspective."

A shaft of light emerged in the dusk. Parted curtains. Nosy Margaret. Could she see me out here with Mr. Pittman? The curtain closed and the shaft of light went away. It would make her so happy if I found a husband. I well recalled her saying that I needed "a man of my own," probably because she seemed to see me as if I competed with her for a place in my father's heart. Which was ludicrous, but typical for Margaret.

No, she would not mind if I stayed a bit longer on the Oaks courting porch.

I showed Mr. Pittman where to sit and there we sat side by side in the moonlight. As we talked over the songs we sang that night, and he shared with me that "Ain't-a That Good News" was his favorite, his hand snaked across the space between us on the bench. I could feel his heat radiating close to my body, almost as if he was asking me a silent question.

I wanted to answer him. I really did. But some force held me back and it wasn't for the first time in my life that I wondered: Was it the hand of one of my mothers? Were they watching me right now with this strange older man, sitting on this porch that was created for just this purpose, visiting with someone who might be more than a friend in the future?

Margaret's whiny tone reached out to us through a slightly opened window. "Well, Portia. It seems as if you are keeping Mr. Pittman so late out here. There is school tomorrow. And you've offered him no refreshment."

His warmth retreated from me, seemingly embarrassed to be caught in the middle of something naughty by the Lady Principal. That was Margaret's title on campus and everyone used it. With capital letters as they spoke it.

"I've no need, ma'am. I'm on my way back to the boardinghouse."

Just as they had built almost all the buildings on campus as part of the curriculum, the students had built the teaching dormitories just a way down the road, toward the town of Tuskegee, but still nestled within the circumference of campus. Father had created an oasis for everyone who was part of the campus community. An oasis of student-built safety on a former plantation site that was just over twenty years old, but never failed to impress visitors. The oasis still reminded me of Father's intent: to make sure the teachers had access to the town, but not so much access that they faced the ills of the outside world.

As I had at Wellesley.

"Are you sure, Mr. Pittman?" Margaret now came outside and folded her hands over her middle where they rested. Like claws.

"I'm certain. I'll be leaving now."

"Well, you are always welcome. Isn't he, Portia?"

I stood, not able to lie, even if I were goaded on by my father's wife. "Of course."

He nodded, making his way to the steps, and walked off into the twilight of the evening.

"A very handsome man," Margaret said the precise moment he was out of earshot. "An educated man with good manners. You could do far worse, Portia."

"I'm not of marrying age yet."

"But you will be. You don't want to be a financial burden on your father any longer than necessary."

"I'm organizing a choir."

Margaret fixed me with a look. "That is not a job that is essential to campus operations. He created it for you so that you had something to do for when you return to your college and wait."

"Wait?"

"Why, for your husband, of course."

"I'm not in a hurry to get married." *Not like you were. Since no one else would have you.* I bit my lips so that I didn't speak the unkind words. I didn't want to disturb my father's peace. Without reason.

Margaret turned to me. "Of course. But really. You don't want to wait too long. A catch like Mr. Pittman all alone on a campus full of accomplished and beautiful young women. Well."

"My plans are to go to Germany after college to study, you know that."

"Yes. Such an expense. And the school always has a need. Do you really think it's a good idea to pursue that path when the money could be put to a more fruitful use?" She stepped back and nodded. "You know what your father would want. Make a careful selection, dear."

She swept into the house, trailing dignified clouds of Lady Principal glory. As she always did.

I opened my mouth to give her an answer, but I sat on the bench there just a little bit longer. My life seemed to fork off into two different directions in that moment. Which one would my mothers want? Father?

And most of all, me?

Portia

November–December 1901

Dear Portia,

I was pleased to hear about the success of your sing-alongs at the school. How soon do you think they will become permanent and then a choir? I cannot begin to imagine how much work that will be for you. But it's a wonderful thing that you are there, not with the horrible bluestockings, and your father can rely upon you.

I'll be that for my father as well. It's clear here at the beginning of his presidency that Mama, for that is what I call her, will not be of much help to Father. He has told me, secretly (how delicious), that whenever he is not able to be present at White House functions, that I will have to step in for him. My brothers, bless them, are terrors and it's all she can do to calm them down and be of service as Father's hostess. So I will have to do.

Which is why he's eager to have me debut. It is set for just after the new year. Isn't that timing great? You can make your way here since you'll be on your break between semesters. You won't be able to find a husband there, of course—there will be no colored men invited—but at least you can see what my ball will look like when you have yours, hopefully next year?

Write me soon, dear friend, to let me know all of your
work down there in Tuskegee, and of your friend there
who sounds as if he's a promising colored man for you
to marry.

Alice

I folded the letter down, ruminating on its contents as I always did after my friend wrote to me. Everyone around me always looked so pleased after I got a letter from the White House, an interesting name if there ever was, especially in the wake of the reaction after my papa went there to sup.

"Well?" Margaret fiddled around me, trying to look as if she were doing something important. "What did she say?"

"Say?" Sometimes it was a good idea to play stupid.

"In the letter, Portia."

"Just the usual."

"What about your father?"

"She's glad I can be here to help out my father because she is there helping out her father. It seems her mama is not quite up to hostess duties."

I put a lot of emphasis on *her mama* so that Margaret would understand just how useful I felt she was.

Margaret waved a hand. "Those society women are so delicate and fragile. It's good that Alice is there and is able to help him. Men who have big jobs need wives to assist them. Now take that nice Mr. Pittman."

"Anyway," I said to deter any more talk of Mr. Pittman, "she thinks that I can attend her debutante ball since I'll have to return to Wellesley for the spring term. It really must be something to have all eyes on you at every moment."

"Well, why not?"

"You see what they did to Papa just a short time ago? What would I go for? To watch Alice and her friends dance? She said that there would be no colored man invited for me. So why should I go?"

"To maintain the friendship, of course."

"Something I can do from the safety of campus. No need to imperil myself needlessly." The debutante ball of the First Daughter would be something to see, of course, but I didn't want to be a wallflower, unable to participate lest it cause another national upheaval. Alice could afford to be a disgrace; I as a Negro who wanted to go to Germany for a year after college to play music could not. The contents of my last meal stirred in the pit of my stomach in the same way as when I had to bear witness to my father's humiliation. I liked Alice Roosevelt, but I did not want to be part of a repeat of that event.

"Let me think on this. Yes, it was a mess when your father went, but he must maintain connection with Mr. Roosevelt."

"And I'm part of that in what way?"

However, Margaret had already left the room, delighted to scheme and plan to benefit my father and the school, in that order. As she always would.

"Those Roosevelt boys sound like a lot of fun," Dave said, his always thin face puckered up into a knot. "They have a lot of pets like we do."

I reached out and pulled him to me, gangly youngster as he was. He would be taller than me soon, no question about that, but always sickly, like his mother. "They do. But their house is many times larger than the Oaks."

"But nowhere near as fine," said my brother Baker.

"Well, Father could tell us that if he were here." He was gone on another fundraising trip, hoping to return before the Thanksgiving holidays.

He usually did, but it would just be for the day before he had to leave again. Bless him.

"You should go, Sissy, and tell us what they do."

"I'm telling you, you can ask Father."

"We did," Dave protested. "He told us that the entire dinner, besides talking of affairs of the race, they only talked about their daughters and how crazy they drove them."

I gave him a gentle shove. A very gentle shove. He didn't like it if I went too easy on him, but it was enough for him to know he was being roughhoused in the same way I would with Baker, for I did not want to treat them differently.

"Be honest, Dave," Baker said. "It was really about Alice. Who is very beautiful, according to what Father said the president said. And he wants to be sure she is married off before she can cause any trouble."

Ahh. Trouble. Of the enceinte kind maybe.

"It's enough to see that certainly, the way she has the interest of the nation." Margaret leaned in over her plate with unsavory interest. "It will be quite interesting to see who she marries."

My poor friend. I certainly wouldn't want to be the center of that kind of rapt attention. Sounded like a dreadful sentence of doom to me.

"That's why you should go up there to find out," Margaret finished.

"I don't want to sit off in a corner not interacting with anyone because I'm colored."

"Why would you do that?" Margaret pounded the table. "I have it. I'll tell you what you'll do. Let Miss Roosevelt know you will be present at her ball on January 3. You can leave on New Year's Day. You can stay with the McIntyres, where your father stays when he's in the capital city. This will work perfectly."

I bent to my task of clearing off Father's desk for me to write my response back to Alice. I just knew that whatever Margaret was planning, it involved deception, which I did not like. God didn't care for it much either.

Dear Alice,

I'm hoping all is going well in the planning for your deb ball, which certainly will be a highlight of the new year. I can confirm that, according to my mother, I will be attending in some fashion. She has some sort of plan that I cannot divine at the moment, but it will bring no awkwardness or shame to you. I would never do that. If it does, then I will send you a message informing you and I'll stay away.

There has been no further development on the front of the man you speak of. We are friends, nothing more. I'm not looking for anything more than that for quite some time, given my musical study, so we are in a fine position as far as I'm concerned. I don't know what his feelings are, but if there are any more developments on that front, I'll fill you in when I arrive there in the new year for your deb ball.

Your friend,
Portia

As I expected, when Margaret told Father her plan, he was fully on board with it and when he put an arm around me after Thanksgiving dinner, he only said, "Trust in the Lord and believe in his steady, unchanging hand."

It was hard to do as he said, but I wanted to be an obedient daughter so I kept my thoughts to myself about the reasons why a path had to be made to reconcile him to President Roosevelt in the first place. On the other hand, Margaret's plan allowed for the fact that all the hatred that had sprung up in the wake of "the Dinner" was foolish at best. There, I had to admit, she was clever. Just as scheming and as clever as she was when she landed my father.

I would get to go and she promised that all the materials I would need to make the costume for my arrival would be covered as my Christmas present.

THERE WAS A Christmas concert with my singing folks. About forty of them lasted and made for a solid choir when we sang on the Sunday before the Christmas holiday. The holiday for us was a spiritual day, a holy day, so everyone had breakfast at their homes and those who were still on campus, which always included some students, some faculty, and of course those of us who lived here, went to the chapel for worship. I was surprised to see Mr. Pittman in the number.

"I thought you were going to go to your mother for Christmas," I said, approaching him after the service was over.

"I saw her at Thanksgiving. I just . . . I felt like staying here on campus to celebrate."

"You must come to Christmas dinner with our family, Mr. Pittman." Margaret swept in between us at once. "I won't take no for an answer. I would hate to think of you eating bachelor rations at the teacher dormitory at such a time. Please join us."

He turned to me and I smiled. What else could I say? "Of course, Mr. Pittman. No one should be alone at the holiday. Please come."

He nodded and once the service was over, we all walked together back home to the Oaks. Lunch was a cold buffet laid out by the students who were left for the holiday, but Margaret wielded her home economics power in the kitchen for dinner. She did a good job. She didn't get that large by not enjoying her food. She knew that my father was partial to possum and had one there, stuffed with sweet potatoes. But there was also a roasted chicken and a ham, with plenty of Tuskegee-grown vegetables: white and sweet potatoes, corn, cabbage, collard greens, and okra, all fixed with ham for a side meat. Mr. Pittman was not the lone teacher who had remained behind for the holidays, so there were about twenty to our number.

There was a nice eggnog with some rum in it for us to drink and a frosted cake as well as a rich pound cake for dessert. My father didn't usually approve of spirits on campus, but because this was Christmas, he permitted the eggnog, which had a spicy hit added to it. I had a small cup. I enjoyed the smooth, cool dairy taste, mostly because our cows produced the richest milk that we enjoyed at table. Running the dairy was also the job of the agriculture students and everything that came from there was fresh, fresh, fresh. For me, the spice interrupted the taste of the eggnog, but I finished it.

"I would like to see you for a moment, Miss Washington." Mr. Pittman came to me and linked his arm in mine, so that I had to come along with him wherever he was going. I looked over my shoulder and I saw my father was enmeshed in some debate with one of the faculty. Of course. Margaret gave me a smug look and dipped her head toward the porch door. Of course. We went out together, shutting the door behind us.

The air in Tuskegee could get quite chilly in the winter, but this year, the holiday had been mild. "Yes, Mr. Pittman?"

"I . . . I just wanted to say a private merry Christmas to you, Miss Washington. And to thank you for . . . Well, for inviting me to sing along with you in your group." The air he breathed out was quite rum infused. We had not touched each other much before, but his touch and his arm through mine were not entirely unpleasant.

"Thank you, Mr. Pittman."

"I also wanted to say, well, I spoke to your father earlier. I asked him for permission to court you."

My heart thumped a little at this news. "You did?"

He leaned in a little closer to me. "Do you like that?"

"I suppose I do."

He pulled back. "Well, good. That's settled then. I bought you a present." He opened his frock coat and pulled out a small black box from his inside pocket. "This is for you."

I opened it up and saw a delicate necklace with one pearl dangling from it folded in the box. "Oh, it's lovely." I touched a hand to my lace collar I was wearing with my Christmas dress, something a little more colorful than my usual somber colors.

I lifted it out and put it around my neck. The pearl slipped into the folds of my lace collar, as if it were meant to go there. "I'm a June baby. Pearls are my birthstone."

"I know. I asked." He put his hands back into his pockets and smiled at me, lifting his eyebrows.

I knew exactly where he found out that information from.

"Well, thank you."

Silence.

"You're welcome."

He closed the distance between us a bit more. "Merry Christmas, Portia."

It was customary for couples who were courting in those days to use their Christian names with each other. I was a little disturbed in spirit to hear him say my name with those lips of his, the ones I had been intrigued with all term long, but the disturbing comforted me, like the spice in the eggnog we had both had.

"Merry Christmas. William?" My voice went up a bit and he laughed, his warm rum-scented breath coming across in puffs.

"My mother calls me William. Call me Sid."

"Oh. Fine. Thank you. Sid." His middle name. Something about a shortened name from his middle name did not please me, but I had no time to think about that as he leaned in more, using those lips to close the distance between us. But then, Dave burst out on the porch and we jumped apart, looking as guilty as if we had been doing something that we shouldn't.

"Portia, it's time to cut the cakes."

I nodded to him. "Thank you, Dave. I'll be inside. I don't want you to linger out here in the cold."

He ran back inside, as exuberant as a lad of twelve could be. I gripped the edges of the bench and laughed a little. "I'm sorry."

Sid wasn't laughing. I looked over at him, curious at the change in his disposition.

"Is there something wrong?"

The storm on his face, a storm of anger at Dave coming out, I suppose, went away as quickly as it came. "Come on. The cake awaits."

He picked up my hand and tucked it into the crook of his arm, but something had disrupted the air between us, and I was at a loss to explain what it was.

Alice

October 1901

Once I had reached the new place where we were to live, what Father dubbed the White House, I was thrilled from the tips of my toes to the tippy tips of my fingers. This, yes this, was the destiny that I foresaw for my father. And me. We belonged here, right here in the middle of everything. There was nothing more showy than this White House and I loved every minute of it.

Mother, of course, wasn't so thrilled. With all the children back now, including me, she was constantly consumed with keeping the bunnies occupied so that they didn't destroy everything at taxpayer expense.

Once everything was unpacked in my room, a rather large suite on the third floor, mind you, I had cornered Mr. Stewart, who was Father's friend who organized his time, to see when I could get in to visit. Meanwhile, I was occupied with planning and coordinating my debut, which would take place in the icy winter holiday break. I also busied myself with selecting my gown. Debutantes wore white, which I always thought was for babies and christenings.

That would not be the case for my debut. I would wear what I wanted and would still be the center of attention.

When I got in to see Father by himself in the West Wing, he ran a hand over his chin. "Listen." When he didn't say the A name, he meant me. Why then would you give the child the exact same name? I resolved not to do that to my babies, but of course, that would mean my death, an unimaginable event.

"Father?"

"I want you to cohost this debut with your cousin Anna."

"You mean Eleanor."

"Yes. That's what I mean."

"Why?"

"Because you are the same age. You should be gracious in sharing your big moment."

"I could never. I'm meant to be the focus."

"When you have your moment, that means that it's more likely that a few beaus will shake out for her and you both could marry at the same time."

I hooted. "Eleanor will never marry anyone."

I could get Father's lips quivering in laughter. Usually. But not today. They were firm and pursed. I tried a different tactic. "I mean, Father, she's got our height, lots of golden hair, and beautiful blue eyes. But unfortunately her chin is weak and they should have fixed her teeth."

"Daughter of mine. You could be more gracious. As a matter of fact, I expect it. It's always better when a pretty girl shows grace. You can do that."

Oh, now he wanted to get serious about this. His posture showed he meant what he said and there was no amount of wheedling I could do to get out of it.

"It should be a great time for all," I said blithely, even as the wheels were turning in the back of my mind as to how to get my way.

"And you need to know that because we are in the people's government housing, we aren't going to be overly lavish. No champagne."

"What kind of deb ball has no champagne?"

"We need the young men who come here to be clear-eyed as to what they are getting into when they meet you."

"No champagne. What about the dance floor? The East Room is dreadful looking as is. We need a proper dance floor. One made of wood."

"I don't think that will happen." My mother breezed in, standing next to my father to strengthen his resolve, no doubt.

"Well. This is going to be a terrible time." I folded my hands, running them back and forth over my knee.

"I seriously doubt that."

"Well, what does one have to do to get a wooden floor around here?"

"Go ask the Speaker of the House. He's the one who will have to appropriate the money." My mother laid her hand on Daddy's arm and he squeezed her hand.

"Now, Mother. Don't joke with her. She really wants a dance floor."

"Any dance worth its salt would have a wooden dance floor. What will it look like for the president's daughter to debut without one?"

"I beg you to remember that the nation is still in mourning for President McKinley. Too many ill-regarded expenditures is not the way we want to begin living in the house, Alice." Mother fixed me with a look. "That's enough now. Time for dinner."

She went swanning out alone. I wanted to stick my lip out but knew better. Father extended his arm and I took it, letting the wheels of my mind spin. Well, I had to give way to have my little doormat cousin around, and I could give up champagne. But a wooden dance floor!

Our government works for the advantage of the people. I was a people and I needed to make the Speaker of the House know my wishes. So I took the opportunity on one fine fall day to take a carriage up to Capitol Hill to see Mr. Joseph Cannon, the present occupant of the office, to express my needs.

I was able to make my way to his office because, even though he was not a fan of my father's, he was a Republican. It was on occasions like this where I felt that my own sex was a distinct disadvantage to my life's path. What was the difference between asking for appropriations for a wooden floor versus making sure that people had fire hydrants or a police station or a post office? None. I was only seventeen, and a female, which meant that I couldn't vote, but I had a voice and I was determined to use it.

I did not know at that point in my life how crucial the Speaker's chambers were to become to me, but when I first laid eyes on it that fall day, I was not impressed. It was dark, wooden, and depressing with a lot of half-filled spittoons sitting around with a dank, musty smell rising from them. Ugh. Some weak-chinned assistant was manning the office. I gave him one sidelong look and knew he would be putty in my hands. "Sir. My name is . . ."

"Why, you are Miss Alice Roosevelt," he said, and I had to give Weak Chin credit for knowing his Washington people.

"I am, good sir. I wonder if it would be too much trouble to get in to see Uncle Joe for a few minutes." I held up my gloved hand and made a small span between my thumb and index finger.

"Well, miss. The Speaker is busy just now. I'll be happy to relay any message."

I moved in closer to him, eyeing him directly. Thank goodness I had been given a rather imposing build, using height, inherited from the Lee side, as an advantage. "In this instance, I need to be the one to relay the message."

I could tell by the way he blinked his eyes that it had been a very long time since someone of the female persuasion had been this close to him. "Yes. Well."

"Well?"

"I suppose a minute or two wouldn't hurt anything."

"There we are." I patted his arm. "I'll follow you inside."

He guided me back through a room with a large table and two pots of imposing palms on either side of a door. A sign over the top of the doorframe read SPEAKER JOSEPH CANNON, as if he were the Lord Almighty himself.

Weak Chin opened the door to where even weaker chin, smaller stature, but substantially older Uncle Joe Cannon sat at a desk. "Well, what?"

I peeked out from behind his assistant. "Guess who has come to visit. Hello, Uncle." I stepped out and came to him, reaching out a gloved hand.

Father always said to make yourself appear larger than anyone else. Intimidation mattered.

"Well, to what do I owe the pleasure of this visit, Miss Roosevelt? I haven't seen you since you were a little girl and now here you are, all grown up. My my!"

I let him examine the full length of my blue dress, so fetching, and my large hat with the curled ostrich plume fixed upon it.

"She certainly is," Weak Chin said, getting his own full look, but it was not as uncle-inclined as Uncle Joe's look was. Now that the underling had served his purpose, I moved away from him to the Speaker.

"I wondered if you had considered the appropriation money for the presidential home, sir."

Uncle Joe blinked a few times. "Well, my goodness. Did your father send you up here, my dear? Or perhaps your mother?"

I put a hand to my clavicles. "Certainly not! My father would turn me out if he knew I came up here to see you. I know that you both don't really get along."

He demurred. "Well, he is the president now."

I stood next to him, elbowing him in a friendly manner. "Sir, I may be a Roosevelt, but I know what all of you said about him. That putting him in as vice president would keep him quiet. And now here he is, far from quiet!"

Uncle Joe's facial expression was quite pained. I would have taken some glee in it on behalf of my father, but I had a purpose here and I needed to take care of it quickly. "No, sir. The reason why I ask, Mr. Speaker, is because my debut ball is going to be on January the third. Now . . . We have no wooden floor for dancing. I know that you have been dancing many a time"—I cleared my throat because that certainly did not look to be the case, but I pressed on anyway—"and you must have a wooden floor. So if there is some appropriations money left in the pot, I was wondering if we couldn't have it for a wooden floor for the East Room."

"Why, bless thee, my dear. I'm so sorry. The pot of money for this year had been with the McKinleys and there won't be another cent appropriated until the middle of next year."

That damn McKinley. Why would he use up all the money and not leave any for us? Of course, I suppose that he didn't know that he was going to be assassinated, but it just goes to show that the very people who you think are not going to be greedy and showy turn out to be just that.

He spread his hands in a show of disappointment. "What if you had your dance in the summer? Then you would get fresh money and have enough to have a dance floor if you wanted it then."

I paused with a finger to my chin, considering a summer debut. No. That wouldn't work. Eleanor would somehow debut before me and that would not work at all. No. I had to be first or at least debut with her so that the contrast between us was crystal clear. "Well, sir, we all know the purpose of a debut ball is to show that a young lady is ready for matrimony. You wouldn't have me put off my husband search any longer than necessary, now would you?"

Uncle Joe shook his head. "Certainly not. It's much too important. Six months is a rather long time in the courtship stage. I remember those days very well indeed."

He was completely and hopelessly in love with his wife, Mary. She probably was the only one who wanted him in the first place, but he could and should remember it any way it helped him. That was my cue. I knew when to retreat and return after some more thought.

"Well, sir. I've used up my minutes. I can see that your assistant here wants me gone. I'm leaving."

Weak Chin stood on first one foot and then another, looking as if he needed a chamber pot.

"Thank you for stopping by, my dear. So sorry that I couldn't help you at this time."

I waggled a finger at him. "I'll be remembering this, too, when I need your help some other time, sir. You better believe that."

He waggled his fingers back and, like Mother, I swept from his office and out of the Speaker area before Weak Chin would ask me for a carriage ride. He would never, ever do for my husband. Heaven forbid that any babies should ever come from me with that weak chin.

Alice

1901

In between Father becoming president and the new year, which meant my debutante ball, I hung around with my friends, the Sloopers. A jolly bunch we were, writing each other crazy notes, making goofy jokes, and loving life. The only prerequisite to belonging is that members could not be married. It was a club we could not wait to depart.

So silly.

Of course, the bunnies never failed to amuse. Now that I was facing my debutante ball, I threw myself into playtime with them even harder, since I knew playtime days were coming to an end for me. When Ted needed help getting the pony up to the family quarters as a surprise to Father, I had to help him—that was my job as his big sister. It was also at this time that I acquired my purse friend, Emily Spinach, a lovely green nonvenomous snake. I knew I would be able to count on her to cause a little stir wherever we went, and she liked it inside of my reticule where it was nice and warm.

Still, I couldn't keep my mind from Portia and her attendance at my ball. I knew not to bother Father or Mother with any of it, so I went to my aunt Bye, my father's sister who raised me up from a small child. She was also the one who had been friends with my mother. My real mother. I could ask her questions when I felt the need to know. Coming to the end of my childhood years revealed that need in me.

She kept her own home in DuPont Circle where, surprise to everyone, she had married so late in life. I say *surprise* not because she was as unattractive as her other niece but because she had a limp from the time she was a girl and people thought that, somehow, this deficiency would keep her from getting a husband. Fools.

Aunt Bye was the sweetest woman, with the best disposition and the kindest heart. She was always there for her nieces, since both Eleanor and I had lost parents.

But I found time to go to Aunt Bye to ask her about Portia one November day after my visit with the Speaker. She hugged me when she saw me and pulled me away from her. "So what aren't you getting at your ball that you want?"

"Aunt Bye. Really. Can't I come and visit my favorite aunt?"

She smiled as if we had a secret. Because we did. "Corinne shouldn't hear you say that."

"I don't care what she thinks."

"Or your Lee aunts."

I waved my hand and embraced her anyway. Her firm body, thickened with middle age, still was stolid enough to calm me. I pulled away from her and slipped my arm into the crook of hers.

"Wooden dance floor."

"Dear child, you've just moved in. Give it some time."

"It's only a couple months away, though." I tried not to sulk, but I knew that my aunt would see this as a disaster, just as I did.

She patted my hand and we sat together on her davenport. "It will all work out for the best, really. Come in here and tell me about your dress."

"It's going to be magnificent. There will be roses all along here and the material is a heavy double-faced blue satin and I will wear gloves."

"Sounds marvelous. I had some thoughts about you having a debut away from your cousins, but it sounds as if Edith is doing a great job so far."

"But for this one thing."

"Things will work out. No more trips up to Capitol Hill in your big imposing hat. You're as bad as your father."

"No one is as bad as Father."

"No one could deny that you are his child and firstborn." When we got inside, she called to the maid for a tray of tea and accompanying sweets. She drew me into the comfortable parlor. "Now, you may confide in me. Tell me all."

I drew my breath. "Once the ball is over, will my purpose be great works?"

"Every woman of society's purpose is to do great works as she is lifting up her husband's name. But in your case..."

"In my case?"

"Well, who really knows, my dear? You're the president's daughter. There hasn't been anyone of your kind in the White House in a very long time." Her brow furrowed.

That was true. And it put me in a rather advantageous position as I looked for a husband. "So what if I did a great work at the debutante ball?"

"Well, I've never heard of such a thing."

"I could begin to get a jump start on things, and because I'm the president's daughter, people will notice."

Aunt Bye's eyes narrowed. "What do you have in mind?"

"I want to invite Portia Washington to my ball."

She sat back, thoughtful, as she waved the maid in with the tea tray. I poured for her, hot fragrant tea with a splash of milk, and I prepared my cup with an equal splash and took up a Joe Frogger in my hand, relishing its spicy sweet taste and scent, for a treat. "Who is that? I don't think I've heard of any Washington family from around here."

"She lives in Alabama. She's also the daughter of a prominent man."

Her eyes widened. "Oh my. Well, you are having many people to your ball. One more young lady couldn't hurt."

"Good. Because she's colored."

"Alice. What? Oh . . . Is she any relation to Booker T. Washington?"

I swallowed a bite of my Joe Frogger. Aunt Bye's were really the best. The White House cook would need this recipe. The family was crazy for them. "Yes. She is his daughter. She's a few months older than me, and having her there—"

"Would allow more of the insanity to continue from when your father imprudently invited her father to dinner last month. No, Alice."

"Aunt. She is a very nice girl. A student at Wellesley, too. Apparently her mother was part Indian."

"I don't doubt that. Her father is a great man. I could not imagine that he would have a daughter who would embarrass him in any way."

"She plays a beautiful piano."

"Aren't you having the National Marine Band?"

"Yes, but I'm not talking about having her in as entertainment."

"I don't know why not. Your father is the president and you saw what they did to him over a mere dinner invite."

I waved my hand, setting down my empty teacup. "People make too much fuss over nothing."

"What is your aim?"

"To show that the colored people of this country can exist with us."

"And what does that have to do with great works?"

"To lift the people up from their desperate state of course, Aunt."

"Isn't that for your father to do?"

"Why, yes. But he can always do with a little help."

"Well then, when you turn thirty-five years old, you can run for president. But until that time, you avoid causing trouble."

I laughed. But Aunt was serious. "I mean what I say, Alice."

I folded my hands, too. "There is just one problem. I've already written to her to ask her to come."

"Well, that was foolish. Really, Alice."

"It would look rude to uninvite her at this point."

"It would. And a bad start to your future career as a hostess."

"Exactly." I tipped my head.

I would get Portia and the floor.

"Have her here, instead."

"Here?" I gestured around my aunt's large, comfortable home.

"Yes. She can stay here in the small bedroom off the kitchen. I don't think she'll be able to attend the ball, but we can have her here for a few days after."

"Well. I don't know."

"Will she have an escort? Has she had a ball of her own?"

These questions stopped me cold. "Well, of course not."

"Do you think it is fair or kind to ask her to something that she cannot fully participate in because of her race? That's not a good work. Not in the least."

Leave it to Aunt Bye to think of all sides of the equation. "I suppose I see your point."

"Well, then, it is settled. I can write to her father and mother so they will know where she will stay. Because she wouldn't be able to stay in the White House. You see that, don't you, Alice?"

"Yes. I do."

AUNT BYE TOOK care of the particulars and a response from Portia came swiftly in return to say she would arrive on January 2 before she had to continue back to school. Aunt would have a hack bring her to DuPont Circle where she could stay in the small kitchen bedroom. The perfect place for Portia.

Meanwhile, Mother and Father had Speaker Cannon to the

house for dinner and Christmas festivities in December. I had another opportunity to speak with him about the need for a floor, and I even took him to the offending room. I opened the door where more moving around was taking place. "You see, sir? The dreadful yellow carpet. It must have been here since George Washington himself!"

I saw his mustache twitch. "He never lived in this house, Miss Roosevelt."

"Well, whoever the first one was." I shook my head. "Imagine, many young people paired up, trying to polka."

I took him onto the offending carpet, dragging my heels as I executed a quick polka step to show him how it just wouldn't work.

"You are very light on your feet, Miss Roosevelt. And I think wherever you choose to dance, the company will be blessed by your grace and beauty."

He chuckled and turned away from me, going back to his holiday spirits.

I sighed and waved a hand at the butler who was stationed there. All the staff were extremely respectful and kind people, the kind of people that Father said reminded him of the way his mother spoke about her life as a southern belle in Georgia. They were caring, devoted employees, steadfast in their service to the president, no matter who he was.

I met his eyes and sighed. "Well, that's that. If I can't get the floor now, there won't be one in enough time for the ball."

The butler nodded his head. "We're going to do the very best for you, Miss Alice. You can count on that."

"I've never doubted it. It's just going to be a little short of what I was expecting. No champagne. No wooden floor. Being the eldest is a trial sometimes, I'll tell you that."

His kind brown eyes softened a little as I started down the hallway back to the holiday festivities. Portia was the eldest in her family. She would understand. I was looking forward to her visit after my ball was over. I would ask her all about her debutante ball, what she would be having, and I could even help her plan if she would let me.

Then it occurred to me.

Maybe she would not be having a deb ball. For instance, my ball was slated to take place at the end of the holiday break, just before the young men had to return to Harvard, Yale, and Princeton so that they can attend without missing their schooling. If the young men one proposed to marry didn't have schooling, when could a person have a ball? Did coloreds have such a thing? I had to find that out from Portia. Then I remembered when we had met she spoke about her music career and not about a husband. The entire purpose behind a deb ball was to say to society that you were ready to find a husband and help him make his name in the world.

But what would Portia do?

I straightened up, ready to go back and preside over the holiday gathering, even with Uncle Joe Cannon present, but my thoughts increased my curiosity to know about Portia's side of life.

Once I knew more, I might be able to help her.

Alice

1902

The floor, the newspapers reported, was the second-most-wonderful thing about my debutante ball.

The first thing?

Me, of course.

That floor, the one that I hated, the one that I wooed old Uncle Joe Cannon for twice but had not gotten from him, was a hit.

I was almost upstaged by old yellow carpet covered over with what the papers dubbed was a "crash" fabric, some kind of waxed white linen that covered the carpet and hardened into a moderately decent dance floor.

Who could believe that it worked? I saw the last guest home from the nine-course supper and dancing in the wee hours of the morning.

And then I went to Portia at my aunt Bye's house and told her all.

My friend took in every single report in silence.

She had not a word to say when I was through describing every detail.

"Well?"

"It sounds amazing. I'm so glad the dance floor worked out." The words coming from her made me remember something.

"It was one of the servants. His name is . . ." I paused. "Samuel. He assured me that something would work out."

"Was he colored?"

"He was. Portia, the staff at the White House is amazing."

"I'm not surprised to hear it. Generations of families serve there. It's the apex of service."

"It is?" I was almost as surprised at this revelation as I was that the floor worked.

She nodded. "There are servants there who have attended Tuskegee."

"But I thought your father's school was to train nurses, teachers, and preachers."

"It is. But there are also people who go to school there who train to become excellent maids and servants. They come to perfect their skills and to be the best that they can be. Part of how my father raises money is to let rich people know that Tuskegee is one of the best places where they can obtain qualified, dependable, reliable help."

I sat back, amazed. We were in my aunt's sitting room, surrounded by newspapers that had accounts of my ball so I could see what people were saying about me.

This was a story that was not reported on, a story that was new to me, a story that Portia, bless her, had insight into that I lacked. "Well, now I know where to get help when I need it when I marry."

"You would certainly do worse if you tried to depend on obtaining your own help. Tuskegee graduates are top-notch."

I nodded and opened another paper. "Mother and Father are not happy with this extensive coverage."

Portia looked a little downcast. "It's not as if you can help it."

"I agree. See? I knew you would see my side of it." I pushed a paper at her, the *Hartford Courant* newspaper, and she took it, nodding. "I know Father would respect your opinion of the matter."

"He would?" Portia's carriage was already impeccable, and would be the envy of society if they had an opportunity to view her, but now, it was even more straight, an unlikely thing. "Me?"

I nodded. "Of course you. He has seen you before. He had much to say about you being the reflection of your father. And he admired your musicianship as well."

"Well. Imagine that." She breathed out all at once.

"It's just Father."

"He's the president of the United States."

I shrugged. "He's not liable to let anyone forget it, either. If you thought he was loud before when he was governor and vice president, well . . ."

"Even more so now?"

I waved my hand. "When they play that song for him . . ." I bent my arms at right angles and acted as if I were marching in somewhere like Father would. We collapsed into laughter.

"Well, he should be proud of his office. Even if he inherited it under a mantle of sorrow."

I nodded my head, knowing that my father would appreciate this more feminine response to his inheriting his office. I well recalled how he reacted when I told him I had hexed the McKinleys and that I was sorry McKinley's end was painful and it left Ida McKinley alone, but that I was joyful Father was president and that I was not going to lie about it, since lying was the greater sin. He looked at me as if I were a curse.

"He did, but the United States is better off for it." I reached my hand out for the paper and as she handed it over, I could see her trying to keep a shocked look from her face. "Listen. No one has managed to say that ever since her husband was murdered by that immigrant Ida McKinley's supposed ill health has vanished." I kept my voice low because Auntie Bye didn't like for me to say that truth.

"It has?"

"Yes. She used to be ill all the time. And by ill, I mean that her face would freeze at dinners." I leaned in.

"A frozen face?"

"Yes, yes." I was impatient to get back to the report in the paper, but I saw that Portia was confused and I needed to make sure she understood. "First of all, McKinley would ensure that, in a breach of protocol, he always sat next to her. Then if her face froze during dinner, he would throw a handkerchief over her face, until she spoke and he would remove it."

"Whatever for?" Portia's gentle face showed genuine confusion. "What was going on under there?"

"Frozen face." I sighed. I could see my help was needed. "Like this." I demonstrated, keeping my nose still from wiggling, lips from talking, and brows smooth and not wrinkled. But it was hard. How had Mrs. McKinley done it?

"Oh dear," Portia finally said.

I let go of my pose. "And there have been people who said that ever since he was, well, killed, no more frozen face. Not one time."

"Maybe because he's not there to cover her face from her fit." Portia began to straighten up the mess of papers.

"That could be." I straightened out the paper in my hands to read. "Or maybe there was nothing ever wrong with her to begin with but her husband."

Portia took in a sharp breath. "Oh no."

I looked all around me to see if my aunt had heard me. She was not there. "Oh yes. Sometimes a marriage can be a trial and I cannot imagine that being married to that sourpuss would have been joyful. That's why we had to come into office. Things are much better now."

"I heard that they had a hard life."

I reflected on this. "I suppose so. Two babies gone before their time. That had to be difficult for her." *That didn't prevent them from being boring though.* I just thought that. I didn't want to say it, lest Portia think I was being too cruel.

"That's sad. Maybe that's when she started having fits," Portia offered.

"No. No. It had to do with being married to a sourpuss, I'm afraid."

"Were there any sourpusses in attendance at the ball?" she asked.

"Well, of course, but I didn't dance with them. I don't want a sourpuss for a husband. I made sure to vary my dance card."

"So one young man for each dance?"

"Yes. Now is the time for that."

"Any particular ones stand out?" She lifted her eyebrows.

I thought about this. "No, not really. Although, like this article said, I was handed from arm to arm and things did not end until the early morning hours. It was wonderful."

"I'm so glad you had a great time." Portia breathed out and smiled. And she really *did* seem to be glad for me. That's why she was such a good friend to talk to in this way.

"Wait. One person was very appealing."

"Who was he?" She leaned in. That was one reason why I liked her.

"Well. His name is Franklin Roosevelt."

"Roosevelt?" She sat back.

I nodded my head. "We're related. Distantly. He's one of the other Roosevelts. From Hyde Park. But it's very distant." I held out my hand, because I could see a growing sense of alarm on her face.

"Well, tell me about him."

"He's very tall. Slender like me. Well-built. He has a good head of hair, too. He's in school at Harvard. Has money. Very important, that."

"Of course."

"We had a waltz. I might consider him further but . . ."

"But?"

I shook my head, not wanting to think of it, but Portia was right here as a sounding board. "His mother is terrible. I could not imagine having her for a mother-in-law. One has to think of such things."

"Absolutely. If there is a parent."

We looked at each other. And we understood. "Yes. But she knows Franklin is handsome and she would be the kind of mother-in-law who would have her claws in him. And that would be a bit much."

"Well, you should try to see him again to see if he would be worth it."

Should I? I thought of Franklin's eyes and his jolly, merry mien. Then I thought of his mother. "No. Now, let me read a bit more."

I read the part out loud about the decorations, skipping over the mention of that darn crash floor, and Portia breathed in. I looked up at her as she set down her teacup. "Well, you know I've had the company of someone."

"Yes, do tell, Portia."

"He's one of the new teachers at the school. An architect."

A colored architect? I raised an eyebrow, something that I was quite good at now, and waited for the rest.

"Father brought him to the school to design more of the buildings and to show the students more about building. Although, given the buildings the students have already built, I could not imagine what else he might show them."

"Students built the buildings?"

"Why, yes. They did. It was one of the early requirements of the school. He told them that if they wanted to earn their keep at the school, then they had to create the buildings. Porter Hall is as sound as a dollar."

"I must go with Father whenever he travels there."

"Oh, yes, you must. I mean, if your father is thinking of coming."

I turned to her and focused on her. "Why wouldn't he?"

"My dear Alice. He is the president. And well, from before."

"From before?"

"From before with your father and my father. Do you think he would?"

"Oh pooh." I shook my head. "That is pure foolishness. Let those people calm down. He'll be there for a visit."

"Some of those people . . . Well, I mean, since my father and your father had dinner, things have happened at the campus, but because the students have done such a good job in making it secure . . . But still . . ."

Now I put the *Hartford Courant* down with its mentions of my wonderful time. "There has been trouble?"

"There is always trouble. It's just that this trouble is a bit more . . . pronounced." A cloud had come into her beautiful gray eyes and it hurt my heart to see it.

"Never you mind. That kind of hatred and awfulness cannot last." I shook my head to clear it of the thoughts of the horrid cartoons of Mr. Washington having his way with me when I wasn't even there! "It will not last. I bet you Father comes for a visit. And when he does, I'll come and see for myself this wonder of a campus of students who build their own school buildings. Also, to see this architect." I straightened the Hartford paper, since it had the best reportage of my ball. I didn't want any newspaper wrinkles on it.

"Oh, Alice. That would be wonderful."

"In the meantime"—I bit my lip because it might be more than a "meantime" before Father and I could travel to Alabama to see anything—"your father needs to keep writing him. Letters don't harm anything and you wouldn't want your father to think that mine was angry or anything. Because he's not."

The storm disappeared from her gray eyes. "I'll let him know."

I smiled and organized the papers in alphabetical order. Mission accomplished.

Good Wives

Portia

1902–1905

After my time at Wellesley as a special student ended, I moved on to Bradford College to attend college. Even though racial encounters did occur, I knew that as Booker T. Washington's daughter, I had to be exemplary in all things. So, even when I came home to Tuskegee during breaks and the summer, it didn't matter how many Sundays that man came to sit in my father's parlor. I was in no rush to be married. Margaret kept up any and all kinds of criticism directed my way about it, probably because she herself had been so desperate to lock my father into the holy bonds of matrimony all those years ago. Well, I didn't look like her, thank almighty God, and did not feel so desperate about my chances to lock in a man. Especially since he was right there. Waiting for me.

Sid Pittman was very handsome, smooth talking, smelled good, and was a professional man who could take care of me. More like my daddy than anyone I had met. Daddy understood just how I felt. After all, he never had any problems getting married—having been married three times.

Also, because we had a special bond with each other, I knew that he was in no rush for me to marry. He had promised me that I could go to Germany after college to study music with the great musicians. People always said he wanted our people to remain maids and janitors, but he had high aspirations for me and my brothers. My study of music could easily be seen as something superfluous and not helpful to the race. He didn't see it that way, and as long as I was properly chaperoned throughout my European sojourn, he was adamant that I should go. Even in the face of Sid Pittman, sitting in the parlor each week. Proclaiming he was dying of love for me.

Alice didn't understand it, either. I didn't want to write the words or say them in the wake of my visit to DC for her debutante ball. However, the mere fact that I didn't have a debutante ball meant my future plans were destined to be quite different than hers. I wished her well on her journey, but my path as a musician was laid out before me.

So when the acceptance for Germany came just before my graduation from Bradford as its first Negro graduate in 1905, I showed my father the letter, and his face shone with pride at my accomplishment. Needless to say, Margaret's firm lips became more firm and Sid . . . Well, he handed me back the letter of acceptance. "Will there be a chaperone?"

"You know that Father would not let me go so far away without being appropriately attended to." I folded the letter and secreted it in one of my skirt pockets.

"It's good to hear that. Because I want my wife to be a virgin."

Something inside of me broke when he said that. I paid no attention to my reaction, though, because I saw Sid's pain and thought that I could heal it. Anyone with more sense, more experience, would have made a different choice. They would have told him goodbye in that moment. We had been courting for years during my college career. What in the world would make him think that after all of these years I would just lift my skirts for a stranger? "You already know the answer to that. I can't believe that you would think that I wouldn't be."

Sid looked to his left, and to his right. Then he leaned into me and kissed me. In a new way. A different way. A probing, questioning way. A way that made my insides sink down into a bottomless abyss of pleasure, a melting morass of sweet sensations that tingled between my legs. He had never done this before. Everything prior was both of us sitting straight up, hands off each other. Now, Sid's hands were on my waist and he kept drawing me to him. Deeper and deeper. This kiss, this feeling that I had gone to the edges of before, must have been the kind of thing Margaret didn't want me to know about, but Sid, for the very first time, took me there. I didn't realize it, but my hands went around his neck and he pulled me down, down, down on the davenport.

I broke away. I had to. I couldn't breathe.

"Portia. I cannot believe . . ." He kept kissing me now on my ears and the feeling was delicious. There was a fog in my brain, as if my senses had left me completely. Where had they gone? Did Sid have them? "If you go we would have to wait for a whole year, even more than that, to become man and wife. Is that what you want?"

I breathed deep, trying my best to ignore those small, tiny kisses he was placing on my ear and trailing down my neck . . .

"I didn't say . . ."

He stopped. "Say what?"

"I didn't say I wanted that."

"So what are you saying?"

I put my hands on his chest, a mistake, because I could feel his hard, hard muscles bulging underneath his shirt. So much hardness pressed against me, pressed against my softness like the fulfillment of some pattern, some rhythm. What would it do for my music if I could peep over the line to glimpse the other side of the knowledge and find out what Sid was talking about? What Margaret meant when she told me to stay away from men?

I gave him a light press with my fingertips, but that wasn't enough for him to get off me. Then I pressed harder, with my palms, and he rose up. "What?"

"Someone could come in." I sat up and straightened my shirt-waist. The material had come out of my waistband and my father, who was in his office quite close by, could get the wrong impression. Margaret probably would not care to see me compromised, in spite of her warnings.

"Besides. You just said that you wanted a virgin for your wife."

"That doesn't include me, Portia."

I fluttered my eyelashes at him. "Of course not."

"Do you expect me to wait for more than a year for you?" Sid stood up, seeming to be in a rush now.

"If you want to marry me. Yes." I nodded my head firmly, even though that fog was still surrounding my brain.

He ran his hands through his silky hair. It was always a thing that Margaret said recommended him well for marriage. *Your children won't have woolly Negro hair*, she would always say. It was something that I never even considered, but now that Sid was so angry with me, it made me wonder if my music career was what I really wanted. I knew I was fond of him, and I didn't want him to be hurt.

But music was what I really wanted. Ever since I was a little girl.

He snatched up his coat, shoving his arms, those big arms, into the sleeves. "Good night, Portia."

"What is wrong?"

"I've already waited years for you. If you don't want to be my woman, all you have to do is tell me that, and I'm gone." Sid made such an angry gesture with his hand, it took my breath away.

"I never said that to you."

"But what you are saying with this—this dream you have of going to Germany is that you don't care about me."

"I do care. Yes, I do. I just know that I have to finish my music study before I get married. There is a reason we don't have married students here. Father knows, just like everyone else knows, that once there is marriage, a woman's attentions are divided."

"I'm almost thirty. I want a wife. Now."

"Well, I'm not, Mr. Pittman."

His gray eyes were wide and wild, staring me in the face as he backed out of the room so fast Margaret fairly came running. Unless she had been standing there listening, which was completely possible.

"What is going on, Portia? What did you say to Mr. Pittman?"

Nothing that is any of your concern.

I put my hand to my head. "I'm . . . I'm not feeling well. I need to go to my room." I moved past her and went up the staircase. My father was so engaged in his work in his office, he didn't look up and I'm glad he didn't.

I shut my door and leaned on it. My eyes filled with tears. The last thing I wanted was for Sid to be angry with me, but apparently, I couldn't prevent that. My wants and desires for what I needed evidently got in the way.

THERE IS NOTHING that spreads faster on a campus full of young people than news of a broken relationship of any sort, especially mine, now that I was a full-fledged college graduate. Mr. Pittman's engagements with other women didn't help any either. He no longer came to dinner and he didn't sit with our family in church services anymore. There weren't many other women instructors like me that he could engage with. The only thing left to him were summer students and there were plenty of those who were happy to vie for the attention of a successful, older, handsome teacher. Young women were there at Tuskegee Normal to learn to be teachers or maids or farmers' wives, but would have been more than happy to steer those skills toward being the wife of an architect.

As for me, there was no shortage of young men who would have liked to spend time with Booker T. Washington's only daughter. Still, Margaret was rather short with me these days, and Father just looked at me with our eyes. After a few weeks, I accepted the invitation of a math instructor to go walking. As we made the campus

circuit exchanging in polite conversation, I saw Mr. Pittman with
a pretty student, just as I feared, heading in the opposite direction
and my heart lunged into my throat.

Well, if he wanted someone who adored him, who was I to say
anything to him about that? No one. Still, when a letter arrived from
Alice, I was glad. TR had been reelected to the presidency last year
and there was now widespread speculation that he felt he had fulfilled the two-term precedent set by George Washington. He would
not seek another term, and planned to hand off the presidency to his
friend, William H. Taft, for the 1908 election. Therefore, he could do
whatever he wanted and that included having my father to the White
House again and this time, he could bring his daughter with him.

I was thrilled.

Margaret was not. She was not invited.

"Did he not say your wife? What about wives? I would not mind
meeting with Mrs. Roosevelt at all. I'm sure we could find something to talk about in light of her good works matched with mine."

"You have many good works here of which to be proud," my father
pointed out without a hint of irony. She did. There was no denying
that. "However, it's noted in a number of places that Mrs. Roosevelt
is often ill and busy with her children. Alice is much less busy and
has become quite the ambassadress for him."

Margaret cut her eyes at me, daring me to even think of such
a notion. I wanted to laugh. She had no need to worry. Even so, I
stilled my face to give no reaction. She would have to think of such
a possibility in the deep, dark night and I did not mind imagining
her discomfort at being usurped. No wonder she wanted to marry
me off to Mr. Pittman.

"Alice is representing him on a tour to the Orient in July." I spoke
up, giving Margaret a directed gaze back in her direction.

"Why, who ever heard of such a thing! An unchaperoned young
lady going halfway around the world?"

"She will be properly chaperoned."

"Well, such a trip will do nothing to help her find a husband to make her fortune with."

I shrugged my shoulders. "Maybe she doesn't want that right now."

Margaret turned to face me, eyes narrowed behind her small spectacles. "Any woman with any sense wants a husband."

She returned my gaze in a triumphant look, as if she won, and to underscore her victory, she left my father's office. This time. I turned to my father. "Is it possible to align my visit with my embarkation to Europe?"

He nodded. "That might be arranged. We can go to the White House and then to New York for a time."

I put my hand on his arm. "Thank you so much, Father. I appreciate this opportunity."

He returned the gesture. "I know that you will do me proud in both areas. Not acting like Miss Roosevelt in any way."

The exploits of Princess Alice were known and documented in the newspapers. Climbing on top of the president's house to smoke when her father forbade her to smoke under his roof, carrying her pet snake with her to scare people, driving a car, visiting the Speaker of the House to advocate for herself, among many others. My father, knowing of our ties to each other, never failed to report Alice's escapades to me. I would always wave my hand at his reportage, even if they did cause a little alarm. Sometimes. But most times, I smiled. "She means no harm. She has her own way of doing her father proud, as I do." I stood on tiptoe to give him a good-night kiss on his cheek and then left his office for him to attend to all Tuskegee matters.

Alone.

Portia

1905

It had been more than three years since Alice and I had seen each other. As part of my traveling wardrobe I had new dresses made by the amazing seamstresses who honed their craft at Tuskegee. They had done a beautiful job and were thrilled to know that the fruits of their labor would be on display in Europe and in the White House of all places. I was thrilled for them, and for me, but still a bit nervous to encounter the president again.

Also I was nervous for my father.

I shouldn't have worried. President Roosevelt was extremely gracious to us both. "Grown up quite a bit, haven't they, Mr. Washington?"

My father nodded, beaming with pride as he usually did with me.

"Well, time passes, Father, as they say." Alice couldn't resist an opportunity to put in her two cents. I could tell she was glad to see me because she was toned down just a bit from her usual position. She was behaving herself today.

"Yes, well, I'm happy to give you a tour, Miss Washington, before I settle down to business with your father."

"She doesn't want a tour with you, Father. That's what I'm here for."

"Oh, yes. Well. Carry on, ladies!" He waved his hand and off he went with my father for their meetings.

"Is the First Lady at home?" I asked Alice, a little disappointed that I didn't get a look at her.

"Where else would she be? We're bound to run into her at some point. Including the bunnies."

She was right. There were a number of the young Roosevelt children around at that time of day, getting into their usual mischief. The boys very much reminded me of Baker and Dave. Kermit was the most like Baker and Quentin like Dave. Her oldest brother, Theodore Jr., was off at school now that he was nearly grown and almost ready to go to Harvard himself.

Alice guided me to a solarium, a room filled with light and many pots of ferns and greenery where tea was set up already. "So we are both traveling. How wonderful."

She handed me a cup of fresh tea with a splash of cream in it. I took it, saying, "I'm happy to finally be going. All those years of studying German at Bradford will have finally paid off. It will be amazing to study the great masters in their homeland."

Lifting her own cup to her lips, Alice gave a half smile. "And what of the esteemed Mr. Pittman?"

I lifted my own cup, shaking my head.

"Oh no. You didn't write of any issue with him."

"I didn't want to talk about it frankly."

"Well, we can change the subject."

I put my cup down. "No. It's been a few months now. I'm much better. Let's just say that he wanted someone who could be more attentive to his needs."

"What man doesn't want that?"

"And that wasn't me."

"You mean he was jealous?"

I shook my head, surveying the amazing assortment of White House pastry in front of us. I helped myself to a yellow petit four, relishing the sweetness of the tender cake and cream. I would have to monitor myself very carefully in England, Italy, Switzerland, and all of the other places we would go before Germany. I didn't want to burst out of my beautiful new wardrobe.

"That's not it at all."

"Isn't it? Let me tell you, I've been surveying all these men who have come to escort me and claim my time since my debut more than three years ago. There isn't one of them that is worth a bowl of piss."

There she was; my old friend was back now that we were alone!

As if she were summoned on cue to reprimand Alice, a beautiful lady rounded the corner and entered the solarium. "That will be enough, Sister."

Her carriage was ramrod straight and her dove-gray dress flowed about her with beauty and ease.

"Oh, look, Mother is here." And knowing Alice as I did, she meant to add "to spoil our fun."

I stood, not wanting to be caught without my manners in front of the First Lady of the land. "Good afternoon, Mrs. Roosevelt."

"Good afternoon, Miss Washington. I hope that you are comfortable."

"Thank you, ma'am. I'm just catching Alice up."

"Yes, Mama. If you must know, Portia had been keeping company with a marriage prospect for years and he went and dumped her because she is her father's daughter."

"Alice. That's not kind."

No, it wasn't. That was Alice. "I don't mind, ma'am."

She turned to me. "Well, I'm sorry to hear that. It's good that you had a prospect. A steady one at the very least. Coming to learn how to be in relationship with one person is an important skill to cultivate. Much better than being a butterfly and floating around hoping to be caught in the net."

It was hard to miss the critique of Alice in her words, and I didn't wish to have my friend be treated as a problem at my expense. I sat back down. Mrs. Roosevelt reminded me of Margaret, something that should not have surprised me. Too bad that they would not get a chance to meet.

Alice piped up. "Well, yes. Sitting around waiting on a man is just the thing to do to get him to marry you. If you're lucky, that is. Because you could sit around too long and he might find a better opportunity out in the great, wide world."

I swallowed, hard, at these words from my irrepressible friend, knowing that the conversation had turned, and something was happening on more than one level.

Mrs. Roosevelt's face took on the appearance of a sunny-day picnic disrupted by a storm cloud. She tipped her head to me. "It was wonderful meeting the lovely daughter of Booker T. Washington. You were right, Sister. She does have something of the Indian princess about her."

"Well, of course," Alice said, sipping her tea, looking elsewhere.

Before I knew what had happened, Edith Roosevelt was gone.

"I'm so sorry for that interruption. So where were we?"

"I hope I didn't offend her."

"No. I did. Given that she sat around and waited on Father for a proposal that didn't come because he met my mother, Alice in the meantime, proves that she has no idea what I'm going through. She never had a bevy of men at her beck and call as I have had and she's jealous."

"She seems to resemble my own mother. Margaret mother. One more thing we have in common apparently." I finished my petit four and took up my tea again.

"It would appear so. So you were saying that Mr. Pittman wasn't jealous?"

"No. He didn't want me to take up my studies."

"Well, there you go. Not only is he jealous, but he wants you to remain stupid." Her hand hovered over a crème cake and she picked it up, biting into it with eagerness.

Well, that was harsh, even for her. "I'm not sure."

"Portia. How many people of your race get to go to Europe to study? Of course he's jealous. I'm sure he is handsome and wonderful and all, but his abandonment of you points to the problem we will have in finding our husbands."

"It does?"

"Yes. Who is willing to marry a princess? I'm sure you have heard how the press has dubbed me as such. You're that, too, but a colored princess. He doesn't want you to show him up in any way, given your background and experiences. As a man, he feels that he must be the one who knows more, and does more. When you come swanning back from Europe all sophisticated and worldly, who will marry you? What colored man exists who wouldn't have wanted to go to Europe himself and have those experiences?"

She had eloquently pointed out a large issue. As blunt and outspoken as Alice was, she was not wrong. I sighed.

"Well, you aren't going back to Alabama, are you?"

I looked up at her. "Certainly not."

"Then you have to enjoy your time in Germany. Every minute. And not regret it. That's all I've been trying to do. There's the very reason that I've been such a 'butterfly' with no steady company. People are extremely intimidated by me, my father, my very existence."

"It doesn't help that you carry a snake in your reticule," I pointed out.

"Well, Emily is quite the protection. She lets them know that I'm not going to put up with just anyone."

"Good point. So are you giving up then?"

Alice laughed. "Certainly not. I have to find a husband. I'm not like you, where I can go be a teacher somewhere. Can you imagine?"

It was hard, imagining such a bright spectacle in the classroom. "Well then, what qualities are you looking for?"

She folded her hands. "It has to be someone who has his own power. Who is on the rise. Someone who isn't intimidated by me or my father. Someone who has his own money. And handsome because I do not want any homely children."

"That's it?"

"That's a start."

"Prince Charming then."

"Exactly."

I shook my head. "They aren't exactly lying around."

"With my father being the president, I'm sure that I'll be married by the end of this final term. Probably here."

"In this solarium?" I looked about me. It was much too small.

"Oh no. I meant here in the White House. The East Room is much better now, with a wooden dance floor that Mother instantly obtained for my sister's debutante ball for a few years from now, but it will also suffice for my wedding."

I nodded. "That will be wonderful. And quite lovely."

"No one wants to say it, but this house is a dump filled with generations of rats who have settled in for the long haul and made homes for themselves. Father has done a great renovation since we have been here. After all, it is the People's House and the biggest and the best. Not to mention the colored staff here is wonderful. Just as you know, several of them attended Tuskegee."

I nodded. "Good. I'm glad they are exemplary. That's the point of the school, to produce the best-trained staff anywhere."

"Well, they have. They are the best."

"And now?"

"Well, my trip to the Orient is in a few weeks. I'll be part of an official party, featuring members of Congress. So I really must be on my best behavior, you see."

"Will any of them be single?" I laughed.

"Of course. But just like you, I'll be properly chaperoned. So no funny business will go on."

"Well, that's good to know." I cleared my throat. "Mr. Pittman told me he wanted his wife to be a virgin."

Alice hooted. "What a bunch of claptrap."

I reared my head up. "It is?"

"Of course it is." She leaned forward. "What he is really saying is that he wants to make sure that his children are his own."

My forehead wrinkled with confusion. "Is that why?"

"Of course. His pronouncement is all about being worried that a woman will trap a man into marriage with a pregnancy that is not his baby. They live in fear of that."

I laced my hands together in my lap over and over again. These were certainly valuable insights that I was gaining from the daughter of the president.

"If there were some way we might be able to be . . . experienced at the marriage bed and not encounter an unexpected happy event, I think men would like if their brides were more . . . frolicsome."

Something then occurred to me. "Alice. Do you mean . . . ?"

She batted her eyelashes. "What?"

I couldn't say the words. I could not speak them to the president's daughter. The look in her eyes was fun and saucy, but she knew so much about life, men, and resources, I couldn't help but wonder what she knew of the whole business.

"Never mind."

"Now that we've had our tea, let's go to my room and I'll show you how my traveling wardrobe is coming along."

I was relieved that she had changed the subject. I didn't want to face the prospect that she might not be a virgin. Not out of jealousy, the emotion that we had spoken so much about in this visit. But because her potential dance with that previous experience was dangerous and might inhibit her search for a husband. There was so much at stake for her, even though she was the president's daughter.

I would not wish that harm on anyone. Ever.

Portia

1905

My chaperone was named Jane Clark, and I had known her from her presence on campus. She was a moderately young woman, around Sid's age, not someone who was unfun but someone whom my father trusted. We made arrangements to travel to England first and see many of the sights there, then Paris, before we moved on to Germany, pointedly Berlin.

The trip was wonderful, and I soaked up all the new sights deep into my soul. Music-wise, it made a major difference to visit the homes of the old English and French masters like Handel and others. Much of those trips set the table for me to go to Germany and to absorb as much learning as I could from the German masters like Brahms, Bach, and, especially, Beethoven. I loved his moody dark sonatas and played them frequently. I intended to honor my teachers when I reached them.

One day while having coffee in a café as Mrs. Clark and I were waiting for me to play for my new teacher, I read an English newspaper and noted that Alice had made her way to the West Coast of the United States, to the ship that would take her to the Orient. She would be in the company of some members of Congress, including a man who seemed to fit all her Prince Charming requirements, Nicholas Longworth, a member of the House of Representatives from Cincinnati, Ohio. I regarded his solemn, sober features. No, he did not look like fun and I wasn't sure he was handsome enough to tempt Alice. Possibly, but his lack of a full head of hair might be a problem.

"That young man over there is staring at you," Mrs. Clark informed me while she took a sip of her coffee drink.

I looked up in the direction that she inclined her head, and, indeed, a young man with a riot of blond curls on his head, dressed in an immaculate blue suit, was intensely gazing at me with his blue eyes. When he saw me look up, his smile broadened, and I immediately went back to my newspaper, feeling the warmth of pure embarrassment wash over me like the waves of the Atlantic Ocean we had just traversed. "Well, I'm not staring at him. It's rude."

Although he was much nicer looking than Nicholas Longworth. He did, after all, have hair.

Mrs. Clark agreed. "You've gotten an incredible amount of attention ever since you've come to Europe. Will it have any impact on your plans for marriage, I wonder?"

I gave her an alarmed look. "I certainly would not marry a young man who looked like him."

Mrs. Clark smiled and sipped again. "He's not bad looking."

He wasn't bad looking at all. He was very handsome. That was clear. But to think of such a man as someone to potentially date . . . well, I knew that I was from the United States in all respects. I would never even consider it. I posed the crux of the problem to Mrs. Clark.

"Would you marry someone who was not of the race?"

She set down her cup. "No. But there is no harm in making friends while you are away from home."

"I don't want to befriend someone who looks like him. Not when he's looking at me as if I were the last schnecke on the plate."

She giggled like a little schoolgirl. We had both become fond of the snail-shaped pastries since we arrived in Berlin. "Are you thinking of your young man at home?"

"I don't have a young man at home."

"You don't?"

She had probably talked to Margaret.

"We ended our connection with each other. I'm sure that a prospect as fine as Sidney Pittman will have no problem finding a suitable wife with the right connections right there on the campus of Tuskegee." I straightened out my paper, trying to read more of my friend's exploits. How lucky she was to travel so far.

"Well, you indeed may have ended the connection. From what I've heard, he's making multiple attempts to forget about you. You may know men often have the bigger difficulty with their emotions and therefore will often be more radical in their behavior."

I put the paper down, thinking of my father. He did not behave in such a way. The husband that I wanted would be like my father, measured, logical, and loving. "Going around campus and selecting a student to date, a student of age, but still a student, mind you, does not show the kind of behavior that I want in a husband. If anything were to happen to Margaret tomorrow . . ." I paused, reveling in the delight of such a prospect. Briefly. Then I went back to reality. "My father would never do such a thing."

"That is my point exactly. And besides, you were young whenever your father was last available looking for a wife. Believe me, many women were in the running to be the next Mrs. Booker T. Washington."

She looked over her cup, sipping like the lady she was.

Then something occurred to me. "Were you?"

"Many of us were," she gently corrected me. "Do you recall Mary Moore?"

I did. "She was Olivia mother's friend and took care of me while I was at Framingham a few years ago." A woman of the same race as Alice, her father, and this staring young man.

Jane Clark nodded at me and my understanding of my father's life while I was a young child gained a new fissure of understanding. Father had regarded Mary Moore as a potential wife? A cold bead of sweat formed around my neck and I patted it away.

Now the young man who had not taken his eyes from me this entire time stood, making his way to our table.

"Well, it is clear that he did not marry her. He certainly could not have married someone of her persuasion. Not if he wanted the school to survive. My father's all has always been about the school. Still"—I folded my newspaper up into a smaller package, so that I could prepare to leave the area—"it's too bad things didn't go further between the two of you. You would have been the superior stepmother."

"Good afternoon," the young man said to the both of us.

"Good afternoon, sir," Mrs. Clark said.

"I apologize for being so forthright for coming to you in this way, but I could not help myself. It is not a proper introduction." His English was rendered with a heavily German accent.

"No, it is not," Mrs. Clark said, giving him a frosty glare. "And yet, you have continued to fix your gaze upon this young woman for this half hour past, correct?"

Fix? Gaze? I wanted to giggle.

I spoke to him directly in his own language. "She means you have been staring at me."

He turned to me, his blue eyes wide with disbelief. "You even speak German?"

"Of course. We're here in Germany. It is just my chaperone who does not, alas."

"What are you talking about, Portia?"

"Is that your name? Portia?" he said in English.

I nodded my head, some of that embarrassment of my name coming through to haunt me.

"Oh." He inhaled and spoke in German. "So that explains why a woman of your beauty and refinement is here in Berlin."

I lowered my head even more. "Thank you," I murmured.

"Now I am even more determined to secure a proper introduction to you." He turned and bowed to Mrs. Clark. "Excuse me."

And he walked away. I could see that he was very well formed as a specimen of the male species. Of his own accord. Comparison was not even in my mind.

"Well, that was strange."

"He said he wants to make a proper introduction."

"He did?"

As much as I wanted to, I couldn't repeat the words he said about beauty and refinement. They did not seem to belong to me. I folded the paper up. "Let's take ourselves to Herr Krause. It's time."

Mrs. Clark nodded. "It is. What a strange segue."

True enough, but as it was time to make my teacher's acquaintance, I could not afford to move my focus in a different direction. I wanted to impress him.

We were not far from the studio of Herr Krause, who would be my music teacher at the academy. We stood, brushed off our walking suits, and made our way across the street to present ourselves. Mrs. Clark rang the bell and a door was opened by a young woman wearing an apron; she curtsied to us, not at all shocked that two women of a brown race should appear at the front door. I nodded to her. There were many things here in Germany I could get used to, one of them being the immediate acceptance of my humanity, without having to think about or consider the color of my skin as a problem.

She went to retrieve Herr Krause while I approached the beautiful piano in the front parlor, a grand one that shone and sparkled like a new jewel. My fingertip touched a white key, then a black one. I didn't think I had ever seen such a fine instrument, and there was no doubt that I was awed by its beauty as well as its perfect tone.

A man, short of stature but built like a bull with a balding head of scant blond hair, stepped into the room carrying with him an instant air of command. "Hello. Is this my new student? Miss Washington?"

Mrs. Clark nodded. "I'm Mrs. Jane Clark. May I present Miss Portia Washington?"

"Ahh, yes, well, so lovely to meet you, Miss Washington. I've been looking forward to your arrival."

"Yes, Herr Krause. As have I."

"Well, why wait? Let us start."

He spread his arm to the beautiful piano and bade me to sit down. I smoothed my brown walking skirt with my arm and sat at the bench before the beautiful instrument.

"Ya, yes. Mrs. Clark and I'll sit here and listen to you perform what you know."

I played my favorite Beethoven sonata, and one from Brahms, and part of an oratorio from Handel that I heard over in England. Herr Krause sat there, listening, making notes on a little pad, shaking his pate back and forth, to and fro. Once I finished the last note of the Handel, I withdrew my hands from the piano and turned to face him.

He finished making his notes and we sat there, facing each other from across the room. When he stopped writing, he looked up at me. "Well, yes." He turned to Mrs. Clark. "Is this what your charge usually plays?"

Mrs. Clark laid an open hand on her chest. "Me, sir? You are asking my opinion?"

Herr Krause gestured wildly. "Yes. You are who I am asking."

"She has practiced these pieces a long time to play for you, sir. I hope that you are not displeased."

He stood up. "That is not what I am asking." He walked back and forth. "What do you care for? I mean. What is your passion?"

I blinked rapidly. I was a maiden of only twenty-two years. What would I know about passion? But I did not tell him that.

I felt the sharp sting of tears. "I've just wanted to come here and learn the great masters in the greatest music country in the world. I practiced."

"I can see that, Fraulein. But you play without a care, without feeling. What have you seen her play with feeling, Madame Clark?"

What does he mean? What could he possibly mean?

Mrs. Clark spread her hands. "Play him something from the choir."

"The choir?" My voice squeaked a bit more than I would have liked.

She nodded her head. I turned back around to the keyboard. I didn't prepare that. Not that I would have to. I knew all that music from my heart. The old songs didn't require preparation. They were a part of my soul.

I touched my hands to the keyboard and played songs: "Steal Away," "Ride the Chariot," "Swing Low Sweet Chariot," "Go Down Moses," and "Sometimes I Feel Like a Motherless Child." When I was halfway through the last one, Herr Krause jumped up and ran over to me at the piano, sitting down and wiping his face with a handkerchief. "These songs. These choir songs. They have a deepness, a beauty of the soul that is anything equal to the masters. But this one, this last one. Does it have words, Fraulein?"

"They all do, sir."

"Why have you not been singing them then?"

"I am here for my piano."

"You must, you must give these songs your full self. I must hear them sung as well."

I wanted to open my mouth and explain that singing was not my gift, but telling that to this man, a white man—the words were not in my vocabulary.

I opened my mouth and sang the words to "Sometimes I Feel Like a Motherless Child." When I looked up, unashamed tears were rolling down the face of Herr Krause. He was not the only one in the room. The young woman who brought him in was there, as well as an older woman wearing an apron, and the man—the blond man with the blue eyes from the café across the street. They were all in tears.

"You see there, Fraulein. That is emotion. That is passion. Those songs are incredible."

"Thank you."

Herr Kause stood. "It appears you have drawn out my family to hear you. This is my daughter, Julia; my wife, Marta; and my son, Karl. Well done, Fraulein."

"Good afternoon, Fraulein." The man who was Karl now stepped forward. "I am finally pleased to make your acquaintance."

He lifted up my hand, turning it over and kissing the warm brown on the back as if it were a rare jewel and not something to scorn. Finally, I got the sense of what Herr Krause was talking about.

Passion.

Portia

1905–1907

I settled into life in Berlin with a great deal of ease. I enjoyed walking about the streets, traveling on the streetcars, shopping in the stores, eating schnecken in the café, along with everyone else—wonderful. It was not like the United States at all because segregation, and its ugliness, was nowhere to be found here. I wrote to my father to tell him of my freedom in going about Berlin, in between explaining the progress that I was making in my lessons. Being away from home made me realize how the unauthored songs of the ancestors deserved to be classified with the greats in American, nay, world music. So I began collecting and arranging them, planning a recital of the music around Christmastime.

Alas, sometime in the fall I was stricken with the flu and had to be in bed for several weeks while I recuperated. I was in the care of Mrs. Clark and our landlady in the boardinghouse where we stayed. I was quite ill, but I never worried because everyone took such good care of me. Everyone was so kind; even the neighbors took pains to come by and see about me and bring me small gifts and treats. Our landlady had taken great pains to tell us our presence was a bit of a rarity, but in a good way, so I received the gifts with the same affection as they were given.

Karl Krause knew I was ill, and he made sure that I got soup, cookies, or other dainties to build me up. It was nothing like being at Tuskegee, because I already knew people there cared about me because of my father. They had to. Here, these expressions happened because I was Portia, on my own, and that made all the difference.

Once my health improved, I learned how to celebrate and appreciate the beauty of a German Christmas, something a little more celebratory and less religious than it was back home. Karl, who showed me around on behalf of his father, would take me to the theater. This was another pastime I enjoyed on a weekly basis with him because it was so inspirational to the music that I loved to play. I even began to dream that I might be able to write some kind of play featuring the music of the enslaved, something that would show their dignity and purpose instead of that crass coon music that now, thankfully, due to the increasing popularity of blues, had begun to fall out of fashion.

We were drinking coffees after a show and I was able to find an American newspaper, where I saw the announcement about Alice. She was getting married. She apparently had fallen in love with someone who was on the trip to the Orient with her. "His name is Nicholas Longworth," I read aloud. *The very man I thought she would fall for*, I thought in amusement. I intuited that very well. "He's from Cincinnati and is worth a fortune." I nodded to Karl over the paper. "That's good because Alice needs that."

"You like to spend the money, too, Fraulein." My friend chuckled.

I couldn't deny that. Coming up with consistent funds to make the seventy dollars per month my father sent me last had become a bit of a problem. Thankfully, Karl was there sometimes to pick up my tab when I ate out and to pay for my tickets to the theater. The money to pay Herr Krause, however, went directly to him from my father. At times I felt a little guilty about Karl's generosity, but he assured me our outings were not just because his father told him to take me, but because he enjoyed my company as well.

"He's so much older than her. He's thirty-six. That's quite a few years," I went on about Alice and Mr. Longworth. My mind reeled back to Sid for some reason, who was eight years older than me. Why was I thinking about him when I was half the world away and enjoying myself?

"I wonder if the president is thinking that an older man will help to settle her down." Karl swiped his fork across the plate where his torte had been.

"Settle her down? Such an age gap just sounds as if he's one step from the grave. I guess it's possible. After all, President Cleveland was twenty-eight years older than his wife when they married." I worked hard to prevent my features from arranging themselves in an unpleasant fashion. Oh, Alice.

"Do you feel sorry for your friend?"

"I don't know what to feel. I suppose I'm happy for her. This was what she wanted. He's a congressman. She won't have to move from DC where her family is. But it just sounds so final."

Karl reached across from where I was and touched my striped sleeve. "A woman must settle down and find herself a protector to marry. It's the way of the world."

I pulled my arm back. "That's not how it will be for me." I folded the paper.

"No?"

"No. I'm studying so that I'll learn how to be a better teacher. To protect myself."

Karl regarded me and my uneaten torte. "Do you never think of taking to the stage yourself, Fraulein?"

Now I poised my fork over my slice of torte. "That would be a dream indeed."

"You could travel all over Europe with your manager by your side. Playing music to concert halls."

Could I? Was I that good? "Do you think that enough people will want to hear the songs?" Karl knew what I meant.

"I do. So does Father."

"Well, I could play them, but not sing. My voice is not that good." I dug into the torte and ate it with enthusiasm.

As Karl walked me back to my boardinghouse, he held my hand. This was nothing unusual, but tonight, Karl's thumb made back-and-forth strokes against my palm and the slight sensation made me shiver. "Why are you doing that?" I finally asked as we stopped walking. We were a few blocks from the residence.

"I'm sorry, Fraulein. I didn't mean to cause harm."

"You didn't. I just wondered."

He moved close to me. "I just want you to know. Know how I feel."

"Feel, Karl?"

Now he was even closer, looking down on me in the moonlight under the streetlamp.

"I think you are one of the most amazing women I've ever met."

"Just one of?" I tried to keep it light. Like a faint ghost, I could sense what was coming. Now.

"Portia. The most beautiful heroine in Shakespeare. You more than meet your namesake." He put a finger under my chin, forcing me to look up at him.

What? Oh dear.

His lips came down on mine before I could even say anything or think about it. He tasted like cherries and whipped cream and I couldn't stop myself from reaching for more, wanting more.

Not like Sid.

And I pulled back. *What would Father say if he knew I was kissing a white man out in the street? What about my dignity as a woman of the race?*

Not to mention Sid. Who wanted a virginal wife.

What Sid wants doesn't matter anymore. Right?

"I didn't mean to . . ."

"No, Karl. It's fine. I mean, I'm okay. I just never realized that you cared for me in that way."

"You couldn't tell? I've wanted to be with you ever since I saw you in the café. My schnecken."

I laughed because it was silly being called a snail after my favorite pastry. But he was serious, so I didn't laugh long.

"Karl, I'm here to pursue my studies. I don't have time . . . I mean, I can't be that serious about a man right now."

"What do you want to do after your studies? You see your famous friend. She's younger than you and she has a husband."

"I mean, I want that, some day. Just not today."

"I'll wait for you, Portia. Until you are ready."

"I'm going back to the United States. I'm not going to stay here."

"Why not? I don't see the trouble. You could learn, and practice and improve and take up touring here in Europe, probably even to the Orient where your friend went."

Me? In the Orient? Like the president's daughter?

He put his hands on my shoulders. "You can do whatever you want with your talent and I . . . well, I can be your manager and take care of you."

I stepped away from him, trying to think. "Karl, there is a lot you don't understand."

"What? What don't I understand?"

"Well, those songs are meant to be sung. The Fisk choir, our choir, the other schools. It's music that a group of people sing together to get them through pain, through hard times. Me playing and singing them on the piano . . . it would seem strange."

"It might be strange at first, but so many of the people would love to hear them in whatever way you presented them."

"And I love it here, but I couldn't live here."

"Why not?" He straightened up. "I'll be finished with my schooling, too, and we can get a town house in the city. With a piano for you."

"Like your father has?"

"Even better than that." Karl reached for my hand again, warming it with his own palm. *Even better than that beauty?* The thought boggled my mind, and mixed emotions washed through me.

"I'm . . . I don't know what to say."

"Say yes. That you want to be with me."

The things that he spoke of seemed strange. Like a fantasy world. Not at all possible for someone like me from Alabama. "I . . . I can't."

"Look. Portia. Say that you will think about it. Please."

"If I were to . . . be with you, I would never be able to go home again. Never see my father and brothers again." The prospect of not seeing Margaret again wasn't that troubling, but the rest? How could I live a life apart from them?

"Couldn't they come here? You said your father and mother came here on a visit a few years ago. That's what paved the way for you to come."

"That's true. But because my father needs money for the school, he wouldn't . . . . Well, he would think it was a waste of money to come here again just to see me and I couldn't ask him to do that."

"There are other ways to get money. They could bring your brothers and they could meet my family."

I put a hand to my temple. "This is all going so fast. I-I need to think about it."

He took my hand and tucked it into the crook of his arm. "You take the time that you need, Portia. I told you, I would be here for you. I'm . . . I'm in love with you."

"But you've only known me for a few months."

"How much longer do I have to know you, my schnecken?"

Years. Like Sid.

We arrived at the boardinghouse and Karl turned his back to

the windows, reached down, and kissed me once more, his lips melting against mine like sweet sugar and beautiful promises. I dared not reach my arms up because I knew that either Mrs. Clark or the landlady would be able to see my hands around his neck and there would be questions. Questions that I didn't want to answer. In the meantime, I could enjoy myself.

Once I went inside, I walked down the hall and Mrs. Clark cracked the door. I could see that she was in her dressing robe. "Making sure that you are in for the night. Did you see the articles about your friend the president's daughter?"

"I did. She's getting married. She reached her goal."

"Yes. What do you feel about that, Portia?"

"I'm happy for her. I'll write her a note of congratulations, and hopefully she'll let me know her new address. I don't think they will live in the White House."

Mrs. Clark shook her head. "No. Too bad you won't be able to go."

I laughed. "I have my studies here. Anyway, knowing her, she would smuggle me in in some strange way." I couldn't imagine anyone who looked like me actually attending her ceremony. Just like I couldn't attend her debutante ball.

Then I stopped laughing. I said good night to Mrs. Clark and went into my own room. That was one thing I forgot to say to Karl. How would all that work? I had been to London, Paris, and Berlin, but would other cities like New York, Boston, or Philadelphia be as understanding about my race? Not to mention southern cities like Richmond, Atlanta, Birmingham, or Tuskegee. He didn't seem to understand that a life with him meant that I could never, ever return to the United States. Not with a white husband on my arm.

When I got ready for bed, I was in a much more somber mood. I didn't want to hurt Karl's feelings but the promise of an uncertain future on the stage for never stepping foot in the United States again seemed like an uneven exchange for a man I barely knew.

Alice would probably come to Europe at some point and I would see her again, but what would she say if I introduced her to my white husband? It was the only thing about that entire scenario that made me smile as I went to sleep.

Just a little.

THEN, I WAS young, beautiful, and charmed, even if I were not completely in love with Karl. Bless him, he thought he could get me there. But there was so much about my upbringing, too much that Karl could never understand, never tap into, no matter how much I tried to talk to him about what it was like to be a Negress in the United States. Being Negro was an integral part of me—the part that brought the songs to life.

One day, months later, I was coming back from the dressmakers who had been engaged to create the perfect frock for my graduation recital. Mrs. Clark had long ago made her journey back to the United States and my father promised to send a new chaperone for my return. The recital would be quite a concert. It was sold out and would be performed in one of the smaller halls of Konzerthaus that held about two hundred people but was still old, splendid, and beautiful. Karl was convinced that this would be my launch into greatness. I was less sure than he was, but I looked forward to it. I had worked hard on improving my technique and was eager to show off what I had learned to the world.

When I arrived at the boardinghouse, my landlady clapped her hands to see me. I thought she greeted me so because of my upcoming recital. "My dear, you have special guests in the parlor."

"Me?"

She scurried away and I followed her to the parlor, the place where the borders liked to relax after dinner. I would sometimes practice and play music here for those who were at the end of a hard day. Here was a place where I practiced the great masters I thought I had come here to study.

When I turned the corner, my hands sweated a little bit and I wiped them on my skirt, peering at who was sitting in the parlor.

Margaret.

But also Baker, my brother. I ran to him and when he embraced me, I could not believe that he was now taller than I was. "You've grown so!" I couldn't stop exclaiming.

I kissed Margaret on both her cheeks. There was another man there, a man of color who was not my father. "I don't have the pleasure of knowing your name, sir." I made a face at this stranger. What was my stepmother up to?

Margaret drew back, peering at me through those small spectacles of hers. "Why, Portia. You've been such a longtime fan. I thought you would know Samuel Coleridge-Taylor in person."

I put my hands to my warmed cheeks. Mr. Coleridge-Taylor was the foremost arranger of the spiritual songs of our people. He lived in London. I was hoping to see him on the way back to the United States, but I never imagined he would come here.

"Good day, Miss Washington." He nodded and smiled.

"Oh, sir. It's so good to meet you. Thank you so much for coming."

"When your stepmother asked me, I couldn't resist. I am so grateful to you and young people like yourself who are keeping the music of our ancestors alive."

"You're here to attend my recital?"

"Well, of course, Portia." Margaret seemed bothered by my question. "He came from London to hear of your progress and great talent."

I was happy, but there was something in Margaret's words that did not help me to feel at ease. She was the chaperone my father sent? Why had he sent her? Didn't he need her at Tuskegee?

There was something behind this. I just didn't know what that was.

Still, it was better to just put a brave face on it and enjoy the company of my Baker and Mr. Coleridge-Taylor, who was far younger than I supposed, but still, an appreciator of the spiritual music that I had perfected in Germany. His father was a Black man who had been born in the United States and was steeped in the music of the enslaved but had traveled to Sierra Leone, studying the ways in which the spiritual songs were like the music of Africa before he went to London and married an Englishwoman there, where Mr. Coleridge-Taylor had been born.

I poured everyone tea and presented them with some thick slices of stollen the landlady put out for me to serve. I would miss her and her kindness.

"I took a tour of the United States a few years ago, and I was thrilled to meet your president, Theodore Roosevelt, and his lovely daughter, Alice."

I nodded. "We are very friendly."

"I wondered. She is an enterprising young woman like yourself, and I was most impressed by Princess Alice. As I am with Princess Portia."

I smiled and shook my head. "I hope to see her on my way back through to Alabama."

Margaret sipped her tea. "You're likely to be far too busy to meet your compatriot, dear."

"I don't see how." I gave her a very direct glare. How dare she try to ruin my plans.

"She is Mrs. Longworth now, and might be busy with other events."

A shudder ran down the length of me. Not that. Not yet.

Was Alice expecting a child? I couldn't think of any other reason she might be too busy to see me, but it was not proper to talk of such matters in front of male company. If it had just been Baker, that was one thing, but not Mr. Coleridge-Taylor.

"Have you seen your rooms yet?" I asked smoothly. "Will you be staying here?"

"Our boardinghouse is just down the way," Margaret interjected.

"Good. I'm glad that you are close by."

I laughed at my brother, wiping his finger across the bread plate. "Now that Baker has inhaled the stollen, it reminds me that it is close to suppertime. Mr. Coleridge-Taylor, do you mind walking him back to the boardinghouse?"

"I don't. We'll see you soon."

After the male company left, and the door slammed shut, Margaret opened her reticule. "When you started making noises to your father as if you might want to stay in Germany longer than your proposed course of study, that concerned both of us, of course, from a financial perspective."

"So Father sent you to bring me home."

She gave a sly smile, one I did not like much.

"On the contrary. Someone more important to your future sent me."

She handed me a letter with handwriting on the envelope that was not Father's. I broke the seal to the envelope, opened it, and the quaking contracted in my stomach.

Sid.

Dearest Portia,

I'm so happy to hear that you are doing well with your studies in Berlin. I am sure that your progress has been immeasurable and I'm so sorry that I could not be there to celebrate with you in person. I've asked your step-mother to be my emissary in sending you these greetings as well as a request on my behalf. I've been praying that you are open to hearing my request, given that the last time that we parted, it was on less than cordial terms.

I looked up at Margaret, who, of course, looked like the cat who ate the canary. The question in my mind was, Who was the canary?

"What is this?"

"I don't read other people's mail, Portia."

I pursed my lips and read on.

I've been hired as an architect for the Black exhibit at the Jamestown Tricentennial Celebration in Virginia. Thus, I'll be leaving Tuskegee at the end of the school year. Since I'll be moving to the Washington, DC, area and its environs, I find myself in need of the kind of companionship that is the making of a man's life. Portia, I'm asking you to return to the United States and become my wife. I have loved you for many years and nothing in the world would make me happier than this. You don't have to send a response right now. I know that the joining of our lives is a large thing, and you deserve the time to think it all through. I'll meet you in Virginia when you come through and give me your answer then.

Yours always,
William Sidney Pittman

I was surprised to feel the prick of tears at the corners of my eyes.

"Well?" Margaret asked as she sipped on her lukewarm tea.

"Well. You must know of Mr. Pittman's future prospects."

"Yes. We are so sorry to see him departing Tuskegee, but always knew that he had promise and the makings to succeed in the larger world. Any woman who would be his wife would certainly be blessed by such a connection."

"So you know that he's asked to marry me in this letter?"

Margaret shifted in her chair.

She knew.

"Mr. Pittman is a man fully grown of some thirty years. I don't suppose to know his business."

I held the letter in my hand. "I can come with you and just as easily return to Europe later, if I wanted to." A goodbye tour to my homeland would be the least I could do if I wanted to return to Europe to be a concert pianist in my own right.

"On whose dollar?"

The question, short and brief as it was, formed an important focus of my current life's issues. I said nothing and left Margaret in the parlor by herself.

My recital was the next evening, and given my current circumstances and the letter from Sid, I played with a lot of . . . well . . . passion.

Alice

1903–1905

Young women who are looking for husbands must display themselves in some way. That's why, at exactly 10 a.m. on the dot, each day during the week, there is a bit of a parade on F Street where young ladies of marriageable age show off their outfits and themselves to the public.

One of the things that was a drawback to being the president's daughter, especially with the mother that I have, was that I could never go. I wanted to watch and see who my competition was if nothing else.

Anyway, there is no denying that my dance card at events was always full—and that I even danced at one with Franklin, my distant cousin who was down from Harvard. He was a good catch, with his sparkling blue eyes and his wavy blond hair. However, he had some problems. One of them was that mother of his. I could never, ever put up with Sara as my mother-in-law. We would fight continuously. It's wrong, so wrong to say this, but she was half in love with Franklin herself and would not let him be with a woman she could not control. So I danced with him, laughed, and tossed my head back, just to spite Sara to make her think I was a possibility. Then I let him go without another thought. If I were more inclined to pray to God, I would pray to whomever had the misfortune of being his future wife, but I was much too concerned with my own prospects.

No, I needed a man, not a boy. So the search continued.

But I did meet someone that night. Marguerite, the daughter of the Russian ambassador to the United States, was in my age range and she was so much fun. I could see that I could easily have a partner in crime, if I so chose. The only problem was that with her auburn hair and her eyes, I might have a problem maintaining a gentleman's attention, even if I am the president's daughter.

Was it better to be the pretty friend and have men come to you? I could hang around my cousin Eleanor and be the pretty friend. Her mother had been one of the most beautiful belles in New York but look at how she turned out after being mistreated by my alcoholic uncle. So unfortunate.

Or was it better to have the pretty friend and see what you might pick up from her leftovers? Leftovers? Ugh, even the sound was unappealing. One of the pluses of having the pretty friend was to prove that I was confident enough in myself to show I didn't mind having a friend with masses of auburn hair and sparkling eyes. Confidence is very appealing and I could play that to my advantage.

I went with the second approach.

So I drew an arm through hers and once the parades began, there we were, quite a pair, walking up and down F street in our different dresses every day.

And as I suspected, the male attention went straight to her first. Maggie, for that is what she had been dubbed by the social elite, laughed and waved, waved and laughed at all the attention. It was then, in the spring of 1903, that I recalled my promise to Portia about coming to her father's campus to see what the students had done. I suppose I felt a little quaking in my stomach.

"You'd better get that sour look off your face, dear. I don't want the men to be scared away."

"I just remembered something that I forgot to do." I cleared my features and tried to arrange them into a more Maggie-like posture.

"Whatever do you have to do?"

"I promised a friend that I would come and visit and now . . . well, time is running out and I may not be able to get to it."

"You're the president's daughter. Things happen. I'm sure they will understand."

A clock in the distance struck 11 a.m. and that was it for the parade. We strolled toward her car and Maggie reminded me of the dinner that evening. "It's going to be quite fun."

"Yes. Quite." I moved toward my own car.

"And don't bring your dour look about your duties."

"I won't."

"Who is this person, anyway? I thought I knew all the people that you know."

"Oh, you don't know her. She's colored."

Maggie laughed her trilling laugh. "Alishuka"—she used the Russian pet name she had for me—"you cannot be serious."

"I am quite." I opened my reticule to check on my snake to make sure she wasn't too cold. She wasn't. Spring weather in DC could be quite changeable.

"You know a colored person?" All the laughter left her face.

"She's Portia Washington, daughter of Father's colored friend, Booker T. Washington."

"I suppose I remember hearing about him. Isn't he half colored?"

I thought of his gray eyes that he had passed on to Portia. "I believe so."

Maggie nodded from her car seat. "That makes more sense. Someone couldn't be an entire colored and do some good in this world. But Portia then . . ."

"She has Indian blood," I put in. And, as it did every time, Maggie saw her in a whole new light. So did a lot of other people. So strange that seemed to matter to people.

"Oh, how thrilling. Still. You either have time from what your father expects of you, dear, or you don't."

I nodded. That was true enough. Now that the weather was clearing up, I knew he probably had a duty or two in mind for me. Something that Mother could not or would not do.

Later that day, Father let me know that he wanted me, and with an appropriate chaperone of course, to go to Puerto Rico on his behalf. A wonderful opportunity that was much better and much more exciting than some of the other places in the States where he had sent me. And this would be a tour! I tried not to look at Mother, because I knew she was looking to catch my eye with some word of warning. I knew how to behave while representing Father, of course, but I knew she would have something to say to me directly.

"Mind you, this is the first time that a presidential daughter will have been sent on such a tour," she said anyway, not caring if she caught my eye or not.

Something in my fingers tingled. It was??

I played it cool. "Oh, I'm fully aware of that."

"Good. Behave accordingly." Then she was the one who got to sweep from the room with no further explanation. Or thanks. She might have said thank you. Wasn't it the job of the First Lady to do such things? Still, it had been a very long time since an administration had an active First Lady to travel on behalf of the president. I mean, there had been Frances Cleveland during those years, but she didn't travel a great deal. Cleveland kept his baby wife close to him for reasons, Democrat rascal that he was. Even though I had been a bit of a fright in terms of behavior, because of my insistence on living my life to the fullest, it was hard to see my trip to Puerto Rico as anything other than a presidential honor bestowed upon me.

OF COURSE, THE trip was a smashing success. Or I was. The two really could not be separated. By the time of my return, the papers were filled with reports of my travels there, including meeting with the governor and approving of the gatherings of the local people. The food, the culture, and every part of the trip was so fulfilling. My cheeks were rosy with my pride at my accomplishment and I could tell that Father was pleased, even two years later, with the reports of my success there.

One day in 1905 he said to me, "You've done well for yourself, my dear. I am thinking about the next thing that I would want you to do." He turned to Mother. "We'll be talking it over and I'll let you know. Meanwhile, we're having a reception for some of the newer congressmen and I need for you to attend. Mother will be there too."

I nodded. "Of course, Father. I'm here to help you."

"You may leave Emily in her cage." He glared at me through his pince-nez.

"I will, Father." He smiled at me. A little. Something in my heart thawed. He didn't smile at me often at all. There was no way that I would deny him what he wanted. Because he saw me.

"There will be some Porcellians there."

With any mention of my father's old college club, Mother's gentle countenance stiffened. Anything from his Harvard days brought back the fact that that's where he met my mother and fell in love with her, leaving Edith mother to fend for herself in New York. She spoke up. "Porcellians mean extensive drinking and drunkards. Certainly not worthy husband material."

"Well, Father was one and look at how well he turned out," I could not resist saying, just to make sure that he would keep smiling at me.

He did.

"Certainly an exception." Mother, of course, took exception to any approval of me.

He coughed, still a twinkle in his eyes. "Well, certainly this will be the case. These Porcellians are the ones who have gotten rich from the United States wine-making industry."

"Whoever knew there was such a thing?"

"Well, now, Edith. We can't let the Europeans have all the fun. The Longworth family of Ohio, I think Cincinnati, found a way to make wine here, and God bless them for it."

Mother cut her eyes. "Drunkards."

Father winked at me. I winked back at him. I couldn't wait.

I made sure to dress in one of my infamous Alice blue dresses. I knew what would make me stand out whenever I had to stand next to Maggie or any other woman, for that matter. The so-called Alice blue, a kind of periwinkle hue, emphasized my eyes as my best feature and helped everything else, so Maggie would be diminished. My sleeves rounded, my skin smooth, and my waist tiny in Alice blue satin, I did not need much embellishment. My youthful, dewy skin would do very well. With my masses of brown hair put in my infamous Gibson Girl topknot, framing my face like a cloud, I could not miss. Even with Mother there in her tiresome scratchy old lady lace.

Once I went into the ballroom, every eye in the place lighted on me. So much fun. I knew getting married was my objective, but I was having a good time in the meantime. I could do this.

I shook hands with the assembled congressmen who were new to the body and made small talk with them. I saw Uncle Joe Cannon there and went over to have a little word with him. I knew it wasn't easy for him to come to receptions at the White House, as he and Father were always at odds even though they were both in the Republican Party, but it was my job as a good hostess to make others feel comfortable. Even Mr. Taft, a friend of Father's, was there. There was something about him that looked a bit like a dog at heel, but I greeted him merrily, as well as his wife, who was a bit uptight, not unlike Mother. I remembered that they had a daughter my age, but she was no fun, so I didn't mention her.

Something made me glance back over at the lined-up congressmen. A man, a very handsome man, had joined their number. I could see from his equally arrogant bearing that he was a congressman. I had missed one. How could that be? Where had he been? "Excuse me," I told Mr. Taft and made my way across the room to this gentleman. I would never be able to describe the way this balding man of some years older than myself with a straw-colored mustache was able to peel me off away from the others, but the energy behind his eyes, the way he held himself as if he were above everything, and his inherent power stance mirrored me in a way I recognized.

Even though I knew it wasn't proper, I had never cared about any of those things before. Now? I couldn't help myself. I saw the male version of me—the version that could have been a ranch hand with Father in Wyoming, and I was drawn to him.

He must have seen me coming from across the room, for when I stopped in front of him, he turned from the other congressman with whom he had been speaking and addressed me directly, using a hand gesture to dismiss him. His colleague fell away as if lightning had struck that spot. Because it had.

Which left us, strangers to one another, all alone without any introduction.

So improper.

I loved it.

"Nicholas Longworth, Princess Alice. At your service."

I greeted him as I was bid to do. "Thank you for coming tonight."

"I apologize for being late, but I had other things to attend to first."

I straightened. "I suppose it is every day that a congressman is invited to sup with the president."

His face relaxed, and then he smiled. "Well, actually, no. But"—he leaned in to me, whispering in my ear so that no one else in the busy gathering could hear him—"I'm the one who will take your virginity away from you, Princess. I wanted to make sure that you would remember my arrival."

All the air went out of the room at these bold words and I had to make quite an effort to look as effortless as possible.

His words tested my hostess capabilities, but I passed.

Barely.

Alice

1905

Who was this man? Yes, Nicholas Longworth, but who was that? I knew that I should be incredibly offended that he would say something like that to me, especially in such a public venue, but it was hard to deny the thrill that ran through me in places I dared not think about, let alone mention.

I wanted to make sure that he would hear me when I spoke, so I cleared my throat. "Sir, I'm the president's daughter and you should not speak to me in such a manner."

He sipped his wine, moving even closer to me. "Strange. After all I've read about you in the papers, I did not take you as someone who followed the rules. Please forgive me."

Well. That was better. The thrill slowed a bit. "You're forgiven, Mr. Longworth."

"Of course, I know that I'm right."

The thrill was back again.

"Even if you are, sir, is this the place and the occasion to say such things? And you are a congressman."

"The perfect cover, isn't it? I've been enjoying myself immensely ever since I got to Washington City. It took some time for me to make my way, but as someone with money, name, and position, I'm going to use every bit of everything I can to engage in hedonism."

"Hedonism, Mr. Longworth?"

"Why, yes, Princess. Seeking out pleasure in all circumstances, no matter what."

I looked about me, sure that Mother or Father would come to my rescue. They were not anywhere around. "I'm Miss Roosevelt, but my Christian name is Alice. You could call me that."

"Oh, I will. Eventually. Since no one else seems to want to."

Something in his words behaved like a hammer of sorts, breaking through the fog, surrounding my heart, grasping hold of it for his own plaything. "How—how did you know that?"

"I know a lot about you. I've studied you."

This was a time I should have brought Emily Spinach, my pet snake, with me. She did not bite, but she could frighten. Was I frightened? By someone who seemingly had read into my heart, mind, and soul? Isn't this what I wanted? What everyone wanted? To find someone who knew you completely?

"Well, tell me some things that you know and I'll see if you've passed the test."

"Smoking on your father's roof after he told you that you could not smoke in his house. So clever. Driving places on your own, when many women wouldn't dare to obtain a license. Carrying your little snake around with you. Pulling pranks with your siblings. The only way that you've disappointed me is . . ."

I whirled on him. "Disappointed you?"

He narrowed his eyes at me. "Why, yes. Is the way you seem to insist on playing games with me. As you are right now. Acting as if you don't want to be a hedonist, too. To cover all the pain you've been forced to deal with since your very first hours in the world."

He had a point. Many points.

"Do I pass the test?" His smile was half hidden by that mustache of his, but I could tell he was quite pleased with himself.

"You've done well enough."

"So, the question is just how long you'll hold out on me."

"Hold out?"

"Why, I mean hold out on keeping your virginity intact. How long will you make me wait?"

My breathing changed again. I must not let him see what or how I was really feeling although I had the sense that he already knew. Damn him!

"Well, isn't that part of the fun, Mr. Longworth?"

He drank the rest of his wine. "I suppose it is." He turned to me full on and leaned down—quite an achievement, since I was rather tall—and whispered in my ear, his breath hot and moist. "Here comes your mother. I can already tell she hates me. Watch."

Sure enough, the First Lady came swanning up next to us. "Good evening. And are you Mr. Longworth? So sorry that I didn't have the pleasure of meeting you in the official line."

"Yes, well, I wanted to make sure I was ready to engage with your lovely daughter here. Alice"—he put a heavy emphasis on my name, on purpose—"is as beautiful as they say she is in the newspapers."

"Well. Yes," Mother conceded. It was hard for her to. Every time.

"Quite bright, too. Alice and I have been engaging in a discussion of ancient philosophy and I'm pleased to say that Alice is able to respond to my questions as an equal."

The more he said my name, the more that he would pronounce it with an extended hiss at the end and it made me think of Emily Spinach. I didn't need to put her in my reticule for tonight, after all. I had a suitable companion already.

"Well, as long as she is behaving herself, I'm glad to hear that."

"Alice is doing a beautiful job of making me more in admiration of her than ever, Mrs. Roosevelt." He took up my hand and tucked it into his arm. "Excuse us, please."

Mother made way for us as he guided me to the dance floor, the appropriate floor now, and glided me out onto it with a smooth motion. "Well," I managed to say as I whirled around, "you handled that well."

"Of course I did. Mothers are a bit of a specialty."

I've never been in the company of a man who literally took my breath away, but this man, this Nicholas Longworth, had many qualities to recommend him. "I don't think my name has ever been said so often in her presence."

He looked down at me, gripping my waist just a tiny bit more. It didn't hurt. It just made me feel more . . . secure than I had before. "Good. It's time that someone did. You are not to blame for the past, you know."

No one had ever said those words to me in that way. Well, Portia had, because she was the only one who understood my situation or came close to understanding it. At least she had her own name. I had to share mine with a dead woman.

For once, I had nothing to say, so I surrendered myself to the pleasure of swirling about in this man's arms, across the right kind of dance floor, slightly buzzed on wine but admired by everyone staring.

I knew this would be a night that I would never forget.

"DID I SEE you dancing with Nicholas Longworth?" Maggie inquired while we were walking F Street after the party. From that night on, I determined to show myself, regardless of what anyone else thought.

"You did."

"Isn't he dreamy?"

I whirled around to her. Quickly. Then I looked straight ahead of me, not wanting her or anyone else watching me to get the sense that I was disturbed in any way. So much for no one else wanting a bald man.

"He's acceptable, I suppose."

"You suppose? My dear friend. He's without parallel. Ever since he's arrived in Washington City he has practically partied nonstop. He has certainly made his mark here since his arrival."

Then why am I only hearing about him now? "I suppose that my trip to Puerto Rico meant that he and I didn't circulate in the same circles."

Maggie gave a little half smile filled with knowledge I did not possess and I didn't like it. "I think it's more because the president's daughter doesn't get invited to those kinds of parties."

The beat of my heart quickened and matched my steps up and down F Street. "What kind of parties? And how would you know about them anyway?"

"He is thirty-five, my friend. These are grown-up parties. Ones with lots of liquor and, well, women in various stages of dress."

"Reeeally?" I drew out the word, but then I should not have been surprised. I knew he was older but he was quite a bit older than me. Women in various stages of dress. "I mean, we did talk about that somewhat."

"You did not," Maggie said flatly.

"We did, mon cheri. He told me that he was a hedonist. We spoke of the philosophy at length."

She giggled like a little girl.

"Oh, he's so wicked and can you believe he's a politician, too?"

"I've seen quite enough of politics to know I can believe a lot of things." The clock in the distance chimed at eleven and our time to parade for the day was over.

"Have you ever been to one of those parties?" I directed at her.

"My dear, I'm part Russian. Russians invented hedonism. We have long had to do a variety of naughty things to keep ourselves warm in the cold." She purred as if she were one of the White House cats we kept to chase the rats away.

Mother was right. I was caught between wanting to slap my mother and slapping Maggie. Neither alternative was a good one, so I stomped away to my car so that I didn't have to look at Maggie any longer. At least not today.

When my car arrived back at home, one of the servants told me Father wanted to see me. He didn't usually make time for me in the middle of the day so it must have been important. Otherwise, he would have waited until dinnertime. I immediately took myself to the president's office and there he was. I tried not to be so surprised, but he fit so well. It always made my heart happy to see him there.

Mother was with him. I should have known. What had I done wrong now? Maybe she heard how I had received Mr. Longworth's words and wanted to scold me about how I should have made more protest at them.

I was about to open my mouth to proclaim my innocence when he held up a hand. "Make yourself comfortable, my dear. I've just finished speaking with your mother about how well you've been doing lately."

Oh. Well then. I sat myself down in the chair he directed me to. "This is very important, my dear. I've been negotiating a peace deal between Russia and the imperial nation of Japan. They've been at war you know."

I knew. Crazy little Nicholas, the czar of Russia, didn't want to look bad in fighting people he saw as inferior to himself, so he had gotten himself all tied up in a mess that he now could not get out of. How typical. Maggie had told me that a large part of Nicholas's problem was that he was short and that short men were always trying to make up for their shortcomings in the world. Oh, and that his German wife was also crazy and no one liked her and she kept having girl babies. I saw no problem with the girls, but that was a problem in a country like Russia, apparently.

"Yes, Father."

"I'm putting together an entourage to go tour the Orient and one of the stops in Japan will involve you, my dear daughter, to make sure that you add your soft touch to seal the agreement between the two nations."

I straightened up. "Me?"

"Yes, you."

"You are willing to have me do this? You feel that I can be trusted to help you make peace between two warring nations?" I gulped.

Mother's face wore a dark look. She surely didn't believe it.

"I've just spoken with your mother. We have both come to see that you have comported yourself well lately. That some of your early spirit has been, well, spent, thank God. You've grown to the point that you can handle this assignment."

"Oh, Father. Thank you so much for your trust in me. And Mother." I nodded at her.

We were not a family that were physically affectionate with one another, so I just let my eyes proclaim their happiness.

When I went back to my room, I gave a squeal and gave Emily a special pat. The Orient! To represent my father on such an important mission. The Puerto Rico trip was quite something but this responsibility was on a whole new level.

Someone knocked at my door. When I opened it, the doorway was filled with an obscene bouquet of flowers and a petite maid was behind it, struggling to get them into my room. "My goodness," I breathed at this latest token of affection. I examined the flowers for a card and finally found it. I opened the envelope and a looping handwritten sentiment proclaimed who they were from. I had to sit down.

The one sentence was on my mind from then on: "Dear Princess Alice, I cannot wait to accompany you to the land of the Orient, the home of hedonism. Nicholas Longworth."

I could not wait either.

Portia

My music program, designed to show my skills, moved between my two worlds. I played from the masters I had come to study in their homeland—my new friends moody Beethoven, elegant Brahms, and thoughtful Bach—to the music from my homeland. I think this is why so many people wanted to come. To see a woman with brown skin play their music was one thing but to hear the music of the United States played with such passion and longing for my homeland was quite another. Karl led the audience in standing for me, which made me smile. They might not have stood if he hadn't done it first, but everyone did stand. Even Margaret stood next to my eagerly applauding brother, but most importantly, my teacher stood, which brought tears to my eyes. Having his approbation meant a great deal to me. Who knew what the future would hold? This might be the last time there would be such focus on me. Or it might be the first time such focus was on me. It was all my decision.

When it was all over, I lounged in my dressing room where many had sent me bouquets for good luck. The largest one, though, was brought forward in a white basket, with fronds of fern, roses, lilies, and other wild flowers. Opening the card, I couldn't register surprise. I knew it was from Karl. I wanted to hide it, but it was so huge, it was impossible. Margaret pushed her way through to the back with my brother. Baker came forward, like the large child he still was, and embraced me, practically stashing me under the pit of his arm. Margaret's eyes wandered all over the room, searching for her and Father's bouquet, which, of course, was there. Still, watching her inspect all the cards of the flowers, she acted as if she wasn't trying to see the card on the largest bouquet of all.

"That was amazing, sister," Baker said. "You played so well."

"Thank you, Baker. I'm glad you enjoyed it."

"Well. So many admirers, Portia. This one, this large one must be from Sid." Margaret looked all through the fern fronds looking for a card, but I had confiscated it long before. Ha!

I said nothing and turned to the tasteful roses and lilies combination she had sent on behalf of the family. "It's beautiful, thank you, Mother."

"You're welcome."

Baker blurted out, "Mr. Coleridge-Taylor loved your playing too. He couldn't stay, but said he looks forward to talking over the particulars with you when you come through London."

"He did?"

He nodded and then looked to Margaret to confirm, but bless him, he didn't know her as I did. She turned to him. "Baker, please make sure the carriage is ready to return us to the boardinghouse. You'll have to be man enough to do it, since Mr. Coleridge-Taylor isn't here."

My brother snapped to attention and went from the room immediately, so happy to be given an adult's responsibility.

"Who sent you this basket?" Margaret was usually more circumspect than that but not today.

"A man." I said it in the same tone as I would say, *None of your business.*

Before I could say another word, a knock came at the door and I swallowed. Maybe it was Baker, though he had just left. Margaret went to the door and opened it. Karl stepped right through, right past her. Usually, I would laugh at someone treating Margaret as if she were my help, but for the way that Karl came right up to me and embraced me as if he were used to doing it.

Then, I had to face the questions in Margaret's eyes.

Portia

1907

She said nothing to me about Karl right away. We were due to leave on Monday morning and she came over to my boarding-house on Saturday afternoon, a time when Karl would usually come and take me to see a matinee. I had told him to refrain this time, since I wanted to rest from the rigors of the recital. He agreed and said he wanted to see me for a performance on Saturday night but I had not said anything to him about whether or not I would go.

"Good afternoon, Mother," I greeted her.

Her lips were pursed and I could tell she was far from happy and she didn't think it was a good afternoon at all.

Margaret got right to the point. "Your father. He didn't want to be separated from me this long, but I just had a feeling that one of us should come. You might have weaseled your way past another chaperone, but you wouldn't be able to pull that off with me or him. And since he couldn't get away from school . . ."

"It had to be you."

"Don't come across with that attitude, Portia. Who was that white man in your room?"

"Karl?"

"Karl." An entire sentence resonated in the way she said that word. "And who is Karl?"

"He's Herr Krause's son."

"I mean to you."

"He's my"—I swallowed—"friend."

Margaret stood. She came over to the davenport where I was

sitting and sat down next to me. I tried not to recoil as I took in her cloying scent of lemon verbena. "What kind of friend, Portia?"

"Someone I go out to the theater with. Concerts. He has some ideas for my future, but I haven't invested too much thought in that."

"Future? You think you have a future with such a man as Karl?" Her lip fairly curled from sneering.

I would set her straight. "If I wanted to."

"If you wanted to. What do you even mean, Portia?"

"He wants me to play in concert halls all over Europe." I left out the other part. She didn't need to know more.

She let out the laugh she had clearly been holding in. "I suppose he would be your manager."

I held my head high, trying not to let the hurt show in my face. "Why, yes."

"And then when you had served your usefulness to him as a pet monkey, what then?"

"Excuse me?"

"I said you would be nothing more than a grinder's monkey to such a man." She drew back from me, folding her arms. "God knows, I've tried to be a mother to you. I had hoped to not speak this way, Portia, but now I must know. I must have the truth. Are you a virgin?"

My eyes darted away from her, filling with tears. She grabbed me by the chin, hard, and forced me to look at her.

"Ouch! What are you doing?"

"Answer me, girl. Are you still a virgin?"

The tears spilled over my eyelids and streamed down my face. "How dare you treat me this way? I'm going to let Father know . . ."

"Do you really want to tell your father you have the attentions of a white man sending you a huge basket like that? Making promises to you? Everything about this little situation smells like the bad times, and it will do nothing but bring him pain and reminders of his own mother and how she thought the Taliaferros of Virginia were going to do something to free them but they didn't. Is that what you want?"

"No!"

Her grip tightened. "Then answer me."

"Yes. I'm still a virgin."

She let go of me and I slumped as she did. She had never treated me like that before. We had always had frosty exchanges with each other, but putting her hands on me as if to cause me hurt? She had never done that.

"You'd better be."

"I am!" I practically screamed.

"That's more like it. Now I'm inclined to believe you."

I reached up and rubbed my jaw, hoping that no marks were left behind. I moved it back and forth. It still moved. I was okay. But Margaret still sat there, glaring at me. "I'm going to move you into my room until it's time to leave."

I narrowed my eyes at her. "I'm twenty-four years old. I don't have to do as you say."

She gave the same look right back at me. "I saw how he touched you and how you were touching him. You may be twenty-four, but you have no idea what you are getting yourself into. The fact that you are about to leave will be too much for you both and you can easily be overcome."

"Are you suggesting that kind of thing happened to you?"

Righting herself, she put a hand to her chest. "If you do not arrive in Alabama, ready to marry Sid Pittman as a virgin, you'll never be able to leave your father's house and you'll disgrace him as an old maid."

"Father would have me stay with him as long as I wanted. I can always teach at the school. I don't have to listen to what you say."

Margaret looked quickly about her and lowered her voice. "What would you do if something happened to your father?"

I drew in my breath. "What do you mean?"

"I mean"—she stared at me—"he's been ill. Not seriously, but ill. The doctors keep telling him to slow down but he won't do it. He is running himself to the ground for the school. He's on borrowed time." She put her hand against the back of the davenport to steady herself, no doubt. She was awful, but I never questioned her love for him. "It behooves all of us to make sure we are secure for any future circumstances. For you, that means marriage to Sid Pittman. As soon as possible."

"And Karl?"

"Do you really think it's wise to put your future in the hands of a white man? What were you singing in those songs, anyway? Do you not understand our long and sad history? I'll tell you myself. My mother thought she could be with a white man—my father. He was a wayward sailor who found himself in Macon, Mississippi. She loved him, gave him ten children, and then he died. We were on the verge of starving to death, Portia."

I looked away from her, unpleasant visions forming in my head. I had visited her homeland with her before when I was younger and it was not a nice place to be. "You recall that my mother gave me to the Quakers because she could no longer afford to feed and clothe me. I had to leave my family at seven years old to make my way into the world. That's what came of her entangling herself with my Irish father, rascal that he was. The lesson? I needed a skill to be able stand on my own and not rely on anyone. You have that now. Go home and marry a good man so that you are even more secure."

I swallowed hard. I had always known what I was going to do, but I cared for Karl. I didn't want to hurt him or his father, who had been a wonderful professor to me. His mother and sister had also been kind to me.

Europe is not like America.

Still. I had racial encounters here and there as well. There was no hiding place in the world away from racial hatred, even if things were easier in Germany. They still were not perfect. I looked up at her.

She only wants me out of my father's house.

She's also right.

Then she spoke the words that hovered in the back of my mind like a ghost, thinking about how stress and worry had stolen my other mothers from me. "All he wants is for you to be secure," she whispered low, as close to me as she dared to get.

That's when I knew what I had to do.

Portia

1907

A t our parting, Karl held my hands and kept his captivating blue gaze on me. He knew better than to try to kiss me in front of Margaret and my brother, but it was clear that he was distraught. His eyes were full of unshed tears and he clearly begged me not to go, even though his un-Sidlike lips were telling me something else. The best I could do was to promise him that I would write. But I never would. It was better to let him think that I would return one day to take up the impossible dream he had for me to be in some far-fetched career. He didn't understand; a career as a touring concert pianist in Europe could never be for someone like me. That's what made my eyes fill with tears, not leaving him. Clearing away my own streaming eyes after one long night, I turned my focus on the road home.

When I arrived to stay with the Coleridge-Taylor family in England, Mr. Coleridge-Taylor's life and circumstances proved me right. His household was filled with love, but it was hard to miss the chipped dishes, the worn corners of the furniture, and the repeatedly turned hems and seams in the dresses that his lovely blonde wife wore. The two young children they had were beautiful, but their clothes were also worn. Money was hard to come by for this man, one of the premier and most talented composers and conductors in Europe. If this talented man could not make a living from performing in concert halls in Europe, what chance did I have?

The voyage from London to New York was relatively peaceful between me and Margaret. I had not written Sid back, but I would see him when I returned, as he directed. I took heart in the fact that he would not pressure me for a decision, but he allowed me to think for myself; that fact made it seem as if Sid saw me as an independent, grown woman.

We took the train from New York to Washington, DC, and I was sorry that I could not stop for a brief visit to see Mrs. Longworth, now that I returned to the United States. DC formed an unpleasant reminder because that was the point where we boarded a Jim Crow car. The fetid air in the car intensified as we traveled south to Atlanta and then to Tuskegee from there.

If I went back to Karl in Europe, I would never have to travel on such a car again. I could travel around in the most fabulous homes and concert halls and I could forget, as much as was possible, my heritage from Africa.

What would that do? Denial of my people meant denial of myself. And, as Margaret suggested but did not say, my father would worry about me every day and the worry would wear him down even faster. The thought of my father no longer walking the earth made my soul feel as if it were cleft in two. I didn't want that. I had to make the safe choice. The choice that would keep my father alive, the choice for my happiness as a Negro.

When we arrived in Tuskegee on the specially run school connector train, it was in the early morning hours. My father waited with the hack by the railroad platform as always. But now, he had company. From behind the comforting shadow of my father, Sid Pittman stepped out into the darkness of the platform. Our eyes sought each other's and that's when I knew.

He was my husband.

"Portia. I mean, Miss Washington. Welcome home." He seemed shy, unsure, not the confident, suave man I had known from before.

"Oh. Mr. Pittman." I stepped toward him and then, I knew, it didn't matter anymore. My father wouldn't stop me. Margaret wouldn't stop me. This is what they wanted as well. I ran into his arms and he picked me up and I was as good as laid bare against him. My heart opened to him, and I knew his heart was open to me and we came together in that moment, together forever.

I pulled back from Sid and his lips, those gorgeous lips of his, pressed against mine and to be honest, the big wedding ceremony in Oaks on Halloween night a few months later was redundant. The knitting together of our souls happened right there in the darkness of that warm summer night on the Tuskegee railroad platform.

Everything that Margaret had told me about Sid was true. But there was much more to it than that. More below the surface. Sid had always been about surface appearances and not taking the time or trouble to make everything else true. Unless it was with his designs.

AT THE TIME we married on the last day of October in 1907, the term was still ongoing, but the holidays were coming up. I wanted to stay in Alabama and have a last Thanksgiving and Christmas at home, but Sid had to get back to work. When we sat at the table at our wedding reception, I guess I thought I could sweet-talk him into one wedding gift. Sid threw his head back and laughed. "Listen, honey. You're Mrs. Pittman now. You have to go where I go. It's not about you being Daddy's little girl any longer."

Margaret was more fine with my leave-taking. On top of that, the talk that she promised me back in Europe turned into a quick "You're going to enjoy it. It won't feel that good at first, but you'll come to enjoy it."

So much for an in-depth talk about men. I really wished we had stopped in DC. A session with Mrs. Longworth about the particulars on my wedding night would have helped, but since we were moving there, I would have more time to consult with my compatriot to ask her the finer points of being married.

Once we left Alabama, we went to Atlanta and stayed at the finest hotel in Sweet Auburn, the Negro part of the city. There had been a racial riot in Atlanta just the year before, where the hotel structure had been compromised. The replacement hotel they had built was new, grand, with state-of-the-art indoor plumbing, and very suitable for newlyweds.

We were taken to the largest suite, after it was explained by Sid that I was the daughter of Booker T. Washington, which was why I deserved the best.

The train we had taken was a late-night one, and I was dragging. I hadn't expected to be whisked away from home so soon after my return to begin a new life as Mrs. Pittman, but I would do my best to adjust.

The door closed and Sid and I were all alone. "Draw me a bath," his first words to me were.

I gave a half smile. "It's five o'clock in the morning, Sid."

He turned to me. "I'm fully aware of what time it is, Portia. But one of the things you will learn to do is what I say. Now. Draw me a bath."

I turned from him, ready to sag from exhaustion, and did as he said, ensuring that the bath was nice and warm, bringing forward a bowl of warm washstand water for myself. "It's ready."

"Good." He stomped across the floor to the bathroom and shut the door behind him, leaving me all alone with my trunks and no energy for me to dig through them to find anything. Fortunately, my travels had taught me to keep something easy in my small grip, so I took out a chemise and I took advantage of the hot water in the washstand to take all the grime off myself from the train.

My husband called out to me and I spoke to him through the closed door. "Yes?"

"Come in here and wash my back."

"Excuse me?" I asked louder. Or maybe I was wasting some time.

"Portia. Come in here."

I opened the door, little by little, to see what he was doing. He was in the large clawfoot tub, arms splayed on both sides, wet all over. I smiled at him. "Yes?"

"Come here."

His voice was deep and low and made my belly quiver. "Okay."

I stood next to the tub and he reached up and grabbed my hand. "See the washcloth right there?"

I nodded.

"Come on and use the soap and wash my back."

I knelt down, trying to look at the wall as I picked up the washcloth and the rose-scented soap the hotel had provided and worked up a lather.

"What's wrong?"

"Nothing." I touched the cloth to his back and worked it from side to side, trying not to notice how well his muscles rippled underneath the cloth as I did what I was told.

"Come on. What's the matter?"

"I just, I have never seen a man before, well, I mean a grown man. Not my brothers when we were little."

"Oh."

Now that I thought about it, his smile was a little smug, as if he knew how well formed he was, but didn't want to say.

"Well, you wanted a virgin wife, as you said. You got one." Everything inside of me, humiliation, embarrassment, curiosity, and, yes, desire were all so mixed up that I didn't know what I would do next. I felt the threat of tears burning in my eyes, but I kept on soaping him, as he directed.

He tugged on my arm and before I knew it, I was in the tub with him, my chemise soaking wet. I shrieked and he laughed at me. "You don't need that silly nightgown with me, Portia." He unbuttoned it, revealing me, and my entire soul, one button at a time.

Well, I thought I was tired, but that bath helped me find renewed energy and Sid Pittman made me a woman in that hotel room in Atlanta. We didn't fall asleep until the cloudy midday November sun dribbled into the room and I lay on my back, bare to the room and to my husband as we both fell into tired slumber, thinking about Margaret's words and wondering how she knew what she knew about the passion I had just experienced, since she had never given my father a baby.

WE WERE IN that hotel room for three days before we continued on to Washington, DC. When we arrived there, we hired a hack to take us to acreage that Sid had bought for our new home, a plot of land just outside of the capital city lines in Maryland proper. "Close your eyes," he said.

In my role as a good wife, I did as I was bid.

His arm draped about me, and I felt safe and secure in a way that I had not felt in all those times when I was away from my family attending school, trying to be a model and exemplary woman of the race. Now that I was Sid's, all I had to do was to keep his home and make him happy while he worked on the designs for his tricentennial project. Finally, a reachable goal.

"Okay. Now you may open them."

As I did, I could see that the shell of the house had been well formed and that it had a similar courting/sleeping porch on it, just like the Oaks had. I breathed out. "Oh, Sid. It's beautiful."

"Do you like it? Really?" He practically squealed in his excitement.

I nodded. "I do." He reached down and kissed me. I kissed him back, so happy that I knew how to please him in the new wanton ways that I had learned in the past few days.

He took my hand and helped me down from the carriage, stepping into the house, smelling how sweet and new everything was, relishing the feel of it all. The house seemed to call to me to help make it better and to make it into a home. And I would.

One of the workmen came to Sid and tapped him on the shoulder, asking him if he could speak with him for a minute. Still transfixed by the beauty of the wood in the parlor, I let go of his hand and paid no attention as the two men exited the room, heading for the back of the house. However, soon, the sound of two loud voices disturbed me from my reverie. I went to the back of the house and stopped in the pantry where I could clearly hear a conflict.

"I got kids! They has to eat."

"I told you I will pay you at the beginning of the week. I'm waiting for some things to come in."

"That won't be good enough. I need my money now."

"I'm on my honeymoon. Can't you wait until Monday?"

"Your wife asking you to wait while you on your honeymoon is the same kind of feeling I got right now."

I withdrew back into the parlor. I didn't want Sid to see me looking at him or acting as if I heard his argument, but later that night at our hotel, he told me that would be our last night there and we would need to move into the unfinished house.

It was November in Washington, DC, a place much farther north than my southern blood knew.

"Will it be warm enough?"

He went over to his bag and took out a bottle and poured the liquid into a glass. He did not offer me any of whatever it was. "What in the world would make you think I would have my wife in a house where it wasn't warm? I'm an architect, Portia. Give me some credit."

I didn't see how, but I just bowed my head.

"I'll work on the house while I'm working on the tricentennial designs. That project is almost finished and then I'll be paid well enough to bring the workmen back on to finish. It'll be a little inconvenient, but it'll be like camping."

I used to go camping with my mother's brothers when I would

visit them and my grandmother in the wilds of West Virginia. I didn't like it then and I was sure I wouldn't like it now.

"Is there a stove installed?"

He whirled on me. "Did you see one the last time you were there?"

"No."

"You're sitting there asking me about a stove when I'm doing my best to get this house finished."

"I can go back to Alabama and wait until . . ."

I never saw it coming.

That's because in all my years as a twice motherless abandoned child, a teenager growing up under the care of strangers, and as a young woman in collegiate institutions hostile to the presence of a young Negro woman in their midst, no one had ever hit me before.

Until today.

I had to wait until someone who was supposed to love me, unconditionally I thought, would lay hands on me. All because I was offering to move out of his way so that he could finish the work on the house.

The warmth of hot red blood rushed to my cheek with a quickness I had never thought possible and I grabbed at my face's flesh with both hands to cool it down somehow.

"Don't. Do not talk about you going back to Alabama. Do you understand? I do not want to hear that from you, Portia."

"I didn't mean to hurt you. I just wanted to get out of your way . . ."

"You would be abandoning me. Leaving me to myself is abandonment. I won't have it. We are man and wife now and we are joined at the hip. We'll never part from each other. Never! No running home to Daddy, do you understand me?"

I nodded, wondering if the hotel would bring me some ice for my hot face.

Sid stepped over to me and knelt down, touching my hands with the same hands that made such a furious attack on my face, and held them with incredible gentleness and kissed me on the spot where he had slapped me. "I'm sorry, honey. I shouldn't have done that. I just... I don't want to imagine a life without you in it. I waited for you so long, don't you see? That's why I acted that way."

I had heard of people, sometimes at the school, who might have done such a thing to their wives, but not in my own home. My father had never laid his hands on any of his wives. Not even on Margaret when she went on one of her crazy screaming jags, he never had done it. *Marriage is not enslavement*, he would often say about the loving way he had been toward his wives.

He was right. It's just that no one had ever bothered to tell that truth to William Sidney Pittman, the man that I was now married to.

For the rest of my life.

Alice

1905

The travel plans involved meant I must prepare for a trip that would take five months. Everything about what I had to learn meant deep involvement and something I had not been involved with before—delicacy. Now, I had even less time to walk on F Street with my friend Maggie, which I guess evened out because I would be seen well enough in the newspapers as I traveled, representing my father.

The trip also meant that I would be in close quarters with Nicholas Longworth, who was part of the congressional delegation that would accompany me, which did not displease me at all. I knew Father would ensure I had the appropriate chaperones: Mrs. Fairweather, a widow, but even more importantly, Mr. Taft, his old friend, who had a daughter about my age. He would exert the heavy paternal influence upon me. He was the secretary of war, so it made perfect sense for him to go as part of the group, and he had been a governor in the Philippine Islands. Mr. Taft, at that time, reminded me of my father in some ways, although he was a lot more rotund and not as charismatic.

The main thing about him and my readily agreeing for him to be my chaperone was that Nicholas Longworth was a bit of a protégé of his, having come from Cincinnati, too. Thus, my connection to that tempting man would be strengthened.

Many of the best DC seamstresses were kept busy sewing new clothing for me to wear during my trip. I would take at least a dozen steamer trunks for my needs. Father groused about it all, but he could say nothing. He was paying my way to go, but dear grandfather Lee could always be counted upon for anything extra in the financial realm and he was happy to pay, because he was so proud I was finally doing good in the world.

Ted was off at school, so Kermit and Quentin resolved to be proper caretakers for my snake while I was away. So I felt ready for anything when I left Washington City on July 1 and made my way to Chicago for the first part of the trip. As soon as we got there, we got word that John Hay, Father's secretary of state, had died. He had been an important man, an old man, since he had served as Abraham Lincoln's private secretary at one point. "Will we have to return?" I asked Mr. Taft with concern. I knew how Father relied on his cabinet and it was important to not look as if we were holidaying with a poor dead man on his hands.

"Goodness, no, child. We'll continue on. I'll telegraph your father. He understands our great undertaking."

I went back to my novel, unbothered. I felt sorry for the man, but it really would have put a crimp in my plans with Nicholas if I had to go back to DC now.

We stepped off the train in Chicago where there was a band playing, flags and streamers and such. Honestly, it was such a fuss, I thought it was for the upcoming birthday of our nation, but there were many signs that said WELCOME PRINCESS ALICE! and WE LOVE YOU ALICE and WE ARE WEARING OUR BLUE TODAY FOR YOU! They even had a barbershop quartet singing one of those hideous Alice blue songs that some composers made up. There were a number of them and none of them were that good as music goes, but it still was quite a tribute to have so many songs composed in my honor.

I preferred ragtime. Now that would have been an honor if Scott Joplin had made up something, but I guess he wasn't inclined. Too bad Portia was in Europe, but maybe she might compose something once she returned to the US. She could show those musicians what real music was about.

Mr. Taft hovered at my elbow in a manner he imagined that my father would have done, as I went to the top of the platform and greeted the officials gathered there. All the fanfare might seem like a bother, but once they guided me back to a room where I could rest before the next train connection, I understood that certain perks of being the president's daughter made up for the bother.

The train traveling across our country kept up a rhythm that matched the wheels going in my head. The worst-kept secret in Washington, DC, had to be that Father was not going to run again in 1908, even though he could have because his first "term" was the one that he finished for dead Mr. McKinley. Not living in the White House or having access to those amazing servants or not having fanfares like this would be difficult to get used to. So why not align myself with someone who would be continuing in the political sphere as my husband? Nick completely met all requirements in so many categories. It behooved me to get ready for when I saw him in California and to do what I needed to do to ensure that we returned to the United States as an engaged couple.

NICK JOINED THE delegation in San Francisco, the port where our ship was docked, and he was, as always, impeccably dressed. He had covered his pate with a bowler hat, so he was more appealing looking than ever. Best of all, I had him all to myself. None of those horrible Capital City hoydens were around.

We were completely surrounded by people when we first saw each other. The crowd behaved as a perfect chaperone, and yet, the reporters here kept shouting out questions to me: "What do you hope to accomplish on this trip?" "Who are you accompanying to the Orient, Alice?"

When he came into my company, he leaned over, whispering in my ear, "So good to see you, fellow rule breaker."

"You wish," I purred, and we both turned on our heels and faced the questioning, pressing throng as we waved from the deck of the SS *Manchuria*. Yes, I could do this. I could be married to such a man who might have aspirations for higher office. Certainly, me being his wife could be helpful to him if he desired such a path.

His hand gripped mine and once we had posed our fill, he tucked my hand into the crook of his arm. We strolled arm in arm like that to the salon, so that I might rest until the ship sailed from the port. I would have liked for everything to have gone smoothly at that point, but I had a terrible case of seasickness. I recalled poor Portia and her biliousness when we first met and felt even sorrier for her. And myself.

Well, Nick was just as capable as a nurse and having him next to me, sponging my head off, holding the bucket up for me meant that after a few days, I was able to get my sea legs about me. By the time we got to the Hawaiian Islands for more greetings and official duties, I had the pink back in my cheeks again.

On a stroll about the deck one evening, he broke off our conversation about the stops on the trip and what lay ahead. "Now that you are all better, my dear, let's take a small sojourn on our own to a special port in Hawaii. I have it all arranged."

"I'll tell my chaperones."

Nick tutted me. When he did that, it made me feel as if I were twelve.

"You'll be fine alone with me. Unless you feel that there is some reason for you to worry." He traced a wayward finger down my sleeve.

I captured it with my hand. "I'm not worried about you. I just don't want word getting around that we went off together."

"Because . . ."

"Because if we do, and our disappearance is noted, then my reputation will be compromised and you would have to marry me." I said the words with a frisson of flirtatiousness, but when I saw his face, he was not smiling.

"We don't have to do anything people say of us. We are in control of our own destinies. And of what we do. Don't you agree, Princess Alice?"

"Well, it is easier for a wealthy thirty-five-year-old congressman to speak about controlling destiny than a young woman of twenty-one years who is in search of a husband."

"You have far more freedom than you suppose, Alice."

"I think you're saying that because of times previous when you used your freedom to your benefit." I traced a finger on the ship's railing, choosing my words carefully.

He turned to me. "What are you referring to? Let us have it clearly."

"The time you came into the late-night dinner party with Maggie on your arm. Just a few months ago."

"What of that?"

"Well, it was a little shocking because Maggie told me she had a cold and wasn't fit to go outside, let alone to a dinner party late at night."

His features moved not an inch.

"I had no idea of that. I contacted her and asked her to come and she accepted."

"Of course." I had completely anticipated this response. "So I suppose you are still shopping around among us then?"

"Among us?"

Now I had him. I counted off on my fingers. "Maggie, Cissy Patterson, Katherine, and myself. You're still deciding who would make the best wife?"

He leaned into me, smiling his irresistible smile. "Maybe one of you. Maybe all of you." He stepped away from me, spreading his arms. "Maybe none of you."

"I see." And I did. But I didn't like it.

"What does that have to do with our outing? None of them are here."

If I believed in a God, I would have thanked him. "Maybe everything. Maybe nothing." Time to give him back a little of what he had given me.

"Touché. You have an hour to decide what you want to do."

He turned and left me, standing along the railing, wrestling with my feelings and with avoiding doing something that would disgrace my father. We had not yet gotten to the Orient. If I were to be wayward in my behavior, then this would be the time to do it, now, before my father could order me to come home . . .

I thought of my father's face, those eyes of his, always looking just past me and never really at me. I was so like her. The other Alice. My mother. *The* Alice in his life. Not me, just being Sister or Baby Lee. The one who was the big sister to his other children. His real children. For, as the offspring of a ghost, there was nothing real about me.

Before I knew it, my face was wet. I wiped it and sniffled a bit. I knew what I needed. A distraction.

One hour later, I purposefully dressed in a lighter day dress and made a casual stroll about the deck. There weren't that many reporters out here, but there were enough. I paid them no mind as I walked past them but went to Nick, who was sitting at one of the tables with an aperitif before him. When he saw me coming, he stood up and bid me to sit down. "Welcome, Princess Alice. Have you made up your mind?" I did not sit down.

"I have. Follow my lead. When it's over, meet me on the upper deck."

His expression was confused, but I knew he would be game for anything I had in mind. I moved closer to the edge of the table and began to create a scene of disturbance. "Well, it seems to me,

Congressman, that you might have made your decision before you left Washington City. I'm not going to be your puppet. You forget whom you are speaking to."

His voice matched mine. "Umm. How could I ever forget you? Everyone knows who Princess Alice is."

"I told you not to call me that." It felt good to get the words off my chest, even if they were based in falsity.

"That's who you are."

I edged myself closer to the pool. "I don't want you to call me that. That's a name that people who don't know me call me."

"Well"—he quirked his eyebrows—"I certainly know you. And am hoping to know more of you on this voyage."

"How dare you speak to me in that way?" I turned on my heel and, putting my hands up to his broad chest, I pushed him with one swift move into the pool. Although I knew that my dress would be caught up and I would end up in the pool, and in his arms, as well.

Perfect.

Alice

1905

I suppose I didn't think through my plan nearly enough when we were thrashing about in the water together. The first thing that came to mind was that my long, long hair was going to be wet. The climate was tropical so it would dry quickly. The next thing was that Nick was taking too long to let me go and began squeezing me in new and private places. I gasped for air in the water, but it was as if the gasping for the air breathed something new into my lungs, something sensual, something salacious.

Of course outside of the pool, everyone was reaching in and trying to get us out, but Nick, man that he was, had the situation well in hand and pushed me to the side and handed me out first, like a gentleman. There was my chaperone with many towels cocooning me. Nick came out after me. I pulled a warm towel over my head to begin the drying process, but at the same time, I turned and looked at him and he winked. Our plan was in effect.

I sloshed to my suite and once my chaperone left me, I began the impossible task of undressing myself—slips, day dress, corset, and all—and left the dripping clothes in the tub. So much for that dress. I toweled myself off, with my hair still lank, and put on another light day dress, no slips. It was much lighter without the corset, which felt much better, to be honest, and I opened the door, looked both ways, and slipped to the upper deck without anyone noticing. There, of course, Nick and the sailors awaited me. We got into the boat and once it was lowered, quietly of course, the two men on either side of the boat began to row as if the very devil was after them both.

"My goodness," I said as Nick and I faced each other. "That was a little more than I thought."

"What part? The part when you pushed me into the pool or the part when I..."

"Hush." I never was one to take the loyalty of servants for granted. They were people too, people in possession of some very important information that a bunch of reporters on the retreating small ship would like to know.

He smiled and touched my wet hair, spreading it about me. "We'll let the sun take care of this." He looked over my shoulder. "We're almost there."

"There?"

"A small island of our own, my dear."

"And what do you propose to do with me there?"

"Well, if you hadn't thought up your little devious plan, you would have never known, now would you?"

"I take exception to that."

"To you being bright? Or wanting to be alone with me?"

That feeling, that thrill, came back to me once more and my insides churned about like the water around the oars. He reached for my hand, which was restoring from its previous pruny state, and held it in his, calming me more than I thought possible. Soon, the little boat washed up on a rocky, sandy shore and I saw there was a small picnic laid out. I'm not the emotional type but I enjoyed this thoughtfulness Nick had shown. "This is lovely." We walked hand in hand toward the beautiful spread, laid out on a thick patchwork quilt, with pillows fluffed up for me to recline on. He handed me down and I sat on a large pillow, so that any potential rocks didn't get me in my behind. Kneeling at my feet, he reached up, grasping my ankle.

"What—what . . . ?"

"Shhh . . . relax. I'm not going to hurt you. I just . . . I'm glad to see that you didn't bother to fully dress."

"How did you know?"

"The shape of your body in your clothes." Nick rubbed my ankles with his hands and it felt better than I imagined something like that could feel. He tucked his thumb into the soft leather of my boot and began to undo the laces, freeing my foot from confinement. "Yes. Just as I thought." He seemed to clearly be consumed in studying my foot.

"You thought?" I managed to say.

"A perfectly lovely foot. Yes."

"Thank you?" No one had ever complimented my foot before, so I didn't know what to say.

He looked up at me and grinned underneath that mustache of his. "Are you feeling shy because I'm studying you?"

"No," I whispered. Then repeated it with more confidence. "No."

"Good." He picked up my other foot and quickly took my shoe off. "Yes. Because I intend to make a study of you for a very long time. Are you hungry?"

I was, but not for food. "No, not really."

He went behind some pillows and opened a case, bringing out a beautiful violin. "Good. Let me play for you."

I could not have been more surprised if he had taken wing and flown off. Nick was playing the violin? Before I could say anything, he quickly tuned up the instrument and played a sweet-sounding melody, striking all the chords deep in my soul as a violin master would. I closed my eyes and the soothing sounds calmed me. The breeze, salty but insistent, blew, creating a deep hunger inside of me, for something that I didn't know I even wanted.

The last note faded away and I opened my eyes to find him looking over at me, placing the instrument back in the case. "You play amazingly. I admire musicians so much."

"I'm glad you appreciated it, my dear."

"How long have you studied?"

"Ever since I was a small boy. If only I did not belong to a wealthy clan, I might have made a career of playing."

"Why didn't you?"

Nick reached into the food hamper that rested nearby, picking out plates of food: bread, pickles, meats, and bowls of tropical fruit. "Because that musician life is already hedonistic in its tendencies. Everyone already believes hedonism of musical artists. This way, I surprise more people, far more often."

He quickly speared a piece of fruit and held it in his fingers. "Taste."

I reached up with my fingers to take it from him, but he pulled his hand back and I knew that he wanted me to take it from his fingers in an animalistic way, like he wanted to feed me.

No. Don't do it.

Then he held the slippery fruit out to me again.

A voice deep inside of me warned me again, but knowing that we were here on this small Hawaiian island, just the two of us, I could do something no one expected. I mean, hadn't I just done that? So I leaned into him and took the small orange bit of fruit from his fingers and my mouth closed around them, the juice from the sweet fruit running down my chin. It was the most delicious thing I had ever eaten, and as the president's daughter, I had access to many delicacies.

"What is it?"

"Mango," he answered, eating one himself and holding another one out to me, feeding me.

You can feed yourself.

I don't want to feed myself. I want him to do it.

I took the mango from him, but this time, I bit his fingers a little with a teasing nip. But rather than pull his hand back in surprise, as I thought he would, he gave me a grin, a lopsided one, a warning one. "Don't play with me, little Alice."

There was my name again. My name, not the ghost's name but the one that belonged to me, shaped new in his lips, well-formed and perfectly sounded and prolonged from him, which made it sound new and special.

I gave a little laugh. "I wasn't and I'm not little." I couldn't help but give him a coy look from under my eyelashes, which, I have to admit, were one of my best features.

He put his finger on my lips. Keeping it there, still. Very risky of him. I could still take a little nip whenever I wanted. "You were. Are you ready to play my kind of game?"

Now I lifted my eyelashes to look at him, the bowl of ripe mango unsettled between us. "You've brought me to an island to be alone with you, and taken my shoes off, and fed me, and you wonder if I'm ready to play those kinds of games?"

He removed his hand and I looked at him, this time taking the mango from his lips. He hovered over me, squeezing the juice of the mango out from his teeth. Then he ate the piece of mango, moving closer to me, closer, and on the places where he had trailed juice on me, he began to lick me as if I were the mango now.

Every single cell of my body vibrated as his violin had, just as it had when he had played it, making sweet music with it. Now, he was seeking to do the same with me, and every time that he licked the mango juice from me, I quivered under his touch. Finally, he faced me full on, and he lowered his lips toward mine, and in that moment, the sense that I had was of the world being just the two of us. There was nothing else, and no one else. I would and could do whatever I wanted to in that moment. Society had disappeared. Completely.

"The sheeeeep! The sheeeeep!"

One of the sailors, frantic with worry, ran up to us. Nick jumped to his feet. "We have to go. Now."

"Why?" I was most displeased at this interruption of real life into my first taste of hedonism.

Nick clipped out the words fast. "The ship. It's going away from us and we have to catch up to it."

Yes. That was a problem. I stuffed my feet back into my shoes and began to pick my way through the rocky beach to get back to the little boat. But I guess I wasn't going fast enough for Nick or the sailors because Nick swept me up in his arms, practically running for the boat. The two sailors were behind us, arms full of picnic hamper, pillows, violin, the quilt, and spilled mango. Nick placed me into the boat, the sailors dumped everything in at my feet, and the three men pushed off, Nick jumping in and the sailors rowing as if their lives depended on it.

I thought I was disappointed at the interruption of what was happening between us, but now, in this moment, I couldn't deny the excitement of being kidnapped off the beach and thrown into the boat with these men rowing, sweating, exerting so hard on our behalf. Finally, after a time, I did see the ship and they rowed harder in that direction. When it was clear that we would catch up, I sat back a little, laughing.

Nick turned to me. "I'm sorry that we had to come back so quickly." He really did look disappointed.

I touched my hair, which was now dry, gathered it into a fist, and swung it over my shoulder. "We'll have other times to get back to where we were when we were interrupted, Nick."

"Will you push me into the pool every single time?"

I smiled and held on as the ladder was lowered from the ship so that we could climb aboard again, hopefully not missed. "You'll just have to wait and see."

He handed me up onto the rope ladder, closely following me, shielding me with his body as we scrambled aboard the ship, which was quiet and still, as if no one had missed us.

I turned, almost going to my room, but Nick wrapped his hand around my waist and kissed me on the lips, and now the full taste of the mango, plus excitement, came across in the taste of him, as he wrapped his tongue, that naughty, naughty tongue of his, around mine.

He was the one who broke it off, and pushed me back, dazed, while I watched him make sure the sailors brought everything back on board, especially his violin.

It wasn't the first time that I would be pushed aside for something else in his life, and it would not be the last.

Alice

1905–1906

I have often speculated that if I were born a male, then I would be the one who would have been named Theodore Jr. and would have followed Father into politics. My brother was the one charged with that responsibility and while I did not begrudge it to him, I knew that he was still quite young and it was unknown whether or not he would be equal to the task.

Whereas I was more than up to the task at hand and performed quite well in all the Oriental places. All of it was a run-up to Japan, to ensure that the peace treaty Father had negotiated was fixed firmly in place, but it was up to me to make sure! Of course, I did that job quite well.

The focus remained firmly on me. Nick made sure that he retreated into the back areas of the delegation because it was for Mr. Taft as the War secretary to be my strength. Poor Mr. Taft, he was quite miserable because he missed his Nellie quite a lot. I didn't miss her at all because his wife was a bit of a scene stealer herself. Had she not been in Europe, she would have minded my presence quite terribly and I didn't want to ruffle her feathers.

So Mr. Taft and I made a good team as we attended to our business in the Philippines and I was so impressed with the gifts—so many gifts they gave to me! "I hope it's not breaking any laws," Mr. Taft fretted.

Bless the man. "I'm not the elected party, sir. So I'm sure it's all right. And the Philippines is our newest possession and it would not be right to offend them by refusing any gifts that they offered to me."

Later that night, Nick grazed my elbow with his. "Looks as if you are the most popular person on earth. No one would be able to give you that kind of attention. I'm sure you won't be satisfied with anything less than the world at your feet."

"That depends," I purred.

"On what?" he purred right back.

"Whether anyone asks me what I want."

"Okay. I'll bite." He made a little snapping noise with his teeth and I shivered as if I had just gotten out of the pool. "What does Alice want?"

"I think you know."

"I need to be absolutely certain. You understand. I wouldn't want to risk looking foolish."

"I would not want to risk that. I feel the same. How do I know you aren't just being attentive since Cissy . . ." He leaned in to me and silenced me with his mouth, in the very best way.

EVERY SINGLE COUNTRY in the Orient had something for me by way of gifts, to the point that when we went back, an extra corner of the ship was stuffed with my gifts and two whole boxcars went back to DC. Father was not at all pleased to have to pay import on all that stuff, but I think people were more inclined to give because it was quite clear that Nick and I made an adorable couple and that love was in the air.

So it was a little surprising to me that when we got back to California to make the cross-country journey home, Nick had not said the words to me yet. Those words. I mean, the words *Will you marry me?* But then I thought about it and I suppose it was not an easy thing to part a man's lips to ask the president's daughter to marry. So instead I said to him on the train, "What should I tell Father about when we will reserve the East Room?"

Nick's mustache wiggled in a funny kind of way and he took me by the wrist. Hard. Harder than I thought he would and stowed me in a small corner of the train station where no one would bother us. I put my arms around his neck.

"I thought I told you that I'm a lifelong bachelor."

"You did?"

"Just because you have the entire Orient and half of the US press whipped up on some love story doesn't mean that I have to cave."

"It doesn't?"

"No. It doesn't. This ends here and now, Alice. I mean it."

Something inside of me sunk down, down as deep as the Pacific Ocean we had just crossed. But I was entirely too used to getting my way. "So you don't want to marry then?"

"That's what I'm saying."

"After everything we've been up to? On the beach in Hawaii? The ship? Everything? Even in fulfilling the naughty prophecy you spoke to me when we first met?"

Beads of sweat popped out on his lip above his mustache. I still wasn't letting him go. "Hedonism. Pure hedonism."

"It was fun, wasn't it?"

"I'm not saying it wasn't."

"Well then, it could be like that all the time."

Now I felt his arms cinch my waist and I tried to focus on his blue eyes instead of thinking: *MINE.*

"You disappoint me. I thought you wanted more out of life, Nick. Especially in politics. Who else is better to get it with than me?"

"That's a good point."

I whispered in his ear, "I'll tell Father to make it my birthday present next year."

He whispered back in my ear with a little lick and nibble at my earlobe for good measure. It took everything in me not to giggle. "And just when is your birthday, dear Alice?"

"February."

He gulped.

"I don't believe in long engagements."

"I don't believe in . . ." I made my mouth capture his. To quiet him. And my beating heart.

"I want you," I told him directly.

"Well. Then I suppose I am doomed." He pulled me to him, grinding himself into me in a very familiar, very thrilling gesture. I could feel him melting against me, hardening against me, daring to seek out the core of me. He bent and kissed my neck and I threw my head back, savoring my victory over him.

"Time to greet the press, my darling." I pulled at his hand to take us out of our warm corner and into the harsh, cold light of day.

"The only possible impediment to our marriage," Nick said to me then, "is my mother."

"Your. Mother."

"I don't know why you are saying it like that. I have a mother."

"I just didn't realize. I mean, I never met her."

"That's because I don't introduce her to everyone in my life. She lives in my house and oversees all my hosting as a member of Congress. She's either going to have to leave or we have to get a new place and there really isn't any money for that."

"There isn't?" That's the first time I've heard those words. Well, maybe not the first time but the second. Grandfather Lee denied me some things as a little girl, but I got them eventually. Little toys and candy and such.

"No. There isn't."

I patted his hand. "I'm sure we will get along so well." I swallowed. I didn't have a lot of experience with mothers. Well, just one. Who resented my very existence.

"You are?" Nick's mustache twitched. "Well, I will tell you, Susan doesn't just really love everyone. She's very protective of me."

"Well, I can understand that," I purred and tucked my arm into the crook of his arm.

He patted my hand. "We'll see. I've been a bachelor for quite a while. You're taking on a lot."

"I think I can handle it." Something in me stilled my tongue about Grandfather Lee as my backup bank. I mean, we weren't married yet, and all Nick had to know about was the Roosevelt connection. Since I had so many siblings, he would surmise that everything was spread thin enough, so he just assumed I wouldn't have means. Maybe that was for the best.

When we finally pulled into Union Station, a band playing John Philip Sousa greeted us, of course, and my father and mother were there to welcome the delegation train and both of us. "Well, well, Mr. Longworth. The one who's going to take Alice off my hands. I've not been more grateful for the presence of a friend than of you, sir."

Father turned to me and kept his voice low under his usually jumping mustache. "What's this, Sister? I sent you on a peacekeeping mission and here you are, cozying up with—with . . ."

"He's a good Republican." I leaned in to kiss Mother's cheek for any member of the press who might be watching.

At these words, I could see that my father was . . . conquered.

MINE.

Nick let his hand rest near the curve of my waist as we went to the carriages for the return trip to the White House. I could tell Mother wanted to speak to me alone. She kept sidling up to me. I tried to stick close to Nick, but once we got back to the White House and I was in my room alone, she cornered me.

"No one is happier for you than I am, Sister, but if you want to back away and break this engagement, no one will blame you. No one."

"Why would I want to do that?"

"He's not husband material. He's got too much of a roving eye. I want you married, yes, but not with him."

"I don't understand how you know that."

"I've seen him. I know the kind of women that he has approached and it's not you."

"Me?"

"For all your bravado inclination to disturb the social order, you are a sheltered, spoiled child. You don't know about men. All you know is that he's older and might seek higher office one day."

I sat down on my bed and clasped my hands to my knee. "Yes. That's appealing." I stared around the mess I had made in my room with all my opened trunks. "Father thinks I did a good job on my trips to Cuba, Puerto Rico, and the Orient. I think I could make a crackerjack First Lady."

I gave her a look to let her know that she was not a crackerjack First Lady.

"The first job of the First Lady is to make a home for the president. Not to go around promoting herself with a whole lot of show."

"Well, then, you've been doing wonderfully." I nodded to her.

She opened her mouth as if she were about to speak. Then she shut it. I heard no more on the subject from her until my wedding day.

Our engagement was announced the next week in the newspapers from coast to coast. The date was set in February, two days after my birthday. Valentine's Day, the day that my life changed with the loss of my mother, would now be a day that changed my life for good in another direction.

ONE NIGHT IN the holiday season, I was due to attend a ball, but I felt my nose getting stuffed up and I begged off it. I retired with a hot brandy and warm handkerchiefs to rid myself of the drip, and then around 10 p.m. I felt a little better. I dressed myself and went on to the after ball. I was having myself a fine time, when, on the stroke of midnight, Nick walked in with another woman casually holding his arm. Not just another woman, but another friend of mine, Cissy Patterson. I looked at the way her arm was on his, the comfortable way she laughed, tossing back her red hair, waist cinched just so in a dazzling green gown, cheeks rosy with cold, or with something else. Nick wore that proprietary air about him and it was obvious. They had been together. IN that way. In that hedonistic way.

A stone formed in the pit of my stomach. A stone of hate toward Nick started forming that day. That day when the words came into my head: *NOT MINE.*

I stood, so they could both see me. Cissy had the grace to look a little shaken but Nick surely did not. A little fun smile appeared on his lips and he headed straight for me. "Feeling all better, my love?"

He reached for me to kiss me, but I gave him my cheek, well aware of my cold. "I was until you arrived with her." I narrowed my eyes at my so-called friend.

Cissy turned as if she was going to go away, but it wasn't that easy. I grabbed her wrist as Nick had grabbed mine. "Where are you going? The whole room wants to see me tell you off."

She fixed me with a look and then laughed. "Go ahead, my dear. Give them something to write about in the papers tomorrow."

"You were my friend. How could you?"

"How could I not, my dear Alice? It's why I'm your friend. I had to try him out for you."

"And what is your conclusion?"

She smoothed down Nick's lapel in a way that made me want to smack her. "He's a very fine lover."

Nick, on the other side of me, just simpered. I let her go, and she walked away from us to fill out her dance card.

He shook his head at me. "I'm not about to be tied to middle-class values and mores. I'm a congressman and I'm entitled to the perks of my situation. No wife, no one, will deny me of them. Is that clear, Alice?"

Crystal clear.

It was also completely clear to me that I was trapped in a cage of my own making.

I resolved to find a way to get out someday.

Alice

1905–1906

Christmas, and all of the season with it, came and went with a whirl. Nick and I were together as much as we were able, between his congressional duties and the wedding planning. Two months usually isn't a lot of time to plan a wedding, but with all the planning and skills of the White House at our grasp it was sure to be a cinch. Oh, the staff seemed to be overburdened, but they had such a special feeling for me, I knew they would work extra hard for me. And they did.

Nick's mother, when I finally met her at the holidays, was an impressive matron of some years who did not appear as if she hailed from the Midwest. She was very sophisticated and when presented to me, holding her hand out for Nick to take, she swept her eyes over me, from foot to head. I've been fixed with looks like that before, but this time her perusal struck me as a little cursory. I stepped forward. "Mother Longworth. How wonderful to finally meet you."

"So this is your Alice? Well, she certainly has spark, not unlike her father." Mother Longworth dipped her head to my father, who was across the room delighting someone with a hunting story.

"Yes. She does." Nick's mustache moved. She stepped forward to me.

"So. Are you going to give me grandchildren then?"

Her perfume wasn't as pleasant as it might have been. She might have gone with a more floral, less fruity scent. I gave a smile. "I hope so."

"Well, please don't have them call me Grandmother. I don't wish for the title." She stepped away, back into Nick's grasp, and he raised his eyebrows as if to say, *I told you so.*

A disappointment to be sure, but our first meeting pretty much sealed the deal.

She would have to leave my house and take herself back to Cincinnati.

MY DRESS WOULD be of my particular color. Just because Victoria wore white when she got married, everyone else wanted to do that, which was perfectly ridiculous. We are not British and I look ghastly in white, so I went with my Alice blue, matching my eyes, with a similarly light colored veil that would wrap about my pompadour, embellished with jewels and feathers.

On the morning of my wedding, I breakfasted on my usual egg and toast and rose to have my hair arranged high on my head and my Alice blue dress puffed up all around me. Many people attended me, including my little sister, Ethel, who, bless her, was a little more than fascinated by me. Once I was dressed, my father came in and proclaimed that I looked bully, of course, but averted his eyes a lot.

He was doing his level best not to become emotional.

Did this day remind him of that other Alice? That more-than-twenty-five-years-ago Alice he couldn't bring himself to speak of or to commemorate in any way? He took me up, and with his usual bluster, we made our way to the East Room where Nick waited with eight hundred people to watch us marry on that cold February day.

Once married, Mother Longworth kissed me with her thin pursed lips and Nick's sisters each got their kisses of me in turn. No wonder my husband had such an amazing rapport with women, having been surrounded by them all his life. When I was a touch lightheaded from all the celebrations, Aunt Bye came to take me to get dressed in my traveling suit, and to recover, so that we could leave for our honeymoon. I was a little surprised to see Mother waiting there for me with my suit all laid out. My aunt withdrew, deferring to my Edith mother. "I'm incredibly happy to see you leaving this house today, even as I wish you had made a different choice."

Something inside of me quivered. I covered it up with another laugh. "Nick's house is very close by. I'll be here so often, it'll be as if I've never left."

She laughed too. "I don't doubt that. What about his mother?"

I sobered. "She's going back to Cincinnati. As soon as possible."

"I hope so. Her presence is not the best thing. I knew Mittie, your father's mother, even though we never lived together." She coughed. Yes. So much went unsaid there. "I wouldn't have wanted to live with Mittie though."

There it was, a little open window onto my past. So many people said I was much more like my father's mother, that sweeping southern belle who had flirted and maneuvered her way into my grandfather's heart. The grandmother I had lost on the same day I lost my mother, dying in the same cursed house, hours apart. Now it was my turn to cough as I adjusted my pompadour after I had donned my suit. "Because?"

"Because. Mothers are protective of their children. Especially their sons. I think of this moment coming with Theodore Jr. and I just . . . can't imagine him taking a wife. With her replacing me in his affections."

I turned to her and patted her hand. "But he will one day, Mother. And I'm sure she will be perfectly nice."

"It would be good to have her moving to Ohio, sooner rather than later."

"After we honeymoon. To Cuba."

"Yes. Always seeking to do your father some good."

"And Nick, too."

We stood there, staring at each other, and then our eyes broke hold. She would never embrace me. For embracing me meant embracing the other woman, the ghost woman who had stolen my father from her. I picked up my reticule. The only other person who understood how that felt was Portia. I hoped she was having a great time over in Europe. Meanwhile, I would be first to find out the answer to all the mysteries, all the secrets that were on the other side. I was eager to find them out. I would no longer have to pretend as if I knew. I would know.

That night, in the Hotel Vienna, Nick made them known to me. So many women spoke in veiled ways about the relationships between men and women and I felt terrible for them. There was nothing to be ashamed of, nothing to hide as far as I could tell. The whole execution of it was like a special kind of waltz, a dance meant to start new life. A new life, even. I emerged the next day, ready to take the train south to the boat to Cuba, with my cheeks rosy and outlook bright.

When I came downstairs, I saw Nick was in the hotel lobby with Cissy, both of them seated at the breakfast table. The nerve of this one, smoothing the sparse hair on the side of my husband's nearly bald head as if he had not gotten married to me less than twenty-four hours before.

MINE, you redheaded witch.

Now that I knew of the intimacies that she had shared with my husband, I wasn't going to allow her to think that she would continue to share them, at least, not in my presence. He stood when I came to the table. "Why, Alice," Cissy said, nodding, "you look as if you are positively glowing, dear."

"I am. I had a wonderful night. And I'm going to have a wonderful life. Without you to spoil it."

"Well, I don't think . . ."

"Clearly. You don't think. How dare you show up here on the morning after our wedding as if you had some claim on him. Leave. Right now. Before I have you thrown out."

Cissy looked around her, but Nick spread his hands in front of him as if he was helpless. Which he was.

She stomped away.

"Well, it was time for the trash to be put out." I sat down, ready to partake of a light breakfast before we had to leave for the train.

"How do you know she wasn't here to help me with some congressional duty?"

"I don't care if she was. She had to go. You are mine, now."

He brought a toast point up to his lips, bit into it, and chewed.

I did the same, fixing him with my Alice blue eyes, daring him to say different.

He said nothing.

Alice

1906

Maybe part of the reason I was so eager to marry Nick was so I could leave the White House, acquire a new name, and oversee my own home.

If I'm being honest, there was more than one reason, like the way my toes curled whenever I thought back to that afternoon on the island when everything between us was perfect and the world melted away.

I did not expect that Susan Longworth was going to be a problem with that part, in spite of what Nick said. She did say she wanted grandchildren, after all.

Nick and I had a fine time having an early spring honeymoon in Cuba, languishing on the beaches together, drinking rum drinks by night until my head had a fine fizzy funny feel about it. Everything was wonderful. We had our own private beach and took complete advantage of the solitary time alone.

Bathing costumes, as we even knew then, were completely ridiculous. So we took moonlight nude dips in the ocean, just the two of us without a stitch of long underwear or pantaloons or camisoles on. Just our naked bodies dipped over and over again in the water, embracing, loving each other, laughing at the sheer hedonism of it all.

With me laughing at how I managed to capture this man for my very own. I began to plot how to get him to his own terms in the White House one day.

Another thing we did was abandon the horrific practice of dressing for dinner and just fed each other simple meals of fresh island fruits, vegetables with bread and cheese. If there was meat, they presented us slices of pork to layer in with the puffs of bread that went down my throat like whispers.

I could have lived there forever, but my husband was an ambitious congressman. So after three weeks we began to make our way back, after a stop to inspect the rum factories and to see the famous San Juan Hill where my father made his infamous charge—after the Buffalo Soldiers went up first to make sure everything was clear, of course.

By the time we returned to Washington, DC, we were in the throes of the Lenten season, which meant better weather and the last time to entertain before the horrible humidity of the capital city summer settled in. I had come to love Washington more than New York over the years, but there was no doubt of its origins as swampland. Everyone knew the White House itself was settled on a former swamp. The summer days made me wish the building had a pool or baths of some kind.

The suggestion never failed to make my mother laugh.

It wasn't funny. Things would change once I got in there myself with my husband.

Now that I was a married woman to an up-and-coming promising young politician, I had to have calling cards and be at home to be seen.

It all sounded so boring.

When we arrived back in the capital after our honeymoon, Nick said we would go to his house, not the White House. He lived in DuPont Circle, a nice neighborhood a few miles from the White House where upper-level employees and congressmen lived. When we came in, a young girl, who looked as if she were Irish, opened the door, her eyes as wide as saucers.

"Princess Alice. I mean, Mrs. Longworth." She curtsied to me. "Welcome home."

I lifted my foot to step over, but Nick pushed me back. "Let me carry you, my darling."

"Oh. Of course." I reached out my arms and allowed myself to be swept up into his. We were the same height, but my husband gallantly performed his duty and when we went inside the elaborate hallway, he set me down and we burst out laughing. Nick could always get me to laugh.

"Bridget, tell her to come in and . . ." My mother-in-law's deep voice resonated throughout the house and she stopped to see us there adjusting ourselves. Nick greeted her with a kiss, and so did I, ignoring her stark expression, not even bothering to mask her resentment.

She had no idea who she was up against.

"Well, you all are here."

"Had a few things along the marital line to do, Mother. Now." He turned to her. "You Mrs. Longworths. Get along. I have work to do. I'm leaving." He gave me a pleading look, but spoke to his mother. He leaned over and kissed me on my cheek.

And he was gone. Just like that.

Leaving me alone. With her.

"I have tea ready if you like." Susan gestured and Bridget bobbed, looking starstruck at me. I had never met her before today.

"No, thank you. I think I'll go to our room."

Susan held up a hand. "Just a minute." She turned to Bridget, nodding. "That will be all, dear."

Bridget left, heading toward the back of the house. "She's new. And young. She'll require some breaking in. I don't know why she's staring like that. It's very rude."

"We've never met before."

Susan stared at me a beat too long. "Yes. We can go upstairs and I'll show you where everything is."

I followed her, our skirts swishing in rhythm together, feeling a bit strange because . . . well, isn't this supposed to be my house?

"This is your suite, with a sitting room, and it adjoins with Nick's room through there."

"We have separate rooms?"

"Of course. As befits your station."

"Well, I had hoped . . ."

Susan shook her head. "Trust me. You'll like this much better. Nick comes and goes all hours of the night. When you are keeping company with people and having duties as a congressional wife, you'll rest easier without him disturbing you."

"But he's my husband. I want him to disturb me." How else were we to be about the business of getting her the grandchildren she said she wanted?

She put a hand to her throat, which was nowhere near as slim as mine, and gave a little laugh. "I remember when I was a newlywed and wanted to be near my husband all the time. But he was not half as busy as Nick is as a member of Congress. See, there's a piano in this sitting room and a stand for Nick for his violin and music whenever he wants to play. Just the kind of thing that's lovely to hear, but at a muffled distance."

"But he plays beautifully." Especially when he has nothing on.

I fixed my own mean smile and looked more attentive.

Susan nodded. "Of course he does."

"Where are you?"

"I'm just down the hall, to the adjoining guest room. So just let me know if you need me." She stepped backward and then turned on her heel to travel the short distance down the hall.

Was that going to be her room when she visited from Ohio? I would have to ask Nick, given that she was supposed to leave for her home sooner rather than later.

MARRIED LADIES LIKE me were made to wait. Wait for the tedium of little cards folded in the corner to see if vapid congressional wives I'd already met on several occasions in the White House would visit me. To gawk at me for who knows what reason. All the freedom I had as an unmarried woman or as a spinster had been taken from me to stay boxed up in this DuPont Circle brownstone waiting for Nick to think of me.

With my mother-in-law who did not get the hint to leave.

Something had to give. And poor Bridget's service could not compare with the attentive Negroes at the White House.

One day, while my mother-in-law was napping, I put on something relatively light, without all my corsets, and with a much smaller hat than I would normally wear, and I took a walk out in Washington, DC. Alone. Fortunately, it was a weekday, so I saw nothing as much as the daily lives of most of the men who worked in the government coming into close contact with one another, eating lunch, exchanging gossip of the government.

I took a deep whiff of the air. This. This was what I had been missing. The stench, the real thick filmy stench of politics at work. I needed to get back in there and dig deep down to get my husband into the kind of power that would get me back into those circles and not shut up in the house like a caged bird.

Before I knew it, I had turned onto Pennsylvania Avenue and I was standing before the White House, not a view that I often had—the view from outside. I was not an emotional person, but a clot of emotion rose in my throat, knowing that I used to live there, knowing that my family still lived there, knowing that I was now the outsider, just like the protesters and mashers in Lafayette Square.

I shook my head, to bring myself back to reality, when someone called my name. One of the staff had my brother's billy goats out on the lawn. He had threatened to cook them a time or two. "Stuart!" I called back and waved.

"Miss Roosevelt! What are you doing looking through the fence?"

"Well, I'm Alice Longworth now. Not welcome in the same way."

He waved an arm to a low place in the fence and invited me to climb over. I did so immediately, so glad to see a familiar face and happy to be welcomed again. "Now you know full well your papa wants to see you. Come on now."

Maybe he did but would Mother . . .

He knew what I was thinking. "She's already getting ready for Miss Ethel's debut. They want to have it before they leave the White House. Lord, I remember you going on about that floor in the East Room." Stu chuckled.

"I . . . yes." I knew that Ethel would have her debut, of course. Still, I was taken aback. Swept aside by the newest Roosevelt girl. I loved my baby sister, but still, being swept aside stung a little.

He escorted me right to the dining room where Papa and Mother were having lunch and my father leapt up. "Well, if it isn't Sissy come to visit." He pounded me on my back and my mother gave me a look through thinned eyelids. "How's everything in the world, Mrs. Longworth?"

"Splendid, Papa."

"Let's set a place for Mrs. Longworth."

He did not have to tell the staff. The wonderful, efficient, prompt maids had already brought me a place setting and a bowl of turtle soup.

I sat on his left across from my mother. "How is married life, my dear?"

"Look at her. The picture of health. How did you even get here?"

"I walked."

"See, Edith? She walked. On a fine spring day. Nothing bad about that. She's in the picture of health and everything is fine."

"Yes, I see her, Teedie."

He drank the last drop of his coffee. Maxwell House, of course. "I'm back to work, my loves. So good to see you, Sister, I mean, Mrs. Longworth. Hope to see you at dinner with your brothers and sister."

Away he went. As always. Probably glad he had a new name to call me.

My mother sipped at her own cup. "So really. Are you leaving him?"

"No." I sat up, sipping at my soup with my spoon.

"Are you expecting?"

"Mother . . ."

She held up a hand as she put her cup down. "I had to ask. You know he'll ask me later."

I knew. He would not have ever asked me such a question to my face. I finished my soup in silence. The maids took the dishes away.

"It's Susan. She's still there."

A slow smile curled about her lips. "And you aren't the queen of your own house. Well, my dear. I can't say that it's rather interesting to see you getting a lesson back."

I knew what she meant. But I couldn't help it. I was my father's daughter, every inch. It was just in my nature to take up the oxygen in the room.

"I wish she would go back to Ohio."

"Is that what you want?"

"Yes. Yes, I do." I dug a fork into the sliced chicken, so tender, so unlike Bridget's cooking.

My mother smiled. "How is your friend Portia? Have you heard from her?"

"She's still in Europe but returning to the United States next year."

"Maybe she might want to come to your house for a visit."

I stopped midchew and looked at her. Mother was not as much of a ninny as I thought. A new kinship took root between us, as fellow married women. "There. That's the answer. I'll write her as soon as I get home."

She dipped her head. "My dear. You're in the White House. The letter will come much faster if you write it after you finish your strawberries. You must have some. They are the best."

I knew. How well I knew. I tucked into my plate, happy to have some decent food to eat.

And happy to have a plan to help me get rid of my mother-in-law.

Good Mothers

Portia

1908

In those days, when you found out about your condition, you stayed at home. There was no such thing as maternity wear. Having a baby meant you took the veil. You came to terms with the acknowledgment that your shape, your new shape, was a shameful thing and it must be hidden until it was all over and you emerged with a new baby.

Hopefully.

No wonder the myth of finding a baby under the cabbage leaves had such a hold on the minds of youngsters for a very long time. Unless their mother was in a constant state, no one was willing to be forthcoming about how women became pear-shaped.

Sid had left for his office, still in the middle of his new commission for the Jamestown three-hundredth anniversary. It was such an honor for him to work on something so important. Things between us had reached an impasse ever since I told him about the approaching happy event. That, as well as his commission, had meant he had not laid a hand on me in the wrong way in months. Thank God.

Still, sitting around and waiting for my baby to come wasn't the most exciting thing in the world. In this state of human creation, I had begun an endeavor myself. I knew that other scholars had gathered the music of the ancestors, but my thought was that not many musicians had done that work. I had begun the project of writing them down and collecting them for myself.

My baby seemed to enjoy the music, as I played on the piano that my father had gifted to us in our new house. The spirit of creation was present in so many and, as long as my husband had everything that he needed, and the baby's nursery was being built step by step, I was free to do something that was just for me. I just wished the endeavor brought in some much-needed extra money.

My rounded front prevented that.

I was in the middle of sounding out "Didn't My Lord Deliver Daniel?," an appropriate song if there ever was one these days, when a knock came at my door. I rose my bulky self to answer it and, to my shock, Alice was standing on my porch, like the bright bird that she was, large hat perched on her head and in an exquisitely designed walking day dress, slender as anything.

When I came to the door, I knew that I wasn't looking my very best in a rumpled apron with my hair sticking out every which way, but she turned and tears rose in her eyes. "Oh, Portia. How beautiful you look."

She had never said anything like that to me before. I instantly swept my hair up in a twist, so ashamed to be caught in dishabille.

"I'm so sorry, Alice. I wasn't expecting you."

Then she was her peppery self. "Clearly, dear friend." She opened my door, reaching through for me and stepping into my home, all uninvited. "You're in quite a different situation than when I saw you last. How splendid."

She clasped her hands.

"It's a . . . good to see you." But was it?

"Don't lie. We've not ever lied to each other. Let's not start now."

"Oh. That's true enough. I'm just . . ."

"Tea would be fine . . ." The president's daughter came into my home, looking around. "This is a darling nest."

"Sid designed it," I offered, not knowing what else to say.

"He did? How clever of him. But he is an architect, isn't he?"

"He is. He's designing an installation exhibit for the Jamestown, Virginia, three-hundredth anniversary celebration."

"Very good." Alice sat down on the davenport in my parlor and I had no choice but to go to the kitchen and put the kettle on. Once the water was hot, I buttered some slices of brown bread and cut them into fancy triangles sprinkling a little sugar on top. It was all I had.

When I came back into my parlor with the tray, Alice was building a fire in the fireplace. "It was a bit chilly in here. I hope you don't mind. You should try to stay warm in your present condition."

"I try to wait until I really need the heat, but if it is too cold in here to you, then I'm glad you started a fire." I put the tray down and served her a cup of tea before helping myself to one.

"Why, of course." She sipped at her tea. "You must take care of yourself now."

"I get so busy around the house sometimes that I don't even notice the temperature. I'm just always moving." I waved my hand.

"What are you doing besides keeping this house spotless?"

"My music."

She nodded her head. "I've always been so impressed with how you keep up your music. That's wonderful. Are you happy in your nest, Portia?"

I took a cooling sip of my own hot tea. "I am."

"That's it? If I were expecting a happy event, I would be ecstatic." Alice helped herself to a triangle of brown bread and a frisson of shame crossed over me, at the meanness of the food I had to serve the president's daughter.

"Things can be . . . hard in a marriage."

"That's true."

A slight silence landed between us. Then I asked the question I knew only I could ask her in as direct a way as possible.

"No events for you, Alice?" I knew she had no children, but in more than two years, it was highly unusual for a married woman to not have had one or two pregnancies.

She set down her tea. "Let's put it this way. At the beginning, we tried a great deal and nothing happened. We try far less frequently these days." She looked away.

"I'm so sorry."

"It's not your fault, Portia. I've gotten used to people staring at me, wondering what is wrong with me. Father making pointed jokes."

"Is it because . . ." I set my own tea down. "Are you scared?"

She shook her head. "I thought of that at the beginning. It was almost as if I wished it wouldn't happen because I was afraid it would mean the end of my life. However, as time went by, the pressure increased. I mean, people are sitting around waiting for me to make Theodore Roosevelt into the world's best grandfather and there's been nothing. Over the past year, it's been my greatest wish, but Nick and I, we aren't together enough to make that possible."

"I see." And I did. I felt the same, even though my own happy event happened quickly and early in our marriage. "I'm scared a lot of the time."

"Oh, Portia. Who wouldn't be? You know I know that. I do take comfort that doctors know more now. Things are different. You aren't in the backwoods of Alabama having your baby. There are many great doctors here."

Not all of them treat Negroes, I wanted to point out, but I knew that was not necessary. Alice was aware of that.

"That's true. I pray about it and that gives me strength."

"Oh, that." She picked up her tea again.

"Yes, that. Have you tried praying, Alice?"

"I don't pray. There is no point in it."

"I have to tell you, it's what gets me through the day."

"It is?"

"Just sometimes, a little whispered prayer helps me. That and the music."

"The music, I can believe. Prayer, not so much."

"You're the daughter of the president. How can you not believe in prayer?"

"If there is a God, he deprived me of a mother's love from the very beginning of my life. And now . . . with Nick . . . well, there it is. No need to discuss it to death. We're bound together for life."

Even the president's daughter struggled. I didn't want to hurt her and go into details about it. I just lowered my head. "There are times when I marvel at that as well. That marriage is for life."

"You do?"

I lifted my head. "Oh, yes. I mean, Sid is not the easiest man to live with."

"What man is the easiest man to live with?" Alice tossed off, teasing. "I can even have more sympathy for Mother these days in terms of dealing with my father."

"Oh, my father is a great husband. It's my mother who could be better in the gratitude department." I rubbed my belly as I felt the baby turn over inside of me.

"I remember well what you said about her. I believe you." She chewed thoughtfully. "It's not what we thought when we were younger girls, that's for sure. But now." She leaned forward. "You know Father is not running for office in the upcoming election. Nick is completely behind Taft. His devotion is a little irritating, to be honest."

"Isn't he nice? I was thinking of telling Sid to cast his vote for him based on your knowledge of him from your trip."

"He's all right, I suppose. He's just not Father. I'm so in the mind-set now that the president is supposed to be my father . . . I don't know what I'll do when they have to move out next March."

"Yes. I could see that." I tried to imagine what it would be like if my father had to give up his kingdom of Tuskegee. He would never do that. It was impossible to see it.

"So, since I don't have any trouble for me to get into these days, how can I help you get into trouble?"

"Oh, I'm content here."

"Stop it, Portia."

"Fine. I'm bored out of my mind." We both laughed at the same time and the baby moved with our laughter. "Money is tight. I wish I could do something to help, but Sid wouldn't want that."

She nodded. "I understand. I'm happy to send you some pastries from our kitchen and some other things, my friend. You must stay healthy for the baby's sake."

I opened my mouth to say no thank you, but I wanted pastries and not sprinkled-on-sugar brown bread. "Thank you."

"Now we've finished our tea, I would love to hear some music."

I stood, still able to rise in a dignified way. "I thought you would never ask."

I went to the piano and sat down at the bench. "I've been collecting the songs of my people." I ran a few chords and sang, in quick succession, "Didn't My Lord Deliver Daniel," "Ride the Chariot," and "Scandalized My Name."

Alice clapped her hands in delight at the lyrics of the last song. "I love that one."

"I thought you would."

She came over and sat down next to me on the piano bench. "Show me the motherless child one."

I picked it out for her, basic note by basic note and we sang it together. That song has always been like a healing balm to me in a way I can't explain. To both of us.

"Ahhhh yes. Thank you. That's what I needed today." She sat back a little. "I . . . can I ask you a favor, Portia?"

"Yes?"

"What does it feel like?"

My heart went out to my friend. We had never, ever, thought to touch, but I turned to her, offering my belly. "At the beginning, it was like that feeling you get across your middle like gas."

"Hah!"

"But now, more and more as the child grows, he has a spirit and personality I'm coming to know." I took her hand, thin and cold as it was, and put it to my belly.

The baby moved and her eyes opened in awe. I saw tears there and then she turned away. "I'm sorry." I didn't know what else to say.

"Oh no. I thank you for that. I was just touched by it. Dear Portia, aren't there some Negro children from around here who might like to come for music lessons from time to time so you wouldn't have to leave your house? You could charge them a very low amount and it might help you in your present trouble. It would keep you in your music."

Her suggestion made it feel as if a sun had broken through the clouds. "I've never thought of that before."

"Yes. They could come here, and you could teach them. Think about it."

I could earn money. How wonderful. What a blessing to have a friend who had ways of thinking about the world that inspired me to action.

When a huge fruit and pastry–filled basket came the next day, it also included the address card of a Negro family just down the road with two children, aged twelve and ten, who would like to start piano lessons. The back of the card informed me their father was in service at the White House.

There was no need to tell me. I knew exactly where their services came from.

Portia

1908

Teaching the White House butler's children how to play the piano worked out well for me. Word spread at local churches and a busy summer came the next month in June when I would have days full of pupils coming to my house and learning their scales on the piano that my father gifted to me.

The baby was due in August and my father wrote me to reassure me he would be there in time to see the birth of his first grandchild, a fact that touched my heart. It was even better that he managed to say, in his usual politic way, that Margaret would not be accompanying him, but was staying behind to oversee campus operations. Good. I knew she didn't care for babies anyway. She never managed, or wanted from what I understood, to have her own, something many, including myself, had always wondered about.

But at the same time, I knew that my father was taking important time away from the campus before school started to come to visit with us to make sure that I would make it through my travail alive.

There was no escaping that particular worry. Alice even showed she felt it, with her overt generosity, sending us elaborate baskets of food every week, baskets that came in a car with someone from her house or in a car inveigled by the White House. The baskets had not just pastries but more substantial fare, like canned meats, cheeses, and fruits and vegetables. Whoever the chauffeur was would help unload the basket into my pantry, and then he would take the huge monstrosity back into the car to load it up with more food for the next week.

Sid had finished his work on the Negro building for the Jamestown Centennial, which was received well with rave reviews. I was so proud of him. Everyone marveled about its beauty and that a Negro had designed it, Booker T. Washington's son-in-law no less, bringing a wonderful highlight to his achievement.

What it did not bring, unfortunately, were any more commissions for Sid to work on. That's why we were running low on money. The piano teaching made the difference for us in a lot of ways, as well as Alice's generosity.

One week, the chauffeur was a few hours later than usual, due to a fundraising ball held at the White House the night before, and Sid was there when he came. "Afternoon, Miss Portia," the chauffeur said amiably. "How's those children of mine doing?"

"Making wonderful progress. It's a delight to teach them both." It was getting harder for me to stand these days, but I made the effort and stood to hold the door open for him. Sid, smoking a cigar on the other side of the porch, just watched the man carry the basket into the kitchen, not offering to help.

"As are you. Looking healthy and strong. No need to help. I know the way."

"I appreciate that. Thank you." I couldn't help but run a hand down my front, calming my wriggling baby just under my untucked shirtwaist. The baby's activity inside of me while I played music reassured me that he or she might carry on in the way of my musical interests.

"Who is he?" Sid's light eyes narrowed as the chauffeur entered the house.

"Mr. Porter. His children have piano lessons here." He brought the empty basket back out.

"You stay healthy now, hear?" I handed him a folded paper and he put it into his jacket pocket, nodded, and headed off back to his car. Or, rather, probably Nick Longworth's car, the husband of Alice's that I had yet to meet in person.

"I will," I reassured him.

Sid watched him drive off without a word. "What was all that? And him saying he knew the way into our house?"

I wished Sid had just confined his interests to drinking lemonade on a sweltering summer afternoon in the humidity of Washington, DC, but unfortunately, he had not.

"It's a food delivery."

"For what?"

"Potted meat, cheeses, some strawberries." My mouth watered at the thought. Wherever the baskets had come from, the fruits in the summer had been exceptional. Probably the White House green-house. It was the fruit that I craved the most.

"You're paying for all this? On our income?"

I turned to sit in the rocking chair on our porch, but Sid had stood and towered over me, not letting me sit down. "I make it stretch."

"Who is providing this food?"

"I don't see what difference it makes. Your belly is full, Sid. That's what matters."

His hands went to his hips, a gesture I had seen many times before and did not want to see now. "No, see, that's where you are wrong, Portia. Someone thinks I can't support my family. You need to let them know that feeding my family is my business."

"I have to nourish the baby inside of me, Sid. There were some times when things were . . . well, sparse and . . ."

"Did you write to your father?"

He grabbed a hold of my arm, not in a nice way.

"No. You know I wouldn't ask Daddy. Every penny goes for the school."

"Well, ever since Andrew Carnegie gave him a million dollars so he didn't have to worry about his living, I know he wouldn't have minded helping you out some, Portia. But you are Mrs. Pittman now. You don't take his money. I don't want no Carnegie money up in my house."

I shook my arm free of his hold. "There is no Carnegie money. Just . . . don't worry about it. Why do you think I've been teaching children how to play? We're doing what we need for ourselves."

"I can't believe you are making that much." He held up a little jar of some preserve. "It's too fancy."

"I make it stretch. That's what a wife's job is." I put a protective hand on my belly. The baby would still at hearing Sid's angry voice. I felt the stillness was its way of protecting me in return, but I didn't like it. I rubbed myself, letting my little one know all was well.

"Whoever is sending this charity up into this house, it needs to stop. I can take care of my own. Understand?"

"I understand."

"You better." He went to the other side of the porch, back to his papers. I closed my eyes, trying to relax the tension in my body. He hadn't raised a hand to me in a few months, ever since he knew about the baby, but the fear he might radiated throughout me.

Another car pulled up to the house and I opened my eyes, and this time, I could see my daddy sitting in the back seat, looking as successful as ever. I stood, struggling a little, and went to the steps to welcome him to my home.

He stood up in the car holding his arms out, and the glare of the sun sparkled off the sheen of tears in his eyes. The gentleman who was driving held up a hand. "Wait now, Mr. Washington. You's precious cargo. Don't want nothing happening to you, sir."

The driver came around and opened up the door for him and my father stepped out, looking a little thinner, as he did every time I saw him. I came down our front steps slowly, my arms outstretched to see him with my own sheen in my eyes, but at this point in my travail, I had no compunction about letting the tears fall at the sight of someone who I knew loved me, just me. Our arms went around each other and I sobbed, so happy to be with my father again. The baby inside of me leapt up and down with an equal amount of joy, I could tell.

He patted my hair as the driver brought forward my father's luggage, since he would be with us for a month. He assured me that he could get plenty done for the school while in DC. Our home would be a hub for him as he made short fundraising trips to New York and Boston while on the East Coast and he'd still be close for the baby's arrival.

As well as whatever happened after.

By the time I had let my father go, the driver had put his luggage into the house, something I was glad to see, because Sid was still looking at him from the side of the porch, not helping in any way. My father was in his fifties and surely should not be lifting so much of his own luggage anymore. The joy in my body shifted to something else. It was quite something to see Sid, a former student whose Drexel tuition my father had covered and who had married his only daughter, sitting on the porch, sipping at a drink with a disgusted sneer on his face.

"Sidney," my father called out. "Good to see you."

"It's a little early for you to be here, isn't it?"

"Well," my father said in a hale voice, belying how thin he was, "one thing I've learned over the years is that babies have their own timetable." His arm was still about me, still protecting me, still sheltering me from the storm of life. I didn't want to leave his embrace, but I knew I would have to. The baby didn't seem to want to, either, wriggling and excited as it seemed to be. I touched my belly, but there was no denying that my baby seemed to know his grandpa.

"They do, Papa. And you are welcome, so welcome," I said, not looking at Sid, but emphasizing the welcome so that my father heard it.

"I'm happy to be here and see you, Portia. You look well and my eyes delight to see you. And Sid."

"My wife has a mysterious benefactor." Sid took another sip from his concoction. "You should see the picnic baskets full of food that are brought here."

Papa looked down at me and snuggled me to him. "Portia has a way of attracting folks to her. I should put her on the fundraising train, myself."

"Hmph." Sidney drained the glass. He put it down and went inside the house. Uncomfortable, the driver made his excuses and drove his car away.

I could see my father's worried eyes following Sid. "These are hard times, child. When a man becomes a father, he has a lot on his mind. I know I did."

My ears perked up a bit at this revelation. The veil stayed completely down over the circumstances of my birth, and I was ever grateful to hear even a crumb of what had taken place. "Really?"

"Yes. Like Sid, I was at the beginning of something. Starting a school. Starting a marriage. So many things beginning and to have another start in the midst of it all. So be easy on him, Portia."

"I'm trying, Papa."

"Good." He kissed the top of my head. "So who is this benefactor?"

"No one but Alice, Papa. She's a good friend."

He nodded. "Yes, she is. As is her father. I'm going to miss when he is out of office next year—not knowing who will come in and be open to our cause. God bless Mrs. Longworth. But if her largesse is causing problems in your marriage . . . you might ask her to tone it down a bit."

I nodded. "Yes, it appears I may have to. I don't want him to feel . . ."

"Burdened." My father put the word in. "I have some leads on some projects for him. He'll find work soon enough."

"Oh, thank you, Papa. That's just what we need right now. Everything will be better once Sid has a new project to work on."

"Good. Well, if you have some lunch in the house for me, I'd welcome it." He helped to guide me up the stairs.

"Yes, of course. You're early, but we have some sandwiches and fresh vegetables."

"Sounds perfect."

Eating lunch with my father on the porch that day was one of the best memories of him that I kept close to my heart for a long time after that.

Portia

1908

August is the worst time to have a large belly in the hot, humid environs of Washington, DC. When I woke on the morning of August 17 with a tremendous backache, I had a thrilling feeling, even though I had never been through anything like this before, that the time had come. I informed Sid, who seemed to be a little disturbed at his sleep being disrupted but he went out to procure help.

Later I learned he woke up my father, and a doctor, not a midwife, was sent for, but I was beyond caring about any of that. It was the pain, the horrid waves of pain that allowed me, for the first time in my life, to join a special sorority of mothers, Fannie Norton Smith Washington, the woman who gave birth to me, and Olivia America Davidson Washington, the woman who loved me and raised me until she had no more in her to give.

I took it all to join them. The whole time, I bore it silently, tugging on the straps that the doctor's nurse brought forward for me to grasp, feeling intimately connected to my two mothers, in a way I hadn't before.

My father was on the porch, reading the Bible and praying, as he was wont to do, that everything would be all right. Half of my heart was with him, because I did not want him to worry, and besides, I quickly understood that screaming would not help my energy to focus on what I had to do—push this baby through my body. So I kept myself as quiet as I could and focused my energy on the task at hand.

At six thirty that evening, I pushed a fine boy into the world. William Sidney Pittman Jr. I named him after his father and not mine because I knew what Sid would say if I did name him after mine. As soon as he was born, and the afterbirth taken care of, I felt as if I could see my father and my husband. I wanted to ease my father's worried heart and show him the fine grandson I had given him.

The nurse who had come with the doctor helped me into a new gown and robe that I had saved for this occasion. I wrapped up my hair with a clean scarf and brought my precious squirming mite of a Willie to my chest. The two men entered and my father, bless him, wept openly at the sight of his first grandchild. "Praise be," he said, and his face wrinkled. "How do you feel, Portia?"

"As if I plowed a field all day, Papa." I reached my hand out to him, grasping his to show him I was strong. "But I'm fine. Just fine."

He wiped his face with a handkerchief.

"Sid? Here's our boy. I've named him for you." My husband hung in the doorsill looking as if he had seen a haint or something. I tilted the baby up a little more so that he could see Willie's small, precious face, sleeping calmly.

"He's mighty light skinned." He peered over at him.

For the first time in a long time, a glint of anger appeared in my father's usually calm features. He never got angry and I was a little surprised to hear him lash out so. "Babies are usually light when they come into the world, son." He peeled back the blanket a bit and pulled out Willie's tight little fist. "See around his nails? That's where his color is. He's going to be a nice toasty beige in a few days."

I laughed to hear this description. I knew it was so. I laid the baby on the bed between my legs and unwrapped him. I could do anything I wanted. This precious boy belonged to me. "Come look at our

Willie, Sid." I grasped his little foot and put it to my lips, kissing the sweet new skin there. He smelled like an angel to me.

"You making him cold opening him up like that." Sid spoke from the doorway.

I turned to him. "It's August. Far from cold. If you lower his diaper, then you'll see . . ."

Sid rushed in. "No, no, no, woman. What are you doing to this boy?" He reached over and put the wrappings back around Willie, albeit not as smooth and snug as the lady nurse had them on him. Both of us had a lot to learn, to be sure.

Sid picked him up, holding him awkwardly. "I'm sorry, son. She doesn't understand that a man's lower areas just can't be exposed so randomly like that. I'm your papa. I know. It won't happen again," he crooned.

I couldn't help but split my face into a smile and leaned against my father, who sat on the other corner of the bed. "Well done, Portia."

"Thank you, Father." He bent and kissed me on the forehead.

Sid gave me the baby back. "I'll take the doctor back home."

My father stepped up. "I'll go with you and send telegrams to your mother and my wife. To let them know all is well."

Father had paid the nurse to stay with us for a few days until I could get used to the baby. That was fine. As my husband and father left, she showed me how to feed Willie, as I eased my shoulder and arm out of my nightgown. When my baby turned his small, soft cheek toward my breast, a rush of milk came in so fast, I almost cried out at the pain. Still, I kept silent because I knew the pain was my sacrifice for my son. He clamped on and the vacuum of his sucking cheeks pumping in and out to gain sustenance was one of the most beautiful sights I had ever seen.

"Mary had a baby boy . . . she had a very fine baby boy . . ." I sang to him from the old song, drawn from the ancestors and their poetry, the very songs that had sustained me from a young age. My singing voice was not wonderful, but I wanted the first song he heard in the world to come from the minds and hearts of our people.

PAPA STAYED FOR another three days and when he was satisfied to see me walk around and stand up, and was reassured I wouldn't slip away from him, he prepared to leave for an educational conference in Virginia. He sat in the window corner of my bed, an arm around both of us, squeezing us to him. "As long as you support your husband in all things, my Portia, things will be fine."

"I believe they will, but once his commission is over . . ."

"It's hard for him, honey. He's out here doing work that Negro men have never gotten to do before. People aren't used to men of our race in his position. Then, he's my son-in-law and that's not easy either."

"We'll be fine," I said with more confidence than I felt. I wanted him to have a good feeling about leaving us. I always hold that picture of him at our bedside in my heart because that was the last time I saw him when he looked like my father and not a ghost of himself.

Once my father left for the South, I began to add my music pupils back into my schedule. It was easy to have Willie be in the room with us and to attend him as I taught pupils in the parlor. Thank God for the extra income, and of course, Alice kept sending baskets, with an especially nice baby basket, after Willie was born. She never did respond well to being told what to do from men.

But her gifts rankled Sid. On the night of our anniversary, which was All Hallow's Eve, I had prepared special Halloween treats for my pupils to eat as they got their lessons. Most of the popcorn balls were gone and Sid pouted because he liked them the best. I teased him a little, telling him I would make more. Willie had been impatient and wanted to feed, so I opened my shirtwaist and let him feed after a long busy day of teaching. Sid just stared at us. "Why does he always have to come first?"

"He's a baby, Sid. We brought him into the world. He didn't ask to come here. We're responsible for him."

"Nothing has been fun since he came."

"Nothing?" My voice went up. "Well, that's because I have to take up teaching. I work hard with my pupils so we have enough to live on."

"Yeah, that and your show-off friendship with the president's daughter sending us food as if we're a charity."

"We are not charity. It's just . . . helpful."

He stood up, slamming down his flask. "I'm tired of her help. And tired of being Booker T. Washington's son-in-law. When will I be known for who I am and for the work that I do?"

"Sid, you've done beautiful work. People know that you are a master at your craft. The time will come when—"

"Just . . ." He raised up a finger. "Just be quiet. You aren't making it any easier, sitting there giving to him what is rightfully mine."

I eased myself back onto the davenport, using my body to surround my small son, to protect him. Sid hadn't laid hands on me in a very long time, but if he did, I would be ready. He wasn't going to hurt my child. He wasn't going to hurt me anymore. I would stand against him, my own husband, if I had to.

Father's words lingered in my mind about my wifely duty. Truth be told, I loved my dear father with all my heart. But, now as a married woman, I could see he had asked a lot of the three women he married. My own mother, Fannie, bless her, had been dragged out into the wilds of Alabama to a dusty old plantation to help him build a school from the ground up. When the time came to have me, the first baby born on the campus, there wasn't proper care for her and she lingered in horrible pain and illness until she died months later as a result.

My mama, Olivia Davidson, already in frail health, worked herself to exhaustion fundraising for Tuskegee in the North with all her Framingham friends. She would always laugh in telling the story of how she had fallen asleep at someone's house once when she was there to pick up a check for the school. Her constant efforts for the school meant that when she needed strength for the two boys she bore my father, she didn't have it. She died within months of Dave's birth, having given her life for Tuskegee.

Even Margaret had devoted her life, as well as any potential children, to unending service to the school. That was one area where even I, her most ardent interlocutor, could find no fault with her. She was always teaching, always speaking, always fundraising to make Tuskegee better and stronger. I would joke when I would say that Tuskegee was my father's best-loved child, but there was something to the jest and something to what he required of his wives. Did Sid require the same of me?

Willie came off my breast with a deep and satisfying sigh. I lifted him to my shoulder to get the air out of him and Sid narrowed his eyes. "Put him to bed. Now."

"I'll get him down. He'll be drowsy after he's just fed . . . I'll be right up."

"Good. 'Cause I've waited long enough."

Once Willie gave off a long satisfying burp, I changed his diaper and put him in his dressing gown and laid him in his crib, humming to him under my breath, to ensure that he had fallen into a milk-drunk sleep.

I dragged my feet to my bedroom where my husband, albeit handsome, had prepared himself for bed already and had pulled down the sheets. I took out my hair receiver, thinking I would take my usual time to plait up my hair and wrap it, but he reached out for me by my wrist, very harshly, and pulled my nightgown down underneath my breasts, groping them, and grasping at my nipples with his thumbs. His rough touch was startling to me in a way I didn't like, in my mind, but my body was responding in the way it was used to and before I knew it, I was on my back, spread open to him so that he could take his pleasure of me.

When 1909 came around, my womanly cycle did not arrive in the new year.

Alice

1909

Fortunately, I did not have to resort to inviting my friend to tea at my house to get my mother-in-law to leave. Susan Longworth tended toward superstition, and she overheard one of the servants say that the reason why I had not given her a grandchild yet was because her essence was polluting the atmosphere. Or some such foolishness as that. Anyway, she believed it and arranged for her return to godforsaken Cincinnati soon thereafter.

Her absence was even more necessary because I had the space to ask one of our servants a few days later if she happened to know what to do if I wanted to get rid of someone.

The servant was an older Black woman, about the age of Edith, and she shook her head vigorously at my request. "That require something very powerful. You wouldn't like something to bring a baby instead?"

I contemplated this during my usual light breakfast of a toast point and a poached egg. If I asked just for something to get rid of someone, then that would look suspicious. I swallowed the piece of toast and drank a sip of the good hot coffee with cream swirled in. "How about both?"

"That cost you some." She folded her hands over.

I did a quick tabulation in my head. I still had some allowance money from Grandfather Lee left. "As in?"

"Fifty dollars."

"Done."

That was a great deal of money for her, I knew, but not so much for me. The next day, she brought me a folded handkerchief. "I'm going to take this up to your bed and put it in between the mattresses. It's been blessed with a particular essence that will put a baby in you."

I nodded my head and held out my hand for the other item she had. It was a little doll, like a person.

"Is this voodoo?" I said.

"That's what you whites call it. It's a hoodoo doll. Put this in their yard and they will go away." She put the little doll into my fingertips and I massaged it. Why hadn't I asked for this kind of thing years ago? I had a whole list of people I could get rid of using my Lee allowance money, like Cissy Patterson for instance, but I better not push it.

I handed over the money to her and her fingertips reached for it just as mine had for the little voodoo doll. The handkerchief drifted to the ground.

LIFE AS A congressman's wife, as well as a former president's daughter, had some advantages. I wangled an invitation to the annual Easter Egg Roll, where many would be busy and not watching what I was doing. I warred with myself trying to decide if I should dress as I would if I were going to call on someone, like my actual friend, Portia, or Cissy, heaven forbid. But instead I dressed down. This errand would involve some dirty work. I went into the gardener's shed and retrieved a small trowel, cleaned it off, and put it into my pink reticule, and then I set out.

April 12, Easter Monday, dawned a little overcast. It had rained overnight, as if the weather were depressed that the Roosevelts were not the ones holding the annual contest. Now, I was in front of the White House gates on the outside looking in without my family being there. Dread swirled in my stomach. My poor father, as it had been told to me, was almost comatose with grief on his big hunting trip, trying to find some satisfaction in a life of ease, but instead, bereft he had given up the White House so willingly. Poor man. They should have had to drag him out.

Well, my hexing had worked before. It could work again.

I worked my way onto the grounds with a group of mothers and children. There were so many children making loud noises, carrying on, screaming and all, that it wasn't hard to just casually act as if I were another mother, happy to come to the White House for the first time with my little darlings. Then I scuttled over to the work barn on the White House grounds. I could still go to the base of one of the trees and do what needed to be done. Fortunately, the rain made the ground soft. I knelt by the base of the tree and took the little trowel out of my reticule, digging a small hole to put the voodoo doll into. There was a soothing rhythm to my work, and I hummed a little tune, one of the piano rags that was going around in proliferation those days, dropped the doll in, and began to drag the dirt and mud over it to cover it up.

A loud cough disturbed me.

My eyes traveled up the length of a skirt and an absolutely dowdy-looking olive-green-and-brown shirtwaist to meet the eyes of Nellie Taft herself.

Oh dear. I had forgotten how much she loved to garden. "Alice Longworth. What are you doing on the White House grounds?"

I stood, smoothing my hands down on my own skirt. "Happy Easter there, Mrs. Taft. How is . . ." I coughed, twisted up my tongue, and made myself say it. "President Taft doing?"

"He is at work, which is more than I can say for you. You should not be here."

"It's just a visit. I thought I could visit less obtrusively during a public event." I stamped my foot onto my muddy little pile. Maybe she didn't notice.

"Well, we'll have to work much harder to make sure our invitation lists are more secure. This is no longer your home, Mrs. Longworth, and it has not been for the past three years at least." She folded her arms. She was shorter than I was, but she had certainly gotten into the habit of carrying herself as a First Lady. Her overbearing ambition had pushed my former chaperone into the White House. Maybe the doll should have been of her rather than him.

"Of course, Mrs. Taft. I was strolling, walking through the park, watching the children enjoy the activities. Reminiscing when my siblings had gotten such joy from the day."

"You would do better keeping yourself to your home, Mrs. Longworth, and seeing what you can do to attend a future Easter Egg Roll. As a mother."

The impact of her words could not be denied, but I stamped extra hard on the ground at her meaning. "Good day, Mrs. Taft."

"Good day, Mrs. Longworth."

We turned away from each other and I was happy that my visit had been a successful one, getting myself as far from the screaming throng of excited children as I could.

When I came down to dinner that night, the little doll greeted me at my plate, with a glaring Nick staring at me. "What is this?" I said, playing it as casually as I could. I kept my face smooth at its reappearance in my house.

"You tell me, Mrs. Longworth. I just know that I had to placate the First Lady because you appeared at the Easter Egg Roll of all places to bury such an object on the White House grounds."

"You did?"

"Yes. You have been banned from the Taft White House. Nellie doesn't want you there."

I rolled my eyes. Nellie could be so dramatic. I doubted that such a mandate would be successful. After all, the staff knew and loved me still.

"I haven't been banned. Just you have."

"Well, of course. The Ohio connection prevails. Bunch of mid-westerners," I said under my breath.

"If I ever hear of you pulling any more of these kind of shenanigans . . ."

"Shenanigans? It's a baby doll, Nick. Look at it."

He wrinkled his nose and looked at the little withered doll made of cloth and covered in April mud.

"It's a wishing doll. I thought it would be fine to be around children and put it where the children played."

Something in his face softened. Hedonist that he was, he never shrank back from wanting to be a father. It's just that he didn't do much about it these days with me, his wife, to make that happen. "And then what?"

"Then maybe the wish would take root and there would be a baby?"

His face softened and I let a breath out. But his eyebrows crossed over each other in confusion. "But why the White House?"

"I told you. The Easter Egg Roll where all the children would be today."

"Why didn't you tell Mrs. Taft that?"

"Because it's none of her business. She hates me because she is jealous that I'm more popular than she or her plain daughter ever will be."

"Alice. That's not necessary."

"But it's true."

He lifted his hand, signaling to the help that we were ready to start dinner.

"I just heard that my friend Portia is going to have a blessed event."

His brow furrowed. "Didn't she have a baby last year?"

"She did."

Our dinner of plain fish and vegetables was brought in and we ate in silence. After dinner on a Monday, we usually had some event that we had to attend, but it being Easter Monday, there were no events, dinners, or receptions.

"Well, Mrs. Longworth"—Nick crossed his silverware on his plate—"I can play some music or . . ."

I raised my eyebrows. "Or, we can go to our bedroom, retire, and see how well this little wishing doll works."

At least, going upstairs with my husband would throw the scent off me and the true meaning behind the little doll.

He used a napkin to wipe his lips, stood, and came to the other side of the table where I was. Holding out his hand, he beckoned to me and I took it. He tucked my hand into the crook of his arm and my mind went back to those easier days on the *Manchuria*, the times when I knew that I mustn't give in to him because we were not yet married or committed to each other, but instead indulged in delicious, languorous play, doing anything and everything to each other except the act that might result in a child.

If I had known how hard it would be to get a child, I might have allowed for him to breach that final barrier. But then I wouldn't have known how completely Nick knew how to pleasure a woman and how well he prioritized that pleasure.

How could we have allowed something like politics come between us? Why didn't he understand that now he was married to a Roosevelt that his loyalties should be to us and not the Taft people? Ohio was a boring place. We were excitement. If it was his future career that he was concerned about, there was no reason for that. Everyone loved the Roosevelts. Loyalty to us would carry him over the top.

In our enjoyment of each other that Easter Monday evening, I made sure Nick knew that in every possible way, without me telling him.

A PERIOD OF such bliss that I never thought possible lasted between us and did not break, even when I discovered a few weeks later that our efforts had not resulted in a child.

No, that wasn't it.

It was when news came in May that Nellie Taft had a stroke that almost killed her. That stroke and her resulting illness was what began to turn Nick away from me and to the Tafts.

That made no sense to me. The doll didn't stay buried on the White House grounds. It stayed in our house, eliminating all possibility of a child.

Until I could think of what to do with it.

Alice

1909–1912

Maybe Taft was too distracted from his presidential duties by Nellie's illness to do a good job. Maybe it was because Nellie, that little firecracker wife of his, bullied him into being president so she could prance around and be First Lady instead of, well . . . someone better suited like me. Maybe it was because my father was bored at capturing game trapped for him to kill already. Maybe Kermit, my brother, was nowhere near as exciting as I would have been on those big-game hunting trips.

Being a woman was not at all fun at times.

But whatever it was, after a few years of boring old Taft in the White House, it was clear that he was not suited at all. Talks began to take place in back rooms of the Republican establishment, but even better than that, they were happening at Sagamore Hill with my father's old group. He was getting back into the game. The prospect of Father getting back into the White House was incredibly thrilling.

Yes, I might have been banned, but I loved nothing more than to take my calling walks past my old home and glare at the occupants in the White House.

Taft, having been handpicked by my father, would just have to move his large girth out of the way.

But then, something went wrong. He refused to move.

None of this made any sense to me.

Taft was much better suited to the judiciary. That's where he really wanted to be. I recall how he spoke about his real love for the judiciary on our trip to the Orient.

What would people think if they knew that the entire presidential nomination for the Republican Party in 1912 was being settled in the dining room of the Longworth home after a fine dinner of beef Wellington?

"What about the judiciary?" I nudged to Nick one evening at dinner.

"What about the judiciary?" Nick repeated like a mynah bird or something.

"Father can promise him a seat on the Supreme Court. That's what he really wants."

Nick stared at me blankly. "No one in the history of the presidency has gone to the bench after having been president for one term. That's just not done. It's a step down. It's humiliation."

"It's not humiliation. It's where he belongs, poor thing. He can take much better care of Nellie from there. You can make them see, Nick. Let them know how much better it would be for them. Really."

"Or make the way much clearer for your father."

What kind of attitude was that? He was a Roosevelt by marriage, for God's sake.

"Well, of course." No need in denying it. I laid down my utensils. My appetite was quite spoiled.

"Well, it won't happen. Your father walked away. If he wanted a second term of his own, he should have run for it." He wiped his lips with his special little napkin wipe. Again. So irritating.

I bit my tongue. Literally. My father wasn't perfect, but that had been his long-standing regret for nearly four years.

"So that's it?"

"What is it?"

"You're working on behalf of Taft and the Ohio people?"

"I am an Ohio person." Nick laughed, pushing away from the table, standing up.

And also a Roosevelt. But I kept that to myself. Disloyalty was an abominable trait. So many of my father's people had gone to support Taft when my father asked them to. Now, he was asking for a simple little favor, for everyone to come back and now this . . . disloyalty popped up. In my home.

"And I am not."

"Not what, my dear?"

"I'm not going to the concert tonight. You go without me."

He practically ran out of there. Of course he loved and enjoyed music, but he was probably also running away from me and our conversation. I would not look forward to reporting what Nick said to my father in my next letter, but it was better he knew where I stood as soon as possible. Father's reinstatement to the nomination did not look very promising from this end of things.

These small skirmishes continued to draw Nick and me apart until it was clear to all in Washington, DC, that our marriage was in name only. Truly, times like these made me glad that my father lived in Oyster Bay in New York and not here. Still, he came to stay at my home when Nick was in Ohio and I hosted him and any meetings he sought to have with any Republican power brokers.

The last night Father was here, we lingered over dessert. I relished the fact that he did not ask me to remove myself from the room whenever he was having his meetings. He wanted me to stay. He sought my honest opinion because he knew I could be of value to him. It was too bad Nick did not seem to see me in that way. "What are you thinking about, Sister?"

"It's not going to be easy." I was not going to lie to him. Telling lies would do no good. Then we would not be able to attack the issue.

"I agree. Taft has a stronger hold than I thought."

"Among many." I nodded, my face downcast.

"Including Nick."

"Including Nick," I confirmed.

"That's how it should be. Taft brought him out of the Ohio machine first. Way before he met and married you."

"But once he did, he should have shifted his loyalties, Father. It's very disappointing."

"Once a woman marries, Sister, she must have loyalty to her husband. I understand."

"No. There is nothing, absolutely nothing that would change my mind. I'm here for you, Father. I support you. Taft is not fit for office."

"I agree. He is, unfortunately, more about the business class, and there is too much left to do for the people. Not who I thought he was at all."

"You're going to win. You'll see."

He turned away from me, seeming to regard the fire. "It's important that you cleave to your husband. He's the one who will be here for you, after . . . well, I know no one likes to talk about the day they aren't there any longer, but a day will come."

"Not for you, Father. I won't hear of it." I didn't tend to tears, but the thought of that day in my future was enough to threaten them in the corners of my eyes.

"He'll be your family. And, well, any children . . ."

Now it was my turn to turn away. Six years later now, it was clear. Children wouldn't happen. And not because of a voodoo doll. "Father. Really. You have a grandchild now." I swallowed and waved my hand. "My new niece, Grace."

He coughed. "It's wonderful for Ted and his wife. But, Sister, I worry about you sometimes. You're a woman. You can't do the same as a man would. I could leave and go into the West, hunt to my heart's content. Go off to Africa, bring back some eleven thousand animals for preservation. But women, you're different. You have the home front to protect and see to, like your mother."

"Father, I'm not the same kind of woman." *Far from it.*

Once again, my quick response closed the door on any kind of information of that other Alice.

"It's Nick's responsibility to protect you. You cannot go off into the wilds to soothe your hurt feelings as I can."

"Yes. I must remain in my home. I've heard you. But women have a different kind of game. Didn't you get to be president because of my hexing? Remember?"

He gripped my arm. "Sister, I appreciate your support. I really do. But a grandchild . . ."

I gripped his arm in return. "One day, Father. But right now, we need to make sure that you are returned to the White House. Anything I can do to help you, I'm here." He patted my hand, made his apologies, and withdrew for the evening.

Nick's timing in returning to our house just a few hours after Father had left to return to Oyster Bay was serendipitous. He was truly Taft's man if he didn't even want to say hello to my father. Nick never liked confrontation, so when he returned, I did the appropriate wifely duty in making sure that he had a hot meal and a bath drawn before I retired to bed.

Alone.

Without him.

The next night, I attended a fundraiser reception for father at another supporter's home. I didn't mind attending such functions, because the kind things that his supporters said about Father warmed my heart. We all sought to convince one another that everything in our country was the worst that it could possibly be, because Taft had betrayed and disappointed us, and all would be put back to rights once my father returned to the presidency.

At nine o'clock, I made my excuses and returned home because I could feel my monthly courses coming upon me. No need to be surprised at this particular time. There was no reason for any kind of hope in them not coming.

There was a light under the door in Nick's bedroom, which surprised me because I thought that he was out at a fundraiser for his own campaign and for Taft. Something, a rhythmic scraping, the wrong kind of sound, drew me to his door.

Dear god. My husband and his hedonism would be the end of me.

I opened the door and there he was, his firm white buttocks furiously pumping away into the backside of my former best friend, Cissy Patterson. She was holding on to the bedpost, plump white breasts spilling forth from the front of her evening gown; Nick's suit pants were down around his ankles.

I bit the inside of my cheeks, trying to keep my anger inside of me, but it spilled forth anyway. "Really? In our bedroom?"

Nick kept his hands firmly on Cissy's waist and sighed, mid-pump. "Where else would you expect me to take my pleasure, wife?" There was no missing the contempt in the way he spoke that word.

Cissy's red hair was all in her face and I fixed her with my own contemptuous look. "When you bed whores, they usually have a place they take their customers."

"How dare you . . ." she sputtered, but Nick's hands stayed firm on her waist.

"No. Cissy. How dare *you*. You know this is my home and you let Nick bring you here. Obviously so that I could see you in dishabille. No. It's *you* who ought to be ashamed."

"We've only gotten started, dear wife. It's not too late for you to join us. If you care to watch. Since you haven't left yet."

I would not give him that satisfaction of thinking he had control enough over me to use me as a pleasure toy as he used Cissy and whomever else. "I'm going to decline and let you continue your little . . . party. I don't think you have it in you to keep both of us pleasured."

His back quivered a bit and I knew my verbal arrow had hit its mark. *Hah.*

I stepped from the room and closed the door behind me, making my way down the hall to my own bedroom suite. I sat down on the bed, burying my hands in my face, waves of despair washing over me. I knew Nick had not loved me for a long time, but seeing proof of his wandering was something completely different.

I wanted to cry but the tears would not come. One thing occurred to me, a throbbing thought that would not leave me alone: Nick wasn't the only one who could take a lover.

Actually witnessing his infidelity with a former friend of mine just gave me the excuse that I needed.

Portia

1909

The sweetness of Willie and the coming child nearly encompassed all of my life. I say nearly because I still felt the tug and pull of music. Even though I was at home teaching so many students that I was booked completely, my students and their parents, bless them, turned out to be great ambassadors for me in the Washington, DC, community. Them, coupled with my father's name, meant other great Black musicians found their way to our doorstep.

I was beyond pleased when the great Harry Burleigh came and brought his friend Clarence White to visit us. Mr. Burleigh had been friends with Samuel Coleridge-Taylor, my friend in Europe who had encouraged me to take up the stage. Mr. Burleigh was well known as the greatest purveyor of our songs, and when he came for coffee one day, we played and sang spirituals deep into the night in a soul-satisfying musical session.

Sid claimed that the music depressed him, but I found strength from the music of my people, knowing that they had managed to forge lives of artistry and poetry in spite of their chains of bondage. I couldn't help but relate to that since I was in the house with another child on the way so soon.

Not all the music was sad.

"I got a crown up in-a that kingdom, ain't-a that good news!" The song of jubilation at embracing the humanity they were denied in bondage brought heart and hope to me.

Of course, the songs of Christmas, even after the holidays, stirred me now as I would sit and rock my Willie boy to sleep. I would sing

"Mary Had a Baby," "Go Tell It on the Mountain," and "Virgin Mary Had One Son" to him as I watched his eyelashes flutter down on his cheeks and finally stay shut. I hadn't wanted to have another baby so fast, as it meant I would miss his babyhood, but what could I do?

When my father visited us around the time of his own birthday in April 1909, I told him there was another child on the way as a birthday present. He was not pleased. Worry returned to have a permanent seat on his brow in that moment. I knew he was thinking of Mother Olivia who had two boys too close together. She paid with her life and even my brother Dave paid with his always fragile health. "I'm strong, Papa. I'll be fine. Really. You'll see."

He nodded, laying a hand on my arm, as if he wanted to make sure what I said was true. "Portia. It's also the pressure on Sid. When you have another, this'll make him feel as if he cannot support you. There must be some project here in Washington, DC, he can complete and still feel as if . . . he's contributing."

"Of course there is. He's very talented." I sent up a prayer in that moment.

Then Mr. Burleigh and Clarence came to visit us and made an interesting announcement. "We're having a recital to support music education, Portia. We want you to participate."

Me? I hadn't been in a recital since before my marriage in 1907. My graduation recital in Europe where it was thought possible by Karl Krause that I should have my own musical career. What was he up to these days?

I shook my head to clear it of the thought of his blond curls and blue eyes. "I don't know if that's a good idea."

"We couldn't do it without you," Clarence said. He was a violinist, a very handsome light-skinned Black man with long, tapered fingers that pulled the most heartrending music I had ever heard out of the strings.

I stood up and poured more coffee for all the men. Sid held up his hand. I could see him tapping his fingers, not a good sign. It meant that he was impatient. About something. It was up to me to figure out what.

"Of course you could. You play so beautifully. It's an honor to be asked, of course."

I could see my father eyeing me. I knew what he was thinking, Victorian gentleman that he was. I should defer in all things to my husband. And I knew, given who my husband was, I would pay for such regard later on. The question was how much did I want to pay.

I put the coffeepot back. "I know that your wife plays, Clarence. She would participate, of course."

Clarence nodded. "Yes. She will participate. But she's not the daughter of the greatest Black man in America." My father gave a slight smile. "People are curious to see what the children of Booker T. Washington do."

I knew that to be true. My poor brothers, bless them. They seemed to shrink from doing much of anything remarkable. The shadow of my father's greatness seemed to make them grow smaller instead of larger and rising to the occasion. The fates appeared to leave it to me, as the only daughter, to be the only one destined to expand under his reputation.

I was a married woman and really should not play in public at this point, in my condition. But as I brought up, so Beatrice White was also married. And she would play.

"It's all to raise funds for the Washington School of Music, of course," Mr. Burleigh put in. "Our students are always in need of scholarship funding."

My father laughed. "I know much of that situation. Certainly a worthwhile cause, Portia."

"Yes. It is." I could feel my fingers itch to roam over the piano. "But as you know, I'm expecting a happy event. When would the recital take place?"

"Next month. Early next month," Clarence put in.

"Well, I probably wouldn't be showing too much by that point."

"Who would watch Willie?" Sid put in, draining his cup of coffee, which I knew had been mixed with something else.

I opened my mouth to let them know I wouldn't be able to participate, but Clarence intervened. "Beatrice's mother will have our boys. It'll be no problem to add Willie to the bunch."

I laughed. "You say that now, but we really should ask her. Three little boys under the age of three is asking for a lot."

"True, but Willie is still a little baby. What about it?"

I demurred. "I have to speak with my husband and see what is best."

They both looked at Sid, gave me a sad sidelong glance, made their excuses, and left, rather hastily I thought. My father patted my arm, looking sorrowful as he wandered off to the guest room to retire for the evening.

Sid went to bed and I cleaned up the cups and plates from our dessert, my mind wandering back to my European recital. What a night of triumph, where I played my music with such passion in front of an audience and Karl. I felt the nerves in my fingers tingle and wander up my arm. Another opportunity for a recital would have to wait, potentially until after I was through having children. Unless it was for the church. Playing for our church was the sole exception that Sid granted me.

I made my cleanup chore last until I was sure that Sid, in a slightly inebriated state, was asleep. I didn't want to discuss his no. I just wanted to hold it to myself a little longer that two musicians I admired thought that I would be able to play in public for people's listening pleasure.

But I couldn't put off bedtime forever. I had to get my own rest, for my baby and for my busy next day. Once I donned my cotton nightgown and headscarf, I slipped into bed, ready to close my eyes.

Sid boomed out into the darkness. "You know that they want to use you."

I screwed my eyes shut a little more, pretending I had fallen asleep. But I had only just slipped into bed. It wasn't possible to fall asleep that fast. Unfortunately.

"I don't know what you mean."

"Yes, you do. They are using you to sell tickets. Told you openly, here in front of me and your father. And you still want to be used. Like a used-up hankie." He turned over. He wasn't drunk enough to go right to sleep. Most unfortunately.

Were they? A little bit of doubt screwed its way into the matter of my brain, trying to move in and build a home in there.

"They'll put it on their posters. Booker T. Washington's daughter. Plays the piano. Like a monkey on command."

I let out a shaky breath, being reminded of how Margaret had insulted me in the same way before. "Monkeys don't play the piano."

"One step up from one then."

"Aren't you tired, Sid? You can go to sleep now."

"I'm not too tired to let my wife know that I don't appreciate it when two damn near-white Negroes come up in my house trying to get my wife to be used to sell tickets to their stupid recital."

Keep your eyes shut.

It would do no good to tell Sid he was damn near white himself. He was not in a listening frame of mind. "Several of my pupils have gone on to the Washington school. They've done well for themselves there. My teaching has been spoken about there and that's one reason why they reached out to me."

Sid hooted. "They don't care anything about your teaching. They care about you as a ticket draw. That's it. The nerve of them. They should have asked me first."

Now we were getting to it. "You?"

"Yes, me. I'm your husband. How dare they come up in here and eat my cake and drink our coffee and not acknowledge me as your husband."

Husband, yes. Master, no.

I could only think that. I couldn't say it. Time to get it over with. "You're right."

"I mean, the complete nerve of them." He turned over.

"Yes." I kept my response short and my eyes closed. It was not worth upsetting him any further.

"Now if I say no, it makes me look like a bad man because they asked in front of your father. Your father is not the head of this house. I am."

"Of course, Sid."

"This is the Pittman home, not the Washington home."

"You built and designed it. Of course it's your home." I repeated one of his favorite refrains. So I could go to sleep and not hear anymore.

"And yet, they come up in my house when your father is here and pull the rug out from under me."

"Sid. It was just coincidence that Father was here."

"Was it?"

"People like to see Father. That's not something that I can help."

"Of course. They want to spread word far and wide of the great Booker T. Washington being interested in their little school."

"The school has hundreds of students." I bit my tongue on saying anything further. The founder of the school was also a woman, a great leader in music education. Speaking about her would only make things worse, but it did make me wonder, How did she do great things being married herself?

He turned over to face me, his rigid body posture almost daring me to speak further. His rum-scented breath went in and out of my face, daring me to open my eyes and face him. I could feel my face grow moist with his breath, knowing that he was doing this on purpose, replacing my breath with his. "Does that mean I want my wife to go and be a monkey right along with the rest of them?"

Keeping my eyes shut didn't help the moisture oozing from them. "Sid. I'm not going to play. Please. Just go to sleep. We both have a long day tomorrow."

He turned over away from me. Now he was satisfied. My no was his.

When I made Father breakfast the next day, he shook his head. "I'm so sorry, Portia. It would have been a nice thing to have you play, but it's really not a good idea in your condition."

I placed a plate of eggs and sliced ham in front of him, pushing another plate of crisp toast toward him along with a jar of jam. "No, it's not."

"Did Sid tell you that?"

"Not in so many words."

The only sounds in the kitchen were of his crunching on the toast. I wasn't hungry, even though I knew I had to eat something to keep my strength up for the baby. I drank a cup of weak tea, waiting for my first student to come.

"He didn't say no?"

"No. He just made fun of the school and their need to have recitals to raise funds for their students."

"Yes, well, since he's an architect, he would have no idea of how the music works to soothe the savage breast."

"Or beast." I thought of the first time Alice had said these words to me about her father. She wouldn't have been caught playing a recital out in public for fundraising purposes. Her example kept me silent on the matter.

Portia

1909

I might have stayed silent on the particular matter of the recital, but a different invitation had come to us shortly before that one that I *had* accepted. My father and I were invited to the White House for tea. Of course, there was no saying no to such an invitation, but the invite markedly was made out to Mr. Booker T. Washington and Mrs. William Sidney Pittman Sr.

"I guess they don't think I'm housebroken or something," Sid lashed out at me while I was trying to get Willie down for sleep.

"No. I think they thought you would be working. Father needs to meet with the president and for me to see Alice a little."

"As if you need to see her. She's not a good example as a wife. Hasn't given her husband any children. What is she waiting for?"

I shook my head, as Willie finished his feed and came off my breast, gurgling with contentment as I turned him around to get the air out of him. "I can move my appointments around, but would you mind taking Willie to the office with you for a bit?"

Sid reared up as if I had beaten him with a stick. "You want me to play nursemaid, too? Oh no, Mrs. Pittman. I'll be working. I'll be in no shape to see to a small child. You can let them know that!"

Father expected as much from Sid, and even though it was wintertime, he told me to bundle Willie up against the cold and to bring him with us. "The president knows about children, and Willie's a good baby."

"Well, Alice . . ."

"She'll have to deal with it," Father put in his gentle way. "For we cannot leave small Willie here by himself."

And so there it was. The solution.

Willie was a most accommodating small guest and when we arrived at the White House, for sure the president greeted us in his jovial way, along with Mrs. Roosevelt and Alice, whose eyes went wide when she saw Willie in my arms. As I stepped forward, I apologized. "I'm so sorry. I could not find someone to mind him and ..."

"I told her to bring young Willie to the White House. Since I know that you won't be here much longer, Mr. President, I thought you might not mind letting my young grandson have a peek at your greatness."

"Mind? God bless the lad. Isn't he something?" The president leaned down into Willie's face and offered his finger for a baby handshake. "Got a good grip on him, Booker! What a wonderful thing to have a grandson."

The room went cold silent for a minute and I wanted the marble to part and swallow me whole. Mrs. Roosevelt opened her arms. "He's a fine-looking boy, for sure. I would not mind if he spent the afternoon with me at all."

"The perfect solution," Alice proclaimed loudly to cover the quiet in the room.

Willie went right to Mrs. Roosevelt, an experienced mother if there ever was one, and Alice linked her arm through mine. "We're having our own tea, Father. Excuse us." She shepherded me down the hall to a small room.

"I'm so sorry, I wouldn't have brought him if I had known ..."

"Known what?" Alice turned to look at me.

"What your father said ..."

"Oh, that. He can never resist getting in a little riposte at me about a baby. He knows full well that I, like him, must be the center of attention. A baby would take that away from me." She squeezed my arm. "I've had to yield attention to my siblings for years. Now that I'm the wife of a congressman and a well-known Washington doyenne . . . well, I don't mind telling you that I couldn't care less."

When we went into the residential area, a small tea was laid out, just for us. "This is perfect," I exclaimed. "Remember the days when we had to go to Aunt Bye's house to see each other?"

"I do." Alice went around to the far side of the table. "And we had some good times, but it wasn't right. I'm so glad that we can make it up to you before we must vacate the White House."

I nodded and picked up a plate, helping myself to some cake and a few sandwiches.

"We'll join Daddy and Mr. Washington in a little while, pick up your baby from my mother, and it will all be good. Trust me. She's happy." She lowered her voice a little as she poured some tea. "She had an incident late last year with a baby she lost. Probably her last chance."

Incident? Then her meaning hit me. "Oh. That's a shame."

"Yes. It's happened before where she lost a bunny. But could you imagine if she had yet another baby before I did? Talk about an attention grabber!"

Well, that was one way to look at it, but it was hard to wish such a woman ill, especially since she was so happy to serve as a temporary sitter to my Willie.

"Besides, you have to do something for babies to come and well . . . Nick and I have fallen far behind in that score."

"Honestly?" I poured tea for myself and sat down to hear Alice's tale.

"Well, when we first married, we were together as often as anyone. But then I suppose he got bored of me. Doesn't happen nearly enough now."

"Oh my. I wish . . . I mean . . ."

"Sidney never gets bored of you? Well, bless you, Portia. I suppose that'll keep you in babies for a while."

I lowered my head and the rush of blood of my Indian forebearers overcame me. I ate my cake, suddenly so consumed with the contents of my plate.

"And another one is coming, right?" Alice peered at me, demanding my truthful response.

"Yes."

"Are you happy?"

I lifted my head. "I would have liked it if things had waited for a bit. It's a bit . . . fast. I mean we are barely used to each other and to have two babies in two years . . ."

Alice ate a cucumber sandwich. "I know. That has got to be . . . rough. Especially with your wonderful piano playing. Still teaching?"

"Yes. I cannot thank you enough for the references. I have quite a lot of teaching going on now. It's very helpful to us."

"Well, of course, my friend. I wouldn't have it any other way. The perfect solution. I cannot imagine it will be easy on you with two babies at once." She set down her teacup. "Oh my. Men can be so inconsiderate."

We finished our tea and nice chat and met up with our fathers for a small tour of the White House. Just as Alice promised, when it was all over, Mrs. Roosevelt emerged with a sleeping Willie. "He was as good as gold. Oh, if we weren't going back to New York soon, I would come out to your place and visit him. Pickaninnies are the sweetest babies."

The blood rushed to my face again, but I bit my lips as I saw Alice cross her eyes behind her mother's head and I wanted to laugh instead of be angry at such a comment. Edith Roosevelt wasn't a southern woman, so I wondered where she had heard such language. Mr. Roosevelt had southern origins—maybe from him?

"A wonderful visit," my father declared as we got bundled into the automobile for the cold ride back to my home just over the border in Maryland.

"Yes, it was. Good to see her."

"And any news from her?"

I shook my head, determined to keep my friend's confidences, even from my father. "I suspect Mr. Longworth is so busy with his congressional duties as well as his support of Mr. Taft, who is coming in now."

"That could be."

"Alice is not a fan of Mrs. Taft in particular."

"I think Alice, I mean Mrs. Longworth, knows that her time in the White House will be curtailed once the Tafts move in."

"I think you are right, Father."

"It'll be important to be a good support to her when that happens."

I knew it would be too much to expect the same in return.

THE VISIT HELPED me change my mind.

I would play. It would be difficult to figure out how, since I had been in the house for more than two years with a baby and a husband. I had nothing to wear to a recital, but the mother of one of my pupils offered to make me a dress in exchange for lessons. Some of me felt lumpy and bumpy all over, as if nothing would fit my changing body that had been used by the males in my life. But the pupil's mother assured me she could create something wonderful for me for the recital, and she did.

My dress was a nice soft butter yellow that went to the floor and pleats fell from my waist in gentle waves so that my growing stomach was nicely covered. The neckline curved in the front and the sleeves trimmed to my wrists. The puffed-sleeve fashion was diminishing, thank goodness, in exchange for a smaller, lighter, more Grecian silhouette and it was one that flattered my growing shape.

As I turned around in the completed dress, the woman offered to do my hair before the performance and I took her up on it. She piled my hair on my head in a smooth updo, billowy pompadour puffs surrounding my head like a cloud, with soft tendrils coming down either side of my head. I did look nice, as if I belonged to play in a recital as I did a few short years ago, but now, I had to practice to be ready to play.

Getting in practice time to play was not easy. Willie had his needs, I still had to teach my students, and Sid . . . well, I think I overcompensated with him so he would be less angry about it all in the first place. My father came back through Washington, DC, in time to attend, of course, indicating he wouldn't miss seeing me play publicly anytime I was in the United States.

On the night of the May recital, I made sure that my family was well fed and cared for. Sid, face downcast and sulky, had been taking some sips from a flask. My father squeezed my hand, telling me he arranged for us to go to the concert hall via a chauffeured car. We did not own one yet, which grated on Sid because he considered himself very much a man of the twentieth century. In spite of Clarence's offer of his mother-in-law to watch Willie, he stayed behind at our house with one of the women from our church congregation. When I settled into the car to ride, I felt like a princess.

The concert would be held in an auditorium at Dunbar High School, the most prominent high school for colored students in the city. I was honored to be able to play in such a large, airy space. Many concerts for Negroes were played in cramped, dark church basements or even worse, in dank pool halls that had been emptied out for the occasion. When we arrived, I was ushered backstage where I saw Clarence preparing his violin, and I flexed my fingers as best I could. I was offered a glass of water, but I declined to take it. This baby didn't allow me much room and I didn't want to have to use the ladies' room before I performed.

There were several others on the concert bill, showcasing so much talent in the city, when a beautiful woman, who looked about ten years older than me, stood in front of the audience, spreading her hands wide, preparing herself to speak. Her skin was a smooth walnut brown, and something in her calm manner stilled me. Clarence came and stood next to me since he had just finished his performance. "There's Mrs. Marshall."

"Who is she?"

"Who is Mrs. Marshall? My, those babies really have put you under a rock. She's the woman in charge of the Washington Conservatory of Musical Expression. You know, the school where I've been teaching for the past few years."

Oh. Yes. I turned to give her my full attention, especially with that name, my middle name. Also, I didn't get to see a woman who did the exact same thing as my father did very often. She spoke in a lilting voice about the mission of the school, to educate Negro youth with the best musical education to prepare them for careers in teaching and, yes, possibly one day to be able to play in operas, ballets, and symphonic halls.

What a wonderful program! And here was Clarence who taught there and other amazing musicians like Mr. Burleigh who also contributed to the school. I would have been much better prepared to handle my European experience if I could have gone to school in such a place instead of Bradford. Well, I couldn't go to this school now, but I could ensure that my son and this little babe, if they wanted to study music, could study the masters as well as Negro music at such a place. Mrs. Marshall finished speaking, and then, I was on!

I was due to play two pieces, my standards: "Sometimes I Feel Like a Motherless Child" and "Etudes." Once I took the stage I spotted my father sitting up front with the lady who had spoken, Mrs. Marshall, and Sid looking as if he would rather be anywhere else than right there listening to me play.

I gulped down the hard rock of nerves in my throat and focused on playing for the pleasant-faced woman who sat next to my father.

What an amazing task before her, someone who had started her own school. By playing well, I was helping her in her endeavor. It would not do to play poorly. I also had students in attendance, making for more pressure.

I sat down, hands poised over the keyboard, and awaited my cue. When I took it, I was swept away, wrapped up in the beauty of the music, expressing, as the name of the school encouraged, my entire self in the sorrow and emotion of the song. When I played "Etudes," the joy my playing imparted went through my fingers and to the keyboard. I never felt as if I were so connected to an audience before, almost as if I were speaking verbally to them.

When I finished, the last lingering note dissipated into the air and I noticed that my forehead was moist and I had no handkerchief. I stood, and Clarence came out onto the stage to help me up from the piano stool. All of a sudden, without warning, the audience exploded into a thunder clap of applause and the babe inside of me wriggled with pleasure at the noise. Looking at the corner where my father was sitting, I could see him wiping his face with his handkerchief, and the woman, Mrs. Marshall, beamed and clapped as hard as she could. I curtsied, as I had been taught to do in Germany. Such a wonderful reception. Scanning the audience even more, I recognized an outlandish hat in the back. Mrs. Longworth had deigned to show up as well. What a surprise!

I was thankful to have Clarence's arm steady me after, because my knees shook a little once I went off the stage to the back dressing room where flowers of all kinds awaited me. "How did people know to send me flowers?" I asked Clarence. "I might not have been very good."

"But you were quite good. Congratulations, Mrs. Pittman."

"Thank you very much." I restored myself with a cup of tea and sat back, relaxing a little to enjoy listening to the rest of the program. Once I finished the tea, I was surprised to turn and see Mrs. Marshall standing there in the doorway of the green room. "My dear Mrs. Pittman. You were marvelous."

"Thank you so much, ma'am."

"I'm a friend of your father's. Mrs. Harriet Marshall. When he told me that you could play, I just thought of you as a-company-in-the-parlor pianist. But you're really quite amazing."

I put a hand to my chest, smoothing to my belly, out of habit. "I really appreciate those kind words. Thank you so much, Mrs. Marshall."

She eyed me. "I see you are expecting a happy event." I moved my hand away and she laughed. "I don't hold with any of that foolishness about women not being out in public during your expectation. I've never understood why we must hide away as if we don't know where babies come from."

"Are you a mother as well?"

A shadow came over her face. "No. Mr. Marshall and I were not blessed in that way. So much of our energy goes into supporting the school."

I wanted to apologize, but I merely nodded in sympathy. "He works with you then?"

"Yes. I couldn't run things without him. And seeing you play, he thought and I agreed that you would make a wonderful class piano teacher this fall."

The beating of my heart, synced with the baby's heartbeat, sounded double time within me. "Oh my." Out of the corner of my eye, my father emerged in the doorway.

"I see that you've met Mrs. Marshall. She's the amazing woman in charge of this school, carving out a place for our people to study our music traditions in our ways." He stood next to me, embracing me to him from the side.

"I was just telling your lovely daughter how wonderful she is. She would be the perfect class piano teacher."

I could see the pride shining in my father's eyes. He squeezed my hand, and I could see the lump in his throat at this idea. "That's an amazing offer, Mrs. Marshall."

"Yes, it really is." My eyes shone too. For a second. And then they alighted on Sid, who was standing in the doorway with a fine sheen of sweat on his forehead. He started doing a slow clap as he walked, albeit unsteadily, toward me.

"My wonderful wife. You were wonderful, wife. That's what I meant to say. Just wonderful." The smell of his favorite whiskey spread over all of us. I sent up a prayer of quick thanks that there was no way for a fire to light in the room, for his breath could be used as an accelerant.

"I...Mrs. Marshall, I'll give your kind offer some thought, ma'am."

She nodded her head. "Of course, Mrs. Pittman. I'm available to talk when you are able." Her eyes took in Sid in an unfavorable way and she turned away, moving swiftly from our party, and I was glad. It would be best to avoid introducing him when he was in this state.

"I'm ready to go, Father. I'm really quite tired and ..."

"I've called for the car. This way."

"Wait a minute. Wait just a damn minute. Ain't no one going nowhere until I hear about this offer. What was that woman talking about? That Marshall lady? What she say?"

"We can talk about it in the car." My hand went to my belly. "I need to get rest and see to Willie ..."

"For once, woman, you are going to put me and what I want first." Sid held up a finger. "Now. Say it. What offer?"

I kept my voice low. Many other performers were receiving their congratulations and flowers and I did not want to spoil their moment any more than mine was being spoiled. "She offered me a teaching job."

"Well," Sid said much too loudly. "Isn't that amazing? Daddy got you a job teaching outside the house."

"No, he didn't. I got the job. Me. Myself."

His eyes narrowed until they looked like snake slits. "No. Daddy got you a job. Sing it, Portia. Daddy got you a job." He made his terrible voice singsongy and taunting.

My father kept his arm around me and pulled me toward the door. "Son, you need to cool off." He put some bills into Sid's hand and swept me away, outside to the car. "He'll find his way home."

I nodded, pulling my shawl about me in the cooling May evening. He would. He had many times over.

Still, that fact didn't stop Sid's voice from taunting me, singing his stupid little song over and over again in my head as the car went down the bumpy, muddy DC street into the night.

MONTHS LATER, MY second son was born. Two sons in less than two years of marriage. Booker Washington Pittman was a beautiful baby and resembled his older brother in so many ways, but how in the world could I possibly pursue my music if I had my hands full with two babies? I tried to see myself playing the piano with them in my lap, my hands. How could I possibly dissuade Sid from coming for his rights as a husband?

Dr. Austin was about to leave my bedside when I brought up these concerns with him. "Is there some way to rest . . . a little bit? To not see you again so soon?"

"Now, Portia." He folded his hands and stared down at us, me and little Booker.

"Doctor, I'm just asking. I need to catch my breath. Is there some way? I mean, look at my father. I'm aging him with worry having

these babies, given his past experience." I spoke quickly, wondering
if I brought in my connection with America's greatest Negro that
the man would hear me.

"I've noticed he does appear different than he did last year."
Dr. Austin stroked his chin for a minute. "I'm going to offer him
a tonic."

"That's wonderful, but what about what I can have?"

He patted my hand. "Rest, Mrs. Pittman, and try not to worry
about something that hasn't even happened yet."

"I don't know how long . . . I can hold off my husband." Tears
seeped out of the corners of my eyes, tears that I didn't even know
were there because it was true.

"Hold him off? You act as if the natural relationship between a
man and a woman is a chore."

"I tried to breastfeed Willie to hold off this one, but it didn't work.
What can I do?"

"Enjoy your boys while they are young, Mrs. Pittman. They will
grow up into men faster than you know."

He turned from me and I wanted to burst into full sobbing. There
would be no more opportunities to share my music with the world.
No more recitals, not for a long, long time. I loved my two boys very
much, but I couldn't take any more. My hands were full.

The midwife came to my bedside. "Aww, honey. I suspect you're
all full up with emotion at having this big boy. You needs to rest.
Pretty soon . . ."

"That's what I tried to tell the doctor but he did not hear me."

The midwife looked over her shoulder. "Before your husband
comes to see the baby . . . look a here. I have a tea mixture I can fix
up for you. It costs some money, though, but if you drink it early in
the morning, it prevents your man's seed from taking root in you."

Something in her words struck a chord in me. I remember my
grandmother Smith talking about something like that. "How

much?" I shook my head. "I don't care. Give it to me. I'll pay whatever you ask for the preparation."

She nodded. "When I come to check on you both tomorrow, I'll bring it to you. Costs a dollar a month."

I would figure out how to teach an additional student or some other way to get the extra money from the household budget; I didn't know how for sure, but I would. There was no way I would do without that tea preparation. It might be nasty, as were most of those medicinal things that my grandmother ran down my throat to make me healthy and strong so that I didn't die at age twenty-six like my mother did. When Sid came into the room, rubbing his hands together exclaiming over another boy like a banty rooster, I smiled, knowing that I would be able to remain strong, even as I yielded to him as a good wife should.

Alice

1912

My intense love for Nick kept dying by inches. Not because I saw his pasty behind in the open air pumping his dead semen into my former best friend. It was his casual invitation for me to join them that did it. As if either one of them would be worth me lowering myself to such spectacle. I was a good wife to him. A great support to his career. A spectacular hostess for his fundraising efforts. Yet all that was worth nothing. Now I understood. His practice of hedonism came above all.

Including me.

I should have been used to being put to the side for something else. It had happened all my life. But that didn't mean that it hurt less. So now, after his casual betrayal of my father, I had to make the effort, the very conscious effort, to show Nick that I didn't care any longer what he did in the way of Taft or his women.

While 1912 brought the happy news about my dear friend Portia welcoming a little daughter to add to her two sons, I had to put the thoughts of yet another fecund friend or family member to the side and focus instead on how to pick off people from the Taft side of things to help my father make his return to the political stage.

Such a focus would require shifting all my attention away from my household, but I was ready to do what it required. Something new was happening. Instead of state delegations deciding the votes for the nominees, people would vote in something called a primary, another election but this time, voters within the party would decide who should represent the party on the ticket. This step still required discussions with state delegations, but now, I knew that my presence would help because it would be the people who would have to make a choice between Fat Willie Taft and my wonderful father—no choice at all, really.

So I went to Sagamore Hill in March of 1912 to talk with Father to help him plan how to attack these state primaries as they occurred during March, April, and May. He needed me, as I knew he did, because Edith would rather not be present in any real or showy way. I also had connections at the Associated Press and they could transmit information to me to let us know whether Father or Taft had won a state.

Nick believed the Republican convention would be the determining factor for the ticket leader and didn't seek to waste time on encouraging anyone in primaries. What a foolish decision. Especially when it came to his beloved Ohio.

Nick and Taft didn't do much in Ohio, because they knew that it was Taft's home state, and they believed that the people there would just give their votes to him. But they did not count on my father's presence and magnetism. Father and I both visited and, of course, with us there to greet people, there was no doubt in who would win more delegates.

When we were waving at crowds and shaking hands one fine spring day in Cincinnati, I noticed a familiar-looking bunch of women with large hats and veils at the edge of the crowd, trying to obscure their otherwise plain looks. "Excuse me, Father," I said and got off the train at the platform to approach the four of them.

"Well, what are you here for?" I said loudly, greeting them all.

Clara, Nick's sister, turned to me and removed her veil, and I tried not to recoil. It didn't work. She still looked like Nick as a woman. "This is most unwise of you, Alice. Why are you here, in our home, undermining his efforts?"

"I'm not undermining his efforts. My husband will easily be reelected."

My mother-in-law fixed me with a glare but kept her veiling on.

Hooray. "You know we mean his influence with Taft. You're ruining Nick's opportunities to become something greater in Taft's cabinet if he cannot win there. You should take yourself home to your husband's side, immediately."

I decided to be kind and not destroy Susan's perception of her son and just smiled. "Nick would never be happy anywhere but in the Congress. He's not interested in the Taft administration, not that there will be another one."

"Thanks to you and the efforts of your . . . father." Clara gestured toward the platform where my father continued to press the flesh. I beamed. He was really having a wonderful time.

"The past four years have proven that it's better to have my father as president. He is the man we need, and he will even bring forward the vote for women."

My mother-in-law recoiled as if I had thrown my old pet snake at her feet, and I had to bite the inside of my cheek to keep from laughing. I knew that would shock her, which was why I said it.

"Your father is sick, sick with ambition and greed. That's abundantly clear," Clara spat out and now I was the one who was shocked. I didn't know that Clara had it in her. If she had not insulted my father, I might have admired the vitriol and hate with which she spoke those words. As it was, she still insulted my father and a response was required from me.

"You all are very fortunate that there is a crowd here and that I'm mindful of that or I would make you pay. As it is, you need to watch your step, as I still might make you pay otherwise. Clara. Susan." I turned away from them and went back to the train platform.

Father took thirty-seven of the forty delegates in Ohio, Taft's home state. Never let it be said that women had no influence in the days before we finally acquired the vote.

I liked these primaries. The only problem was we had to depart Ohio rather quickly when the result was announced as the Taft people were, understandably I suppose, rather angry at the result. Imagine them being angry enough to want to harm either one of us! Nick surely had cause to be angry since he barely squeaked out a win in his primary, and he had cause to blame me. He was looking for someone, anyone, to blame for how the wind was not blowing in either his or Taft's direction.

Once we reunited in Washington, DC, before the Republican convention, I went right back to doing what I knew how to do. Being Nick's wife. Making him a comfortable home. Ensuring that dinner was all ready.

But we didn't speak. We had nothing to say to each other, even though we ate our filet of sole at the exact same table, far, far apart from each other.

When we'd each eaten of the delicious floating island dessert, Nick pushed back his chair. "I have a Taft fundraiser. Do you care to come with me?"

"Me? No, I do not." Where had he gotten the gall to even ask me?

He sighed. "So this is how it is to be between us then?"

"I'm not sure I entirely make out your meaning." I folded my napkin and put it in my lap.

He stood. "I mean. Are you married to me or are you married to your father?"

Now I stood. "I shouldn't be surprised that you would make some filthy accusation like that. You disgust me."

"Me? After you sat on Hiram McTreackle's platform?"

I waved my hand. "I don't know who all your Republican opponents are. This whole primary system is new. Your seat is safe. Besides, you shouldn't have been so busy running after Taft trying to catch up to his every single whim. What kind of man are you anyway?"

"How can you say that? And expect me to believe it?" He pointed at me. "You have the shrewdest political mind I have ever seen in anyone, man or woman. And yet you refuse to use it to help me, your own husband? I curse the day I ever married you."

"I completely agree. And I can tell you this. If you lose, I'm not going back to that hellhole you call Ohio. Clearly you are all washed up, Nicholas. Marriage to you has done nothing but debase me."

He sputtered like the simpering fool he was. "You are debased? I was almost defeated in my home district and you sat with my opponent? All because of you and your damn father," he shouted.

"I told you not to support Taft. If you believe that I'm so shrewd, then why don't you listen to me?"

"Because, even though you have a shrewd mind, when it comes to your father, you lose all sense. All you want to do is please him. Everyone else can go to hell, including me. Which is why I have to spend more time now, back in Ohio, to make sure that I don't lose!"

"No. If you have to do all that, then it's because you are a bald, ignorant fool!"

I could tell by the sinking look in his eyes that my words hit their target. Why is it the people we love know how to hurt us the most? What had happened to us? He sank back down in his chair, covering his face with his hands, running his fingers down his mustache over and over again. "I can't live like this anymore. I won't."

"Neither will I. I want a divorce."

And there it was. The word that people in my world never dared to speak.

He looked up at me. We hadn't made a practice of dining together often for years, but his gaze on me this time burned a hole in my soul. I could not help but feel a sense of victory in that gaze. Now he understood how I felt. How deeply my pain went from his casual, horrific, terrible treatment of my love.

"What about the convention?"

"Oh, I'm going to the convention. I just won't go with you. I'll be with Father the entire time and let every reporter wonder why I'm nowhere near you."

"You cannot do that. I mean, Alice, you just . . . you can't."

"I can and I will." I pushed back from the table, feeling stronger every minute, and then he ran to me and clasped me by the arm.

"No. Alice. We can work this out."

"How? How do you propose that we work this out? It's our marriage. You don't want me anymore. Just admit it. Just say it out loud."

"That's not true."

And a little joy, just a little beam of it, leapt in my heart. Then I quashed it. *He only wants your popularity to help him. Fool.*

"What is true?"

"I told you when we met. I'm a hedonist." He let go of my wrist. "That's the freedom to do whatever I please." He sounded more like a whining five-year-old now. "Whenever I please. With whomever I please. I don't understand. I thought you wanted the same. The way you smoked on the roof of the White House, defied your father, carried a snake around, talked to my mother in a rude way . . ."

"All of that you appreciated, I suppose. Because you never had the guts to stand up to her yourself. You married me so I could do it for you."

He stood. "Well, I've booked our tickets to go to Chicago. Together."

"I'm going with my father."

"Alice. He's going to lose. The party establishment have said that they are giving it to Taft. What would it look like for them to change horses in midstream? To just abandon the president of the United States? It isn't done."

Something inside of me twisted at his betrayal of my father. "My father was president. A better president than that fat fool ever was. And he will be again." I pointed to one of the side tables. "Leave my ticket here. I'm going to leave for Chicago from New York as part of Father's party."

"I'm going to leave for Chicago tomorrow." He turned and walked out of the door. "We can be as you like, but there will be no divorce, Alice. Ever."

I shut my eyes. To hold back any weakness that might leak from them. "Don't forget to take Cissy with you."

The only response to my riposte was to hear the front door slam. Only once I heard that final sound did I dare to slump to my chair, my own mind agog at my own audacity.

For once.

THERE WERE FAR better places to spend June than in the overcrowded, overheated, overbearing Chicago Coliseum, but there was nowhere else I would rather be. Politics, sweet politics, was in the air and even though the air was thick with the stench of cigar smoke, I couldn't wait to advocate on behalf of my father.

In spite of my threat, I was forced to come to Chicago on the train with Nick. My father told me not to come to him until he got to Chicago. It would be too much to arrive with him, even though Edith stayed home in New York. If I did not come with Nick, that would be enough to get tongues wagging.

Nick and I had to go straight into sessions and even though women were not allowed in certain areas, I just bullied my way through. No one would dare to stop me, because they all knew who I was. My person, although thin and lithe, blocked Nick's way if anyone came to talk with him. One man surveyed his way toward us. "Good afternoon, Mrs. Longworth. It's a beautiful day."

"Who are you?" This man was as tall as I was but bent over to reach for my hand to kiss it. I looked down my nose at him. A charmer. Although I was not as charmed by his graying hair and caterpillar-thick eyebrows.

"Warren Gamaliel Harding at your service, ma'am. A son of Ohio. I hope to have some words with your husband about an opportunity for him in his home state."

Nick stepped around me to the man, reaching his hand out to

shake it. "Ahh, yes. I've heard of you. From the state legislature and you're running for the Senate. Excellent news. Good to meet you."

I peered at this man. There seemed to be nothing remarkable about him. At all.

"Well, there is an opportunity for you to be governor, next cycle. If you are interested, Mr. Longworth."

I grasped Nick's arm. "We are not at all interested in going back to the heathens in Ohio, sir. Have a good day."

Nick laughed. "Mrs. Longworth speaks the truth. But let me ask you instead. Are you a Taft man?"

"What else would I be?" Mr. Harding perked up and they engaged right away. I picked up the hem of my afternoon dress and edged myself away from that conversation.

Once I found our accommodations, I waited there until word came that Father had arrived. That's when I packed and arranged for the hotel people to transfer my things to Father's quarters. As was appropriate, his suite was full of men, including my younger brother taking time away from his young family and my father's first grandchild to help in the necessary pressing of the flesh to help Father win the nomination.

As much as I loved Ted Jr., he was not suited to this purpose as I was. When I got there, I saw my luggage was stacked in the corner of the room, not in the other bedroom of the suite. I didn't want to ask him why it was outside of the bedroom, because Father was busy. He had a new man in to help him with his campaign since his previous man, Colonel Archie Butt, had gone down with the *Titanic* a few months before. It was a time when my father and Taft had come together of one accord because he had been friends to both. I wonder whose side he would have taken.

I was the lone female in the room. I certainly couldn't carry it. My brother came back into the room so I asked him. "Why are my grips not in the other bedroom?"

"Because I'm staying there."

"You?" I had to clamp my lips together to keep from laughing. "Why?"

"I'm here to help on the campaign."

"That's what I'm here for."

Now he laughed at me. I was about to raise my voice to him, when Father stepped over to us both. "Now, Sister. Don't go getting mad at your brother. You can't stay here and you know why."

"No, I don't."

"You have a room with your husband, correct? You're his wife. Go back to him." My brother waved his hand in the air to dismiss me. As if he could.

I stepped back from them and pulled out my hatpin. "I'm not leaving until Father gets this nomination. I'm here to help him in every possible way to do that."

Father looked delighted. Teddy less so.

I wore a track in the carpet between my father's suite of rooms and the Chicago Coliseum. When it came time to sleep at night, Teddy went to the bed in the suite and I curled up on the davenport. My father said nothing. Teddy should have yielded the bed to me, of course, but I was willing to prove my loyalty by staying on the uncomfortable, narrow davenport. I went back to my room during the early morning hours, a time when I knew that Nick would be elsewhere or not awake yet, to refresh myself and change my clothes.

The lead-up to the counting of the votes was a night full of excitement. Still, I could see something in my father's eyes, but I was there to make sure of the end result. I stuck by his side while my brother was the one who went to do the tabulations and had been charged with letting him know what the ballots were as the states came in. People might think that he had the more important job, but I did. I could intercept the information as it came into the room to him. No one was more critical to the operation than I was.

Once, I went to the door, thinking my brother was coming with some figures from the west when instead, a man of my exact height approached me. He had a huge head with gray hair that went all over, and not in a neatly combed fashion. His face was not at all handsome, but his brow was prominent with one graying bushy eyebrow that went straight across his forehead. His lips were quite thin and not obvious and his nose a little too rounded and bulbous. It was the nose, I decided, that kept him from being too appealing.

"Ahhh. President Roosevelt, please," he said, and at the sound of his incredibly deep voice, everything I had just thought about his appearance left my head. I knew I had never met someone more appealing.

I gathered myself. "He's busy right now. May I convey a message?"

"Mrs. Longworth, I presume?"

"I am." I nodded, assuming my best princess pose. Why did I want to impress this stranger? What was it about him that struck a chord within me, a chord of a song I believed had been silenced?

"Senator William Borah of Idaho at your service, ma'am. Coming to talk to your father on behalf of the Idaho coalition."

I opened the door a little wider, even though it went against what I would have usually done.

He stepped in, and I could see that he was not a thin man, but broad, like a bull in a china shop.

Like my father.

He went past me and went to my father, who greeted him heartily as if he knew him. I later learned he did. Senator Borah had been in the Senate during my father's second administration. He was coming, I suppose, to defer to my father and to let him know which way the Idaho delegation would vote.

To eavesdrop on the conversation, I went over to the davenport where my father was sitting. Father wouldn't mind if I sat in, because he trusted me, but for a stranger, having a woman sitting so close might be difficult.

"And more in the delegation are looking to back Taft since . . ." The senator stopped speaking in that glorious voice of his and I leaned forward, hoping he would pick it back up again. "May I help you, Mrs. Longworth?"

"Please go on. I'm my father's greatest confidante."

He turned to give my father quite a gaze and he nodded. "Well, I had no idea."

"Is there a problem, Senator Borah?" I asked him in a more pleasant voice than I might have, if his brief oratory had not been so, well, thrilling.

"It's just . . . I'm not used for women to be in the room. My own Mamie . . ."

"Your wife, no doubt?"

"Yes. She's very retiring and wouldn't dream of being where men are discussing political matters."

"Well, I find it very strange that you have never come across a woman with any kind of brains to be able to engage in politics. Aren't you still in your first term, sir?"

"I am."

"Well, I think that now that you have had some seasoning as a senator, you might meet a wider variety of women."

"I prefer to read and study in my library to socializing in the wilds of Washington, DC."

"No wonder you only have your Mamie for your example. It's good you've come to the convention here in Chicago to be more readily exposed." I settled into my chair and clasped my hands together.

He laughed a little bit. "I've heard much about you, Mrs. Longworth."

"I'm sure. But don't hold that against me." I smiled a little bit and found that, sparring with this man, flirtation came easier to me than it had in years.

"Oh, no. Just what I've read."

"Since you are a reading man."

"Yes. Exactly."

"I love to read as well."

"We should exchange lists at some point."

"I look forward to that. To make sure that you know enough about women."

My father fixed me with a look, a strange look that I had never seen before. "Is that all, Senator?"

"Well, I just don't know if I can bring them round. It's a shame, but mostly they seem to be for Taft."

"Split them then, and let those who will speak for him do so. There will be other coalitions where we can pick up more votes," I declared and Borah gave me a look, raising up his eyebrow.

Father spoke up. "There gets to be a time when the handwriting is on the wall, Sister."

A knock sounded at the door and it was my brother this time, bringing more news that was quite opposite of what we had hoped. Soon after he delivered it, he went back out, and Borah stood. "I won't detain you any longer, Mr. President. I just wanted to let you know of my efforts."

"I appreciate that, Senator. Thank you."

"Let me see you to the door," I said. I had no idea where those words had come from. I was not in the habit of seeing people to the door. But I wanted to walk alongside of him; even that brief trip across my father's suite was quite pleasurable.

"Thank you, Mrs. Longworth. I regret to say that I did not have good news to bring to him." He gestured toward where my father huddled with another clerical worker.

"He'll make it somehow. He has to. We cannot have another four years of Taft."

He nodded and stepped to the doorsill. "It may well be what we expect. Better Taft than a Democrat."

I straightened up. "I'm not so sure about that, Senator, and I'm surprised to hear you say so."

"I admire your loyalty to your father. I suppose that Congressman Longworth is aware of your support?"

"Oh, yes."

"He permits this?"

"I'm not a dog chained on a leash, Senator. I'm not sure what . . . Mamie, is it? . . . endures from you, but be assured that I'm a very independent woman in my marriage."

"Now. As to what I've heard, Mrs. Longworth. That's what I was referring to. That you have an independent streak in you."

That voice. What had I been missing staying in the House chambers all these years? I needed to visit the Senate more often to hear this man speak in that voice of his.

He leaned forward toward me. "The question is, just how independent are you?"

To this day, I don't know how I managed to keep standing, but I did. My entire body transformed into a quivering mass, in such a way that brought to mind my first island adventure with Nick, oh so long ago on the island beach when I was still a maiden. Who was this man talking to me, Mrs. Longworth, in such a way? How dare he? Was I offended?

No.

Should I be?

Yes.

But I wasn't.

I leaned forward to him and said just one word. "Very."

"Good," he said, then he turned on his heel and walked down the hall, turning the corner, giving me no opportunity to digest what it was that he said.

Alice

1912

The unjustified rejection by the stupid Republicans meant that my father had to resort to another means to secure the presidency. Another party. He formed it himself, called it the Progressive Party, and a convention was hastily arranged in the Chicago Coliseum in August. This time, there would be no contest as to who got the nomination, no disrespect of my father shown by those Taft people. It was all Roosevelt, so we had a glorious time.

Because the end result was known, we didn't have to have a long convention, just one good enough for two nights or so to make everything official. This time Edith came, so I didn't hang around my father as much, so that I did not have to endure her presence, but I had my own suite with all my brothers and my sister gathered as a family to celebrate my father.

Looking back, I could not have known that would be one of the last times that we would all be together like that, save Nick, but we celebrated Father and his new Progressive Party as if we were the real thing.

The Progressive Party needed more members, more fire, more movement. Senator Borah was on the floor as my father made his speech. I managed to get a peep at him as Father accepted his nomination and spoke about carving a new path forward for the workingman.

Borah looked back at me and smiled in my direction. I used my hat to tip him out of my vision, trying to breathe normally, willing myself to calm down.

Why did this man have such an impact on me? He was not much to look at for sure. It was the way that he spoke a truth, his truth. Right then, I resolved to get him for the Progressive Party, no matter what I had to do.

Once the speech was over and the convention completed, I made my way to where he had been standing, watching the proceedings. "Senator. So nice to encounter you again."

"Mrs. Longworth. How are you?"

"Doing splendidly. Now that Father has his nod and we can campaign."

The senator rocked back on his heels. "Yes. It's a fine celebration for him. I'm glad to see that for the old Bull Moose. But you know it's a last hurrah."

"I don't know any such thing."

"Mrs. Longworth. I've done some reading about you since our last encounter."

I pulled back farther into the shadows to stand next to him. It was hard for a person like myself to retreat entirely, but I was willing to try to hear his justification.

"You have? Why?"

"Because I wanted to know more about what goes on underneath those outrageous hats you wear."

I ignored those words. "And what did you learn?"

"If you were a man, that would be you up there, no doubt."

"You flatter me, entirely too much. I'm not thirty-five."

"I'm completely serious. Your mind, your acumen. It's amazing."

"Thank you. I'll be just as satisfied getting the vote."

"And after that, watch out!"

"Exactly." I lowered my voice a bit, so just he could hear me. "Did you like what you found out?"

He matched his tone to mine. "I came here to Chicago, on the way to Idaho, to tell you to not build your father up too much. But I come here to see that it's all too late."

"So you are no candidate to join the Progressive Party?"

"I am not. And neither should you." He turned to me, voice even lower. "Don't throw yourself away on this."

"Throw myself away?" Now I was a bit indignant. I wasn't used to being talked to in this way, this stripped down, bare-bones way. By someone I barely knew. Who seemed to know the impact he had on me.

"Yes. Let him have this last hurrah, but keep your cards close to your chest. Don't make too many enemies in the party. You'll need them someday."

"Quite the advice. Thank you."

"I hope I didn't offend you, Mrs. Longworth."

"Not at all. How can I be offended by advice that came all the way from Idaho?"

"Good. I wouldn't want to be on the wrong side of someone like you." He bowed. "I will leave you all to your celebrations while I continue my travels."

"Thank you, Senator." I turned from him and intended to walk away to make a clean break of it with him, but he captured my free hand in his.

His touch, rough and manly on my hand, felt as if he were slough-ing off my skin. I had never been touched by a hand like that be-fore. I wanted to pull myself away from him, but if I did, more of me would come off and I would be left bare to him.

I would not, could not, be that way for him. He was not my husband.

Why do you care? If it gives pleasure, do what you want to do.

For a split second of a second, I thought about Nick but then Nick went away and all I saw was Senator Borah.

The look on Borah's face, that broad, not-handsome-at-all face, but intelligent and intuitive face, read my every single thought and he knew. He took my hand up to that face of his, staring at it, and turned it over, kissing my palm along the edges of my wrist. Repeatedly.

Every kiss that landed on that inside seam of my sleeve went straight to my heart and jolted that dead thing alive once more. I had not known that I was dead inside until those light, feathery kisses were applied to me. On me. Suddenly, it struck me, all at once, that we were in the most public of places, surrounded by hundreds of people in midcelebration.

And I did not care. I saw nothing. I knew nothing. I wanted nothing but this man.

"Goodbye, Mrs. Longworth," he said and dropped my hand, and the cold of the world, a cold that I had become accustomed to, surrounded me all at once. I could do nothing but watch Senator Borah retreat from me, on his way back to Idaho.

All of a sudden Idaho sounded like a paradise to me. I started to follow him, to walk in his footsteps, but my brother Kermit grabbed me, elbowing me and pulling me into a circle of my siblings shouting and screaming, "Father won! Father won!"

Well, of course he did. We set it up that way.

For the first time in my life, I did not care about what pleased Father. Something, a primitive instinct I suppose, took hold of me and shook me so that everything in my world turned from a dull gray color to vivid, intense color. My siblings were telling me that there would be a spread in Father's suite.

By the time I came to myself to understand their words, Senator Borah had walked away from me and it was too late.

You could go to Idaho.

I could. But where in Idaho? What would I look like, wandering about an entire state looking for one man?

I'd missed my chance. An opportunity. Nothing to do but to keep on working for that long-desired approval from my father, which now came across as a cold and unappetizing biscuit. I could hardly believe in that moment . . . I had been chasing a cold biscuit all my life.

FATHER INSISTED I go, and I was happy to, back to my home in Washington, DC, to consult on his campaign moves from there. At least in Washington I knew that I was breathing the same political air as Senator Borah, and that eased the ache in my heart for him a bit.

Nick, going back and forth between the capital and Ohio to his district to campaign, noticed nothing of me and did not care about what I did. On election night, I went to my friend's offices at the AP and monitored the results by telegraph there. It was not long before it was obvious that Father was going to lose, spectacularly. And so would Taft.

Our new president was going to be a pinhead from New Jersey, Woodrow Wilson, who had three daughters, none of them prize beauties to be sure, but who still would capture all the attention of the press that I once had. At least with Taft he only had the one daughter and she was already married. Senator Borah was right. All was lost.

I came home in the car and the house was completely dark. I had not stayed with Nick for him to obtain his results. The fact that Taft lost was not a good sign for the rest of the party.

I was right. When Nick came home, he was completely drunk. I didn't want to see him, but I still went down in my dressing gown to get the results while he helped himself to more brandy, stinking of rye and Cissy or some other whore.

"It doesn't look good, that's for sure. It's entirely too close for comfort."

"The entire Ohio machine?"

"That's what it looks like, Alice, my dear wife. Thanks to you sitting with Hiram on his platform there."

"I'm just one woman. No one cares what I say or do."

He tossed back the liquor. "That's not true and you know it. Too many people care." He pointed a finger at me. "So it will be interesting to see which one of the Wilson girls takes over the spotlight from you so no one will care any longer about Princess Alice."

"Shut up, Nick."

He laughed. "Serves you right. Now, you'll have to come back to Ohio with me and live in our house with my mother."

I folded my dressing gown over my front again, closing my eyes to the very thought of that. It sounded like hell to me. Ohio. A buried coffin of a word, where I would have to be committed to the Longworth home for long days and nights, trying to speak kind words to the awful Mrs. Susan Longworth.

Life was incredibly bleak and beyond unfair.

The reason for hedonism, according to my drunken husband, was because it prevented life from being bleak and hopeless. Always getting what you wanted made existence more meaningful, because what you wanted must be for the best.

Nick, slumped over and snoring, was not what I wanted, nor was going to Ohio the best thing for me.

I went back upstairs and dressed plainly in a white shirtwaist and dark blue skirt. No hat. No Alice blue. Just me. Simple and straightforward.

After lacing up my boots on my own, I wrapped myself in a plain wool shawl and went out of the house, relishing the quiet of the cool autumn Washington, DC, night, but as I continued my walk out of DuPont Circle into other neighborhoods, I could see that there were many Democrats, hang them, who were in full celebration mode. The Republicans, morose and quiet, contemplated what their fates were now that they were going to lose their jobs and have to return to places like Ohio.

Crossing DuPont Circle into the northwestern part of the city, I knew where my feet were taking me. Where they wanted to go. I could just sit outside and wait for him. I would just sit there and wait all day and night if I had to, but just sit there to let him know or convey how much I wanted him. Maybe if I were patient he would come out to me and . . .

What about Mamie? What if she saw me waiting out there in front of her house? Waiting on her husband? Like a spider in a web, wanting to spin him into my personal prize.

Cissy hadn't cared what she did with my husband. Or Maggie, as I came to find out. Or any of the other hundreds of women Nick had been with. Why should I? I was past caring about what Nick felt or thought. The only person I cared about was Father and he was in New York. Now that he had lost the election, I didn't have to behave anymore. I didn't have to be the country's princess anymore. The Wilson girls would come in and take over and then I could . . .

Engage in hedonism and do as I wanted. Take what I wanted. Be what I wanted.

Before I knew or fully understood, I stood in front of the Borah house. A small stone bench beckoned and I sat on it, wrapping my shawl about me, waiting, waiting, waiting for my love to emerge.

Alice

1912

Later I learned that Nick lost by ninety-seven votes to a small-potatoes lawyer by the name of Stanley Bowdle. Less than a hundred people in miserable little Cincinnati, Ohio, had determined my fate, and now I would have to move back to their dreadful town to live with my cheating husband and hateful mother-in-law, no matter what I had said. I could never bring the disgrace of a divorce on my father, especially after he had lost the election. But, in that moment, I did not care if Nick won or lost. All I cared about, with me as a very well-known woman, was my hind end freezing on the cold stone bench in front of the Borahs' house waiting for . . . him.

So desperate. So sad.

The energy emitting from the large gingerbread house was low, very low. Whoever Mamie was, she was not as energetic or as bright as I was. He needed me. That's why I was there. He needed me to talk to. Be with.

Or was it that I needed him? He tried to tell me what was going to happen, and I had to let him know, somehow, he was right. I had to pay homage to someone whose political instincts were better than mine. He had seen this coming.

After what seemed to be a long time, light flickered on in the front part of the house and a moment later, the door opened. I did not believe in God, but some force was looking out for me.

Thank you.

Borah. At the sight of him, the fire in my heart lit anew. This nearly fifty-year-old personage, in contrast to my twenty-eight years, ran to me faster than I thought possible and I knew he felt the same way. "Mrs. Longworth. What are you doing out here in the cold?"

I tried to speak but my teeth chattered. He helped me to stand. "Come in. Let me fix you some coffee."

"It's so late," I managed to say.

"Tea then. Let me get you something warm."

He guided me into his home and it was all just as I thought. Heavy, depressing, dark wood oak surrounded us. Nothing on the walls. Nothing colorful inside. Just empty.

He's not happy. You can make him happy.

Instead of making me unhappy for him, that fire glowed inside of me and I was warmed.

"Please. Sit in the parlor while I . . ." His voice was low. I guess given the late hour, Mamie was sleeping.

"No." I kept my voice low too. "I'll come with you."

"We can speak better in the kitchen."

He led me into the back of the house where a variety of fascinating objects were. I didn't have much interaction with kitchens, but it just showed what an interesting man the senator was, to be able to light a stove and put a pot with a curved handle on.

I sat down at a small wooden table in the corner and watched as he opened cabinets, bringing forth items for tea. "I apologize, Mrs. Longworth." He said this in a normal voice, so I presumed it was okay to speak as he did.

"Why? You didn't know I was coming."

"We don't have help sleeping in. It's hard to afford that here in DC."

"I understand." I really didn't understand a life that meant limited money, but I wanted to respond to him in some way.

"I was about to go to bed after reading in my study when I saw you on the bench. I'm glad I did. Why didn't you just knock?"

"I didn't want to disturb your household. I just . . ." What a fool I was.

He slid into one of the wooden chairs opposite of me. Not the one next to me. Which is where I wish he would have sat. "I've heard the news. I'm so sorry."

"You tried to tell me. Back in Chicago. How I wish. I wish I would have listened to you. But you see, I've never met anyone like you before."

"Like me?"

"Someone whose political instincts were so in tune with mine." I lowered my head. My neck began to hurt a little, because I wasn't used to holding my head in such a posture.

He spread his hands. "I didn't want to be correct. I knew splitting the party so would hurt us. But now, here we are with Wilson in the driver's seat." I could hear water bubbles in the pan on the stove start to grow and break apart.

I played with the fringe on my shawl. "That would be terrible enough. Father is bereft. But the worst of it is that Nick has also probably been swept out."

When I said these words, his head had faced the stove, but now he whipped around to face me. "That's terrible news. Forgive me, Mrs. Longworth. I did not know."

"Thank you. We'll have to return to Ohio."

He stood and removed the pot from the stove before it bubbled over and poured hot water onto a cup of leaves that waited nearby. "Would you like sugar or milk?"

"No. Black is fine."

He placed the cup in front of me and I put my hands around it, letting the warmth seep into and through my chilled fingers. "This is worse than I thought. The cause of the progressives will be set back for decades now without a champion like Nick in the House."

I raised my neck to its rightful position so that I could sip on the tea with the leaves settled into the bottom. "Yes." I sipped and the liquid warmth spread throughout me. "Very good. How is it that a man like you can make a good pot of tea?"

"I'm not rich, Mrs. Longworth. I've not always been a senator. I've been a lawyer with a one-man office and before that, I've done time in the silver mines. Many a night I've had to fix coffee over an open fire. It's not hard to fix tea."

It isn't? I continued to sip.

"A new world is in the offing indeed."

"I came. I came here because . . ." I lowered the cup from my lips so that I could speak. "I wanted to say goodbye before I returned to Ohio."

These words had to sound perfectly ridiculous to a man I had met exactly thrice in my life. But his rugged features were sober, and smooth. He nodded. "I'm glad that you did. It's a strange time of night for such, but I'm glad, nonetheless."

"You are?"

He nodded, as sober as Nick never was. Something inside of me, something that had been glazed over, cracked open and saw the sun. All of a sudden, he looked like Adonis to me. I knew he wasn't, but that's what he seemed to be in my eyes. The god of love.

"Yes. To tell you . . ." He moved closer to me. To the seat where I wanted him to be in the first place. I was willing to let the tea get cold. "Your father's career is over. But you, as well as Nick, are just getting started. It may seem as if two years is a long time, but it isn't. Be disappointed now, yes. Cry if you want to now, but two years is enough time to plan a return. Ohio sounds as if it is far, but two years is enough time for someone as smart as you to learn that Ohio operation and plan a comeback. Didn't your father win that Ohio primary? But it does depend on what Nick wants."

"Oh, yes. Without question. He's a House man."

"I thought so." He slid his large hand over the top of mine. "He appeared that way to me."

"He did?"

"Well, of course. If I studied you, I've been looking at him also."

"And?"

"He's got potential for House leadership. People like him. But you're going to have to help him. He's not as smart as you are. He'll need you to figure out the relationships and you'll have to smooth his way to make it happen."

His hand felt like a blanket of warmth on top of my hands and, honestly, his handhold was better than tea. "Yes. A lot of people like him. Too many people." I took in a sharp breath. "I've asked him for a divorce."

He pulled his hands back away from me. "Why?"

"You don't understand. I've seen . . . I mean, I've caught him in flagrante delicto."

"Is he in love?"

"Excuse me?"

"Is he in love with the woman?"

"I don't think so. He didn't say. It doesn't help that she was a friend of mine at one point. Cissy Patterson. Nick had been trying to make up his mind between us and then went back to her." I left Maggie out of it all. It was too complicated, even for me.

"Cissy Patterson?" He peered into my face. "My dear Mrs. Longworth. There isn't a man in Washington who hasn't had relations with Cissy Patterson. I'm not a man who regularly strays from my wedding vows, but even time to time . . ." He coughed.

Now it was my turn to peer at him. "Yes?"

"It was a very long time ago," he confirmed.

I sat back in my chair. Stunned.

My friend was no better than a whore. A welcoming committee for all of Congress.

The senator said, "Leave Nick to his practices. There's no need to be thoughtless. He's going to need you to help him return to Congress and to adjust himself to take up a position of leadership. Our return to power will take time, patience, and effort. So two years"— Borah snapped his fingers—"will go by just like that." He put his hands back over mine. "When you go back home, I want you to impart this to Nick, but you don't have to tell him I said it. We can make arrangements to have dinner together before you depart for Ohio, if you like. You'll meet Mamie and we can have a bit of a powwow."

Was that a good idea? Maybe. Still, I felt warmed at the thought that I had a purpose now. Senator Borah had given me a task and a purpose and a direction. Yes, that direction still involved being married to Nick, but that was better than being rudderless as I had been before I came here.

"That sounds like a plan. A good plan," I said slowly.

He patted my hands. "Do you feel better now?"

"I do. Thank you. I feel much better."

And I did. "Now. We can arrange to get you back home."

"How?"

"I'll call a hack. I would drive you myself, but I don't have a car. I walk and use the transit most of the time."

"Transit?"

"Yes. Public transit here in DC. Very handy and accessible but it doesn't run at this time of night."

He excused himself to go to his study and I finished my tea in the meantime. How wonderful for him to be so self-sufficient. I knew of this side of life from my dear friend Portia, of course, but I assumed life existed in that way for people of her race because they had no other choice. For a man, a powerful and connected man like Senator Borah, to live so independently . . . that was a whole other thing.

He returned quietly. "There. They'll be here shortly. I know it's cold but we can wait on the porch."

I stood and followed him back to the porch outside, where he had spread a quilt on the bench, wrapping me in it as he sat with me and waited for the hack to come. I don't think either one of us noticed, but he covered my hands with his hands and he leaned into me with his big, warm body. In the still darkness, we heard the distant echo of a car, hiccuping its way toward us.

"That's probably the hack."

I nodded. "Thank you for all that you have said tonight, Senator. I'll think very carefully on it."

"I know you will."

There was nothing more to say. Except.

I turned my face to his and he did the same. Why had I ever thought him unlikely looking? What kind of fool must I have been to not see the warm, radiant kindness in this man's soul? I'm usually perceptive and not so blind.

His breath exhaling in the cold was visible and mine far less so. I gave a little smile, just the tiniest, and leaned forward, inch by inch, until I was pressing my lips to his. In gratitude.

But once I kissed him, my entire world changed. Everything in my life opened anew and my world, so dark and cursed, shifted. Into the light.

At first, I was kissing him, my lips on his surprisingly soft mouth. But then he opened his mouth and the kiss became some other kind of wild, forbidden thing knotting me to him.

The hack pulled up and he tore away from me, taking me by the hand and helping me into the hack, unwrapping me from the quilt as I got in the car.

"Good night, Mrs. Longworth," he intoned and stepped away, so the car jutted forward, carrying me and my newly sprung love for him along with it.

All the way back to Ohio.

Liberation

Portia

1909–1912

After the recital, something within me died toward Sid. I prayed about it. I would clean his clothes, fix his meals, teach my students, and lie there and grit my teeth while he would rut on top of me whenever he wanted. But that day, just a few years into our young marriage, it was over.

I was Booker T. Washington's daughter. I had to do him proud. Once my drunken husband had humiliated me at the recital, I never went back to the Washington Conservatory. I couldn't look into the kind eyes of Harriet Marshall or stand tall and proud as a teacher on her faculty. My father, bless him, didn't press the issue. I got the sense that he understood.

Fortunately, my baby boy, Booker, was my most musical child. He kept his movement going whenever music played, and in my house, that was a lot of the time. His entire goal in walking was to reach up to the piano stool so he could get on it and touch the keys. Willie was far more quiet, more studious, more like my father, I thought. It never failed to be a source of amusement to me that I had named my children incorrectly. But Sid would have never stood for naming my first son after my father.

Those years of the Taft administration went by in a blur. How could they not when I had two busy boys and a teaching practice on my hands. I couldn't spend as much time with my friend as I might have liked and that saddened me. I knew that she was not happy, either. I didn't know why she was unhappy; I mean, she didn't have money troubles as I did, but I suppose that saying that money isn't everything was true.

One day in 1911, I was alarmed to get a telegram from my father, asking me to come to New York as soon as possible. It shocked me, because he might have summoned my brothers or even Margaret, but he asked for me. I made arrangements with another one of the women in our church to take care of the boys. I knew that I couldn't trust Sid to do it. I went to New York on the first possible train.

Once I got there, I went to the address my father directed me to, and to my shock, he was in jail. How could this be? The great educator in a prison cell. I made arrangements for his release at once and when he was remanded to my custody, something in his eyes, the light in them, had dimmed. "Thank you, Portia. I knew that I could trust you to handle this matter with discretion, without making the press aware."

The skin from his neck hung in a new way, a way that meant that he was losing weight, and I did not like the way that it looked. My father, my great father, was getting older and it hurt me to see him age, even though I was warned this was happening. "Of course."

He was renting a room in the Negro part of town, his usual practice. I obtained a hack and we both went back there. When he let me in, the room carried a small, closed, sad air about it and I could see how much he had sacrificed of himself to keep staying on the road, fundraising for the school. Something about the situation brought a tear to my eye, but it wouldn't do for him to see me cry. I whisked it away and sat down in a small hard chair next to a dresser.

"Thank you once more, daughter. I appreciate that you didn't harangue me about why I was in jail."

I nodded, even though I gripped the edges of my reticule, because I wanted to know.

"They accused me of compromising the honor of a lady. A white lady."

Now I gripped the edges of the chair that I was sitting on. That was not possible. "How?"

He waved his hand. "I should have known the old accusation would catch up to me. Someone who wanted to discredit me and the school by extension. I would never..."

"I know that Papa. You don't have to explain."

He brought a hand around to his neck, rubbing at a spot of tension there, no doubt. "How foolish I was to think that those things could never happen to me. Did I think I was better than my fellow Negroes, that I was above it all? Just because I'm friends with people like Andrew Carnegie and Theodore Roosevelt?"

I patted his knee. "No, Father. You've worked so hard. That's all. They wanted to discredit you because of the success of the school."

"While I was in there..." His voice broke off a bit. "I thought, maybe I should resign. Let someone else run the school."

My heart beat fast at these words. "Oh, Papa. No one else could run the school but you. How could you think that?"

"I just... I felt more helpless in that closed, cut-off cell than at any other place in my life. I thought of all kinds of things. Portia, I would never bring harm to the school. If this got out, so many would be deprived."

"That's why I came as soon as word got to me. It'll be fine, Papa."

His hand covered mine and clasped it. "How are the boys?"

"Active. Busy as all boys would be."

My father laughed. "I remember my last visit when I gave little Willie that five-dollar bill and he flung it into the fireplace saying 'pretty fire'!" I laughed with him, relishing the feeling of his attention and need of me, on me. "When I was going to sleep in the crawl spaces underneath salons on my way to Hampton, dreaming of fried chicken, never did I ever believe it possible that I could have enough money for my grandson to burn."

Then he sobered. So did I.

"You should go back to your boys."

"You should come with me, Papa. You know they would be glad to see you." I squeezed his hand.

"That might be true, Portia, but your husband, less so. How is Sid?"

Now it was my turn to be downcast as I reflected on the prison of my own making. "He's working on the YMCA building for the colored in Washington."

My father nodded. "Good. It's good when he is busy. No. I'm going to go back to the school and make sure all is well. You go on home and see to your boys, Portia. I'll be fine."

I stood and gave him a hug. His body didn't feel the same in my arms. But I maintained my cheer and kissed him on the cheek, saying a farewell to him, holding my tears until I got on the train to return to Washington, DC.

By the time I returned, it was late at night. The church ladies had made some smothered pork chops for dinner, ensuring that my men ate, saving me. I was completely grateful for their support. Once they left, I put the boys to bed, reading them stories from the Uncle Remus tales as they loved hearing about the tales of Br'er Fox, Br'er Bear, and Br'er Rabbit so much. They went down rather quickly.

I then closed their door and took myself to Sid's study, his place where he hid away on his benders. I tried not to venture into his place very often but after a full day seeing to the needs of others, I had to check on him.

I gingerly tiptoed to the door and pushed it open. He was there, slumped over on the davenport. His breathing was even, and I thought he might have been sleeping his drunk off, but then he spoke. "Come in."

"I was checking on you to make sure you had some dinner." I did as he bid me to and came into the room, standing over him, trying not to be disgusted at how badly he reeked of alcohol and unwashed body.

All of a sudden, he lashed his arm out and grabbed me by my wrist, holding it tight, tight, tight and his hold made me want to turn myself loose. "Stay," he said, holding me harder.

"I don't want to." An ancient response rose within me.

He lifted his head and his eyes were completely bloodshot. His collar was loose and his usually slicked-down hair stood all over his head. "You're going to do as I say for once. Hear me?"

"Sid. I usually do what you want."

He stood, facing me. "You lie. As you do. Get on my nerves with your lies."

"Let me go." I kept my voice calm, as if I were talking to one of the boys, but I couldn't hide what I was feeling now.

"Daddy ain't here to save your sorry ass. You gone do as I say, Portia. You're my wife, and you do as I tell you to do." He pushed me to the davenport and began loosening his pants.

Dear God.

I swallowed hard. Not this. Anything but this. Our times together had been less frequent because he could tell I was disgusted by him. To be honest, the tea had become less necessary and I stopped taking it, thinking that I could control the situation just by avoiding this with him. I scrambled to the other side of the davenport. But my moves to get away seemed to make him stronger, and he pulled his pants down, exposing himself, completely erect.

"Pull up your skirt, Portia."

I grabbed fistfuls of my skirt into my hands, keeping a tight hold on it, either side of it, to keep it down, down, down.

"Do as I say, woman."

I bit the inside of my cheek. What could I say to him that would make him understand that this was not necessary. Indeed, that it was hateful. "Sid . . . I haven't been taking the tea." *Stop shaking.* "You know, the tea that stops a baby. What the midwife gave me after Booker came. So we really . . ."

"I know you heard me."

So he wasn't going to be reasoned with. Not this time. Not in this state. My eyes cast around his study, desperately thinking of, planning for, attempting an escape. But this was his lair. There was no way out.

With trembling hands, I lifted my skirt as he told me. He grabbed me by the waistband of my drawers, yanking my body up to him, and flipped me around as if I were a rag doll, pushing my face into the davenport; then he bent me over, using me, roughly as hard as he could, repeating the words over and over again into my ear. "You. Do. What. I. Say."

What could I do but hold on to the side of the davenport and pray that it would all be over soon? He clearly only wanted to think of himself, and not of me. After what seemed to be an eternity, he collapsed on top of me with a groan. He pulled out of me and I could feel the shame and humiliation dribble down my legs.

I pulled up my drawers, trying to get much of the hateful fluid absorbed in them, but back in those days, the cotton wasn't as absorbent as it could be. So instead, the wet spots stayed cold against my legs as I pushed my skirt down.

"There's a plate of dinner in the stove." I kept my voice steady. "You really should eat to take the edge off your inebriation."

He lifted his head, staring at me. I could be as saucy as I dared now that he had used me. I walked away from him as swiftly as I could, hoping to cleanse myself of him and his use of me.

The next year, in a presidential year, I welcomed my only daughter, Fannie, named after my mother, into my world. She was the last beautiful thing to come from our tormented union.

Portia

1913

With three children under the age of five, it can often seem as if a mother is in an us-versus-them situation. Or in my case, a *me*-versus-them situation. I loved them all but they were all so young. Poor Willie, as my eldest, had to take on a mantle of helping a lot more than he might have otherwise. I also could not afford help, so I soldiered on during that first summer with Fannie in my arms while young Booker persisted in trying to play the piano I needed to teach a student for much-needed money and Willie played with a train or building blocks on the floor.

"Come on here, Book. Play with me," Willie would tell his brother, but my baby boy cared nothing for those blocks as Willie used to. He just wanted that piano. Only when I cobbled together a set of drums out of some empty containers would Book be occupied away from my instrument. At a very young age, by the time Fannie came along, Book would seek out empty containers of a certain size and range to create the sound he wanted. Yes, he was the musical one.

In the middle of all this, I was still trying to figure out Fannie. She was the one, in looks and temperament, who resembled Sid the most. She was the fairest skinned of all my children, and her hair grew into glossy black locks, maybe harkening back to my Kanawha Indian heritage. When she wanted something, she would let us know and scream relentlessly until she got it. She also received my father's light eyes and even as a baby, I knew she would be a very beautiful woman one day.

The thought filled me with fear.

After Christmas, in early 1913, I received a letter from Alice that she wanted to call. Her husband had been defeated in the wake of Taft's loss and she was going back to Ohio with him, "a fate just like banishment in the ancient days—worse than death," as she put it. Of course I was busy, but I moved some appointments to make time for her.

I told her the best time to come was while the baby napped, and she obliged. Book was coming out of the age of napping, but I still put him and Willie into another room for "quiet time" while I visited with my friend for an hour or so.

Alice appeared as her usual ebullient self, but as I knew, things were turbulent on the inside of her life. "I suppose putting that voodoo doll of Taft onto the White House lawn was a bridge too far . . ."

"Alice." I sipped on my tea while I fixed my friend with a look. I made sure there was plenty of warmth in our stove in the parlor, much before she came.

My friend reached for a cookie and chomped down on it. "I couldn't help myself, Portia. I wanted to get the Tafts out of the White House! Then she had a stroke and I thought, well, maybe that little doll was a little too strong. And then Father lost and Nick lost on top of it too. It never occurred to me that the fates would reverse in my direction . . . unless . . ." She licked a crumb from the corner of her mouth and abruptly smoothed her hands down her gorgeous lace day dress. "Oh well. No use worrying about any of that."

"Maybe now in Ohio your life with Mr. Longworth will be less busy and . . . well, as they say. Grass cannot grow on a busy street."

I didn't want to be direct and talk about the missing children from her life after seven years of marriage, but I shifted the topic a little to let her know I was open to discuss that situation if she cared to talk about it.

But no, it was the rakish Alice who was present and she picked up another lemon cookie. "You mean my husband's pate?"

I couldn't help myself. I covered my mouth and she laughed out loud then covered hers. "I don't want to wake the troops."

"What will President Roosevelt do now?"

"Big hunting trip with my brother Kermit. As long as he can go big-game hunting somewhere, if not in Washington then the darkest jungle, he'll recover. He does not want to go back to Sagamore Hill and sit around with my mother, that's for sure."

I nodded. "I've always wondered if that's why my father remained so busy. The school was an excuse, of course, but getting away from Margaret was probably another reason." I drained my cup of tea, ears perked for the sounds of my children. Silence. Not necessarily blissful, because that could mean Book was up to something.

"One more thing, Portia. Before I go and your troops come in to you. There will be a march in the streets of Washington, DC, when that fool Wilson comes into office. A march of women will take the route of the inauguration the day before on March 3. We should go."

I put a hand to my chest. "We?"

"Yes. Let's go. Join the women to make our voices heard. Wilson has three daughters, but none of them can hold a candle to me. That's why he insists on keeping women in their place. Come on."

I pointed a finger upstairs. "What of them?"

"You can get a sitter. Oh, come on. Let's just do something for ourselves. One more time."

"I confess that I was sorry that Wilson got into office. I know Sid voted for your father, especially now that we have Fannie . . ." But had he? I couldn't say for sure. Sid never discussed with me how he voted.

"An even better reason to go. I know there will be talk about voting, but this is about . . . I don't know. Being seen."

I shook my head. "Yes, my dear Alice. I know how you relish that." We both laughed a little, still cognizant of my children.

"Okay, fine. I'll come."

"Wear white."

Once again, the issue of our different racial heritage came to mind. My mind. "Where will we march in the procession?"

"Leave that to me. I'll figure it out."

Just as if it were on cue, my Fannie Virginia cried out. Hopefully Book was not pinching her toes.

Alice stood. "I'll leave you to it, my friend."

"You don't want to meet Fannie?"

She waved a hand. "Once you've seen one baby, you've seen them all." I nodded, knowing what she meant. "I'll be in touch."

WE WOULD JOIN the march in the teachers' section. That made the most sense for me. I'm not sure what it would do for Alice. She explained to me later, "There isn't a section for socialites, princesses, or congressman's wives, so teachers will have to do."

The cold March morning forced me to layer long underwear under my white dress and I put my coat on. I warred with myself over the sitter. It would be too early to call on one of my church ladies or even one of my young students to come over and see to breakfast for all my children. Sid had no projects. He wasn't working. Why did I need a sitter? Why couldn't their father watch them?

So I left Sid a note.

"Dear Sid, I'm sorry I could not explain this to you in person, but I'm going to attend the Women's Suffrage March with Alice in the city today. I'll be home when it is over to make dinner, but you must be responsible for the children until then. I will not be here to feed them, play with them, or take care of them all day. You must do it. Portia."

He did not stir as I prepared myself for the march, and the quiet of the still-dark morning air was a balm to my aching heart as I waited on my dewy porch for Alice and her driver to come. Would

Sid wake to take care of his children? How could I leave three children so young all alone? With their useless father?

In the distance, the chugging of a long car sounded and became louder and louder as it came closer. The car pulled up to the house and Alice opened the door, offering me a warm lap robe to cover my legs and a Dewar flask filled with coffee. "Drink. It has something with a kick in it. For courage!"

I laughed as loud as I dared and as the car pulled off into the darkness, Sid came running down the front steps of the porch in his long johns, yelling and screaming, matching the screams of his baby daughter in the house. Good. He was awake.

After the historic march was over, I read much coverage about how the Negro women were not permitted to march. But that was not entirely true. The march did not want a group of Negro women to march together. The group of Negro women who requested a place to march had been relegated to the back. It would have been better if they had broken apart and scattered, because it would have been harder to stop one or two of us joining in here or there. Of course I was in the company of Princess Alice, daughter of a former president who many wished were in office again, as well as a congressman's wife who had made a connection through her well-placed friends to secure our places among the teachers.

No one said a word to her about me, or her, in the march as we stepped along, having to stop some of the time because the large crowd kept closing in on the parade route. It was annoying, merely. Alice had said many times that she did not agree with women having the right to vote, because women could be mean and small, but if it came down to showing herself in public to make the point that women were just as good as anyone else, she would be there.

On our way back, we had a picnic of prepared sandwiches and refreshment in the car before she took me back home.

"Did you ever consider running for office yourself when Nick lost his seat? To stay in Washington, DC?" I asked her.

Alice hooted at the thought. "A woman? In Congress?"

"Why not? There have been some women who made it to some state houses in the West," I pointed out.

She sobered. "That's true, but I don't see anything happening like that, although wouldn't it be grand if I were the first? I do love it here and I dread the wilds of Cincinnati with my in-laws, but I'm someone who likes to pull strings, not someone who takes power. I know the difference. I'm good at what I do, but I have a feeling it's not over for Nicholas. We'll be back."

When we pulled up to the front of my house, the children, all three of them, were bundled up and playing in the dirt in front of the house. Their noses were all running but they were alive. "Dear ones," I said as I alighted from the car and embraced them all. "Why are you playing in the dirt?"

"Father told us to get out, and so we did," Willie said solemnly and waved at the lady he called Miss Alice.

I'll just bet he did.

"Well, Portia. I cede you to your troops. I know you will make it through the wilds of the battle that is motherhood unscathed."

I picked up Fannie, wiping her off as best as I could, and perched her on my hip, facing my friend. "Thank you. And I wish you the best, Alice. Thank you for today. She thanks you as well."

For once, Fannie was quiet, staring at the long shiny car and Alice's large hat in wonder. Alice nodded, and I thought I saw a trace of something shining there in her eyes, but she shut the door and directed her driver to pull away.

I didn't know it then, but I would not lay eyes again on my friend for almost twelve years.

When she finally became a mother.

Portia

When I came home, Sid said nothing to me. For days. I kept my silence also and did everything that I was supposed to do as a good wife. His silence worried me, I had to admit, but the quiet also allowed me to reflect back on my experience out of the house. I enjoyed my time among people my own age. I don't know if it was because I was with Alice, but the other teachers I marched with seemed to be fine career women, well-dressed and well-spoken, who were treated with respect. If I had been permitted, I could have been a teacher at the Washington Conservatory, which, by now, had grown in numbers and was well regarded. I had helped several of my home pupils go on to further education there.

Harriet Marshall was also at the parade. I saw her from a distance with some other Negro teachers but I did not approach her to speak to her. First, I thought it was better to not draw notice with too many of us congregating together. Second, I didn't dare leave Alice's side, as she was my protection from slights and name-calling that I saw that other women, no matter their skin color, had to endure from some men who had assembled on the sidewalks.

But I was also afraid that she would remember that night after my recital when my husband was so drunk and bent on humiliating me in those musician circles. He had succeeded. Once I had Fannie, I stayed home with her and Willie and Book and had not moved a toe out of place for years. Sid's rough treatment of me resulted in Fannie. Three children were enough.

ONE NIGHT IN April, I served a dinner with no meat. I was not happy to do so, but it was becoming more difficult to obtain some of what we needed from my teaching money and from Sid's too-infrequent work as an architect. He bowed his head, reciting the prayer, but ate the meal quietly, saying nothing, not asking me where the meat was.

Once he wiped his plate with the light bread I had made, he sat back and reached for Fannie, a rare gesture that pleased me, holding her in his lap. "I've an opportunity to design a Mason hall."

I put my fork down. "That's great news. I'm glad to hear of it, Sid. When does it start?"

"Next week. In Dallas."

He was leaving me to go to Dallas? My silent tiptoeing around and quiet could stop. How long would I be free? Instead I said, "How long will you be there?"

"We are moving there."

The inside of my mouth transformed into cotton. "Excuse me?"

Fannie twisted herself away from him and he put her on the floor, where she began to crawl around. Smart as a whip, she saw her brothers walking and wanted to do the same.

"We're moving to Dallas. I have to be there in a week, but you'll pack up this house and come on the train with the children as soon as possible."

"But this is our home. You built this house for us. How can we leave it?"

He spread his arms. "Simple. I'll sell the house for money. We pack up our things. Leave the furniture, of course. We'll get new furniture in Dallas."

"My . . . piano. My father gave it to me."

Sid slammed his hand down on the dining room table. "I knew whatever objection you would have, it would be something about your damn daddy."

"Please. Don't swear in front of the children." Book's and Willie's eyes widened as they watched their father explode. They knew it was coming. So did I.

"I'll say whatever I want. I have told you. I have shown you. And now I'm showing you again, Portia, cause you are hardheaded. You're *my* wife, not your daddy's." He stood. "Honestly, I can't wait to get the hell up out of DC. I've had to be his son-in-law for all these years and I'm sick of it. I'm a man. I can do my own work and make my own way." He pointed a finger at me. "We're going somewhere far away where a man can make a new path of his own."

"That's not ever been the case here. I love it here."

"As I said, you're coming to Dallas with me."

"Our church home. This house." *My piano.* My heart thudded in my chest as if I were Br'er Rabbit under Br'er Fox's paw.

"One week, Portia." He stomped off to his study and slammed the door.

"What he talking about, Mommy?"

I smoothed down Willie's hair. "Don't you fret, son. Your father is just saying some things." He was about to start school. If we moved to Dallas, he would start school in that place. A strange place that I knew nothing about, somewhere I had never been.

Fannie was about to put a ball of dust into her mouth and I took it from her fist and she began her usual screams. I held her close to me and rocked her, wanting to scream myself but just crying silent tears.

There was nothing else I could do. I packed up our movable belongings to leave our dear Fairmount Heights house and followed my husband halfway across the country. He had a point. Texas, as a newly settled place, meant many more opportunities for an architect. The Mason hall he had been recruited to build, independent of my father, was a large project and he was being paid well for it. Maybe this was God's will, to help Sid feel successful. Then he could be rid of the demon alcohol that had such a hold on him and maybe . . .

So many maybes. Maybe was exhausting.

ONCE I REACHED Dallas, I could see it for what it was. A cow town that was transforming itself into a city. Yes, there was opportunity here. The fact that a Negro Mason had hired Sid, a Negro architect, to design their building meant that there was enough of a class of us who aspired to the finer things in life. Like piano lessons for their children.

The house that Sid found for us was located a few blocks away from the building site and a few streets over from the school where Willie would attend. The neighborhood was pleasantly structured with lawns, trees, and houses of a nice size. Of course the neighborhood was segregated, which was to be expected, but it was a promising place.

Our first Sunday in the city, we were able to visit a church in our same Christian denomination. They were happy to welcome us. "They are looking to build a new church soon," Sid whispered to me and a thrill went through me. *Praise God.* He was right about something. This opportunity, finally, after nearly six years, looked more like what I had expected my marriage to be. As Fannie cooed, I slipped my hand into his on the pew and we sat there, content for a small while listening to the minister's sermon.

"I would like for anyone who are visitors—please, you're welcome here among us—to stand and let us know who you are in the name of the Lord."

Sid stood right away and the minister, a kind-faced man who

was in his early forties, nodded at him. Sid said, "We bring you greetings from Maryland. Just across the border from Washington, DC, our nation's capital. Our home congregation was Fairmount AME and we've been looking for a church home ever since we've moved to Dallas. I'm William S. Pittman. You can call me Sid. This is my wife, Portia. She's holding our youngest, Fannie. These are our boys, Willie and Book." He sat down, looking pleased with himself, tucking his hand back into mine.

A humming murmur spread throughout the congregation. The minister tipped his head, spread his arms toward us, and said, "Welcome to the Pittmans, our brother and sister in Christ. Could it be that Mrs. Pittman is the daughter of the great educator Booker T. Washington?"

Sid dropped my hand as if it were a hot coal and I could feel the frost emanating from him at the question. I leaned forward to answer, but he put on his happy face again, standing and smiling. "You would be right at that, sir."

"Praise God! Welcome to our congregation indeed. I was pleased to meet your father some years ago and we have several Tuskegee grads in the congregation. We're pleased to have you in our membership."

I nodded and tried to slip my hand back into Sid's once more, but he put his hand into his suit pocket, no longer interested in loving me.

Once church was over, we were mobbed. I carried Fannie on my shoulder, as she was taking a nap. She was getting to be a big baby, but Sid was apparently satisfied to let me carry her. An older woman came to me. "Oh, Mrs. Pittman, I've heard so much about your musicianship."

"You have? How?"

"Why, people wrote about you in the newspapers when you

went to Europe to be educated. Our music program here is just starting and it would be the making of us if you took it over." Something in me thrilled.

"My goodness. I've, well . . . thank you for that offer. I would need to speak to my husband about that."

She spread her arms. "We can arrange for care for your children. As you can see, we have several young families as part of the congregation. We want a choir here and our organ sits unused."

"It's been a while since I've played an organ."

"But you know how, right? And you see our piano there?"

Oh, I saw it. I noticed it first thing as we came into the church. My fingers ached to touch it, since I had to leave mine behind. This piano wasn't a home instrument, but a more grand public one, clearly designed for playing in the name of the Lord. I nodded. "I'll speak to my husband and I'll let you know."

"Thank you, Mrs. Pittman. We appreciate any consideration you can give to us."

I dared not say a word on the walk home, or while I prepared a dinner of ground steaks, mashed potatoes, beans, and slabs of dried apple pie. Once Sid pushed back from the table, filled up from the delicious meal I made, that was when I would make my plea.

"What did you think of the church today? They seemed nice, didn't they?"

Sid shrugged his shoulders.

"You were all for them when you said they were looking to build a new church that they would need an architect for."

He sipped at his coffee. "There are many churches who have that need."

"Yes. Enough work to keep you busy for a while." *I hope.*

"That's why we don't have to join there. They're a little too country. We can choose somewhere grander. Imagine belonging to a church that doesn't have the basics."

"I liked it there," I put in more firmly.

Swigging back his coffee, he slammed the cup to the table with more force than necessary. "You would. With all the fuss they made over you."

"I wasn't looking for fuss. They seem to need help and I . . ."

"You're not the one who will fit the bill. They need someone trained, Portia."

"I'm trained."

"I mean the right training." He stood. "God, you don't get it, do you?" He stomped off.

Get it? I knew what I was getting.

MY CHILDREN AND I showed up on Tuesday. I took charge of the music program, becoming their very first director of music. It wasn't the grand concert halls of Europe but I relished the opportunity to use my skills to organize a choir. I didn't have a piano in my home, but I could come to the church whenever I wanted and play that beautiful piano in the Lord's house.

Sid was often too busy at his construction site to attend church and rarely came to hear me play or to hear my choirs sing. But I expected that by now.

Alice

1913–1914

The two years of exile in Ohio sped by, just as Borah said they would. I spent much of my time in my room, reading, writing letters, plotting, only having to suffer the company of my intolerable mother-in-law and sisters-in-law on very rare occasions.

When I wasn't inside, I was outside of the house in the city, charming city operatives as Princess Alice and moving people to work on Nick's behalf to get us back out of Cincinnati to return to Washington, DC. Nick went back there to visit the House just once, when he announced he was running again and people were glad to see him. Except his opponent, of course.

One thing that I didn't like during my exile is that it pushed me further away from my father. I didn't know it directly, couldn't sense it, but I got the feeling that he thought, somehow, that I was to blame for his loss. I didn't know what I had done wrong. Was it by sticking so close to him? Had I embarrassed him? By encouraging him to go it alone, separate from the Republicans?

I couldn't ask him. He had taken my brother and gone off into the wilds again, hunting to round out animal collections in the United States. As much as I loved him, it was the one activity of his that I did not understand. He had done so much to preserve the lands of the country so the wilds would be left for people to love and enjoy as he had. And yet he could go to strange places and slaughter thousands of animals? Words were not directly said, but yes. There was something between us. An increased tension.

Also, as much as I didn't want to admit to it, Father's distance from me didn't hurt as much as it used to. Was it because of Borah?

I wrote the senator, of course, during my exile. He wrote me. Our letters were very pedestrian. Safe. He was my friend. No mentions of the kiss we shared, or the passion between us. Of course, the possibility also existed I was the one who felt passion and he felt nothing for me. I might have overplayed my hand. I probably met the only other person in the world who did not care a fig about Princess Alice. Besides Nick, of course.

Which was terribly unfair, because Borah consumed me during that time. I had a newspaper clipping agency send me every single word about him, so I could keep track of what he was doing and saying in the Senate. I knew when he was in Idaho and when he was in the capital. Oh, how I wish I would have gone to him in Idaho. I thought of it, many times, but I knew that if I showed up in a place like potato-heavy Idaho, I would have stuck out like the fancy bird I am. No, the only place where I had the slightest chance of going incognito, even being Princess Alice, was in Washington, DC, where all the other show-birds lived. I worked, worked hard to get myself back to DC on the arm of Nick, to get him into leadership, and then I could launch myself into Senator Borah's arms. Life had, after all, denied me nothing.

When Nick won in 1914, the moment it was confirmed, I told him I was going back to Washington, DC, to look for our new house and to make it ready for him. He waved at me, probably too happily. There was no Cissy Patterson in Cincinnati, but she had many similar sisters willing to step into her Nick-pleasing shoes.

The only thing that displeased me about having to return to Washington was that I would be staying with my cousin Eleanor and her husband, Franklin. Franklin was also our cousin but very distant from us both. At least it pleased me to think of it that way. I would have never married him, but I suppose a cousin-husband was the only option available for poor Eleanor. I was all prepared to take up a hotel suite to stay in until I got a look at three houses that had been slotted for my review, but she would not hear of it. At least I would only be there for a few weeks.

Franklin had the temerity to be in Wilson's cabinet, a Democrat, another thing that was distasteful about them, and then, they had so many children. She had kept popping babies out every year in the most unseemly fashion and my father kept pointing out to me how fecund she was. Who cared? Did the children look like anything? Also, it was bound to be noisy there. The only comfort was for me to finish my business and get into my own home as soon as possible.

Then, Borah.

Nonetheless, we were family. As I thought, it was hellish and noisy in that place. Eleanor never had any sense about housekeeping. I still don't understand to this day how I had gotten a better sense of how to keep house than she did. But she was also under the thumb of her mother-in-law, Sara, a hateful harridan if there ever was one. When I had returned from securing our new house, a block away, Eleanor ordered tea and expressed her pleasure. "Now we can go to soirees together. You're so much better with people, Alice. I don't know what to say to them."

"I'm not the biggest fan of calling myself. All of that card folding and whatnot. Ugh." I referred to the continuing stupidity of how one had to leave calling cards folded in certain corners to leave messages for the lady of the house, who might not be home because she was out calling herself.

"As a cabinet wife, I get squeezed in. Tuesdays are for women in the House, Thursdays for the Senate, and Friday for the diplomatic corps."

"I will not partake in any of that foolishness. I'll go see who I please when I please." I sipped at the tea she poured for me and helped myself to a ginger cookie.

"I think you are just about the only person in this town who could get away with that." She gave me a smile and sipped at her own tea.

"Even after all these years? I mean there are the Wilson girls."

"No one can hold a candle to you, cousin. You know that."

I continued to sip, reassured. "The calling card business is so pervasive, I daresay that I'll probably have to make a call to see Nick when he arrives."

"Would that I would see less of Franklin. We've just had our fifth, but for our little Franklin." She lowered her head. They had a baby son who'd died a few months after his birth a few years ago. I nodded, not knowing what to say to her. I might have pointed out that her fertility was rather like a woman from the Lower East Side but I refrained.

Instead, I said, "Do you do anything to stop them from coming? What do you do?"

"What do I do?" Her blue eyes blinked at me without understanding reaching them. "Nothing. I love our new baby—I mean, this new Franklin Jr. If it weren't for Mama, I would not know what to do with myself. Babies aren't the most amenable to sitting still as I do my charity work. Except for Anna. But I suppose that's because she's the oldest."

"I'm no fan of babies myself. They are so . . . weird looking. But Anna, she seems to have quite a spirit." I was always compelled to say this, as an explanation for my childless state after so many years.

"Much more than I do. More like you, cousin." Eleanor gave a slow smile.

"Heaven forbid!" And we both laughed, in a companionable way that, years before, I would not have thought possible. I could not believe I was sitting here having a cup of tea with her like an old friend, as if she were Portia. We had been pitted against each other so much of our lives.

"But you. You . . . don't have any. How have you managed?"

"Well. Dear cousin, I just . . . I don't. Manage, that is. It's just not happened for me. That's all."

She put a hand to her mouth. "That's so sad."

"Well, it isn't for me. As I've just said, babies look weird. Like little frogs. I don't believe in your God, but somewhere something knows that I have no business being anyone's mother. So I'm not."

"There is nothing that you've done . . . to prevent it?"

"I've heard of some things." I swallowed the rest of the tea, put down the cup, and went to work on my ginger cookie. "But I haven't had to use them."

"Isn't that strange?"

I never gave any thought to it, to tell the truth. I had just spent the eight years of my married life relieved, and glad of it, ignoring my father's pointed references to Eleanor whenever he made them. I would not have been able to jet around Europe with him a few years ago if I had been saddled with an annual baby like poor Eleanor. "Maybe we just can't."

Maybe Nick and I were barren. Figured.

"I know you aren't a believer in God, cousin, but there must be some purpose in why you haven't been blessed with children."

I chewed thoughtfully on my cookie. "The plan is to get Nick to be the Speaker of the House."

Her eyes went wide. "Oh my!"

"Don't tell me you are just satisfied being the wife of the assistant to the secretary of the navy."

"I have no idea what Franklin wants. That's not for me to decide."

"Just him and his mother."

A sad look dawned on her face. Bless her. She loved him so. It was always so sad to see those couples where one person was so much more in love with the other. I had an idea and I offered it up to her.

"Part of it is . . . Well, Nick and I, we don't come together that often. What about that?"

Her eyes brightened for half a second. Then the light dimmed. "Oh, if only that were possible."

"What do you mean?"

"He . . . well, insists on activity. A certain amount. A few times a week."

I swept some crumbs from my lap. "There's an advantage in marrying an older man. Time slows them down. Even Nick who . . ." I didn't want to confide that much in Eleanor. She wouldn't be able to take in too much information about Nick's hedonistic tendencies. "He'll slow down," I said more firmly.

She breathed out. "I look forward to that day."

"Don't you like doing it?" I kept my voice from squeaking too much in shock.

"No. Do you?"

Did I? Oh yes. I did. There were times with Nick, early on, where I wanted him. He always seemed to like it when I would show him my near desperation for him. And then when I saw him with my friend, that want for him died in me. Until I had seen Senator Borah. I thought that part of my life was over. Maybe it was over in all but name. Best to look at it that way. I kept my response muted, lest she sense something heated in my words.

"Once upon a time, yes."

"It's just part of being his wife that I have to endure." She reached for a cookie herself. An unlikely gesture from her that meant she was embarrassed.

Endure? Oh my poor cousin. I didn't know whether to feel more sorrow at this revelation or at the loss of her baby.

The revelation of having to endure was the heavier burden, I decided. She had enough babies. Her God could be as merciful to her as he had been to me.

"You'll come to our Christmas soiree, of course? You'll be in your house by then?"

"Of course. I wouldn't miss that."

"Will Nick be here then?"

"He won't come out from Ohio until the new year."

She leaned forward and patted my hand, when honestly, she was the one in need of more comfort. "Well, then you must stay and holiday with us until he comes back, for I know you must be lonely."

I wouldn't admit it to her in person, but she was right.

Alice

1914

I was only in the Roosevelt household for a week. My efforts to get into my own home, just a block away, made that much easier. I could interview household staff, arrange for furnishings to be transported, and set up something at least habitable, which made my hard work worthwhile. I had to get away from all the noise and babies. I wanted to revel in the quiet of my own home. Until Nick deigned to come.

The evening of the Christmas soiree, I had a delicious new velvet evergreen dress and used part of the fabric as an ornament for my hair instead of one of my signature hats. People wouldn't know who I was. Indeed when I swept into the room, my appearance took several of the Wilsonites by surprise, and some of them managed to be intimidated. But I made sure to show reflection of the holiday spirit so that they could see that I didn't hold any hostile feelings. None that I would showcase, anyway. Just as long as I wasn't forced to engage with Wilson himself. I had enough of that at the very beginning of his administration when I went to tea with his wife, who wasn't very merry, nor did she keep a good table. She died shortly thereafter but it wasn't my fault. People in this town would find a way to blame me for anything.

Unfortunately, the children were running around underfoot and Eleanor was forced to bring her new Franklin forward before he went to bed. Many were charmed, but I used the opportunity to take up another holiday drink. Attention to a months-old baby instead of me was a phenomenon that didn't happen too often and

I retired to a corner. Until I saw that one of the new arrivals to the party was Senator Borah.

The drink went down my throat too fast and I coughed. Anna came along and patted me on the back, gently enough for me to get my bearings. "Thank you, dear." A most resourceful child.

"You're welcome, cousin. Do you need anything else?"

"No, my dear. I'm fine here, thank you." She seemed to sense her dismissal. I was glad. Since everyone was making a fuss over that baby, I could stay in the corner and watch the senator, accompanied by a petite woman wearing the most drab brown town gown I've ever seen. Mamie. A plain brown wren indeed.

She was the one most taken by the baby, angling to hold the drooling thing. Her husband, however, only had eyes for me, stowed away in the corner, and he made a beeline for me right away. "Mrs. Longworth," he said as he bowed and made for kissing my hand, but I kept my hands to myself.

"No. No, you don't." I kept my tone frosty to match the December weather.

He stood and looked into my eyes, his gaze soft and curious. "What is the matter? Have I offended you in some way?"

"What are you doing at this party full of Wilson folks?"

He smiled. "The same thing you are. Gathering intel on how soon Wilson will want to join what is going on in Europe."

I startled a little bit. I had just come from Europe a few months previously. I didn't think intrigue was possible. "You think that I'm here for that?"

"Aren't you?"

"The Roosevelts are my cousins, you know. That's what I'm here for."

His eyes now, not as soft as they were but instead heated, made a slow circuit up and down my new Christmas frock. "I seem to recall that."

Me. He was here to see me.

"What do you want?" I whispered, grateful for the distraction of new Franklin for once.

"Will you force me to tell you? When I'm in the same room with my wife?"

"Would you tell me if we were alone?"

"Repeatedly." He turned and stood next to me facing the room so that we were still in each other's personal space, but looked as if we were more distant from each other.

"We might as well be. Your wife, is that her? Seems to be enthralled with my newest little cousin."

"He's why she's here. She would have stayed home otherwise." He spoke low, effectively tossing his words across to me, not hard to do since we were exactly the same height.

"That's sweet." I put my glass down. "Do you have children?"

A look crossed Borah's face. I couldn't read it in that moment. "She isn't able to."

I shrugged. "There are worse things in the world. She can enjoy my little cousin and give him right back to his nurse when he does something embarrassing. Even if he's a relatively good baby. If you like that sort of thing." I turned to him. "And I can't, either, so I know what that's like."

He nodded. "Your childless state has been remarked upon in far more corners than my Mamie's."

"Why not adopt?" I sniffed a little, peering at him.

"There might have been a time, about ten, twenty years ago. Now, we are getting older and it wouldn't be fair to a child."

"Senator Borah, I assure you, you're in the prime of life." I kept my tone flat, without any change, so he knew that I was serious.

"I appreciate that insight. If I were here alone, I would thank you for that."

"How?" I tossed off.

"I would show you what I wanted to do with you and that green gown you are wearing."

I laughed, lightly. That was all the air I could manage to get from my lungs. "What's stopping you now, Senator? Propriety?" I looked around me. "Are there any constituents here from Idaho of all places?"

"Don't toy with me, Princess Alice."

"I can assure you, I'm not that familiar with that kind of game. I'm no Cissy Patterson."

"I'm glad to hear it. I have not kept company with her in years."

"And others?"

"I've told you before. I go home to my library to read."

I did recall him saying such a thing. *He really is here to see me.* Warmth spread through me at the thought that this amazing orator and senator had come to see me instead of my newest cousin, who was probably filling his diaper as we spoke.

"Let me tell you what." I spoke across to him. "I'm going to tell my cousins I have a headache and I'm going home. To my home. You gather your information from these Wilson people and I'll be in a position to hear a report from you in . . . say an hour?"

"Make it an hour and a half." He swallowed the drink he had in his hand, putting down the glass on the edge of the overladen dining room table.

"My new home is . . ."

"I know exactly where your new home is," he told me and strode away from me, without looking back at me, even once.

BACK AT MY new home, where sheets had not even been put upon my mattresses yet, I found the love of my life and knew I would never be lonely anymore.

THANKFULLY, ELEANOR HAD insisted on giving me a basket of food before I left the party. "You didn't eat, cousin, and I know that you don't cook. So I have had Anna pack you some goodies in a basket."

My young cousin had packed sausages, Scotch eggs, cookies, fruit, rolls, and half a ham. Bless her.

"I guess she thought I would never come back again." I now peeped into the basket, bringing it forward to share with my new lover.

"Whatever she thought, she was thoughtful," my Borah said.

I didn't know what to call him in this newfound state that we found ourselves in. All I knew was he found the very thing, the irritating itch I needed to have scratched, and he scratched it. The relief and joy I felt was unprecedented.

Most pleasingly, he said my name, without a shred of sorrow. Musically. As if I had never heard my own name before. Which I never had, when I thought of it.

The only thing I had to drink was some champagne, so I shared that with him, dividing the bottle, daring to drink straight from it after he did.

"I think Eleanor knew." I stared straight ahead.

"How was that possible?"

I could not give my new lover intel on my cousin. Not yet, anyway, but I slid down to the edge of the bed, crossing my ankles like the lady that I was, with the rest of me in the state I was born in, completely bare to him, with the new winter sun about to dawn. "She's smarter than what she appears to be."

He munched on a little sandwich he made out of one of the sausages and one of the rolls. "I'm glad. A man of my years needs this sustenance after such complete exercise."

I threw my head back, shaking my hair across my shoulders, and laughed. "I think that you do just fine for a man of your years, as you say."

He had not laughed. I turned over on my side, letting my long hair drape down over my body like a cover. "Please. I didn't mean . . ."

"You're apologizing to me?" Borah chewed the last of the sandwich and took a swig of champagne.

"I would not hurt your feelings. I cause a lot of hurt feelings for a lot of people, but not you."

He drained the bottle, put it down, and stretched the length of his body to be exactly parallel to mine. "There's no need to apologize. It's just something that I, well, have to consider. I'm so much older than you are."

"So what?"

He smoothed my hair, which ran down my body, coming to the end of its length, tantalizingly close to the special place so recently delighted at his rough, tender touch. "I don't want you to be disappointed in me."

I reached out and smoothed down his gray hair that went every which way like a mane. My lion. "I have not been so happy in many years, Borah. I tell you true."

For some reason that I never knew or could completely understand, a shine appeared in his eyes. I had never seen someone have emotion for me inside of him, certainly not a man. I pulled myself to him and under him, running my hands over his body, wanting him close, even closer. "Now, tell me all about the war talk."

He did, whispering it all in my ears and to my face, into much of the next day and evening. By the time he had told me everything about that horrific Wilson, I knew I would have to stop him in some way, so that a Republican of our choosing might regain the White House, but the way had not been revealed to me just yet. I did not want to enter into the calling card circuit, but I would do it if it helped my cause. Truly, probably the only wife worth calling on would be if the president got married again, since his first wife had banned me because she heard I had made fun of her daughters before she died.

I would find my way around that ban. Somehow.

Portia

1914–1915

Sid and I didn't necessarily grow closer during this time in Dallas, but we reached a rapprochement in our marriage that pleased me. The children were growing up so fast, and I was pleased at how Book, especially, took to his piano lessons I shared with him in between my own students at the church.

I worked out of the church so often it seemed illogical for me to have a piano at our house, which did not resemble my past situation, but I grew accustomed to it. It was during one of these sessions in November of 1915 when I was teaching a student in the after-school hours that my Willie came running into the church vestibule with a message clutched in his hand. "Son, you know better than to disrespect the Lord by entering his house in this way," I chided him, but I patted the top of his head anyway.

I loved my children and never held back from an opportunity to show them love, because Sid was much tougher and withheld his affection from them.

"Mr. Patton at the store said to run straightaway and give this to you."

"What does it say?"

"He told me to give it to you and not even take a moment to read it."

My heart pounded at that. For some reason, the kindly Mr. Patton didn't want Willie to know what the message said. My Willie was a good and obedient boy and he did what he was told. Book and Fannie would have looked. With dread dripping down my arms, I opened the paper and saw it was from Margaret. "Father. Dying. Transport. From. NYC. To. Tuskegee. For. Last. Moments."

I took in a gasp of air, one designed to help me breathe, but instead was on the verge of taking my breath away. Father.

Willie's small face was a brown oval of concern. I hated having to shatter his world. He loved his grandfather very much, the only grandfather he had ever known. The heartbreak was not mine alone. I turned to my pupil, willing to keep my voice from shaking. "Flora. I'll have to make up this lesson another time. There's an emergency."

Flora, a young woman of twelve, also looked concerned. I knew what she would hear would spread like wildfire among the church members because her mother was the biggest gossip in the church. I laid my hand on Willie's small shoulder. "Grandpa is going to see Jesus soon. I must go to him."

Willie buried his face in my side and I put my arms around him, his small body providing as much comfort to me as I was giving him.

"I'm so sorry, Mrs. Pittman. We'll be praying for you all in this time of sorrow."

"Thank you, Flora." I grasped her hand, squeezed it, and let go. Willie and I walked out of the church, arm in arm, going home as fast as my hobble skirts would take us both. Once home, I went straight to my bedroom to pack a grip. Just as I thought, Flora's mother knocked on the door by the time I finished packing, offering to watch the children and to set up a schedule for meals and babysitting. She already knew that Sid would be on site for his third building in Dallas and wouldn't be able to take care of the children. I didn't even leave him a note. He would find out like everyone else did. Not that he cared.

My work at the church meant that I had my own money to buy my ticket for the long train ride from Dallas to Memphis and then to Tuskegee. The time to myself was usually something I desired, but I was morose as I tried to imagine an existence without my father in this world. I would be completely orphaned, because Margaret had been no kind of stepmother to me, even though I did appreciate the love and care that she showed to my children over the years. She was a much better grandmother than stepmother.

The rainy weather in Tuskegee reflected the sad events. That a car had been sent for me, I noticed, not a mule-driven hack, already reflected change at my father's school. "He's not gone yet, Miss Portia. He's waiting on you," the driver, a student, reassured me. What would happen to those students now? I wondered.

"I bet he's fighting. Father has so much left to do."

The student nodded, cranking up the automobile once he made sure I was settled with my grip in the back seat. I never could get over the way that I was treated when I came into the Tuskegee air. Living as a Negro woman in the world and coming into the Tuskegee world were two different things. My father had created that rarefied air for everyone on this campus. Now that he was ailing, reality would come here. More change.

It was morning, and when I arrived at the Oaks, Baker and Dave, my grown brothers, were there. Baker stood in the parlor with his wife and her rounded belly, and Dave sat on the porch with a lovely young woman he had indicated he would marry soon. Without words, we embraced one another and they handed me off to go upstairs to where my father lay.

My poor father was noticeably thinner than he had been the last time that I saw him. He had two doctors attending him, and Margaret was by his bedside, clutching her handkerchief, looking older than I had ever noticed before.

"He's been asking for you." I knew how much that gutted her. I went to the other side of the bed from where she was and grasped Papa's hand, which was so, so cold. The tips of his fingers were gray, where clearly the blood was drawing away from them. No, my father was not fighting anymore. He had earned his rest. Trying to prolong his life was not going to do him any favors. The best thing I could do right now was to tell him I loved him so he could go.

"Thank you," I told Margaret and gave her a dismissive nod. She did not get the hint.

"I need a moment with him."

Margaret crumpled up her handkerchief and wiped her face with it. "The doctors say he may not be long."

"I understand. But I need a moment. Just one."

She still stared at me.

I stared back, then I said, "Have you had breakfast yet? If not, this would be the perfect time."

"You don't understand. I want to be here when it happens."

"I understand better than you think. If something happens, we'll call you." I gestured to the doctors.

Margaret stood and I noticed that her knees were a little shaky. If I were on the same side of the bed, I would have helped her, but she righted herself and went to the door, stepping over the doorsill and into the hallway.

I turned back to my father and grasped his hand. His eyes, those always distinctive eyes of his, lighted on me and a flicker of something, life, came into them. "Portia. You came."

"Of course I did, Papa. I came as soon as I could."

"The children."

"They are fine. They worry about you. As do I."

It took some effort, but he shook his head. "No. No worry. Sid?"

"He's in Dallas."

"He didn't come with you?" A storm cloud entered his eyes. I couldn't form the words. I shook my head.

"Listen. Margaret needs the Oaks. I hope she can stay."

"I'll do my best to see to that." I had to confess to some relief. I didn't want to take Margaret in, and I hoped he wouldn't ask me to.

Not that she would leave campus anyway. His departure was probably her prime opportunity to take over.

"You."

I squeezed his hand. "Me."

"You. Take your music on. I'm sorry."

"For what, Papa?" My mind filled with possibilities. Is that what had kept him alive for me to get here? That he was sorry for something? "You've given me so much."

"You didn't stay in Europe," he rasped.

Tears pricked my eyes at the thought he was thinking of that time now, at his last. "I didn't want to. I wanted to come home." Remembering very clearly that Sid had lured me back to the United States with promises. So many promises. Ones that were just beginning to be fulfilled but still fell short of the mark.

"You can do so much. Music. Please. Don't stop. Our people need that."

"You can count on that. I won't stop. I'll do all I can."

He smiled. That was something he hadn't done nearly often enough in his life, so full of hard work and striving. Smile.

His breathing sounded strange now, and I leaned in, thinking he would say something.

And then.

Silence.

Oh dear God.

"Papa?" I called.

He did not answer. I wrapped my arms around him, feeling his spirit, large and special, depart from him, and a pain coursed through my body, as if I were cut into two. "Oh, Papa." My voice broke.

There was one more thing he had to know. I whispered in his ear, hoping he heard me, "Kiss my mamas for me. Please."

He was no more. Margaret came into the room, screaming at

him to come back to her. With a strength that I didn't know she had, she pulled me from him, wrapping herself around him, weeping loud, obnoxious tears.

My brothers hovered at the door and I went to both of them, wrapping my arms around them both. "He's gone."

We made a circle, the three of us, clinging tightly to one another, orphans united in the bonds of my father's death.

The funeral, days later, was fit for royalty. Thousands showed up in Tuskegee. Alice and her father sent a lovely spray of flowers to show their respect. So did William Taft. Woodrow Wilson sent nothing, but that was no large surprise to me.

Sid came, bringing the children with him, and I had to remember that he had to mind them all the way, a bit of progress for him. The school choir sang at the funeral, of course, and I was glad for those amazing young voices who helped me grieve with their beautiful tone and execution of our music. All the students, in the way that my father had set for them, did him proud in how they took care of us and executed everything perfectly.

We stayed for Thanksgiving and muddled through a strange dinner where Father's chair was empty. We were all afraid to sit in it.

Margaret, who had always had a little extra weight to her, looked gaunt and lost. The truth of how much she had loved my father was there in her face and for the first time, I felt sorry for her. At least I was going home with Sid, though he didn't love me. The possibility of repairing our marriage existed. Once we all left, there would be no one and nothing for her.

"I'm stepping down from the board of trustees," Margaret announced as we ate our dinner.

"You aren't working for the school anymore?" I had to admit to being stunned.

"No. I'm continuing my community work. But no more school

work. Whoever is coming in, and that's thought to be Warren Logan, deserves a clear path without my interference."

I swallowed. Hard. Her statement was more logical that I thought her capable of being.

As we readied ourselves to leave, another blow came. At the discussions of the takeover among the teachers, one of them, Adella Hunt Logan, Warren's wife and a longtime family friend, ran over to one of the windows in Porter Hall and jumped to her death.

The campus reeled in shock at the loss of one of the most important math teachers. She had long been unbalanced, but no one was expecting that kind of end for her. With that, Warren Logan withdrew his name from consideration in taking over. Robert Moton stepped up to the plate instead.

I did not know it at the time, but his takeover would be incredibly meaningful for me one day in the future.

But now, I returned to Dallas with my husband and children to honor my promise to my father to keep the music going.

Portia

1915–1924

Our train ride back to Dallas was somber. Once the boys were bedded down together on the bench facing us and Fannie slept propped up against me, Sid whispered to me in the darkness. "I've been thinking. Once I'm finished with this church, I think I'm done with being an architect."

Well, this was a surprise. "Why?"

"It's mighty hard as a Negro man, begging people for work. I'm done with it. As a matter of fact, the whole way my career has been going has made me think of what I really want to do." *We moved from Washington so you could get more work as an architect.* The thought, a betrayal to be sure, crossed my mind as soon as he said those words.

"What do you really want to do?"

"I'm going to be a journalist. Start a newspaper. Talk about what's keeping the Negro down in this country."

The words I thought came out of my mouth because I had three mouths to feed. "A journalist? That job makes even less money than being an architect."

He turned his head to me swiftly, not thinking of little Fannie, stirring in her sleep. No, he didn't think of the children—ever. "That's not true. I have many connections in the Dallas community now. Plenty of folks who are willing to read and hear the truth about the suffering of our people. When you think about it, it's kind of like what your father did. Now that he's gone, I want to continue his work in some way. Being an architect won't do that."

Now he talked about continuing my father's work? When he never missed an opportunity to disparage him in some way? I spoke up. "Yes, it does. This is where folks got my father all wrong. People thinking he only wanted for us in the race to serve white folks. That's not true. He knew that some of us would be in those positions but he also knew that others would be in the professional classes. He knew it would take a longer time for people to accept us in the professional class. That's why you can't quit being an architect. More folks need to know that we can draft, design, and build beautiful buildings and churches just like you."

Every time I thought about how people, even his son-in-law, got my father wrong and instead gave more credit to Mr. DuBois, it made my blood boil. If people really knew about Mr. DuBois and some of his beliefs . . . Sid was not wrong in one way. Dreamers needed live people out front pushing for those dreams, and I really didn't think Robert Moton was the man to do that. My father was a dreamer and now he was gone; there was no one left who would fight for opportunities for everyday Negroes as he did. Something rumbled in my stomach and I prayed not to get sick on the train.

"A pretty speech. But it doesn't work for me. Or us. I need more, Portia. Let me try this. Let me try this for a year and if it doesn't work out, I'll go back to being an architect."

"How are we going to eat for a year, though?"

"Isn't something going to come from your father?"

Ahhh. That was it. He thought I was going to be a great heiress, probably because of the Carnegie gift. His face wore a keen and invested expression. This was why he stayed by my side all these years. He wanted to coast on my father's money.

"There won't be anything coming from my father."

"How do you know that?"

"Because anything would be going right to Margaret to support her. And if not her, then the school. I honestly don't want anything coming to me, because I don't want Margaret or the concerns of the school coming to me. They can have it all."

"No, they can't!" Sid said entirely too loudly.

The boys stirred on the bench and I know I saw one of Willie's long eyelashes flutter. Sid wasn't thinking of them, either.

"What are you going to do about it? It's not yours, Sid. Father paid for you to go to Drexel and be an architect. He gave of his largesse to you years ago and this is how you thank him?"

Sid stared out of the window and got quiet. Good. He didn't need to say anything else. I was tired of hearing his nonsense.

Once we reached home in Dallas, Sid seemed to recover his good sense and went in pursuit of more architecture commissions and steady work. I was grateful for this because the boys kept growing fast and were in constant need of new clothes and shoes for school. Fannie was also growing up and needed more clothes and dresses befitting the granddaughter of Booker T. Washington.

JUST AFTER CHRISTMAS, in the new year of 1916, one of the teachers at the Dallas high school named for my father went out on leave for an illness. I heard about a substitute teaching opportunity from one of the people in our church. They were looking for someone to finish out the year.

Me.

I didn't approach Sid to talk about it. I just told them I would do it. The only one who would need care was Fannie. I would drop her off at the sitter's house on my way to work. The boys would be in school. They could come to the high school after they got out of their school and sit while I finished class.

The first morning of my new job, Sid noticed I dressed in my walking suit. "Where are you going?"

"I'm starting a substitute teacher job at Booker T. Washington High School for some extra money."

"You said nothing to me about it."

"I didn't think you would disapprove of me earning some extra money seeing as how you wanted more money from my father coming in to our household."

He turned away from me, grabbing his lunch, and headed to the construction site. Fannie and I left for the sitter's place, since the boys were already at their school just a few blocks away.

The schedule worked so well. After school, the boys came up to the high school, just a few blocks away from their elementary school. They would sit themselves in a corner of the high school auditorium and wait for me to get there. Soon, as I settled into teaching there, I started some after-school activities, taking on directing the school choir for more money, and my boys would wait for me through that, too. Of course, Book was fascinated with all the choir did. If practice went too long, they picked up their little sister and brought her to the high school. Many of the students loved Fannie and her antics and I never ran out of people who were willing to be supportive of us.

Even though things were rough between Sid and me, we came to enough of a truce to maintain a smooth running household and I was able to save money, as well as provide for us. It felt good to finally be solvent.

THE CHILDREN GREW up in this way, adhering to the personalities they had as children. Willie, somber and industrious, expressed an interest in architecture, much to Sid's chagrin. Booker learned the piano, quickly—too quickly and it bored him. He began to show an interest in the woodwind instruments. I wished he maintained an interest in the piano, but I was secretly delighted at his musical prowess. Fannie took to the piano and had a lovely soprano singing voice. My singing voice was not nearly as nice, and so Fannie, while being musical, managed to do something different and be unique unto herself. She also, as I predicted when she was a baby, grew to be incredibly beautiful with the large mesmerizing eyes that her grandfather had. Her beauty frightened me. Texas was still the South and she was a young Black woman. There was not a time when I didn't fear for her—even before she came into development as a young woman, because her engaging persona, coupled with her beauty, made for a dangerous combination. As much as I loved my only daughter, my prayers for her safety kept me on my knees at the Macedonia AME church.

At the turn of the new year of 1919, the news came forward that former president Theodore Roosevelt died in his sleep. I wrote a long letter of condolence to my friend Alice, knowing she was undoubtedly as devastated to lose her father as I was to lose mine. Unfortunately, no one had been there at the end, for he died in his sleep after a struggle with ill health the previous year in the wake of one of his many jungle illnesses.

After a time, a long time, she wrote me back and spoke of her longing for one of our visits. Our lives, both of them, kept us busy, too busy to engage with each other in person. I had hopes of returning to see her in Washington, DC, ever since Mr. Longworth had been reelected and "brought out of the wilderness like the children of Israel," as she put it, and had risen in House leadership. She was busy "pulling strings" as she liked to call it. Any meeting in person was not possible in the short run of time since I lived in the wilderness that was Texas.

THE YEARS PASSED and one day, the principal called me forward and spoke about an opportunity to put together a choir for a visiting national convention. The officials had gotten together and agreed I should be the one to direct a special choir welcoming the delegates to Dallas. They envisioned a choir of some six hundred members, singing "home songs," as they called it—the spirituals that they knew were my specialty.

When I let Sid know of the opportunity, he waved a hand. "Someone has to do it. Might as well be you. Are they paying you?"

"Not nearly enough."

The effort was pulling together all the members I directed, of course, from the high school, the two local club choirs, and the Macedonia church, as well as additional people. Directing from my repertoire would make things much easier, as those members would help guide the others new to my methods and practices. Still, the rehearsals, of which there would be two before the big event, would be a lot to manage.

Fannie was of a young age, but her sweet voice made for an excellent addition to the choir. The event, strangely enough, would be held at the Pythagorias Hall that Sid had constructed, as beautiful a building as any. Every time I entered it, the wide marble halls and open, lighted spaces gave me a thrill, even though I had long fallen out of love with its creator.

The challenge of pulling together so many voices into one smooth coherent whole was daunting, but I knew my heavenly father would help me.

We started off with "Oh Mary Don't You Weep," and continued with other spiritual tunes of note, like "Go Down Moses," "Swing Low, Sweet Chariot," and "In That Great Getting Up Morning." The entire cohort of superintendents who had gathered for the National Education Association conference gave us a standing ovation that lasted for quite a long time, or at least it felt that way. Even the *Dallas Morning News*, the white newspaper in the area, spoke about the accomplishment, praising me and the choir by saying that we had taken the "audience by storm," and that the musical numbers were such that "Southerners had not heard their like in quite some time."

White newspapers very rarely noted the comings and goings of Negroes, so for me to be listed and mentioned as well as my choir at a conference primarily for white professionals was quite an achievement. My children were very proud of me and told me so.

Sid had nothing to say.

My husband and I had grown further and further apart and so it occurred to me that this would be a good time to visit my friend. My son was beginning his studies at Howard University as a special student, and I, instead of Sid, could go with him. I thought I might then visit Alice, along with my daughter, who was quite a young lady by now, taking her to meet a grand lady of Washington, DC, the wife of the House Majority Leader.

Portia

1924

A lice did not live in the same house as she did before. The Longworths had moved to DuPont Circle and it was a little riskier for us going there. We had made sure Willie was settled at Howard University before I came to the neighborhood full of traditional Victorian gingerbreads with side entrances, specially built for colored servants. I knew better than to have us take a car, so after we had lunch with Willie and dropped him off at school, Fannie and I took a trolley there, sitting in the appropriate space. Washington, DC, was still very much a southern city.

A Negro woman and her younger child, while quite pretty, did not draw any extra attention. I made sure that our dresses were nice, but not extravagantly so. It would not do to appear dirty from the trolley. Once we got to Alice's house, I stood in front of the house, but with Fannie next to me, I was not willing to take foolish chances. "What is it, Mother?"

I moved quickly and she followed as I knew she would. "We need to go to the side. Just to be safe."

Her smooth eyebrows furrowed, and we pulled the bell at the side door. A maid, only a few years older than Fannie, answered and guided us in, telling us, "Mrs. Longworth has been expecting you."

She took us to the sunroom in the front of the house where a bit of the dreary day dribbled in through the curtains. Alice was there, seated in a chair, like the princess she was with a big belly.

When had this happened?

She had written absolutely nothing to me of this happy news. She must have had a reason for her silence. So when we came in, I went to greet her, nodding, standing before her saying, "Mrs. Longworth. It's been some time. So good to see you again."

Her hands clasped at the sides of the chair. "Equally, Mrs. Pittman. Is this your Fannie Virginia?"

"Yes, it is." I gestured to my daughter and she curtsied, her lovely features arranged in awe at meeting a famous person.

"She's quite beautiful and changed from the last time I saw her as an infant in your arms with a runny nose." My friend's mischievous smile tugged at the corners of her mouth and we both laughed in spite of ourselves. Fannie laughed a little too.

"Are you both hungry? I'm not quite ready for tea yet." She gestured with a hand that seemed a little puffier than it should. I was used to everything being lean on Alice.

"We just ate lunch," I informed her as I sat on a davenport.

"I can have something," Fannie put in and we both laughed again. Alice rang for the young maid who had let us in.

"Please take Fannie back to the kitchen, Amelia, and give her something. Like ice cream, maybe?" Alice suggested, tapping her chin with a finger.

Ice cream was a rarity, reserved for the rich, and Fannie's eyes lit up in wonder. "You may have some, too, Amelia."

Both of the younger women practically ran from the room, eager to indulge in the rare treat.

"Look at that energy, Portia. Reminds me of us when we were young. Not as young as Fannie, but Amelia is about that age when we first met." Her hand dropped to her rounded belly. "I don't have much energy these days as you can tell, dear friend."

I wanted to scold her for keeping the happy news to herself, but I still was so shocked at seeing her in a family way, I didn't know what to say. "It's quite some news, Alice. After . . ." I quickly tabulated the years in my head. I had been married to Sid for seventeen years this year, which made almost nineteen for her and Nicholas.

"It's not Mr. Longworth's child, Portia. If you are doing math."

I gulped. *Dear Lord.*

"Is that why you didn't write me about it?"

"Well, all Washington is calling this the miracle child. We've been married for almost nineteen years. Then all of a sudden, this. Many people, including Father before he departed this earth, blamed me for the lack of a child, but apparently, I'm quite fertile when I'm with the right man. No, it's my husband who . . ."

"Who?"

"My dear Portia. There are just some things that are not for your Christian sensibilities." She sighed. "I would want us to remain friends."

"Of course. I'm not one to judge you. I mean, if you are talking about my faith, that is something we usually did not do."

Her eyes twinkled. "Oh, yes. That's right. I remember Father talking all about that forgiveness stuff as well. Is that all a part of it?"

I leaned in to her. "Of course it is."

"Well, I don't need forgiveness. My marriage. I mean, my situation. It's been far from ideal. I have stayed in it, so that Nicholas can succeed. If the Speaker wins his election to the Senate, Nick is next up to be Speaker of the House. It's not president, but it's closer than many thought he would be. It would devastate his opportunities if our marriage were to break up. So we have stayed married. But we have each had our own . . ." She gulped and came closer to tears than I had ever seen her. "Pleasures. Except mine hasn't been so pleasurable."

Well. "I suppose adultery isn't supposed to be pleasurable."

She focused her gaze on me. "The father of my child is married to someone else. And he, as an important man, cannot divorce either."

I laid my hand on hers, squeezing it. "I'm so sorry. So very sorry, my dear friend."

She laid her thumb over my hand. "It's really quite funny. He's also a politician. Leaving his wife would end his career. But the strange thing is that he doesn't have any children either. One of the reasons that he talked me out of doing something about the situation. I would have if he hadn't asked me not to."

"That does make it harder."

"His wife, she had a child but then it died and she couldn't have any more babies."

"Is that why . . . you both?"

"No. That's not why." She inhaled. "We could talk to each other. I suppose I fell for him because he loved to talk about Father." She laughed a little. "That's one way to get to me. I was feeling so sad and lonely after Father died."

I nodded. I was so grateful for the opportunity to teach after my father died. I had something to turn to, a purpose to consume my time.

"We're very similar political animals. Same outlook, same point of view about things. Not the handsomest man in the Senate, but still, his oratory . . ."

"He is a senator?" The father of her baby was a senator while her husband remained in the House? Oh my.

"They call him the lion of Idaho." She paused. "Of course you remember how often they called my father a lion. How could I resist?"

All I could do was nod to encourage her to continue talking and she did. "Then this happened. I mean, in so many ways, the worst possible thing. Because as you know, I'm not incredibly fond of babies until they get to be people."

"I know."

"And it meant that, well, in terms of our trysts, I had not been discreet. Not to mention that I'm an old mother. So now you know. I'm terrified."

"Which you should not be. You see, I've been through it three times and have come out the other end. And yes, you are an older mother, but you'll be fine."

"I appreciate the kind words, Portia. I suppose, well, given your Christian sensibilities, I have no right to unload my burdens on you like this and expect you to understand."

I closed my eyes. "These years with Sid have not been easy. I expect you knew that when I still lived here. I thought moving to Dallas would mean more work for him, easier times. That wasn't true. It got harder. I was forced to help out, to take on teaching and private students. The more I helped out, the more he resented it. And me. He hasn't touched me in . . . oh, a long time now. I've thought about moving out into a different bedroom because he drinks. Often. He gets so absorbed in his work that he'll go unwashed for days and let his hair grow out until he looks like he's insane."

I didn't want to open my eyes, because I hoped that would stop the tears from falling, but it did not. I was so ashamed at how I let so much go past me. And for what? For my children. For Fannie and Book, still at home, to have their father. The both of them could be a lot to handle and I needed help with them. If it hadn't been for the two of them . . . could I divorce Sid? Even though we were in the midst of the Roaring Twenties, a time with a different set of standards, I still was a Christian woman. My beliefs ran deep and one of those was supposed to be for me to stay married to Sid until death parted us.

"It's not been easy for either one of us." Alice patted my hand. "I'm so sorry, Portia."

I wiped away my tears. "But my teaching. That's been my joy. And look"—I pulled the newspaper clipping from my purse about the concert. I didn't know if it had made it to Washington, DC. I handed it to her, and Alice, a lover of all news, took the thing into her hand and read it eagerly.

"This is amazing, Portia. Six hundred high school students? It must have been like herding cats!"

"Something like it"—and we laughed together—"but well worth the effort."

"This is wonderful." She handed me back the clipping, eyes shining. "You have something. Something of your very own. Something real and tangible. Don't let that go. You have to keep it for yourself. Nurture it. I've always admired that in you."

"You have?" This was the great president's daughter saying those words to me, her Negro friend.

"Yes. Your music. So important. I know why you came back to the United States. It was for the same reason I came back with Nick and a ring on my finger. People don't think that women have feelings or needs. It's one reason why I love these flapper women. They're telling it like it is. Women after my own heart."

"Of course."

"Your Fannie gets to grow up in this time. How lucky she is."

"And your child."

Alice shook her head, spreading her arms wide. "Yes. This. Too."

"How about some music?" I gestured toward her Steinway. "Is it in tune?"

"How am I supposed to know that?"

I stood. "Let me take a look." I ran my fingers up and down the keys and made a few adjustments. "Remember when we first met and I played for you?"

"I recall it well. The home songs. I would love to hear them again."

I played the concert bill for her. Fannie came in after her ice cream, thankfully, and she sang. The calm of the music relaxed my friend and we passed a delightful afternoon until we heard a deep male voice intrude. "Well, isn't this a lovely party?"

The famous Mr. Longworth appeared before us.

The look of shock on Alice's face was unlike anything I had ever seen. She looked cowed by him, almost. Not at all the saucy Princess Alice. "I wasn't expecting you home so early, Mr. Longworth."

"I must have intuited that music was playing in the house, dear wife. You know how fond of it I am."

"I know you have never met. Mrs. Pittman, this is my husband, Mr. Nicholas Longworth III of Ohio. This is Mrs. Pittman's daughter, Fannie Virginia. They are from Dallas, Texas."

"My. A long way from home."

"We brought my son for his term at the Negro college, Howard. I wanted to stop by and visit Mrs. Longworth."

"Mrs. Pittman, as you know, is the daughter of Booker T. Washington."

"Oh, yes, now I remember. I recall you said you knew her."

Alice's face returned to its usual posture. "She has been my friend and compatriot these many years."

"Ahh. Compatriot. Interesting use of the term, my dear wife. You're from the same country."

I turned to her. "Yes. I think that's the exact word."

"Beautiful. As is the music." Mr. Longworth stood. "Mind if I join you both? I don't get to play my violin as much as I like in this political jungle."

I opened my mouth and then closed it, not sure what to say to his request.

"She plays the home songs of the Negro people. I'm not sure you know that music, dear husband."

"I know many European concertos if you prefer, Mr. Longworth." I picked out a Chopin and he nodded.

"Yes." He retrieved his violin from a shelf and began to prepare it, rosining his bow and tuning it. "So rusty, my poor fellow. Come, Mrs. Pittman. Let us play music for my lovely wife so that she might relax her mind about her impending event."

I cleared my throat and played on, knowing that choosing silence was better than saying anything at all.

Alice

1917–1919

My Borah and I could not stop that man from starting a war, no matter how much we tried. Before he did, he went and found some terrible widow to marry after an indecently short amount of time after the death of his wife. They waited a year and some months after his first wife had died, but it was obvious to all that was a ploy to make it appear as if he hadn't fallen for a Cissy Patterson type so quickly. I mean, even if Ellen Wilson wasn't a very interesting woman, she deserved more regard from him than to be swept aside like yesterday's rubbish.

The senator and I had been having regular assignations for three years and I had speculated with my Borah that Wilson probably had her poisoned. "I mean, he is the president after all."

"Alice," he said in his dear voice, as I rested in the crook of his arm one afternoon after Wilson had been reelected to another term, much to our displeasure. "What in the world would make you feel that he would do that? Just because he is a Democrat and beat your father in '12?"

"That. His beady eyes behind those spectacles he wears and because he just seems to be the type."

"Some might look at the two of us as we are now and say we would be in the mind to be rid of our encumberments."

I stroked his face, looking far too hound-dog unhappy after we had just been together in such a special way. "I doubt that, my love. They don't understand how much we like our situation as it is."

He said nothing and turned from me, taking up his arm.

"I mean, don't we?" We were of one accord in so many ways, I was a little shaken to hear him disagree.

"I know that Nick is your"—he gulped—"husband. I know that you don't . . . with him. I mean. You aren't like this with him." He spread his arm around our bed. Well, my bed during the day. "And you say he doesn't care if we . . . continue."

I surrounded him with my body. "He doesn't."

"I still don't like that he is your husband."

"I don't mind about Mamie," I whispered.

"I know that."

"She's quite kind," I offered. She was. She was a kindly little wifely person a senator needed. I could never be that.

"Yes. As a matter of fact, she's been hinting that you and Nick should come over sometime."

I took in a breath. "What did you say?"

"I said we should have you both. What do you think I should have said?"

"Well, you might have asked her why us."

He clasped my hand. "My dear. She knows who you are. She re-members you from the Christmas party and wants to sup with you."

"Oh. That."

"Yes. That. Well?"

"Sure, why not?" I patted him on his bare back. "It sounds like a fun evening."

"If I see Nick treat you poorly, I'm afraid I would not be able to refrain from addressing it."

I squeezed him. "You would and you will. Let her know it's fine to make the contact."

HE DID AND, faster than I thought, we were going to have dinner with the Borahs in their home, blocks away from ours.

Nick had a fundraising reception after, so he would be able to leave sooner than I would, but Borah told him that he would make sure that I got home. I certainly had no objections to a little night-cap with my Borah.

Once we were there, I felt a little nervous. Borah came and shook hands with Nick, nodding to me. I was glad that he didn't shake my hand. I would not have been able to act nonchalantly at his touch.

His wife came forward, untying an apron from her small person. "Hello, Mr. Longworth. Mrs. Longworth. Welcome to our home. I'm so glad you've come to visit us. I've wanted to meet you for so long, but Willie said that I mustn't impose."

Willie?

"We are grateful at the invitation." Nick nodded. She swept her hand to the table.

"Please, have a seat. I've put name cards down."

"And you managed to cook?" I gulped a little.

"Oh, it's nothing really. I've been cooking most of my life. I was a governor's daughter, but we had no money. I've had to know basic housekeeping skills for a while now."

That was interesting, to be sure.

Yawn.

The dinner she served was a roast, potatoes, and asparagus. A fruit compote rounded out the meal. It was served nicely by the maid Borah told me they had hired for the occasion, who I supposed had to stay longer to accommodate so that Mamie didn't have to serve, and we passed a very pleasant evening, talking and mostly decrying Woodrow Wilson.

"I cannot believe that he got us into a war after he said he wouldn't. What kind of man is he not to keep his word?" I put my spoon down after I finished my fruit compote.

Mamie put in, "I completely agree with you, Mrs. Longworth. It's hard to respect a man who makes a promise and then breaks it."

I swallowed some of my wine and avoided the gazes of both my Borah and my husband completely. "What kind of man is he, newly married to Mrs. Galt now and with three daughters of his own but refusing to help women get the right to vote?" Little Mamie said with more credit than I would have given her. Did her husband have her entirely right?

"I've often wondered that myself."

"We may get it to the states yet, ladies." Nick just loved to lay it on thickly to women whenever the issue of suffrage came up.

"I know you are a supporter, Mrs. Longworth," Mamie pointed out. "I have to tell you things have long been different in our western states. I've voted before."

I turned to her, feeling as if I were in a comedy of manners story. This little woman had voted before? "Isn't that amazing?"

"It's our right as citizens of this country." She stood, although it was hard to tell. "Please come to the parlor. We can better enjoy our conversation there."

Nick stood as well. "I must leave for my reception obligation. Mrs. Borah, this was a fine, fine meal. I've enjoyed your cooking and it's been a pleasure being in your company." He took her hand and shook it and something, I don't know what, curled in me.

"Thank you so much, Mr. Longworth. I hope you can come back when you can stay longer and join us in the parlor."

For the first time, I gave a cursory glance at my Borah but his eyes did not meet mine. Not once.

When we retreated into the parlor, the conversation turned to books and both Borah and Little Mamie were very knowledgeable and Mamie just laughed as she worked on knitting a sock. For her Willie. "We've established several libraries in Idaho. I long to do something similar here. I know that my husband has been here for two terms now, but the fluid nature of politics makes me a little wary to do that kind of charitable work here."

"Oh, you mustn't feel that way," I insisted. "You should begin some charitable endeavor. It would be good." Anything to keep her busy.

"Well, maybe you can come around with me. I love to go calling to the other Senate wives on Thursdays. Since you are in the House, we can go out together on Tuesdays to see who else might want to join us."

Accompany Little Mamie Borah on calls? I would rather tell Eleanor I would be happy to volunteer to babysit her newest son, who was a terror just two years old.

HOWEVER, MAMIE WAS completely serious and set a time for us to go calling in July of 1918. Even though the humidity in Washington, DC, was unbearable in the summertime, with Nick in leadership positioning, we still went out. Idaho was also very far away to visit, so the Borahs did not go home during session breaks as often as they might.

Or maybe they were here because I stayed in DC. Nick was the one who would go back to Ohio. I never had any interest in going back there for any reason.

Still, we made visits to several congressmen's wives. I allowed use of my car and driver and Mamie would jump out at every stop, excited beyond belief to leave her calling card for absent wives to let them know about her latest charitable endeavor with providing books to the poor. After a time, I just stayed in the car.

I had no cards, for the sheer purpose that I did not need them and I knew that some of these wives would consider it quite a coup to have me in their parlors and I did not relish being a prize for anyone. When we dropped Mamie off, she thanked me profusely and said that we must do it again.

I said nothing, since I knew we must not.

Dinner was one thing, chatty Little Mamie a whole other thing.

When the driver brought me home, Nick came outside of the

house, a rare event, but the look on his face said he had terrible news.

"What are you doing here?" My heart pounded inside of my chest. "Is it father?"

Nick shook his head. "Quentin. His plane went down in France. He's been killed."

I don't remember much after that. I do know that I screamed. I knew what Quentin's death, my father's youngest child, the most mischievous brother of mine, would do to him once he found out. Nick had the maid pack my grip for Sagamore Hill and we left on the train at once.

I was right. When I saw Father, he looked as if a great force had taken a straw and sucked life from him. We were not a touchy family, but I could not help but embrace him, trying to pass some of my vigor back to him.

Mother was her same, wan self. She barely responded when I greeted her, but she came alive when Teddy Jr. and Ethel, now Mrs. Derby, brought their children forward. Since I had no children to bring forward, my embrace and greeting were less welcome, I suppose.

I was able to focus on making sure things went smoothly since Father's usually bright personality was much sobered by the loss of his youngest boy, who really had been the country's boy from our years in the White House.

How I wish my Borah could have been there as a support for me, but I knew I had to be there for my father. And Mother by extension. I did my level best to support them both and by the time I left, my father sagged in relief, not saying thank you but conveying his thanks in another way—by not harassing me about my missing children. I was grateful.

Still, I felt an impending sense of doom when I was on the verge of leaving him. He was not well because of all the diseases he had caught in the jungle. Those illnesses, topped with the loss of my younger brother, troubled me. I could not draw him out to talk about politics, either. All he said to me was "If I had been the president, that blasted war might not have ever started."

Which is when I knew, and I felt, that somehow I was to blame.

So when the telegram from my brother Archie came in the new year of 1919 that said "The Old Lion is dead," I had already done my mourning. I had already done my weeping when Quentin was gone. For my father was not quite there and as always, and as ever, I, his oldest daughter, was not enough to ease his loss.

The difference this time, in 1919, was that I had my Borah, and even though I was in his arms when the telegram came, I traveled to Sagamore Hill with him at my side, instead of Nick. Now that my father was gone, I did not care who saw us together and what they would say.

For the only person whose approval I cared to obtain had gone to his reward.

I was finally, perpetually, free to do as I wanted.

Alice

1919–1924

The year 1919 started off as a bad one, because of the loss of my papa, but it improved. Wilson put himself out there when the war ended as if he were the savior of the world, but he wasn't. I could see through him, plain as day, and I found it irksome that he was out there trying to get credit for making the peace. He had not. It was one of the chief topics between my Borah and me when we were alone.

"This League of Nations foolishness is the next thing," I burst out. "He thinks that he can pull it off."

Borah had interlaced his fingers across his broad chest. I loved stroking his hairy chest with those surprisingly silky hairs on them. People may not have thought Borah handsome, but to me, he was beautiful and all *MINE*.

Except for the small portion of him Little Mamie had.

"He can't do it without the Senate."

"Excuse me?"

"He cannot join the League of Nations without the approval of the Senate."

I sat up in my bed, twining my hair about my fingers. "If only the Democrats didn't have it."

Shaking his head, Borah sat up, too. "That makes no difference. He won't have the numbers, my darling."

"It would be defeated?"

Now it was Borah's turn to play with my hair. "Is that what you want, sweet Alice?"

I thought of my father, who had won the Nobel Peace Prize, going down in history as the peaceful president without Tommy Wilson, what I liked to call the current occupant in the White House, in the way. "Yes."

Borah's rough touch trailed up my arms to my lips. "Then it's yours." He reached out to kiss me and because he was my champion, he got the reward he had been seeking.

Tommy Wilson never even knew that his downfall to being considered a peaceful president had been carefully plotted out in a DuPont Circle bedroom.

It was time to consider who would be our next Republican president, since Tommy was on his way out. I faintly recalled meeting Warren Harding at the convention several years ago. He was also the topic of many a plotting conversation between us.

There had been some rumors about him, like that he was as bad as Nick as a lover man, probably had Cissy himself, too. Still, the one that I liked the best was that he had Negro blood. I wrote about it to Portia in one of my letters to her during that year and she told me that was one of the best reasons to support Harding because he would be the first of their race to reach such a high station.

Nick knew him, of course, but so did my Borah, because Harding and Borah were both in the Senate. I made a habit to visit the House on certain days and the Senate on others. So I had seen him, conducting business there. I suppose that he was handsome enough, but once, around the end of 1919 when I took lunch in Borah's office with him, Borah told me that Harding had had a baby with another woman back in Ohio. A young woman. Very young. "This might ruin his chances of running. Some of the officials are concerned."

"A baby? Isn't his wife, well, old?" I had only seen Florence Harding from a distance, but it was enough to know she was much closer to mutton than to lamb.

"It's some young woman in Ohio who is the mother. Apparently, they've had something going on for a while."

"Well, isn't that something." I paused. "Old Cleveland had something going on like that, too."

Borah stroked his chin. "I believe he did, yes."

"Well, that didn't stop him, did it? Is the young woman married?"

"No. She's just a young woman living on her own with this . . . little girl."

I waved my hand. "That's nothing. My goodness. The father could be anyone. I'll go look into it at the Library of Congress to see what they did with Cleveland, but a young woman on her own? That can be put down with a few well-placed sources."

And it was. No, Warren Harding never thanked me directly for his being elected president, but he did thank all the newly enfranchised women voters who put him into the White House, so I considered that gratitude enough from him.

Still, something about the Harding baby lingered in my mind. I brought it up to Borah one afternoon during one of our assignations. I wasn't feeling bad about Nan Britton, which was the name of the young woman in Ohio, but because after fourteen years of marriage to Nick and now having been with Borah a few years, there was nothing. "What if, not saying this were to happen, but what if that happened to me?"

He propped himself up on one elbow. "What if what were to happen to you?"

"What happened to Nan Britton in Ohio."

"A baby?"

I nodded. "Yes. I've wondered for a while, why she just didn't . . . well, have it taken care of. There are such procedures that . . ." Suddenly he gripped my arm. Hard. Surprising me. A strange look came on his face. A look that I've never seen before.

"You're different. Don't compare yourself with her."

"I understand that. But Harding could have had someone come in, someone with the best money, and there wouldn't have been a baby."

"Sometimes you can have all of that and still have a bad outcome." He faced me. "Promise me. Promise me right now if that ever happened you would tell me and not deal with it like that on your own."

I had never seen him so angry at me before. I put my hand on his arm. "Borah. Please. Sit down. Calm yourself. It's me you are speaking to."

I didn't want to get angry back at him, but I didn't understand where this passion was coming from, especially since he had never espoused any interest in babies before. He did as I asked, and I was glad for it.

"I just know you. I know you would do something and not tell me." He put his face in his hands.

"That's not true. I tell you everything."

"You do. But you would find a way not to tell me about that."

"I don't understand. What has caused this emotion in you, my dearest?"

"I've never said this to anyone, but"—he took a deep breath—"when Mamie and I first started dating, things got out of hand quickly. I hadn't resolved to marry her, but her father, who was the governor, could not have a pregnant daughter as a scandal, so he made arrangements for her. The best of everything. She did not tell me about any of this.

"The procedure destroyed her insides. That's why we don't have children. It's not because we didn't want to. It's because we can't."

"But when did she tell you?"

"After I married her."

I sat down next to him, reflecting on how Mamie went nuts over my little cousin Franklin at that Christmas party a few years before.

I laced my fingers with his. "I'm so sorry. I didn't mean to bring up something that caused you pain." I leaned on his shoulder.

He patted my knee. "I knew that you didn't know, my darling. I'm not angry with you. I just . . . Thinking about it brings back much of what I did then. Such a terrible mistake in my life. So many people don't understand, how there are worse things in the world than a baby born out of wedlock."

"You're right. A little incident won't hurt our man. Besides." I stood up so that I could get dressed. "I've been barren for years. Nothing like that has happened and nothing like that could happen."

What is the saying? Man plans and God laughs? Well, I had never believed in God, but, given what happened, he surely believed in me.

No, not because Harding later died in office in 1923 and brought my friends, Grace and Calvin Coolidge, to the White House. I'll never understand why people gave that man a hard time. He was a good man and their election meant that I could go visit my old home whenever I wanted. Grace had much good sense and I enjoyed my time visiting with them. I loved that she had a pet raccoon, named Rebecca, and she enjoyed teaching that rascal tricks.

GRACE COOLIDGE ALSO was the mother to two well-mannered, interesting young men. I thought of my cousin Eleanor's Anna, becoming quite a young lady and still in the city for the summer of 1924. I would introduce her to the boys. It's always a good thing to establish networks, if not for marriage then for other purposes. I had thoughts of having her accompany me to the White House to have tea with the First Lady one day when the most dreadful news came. Calvin Jr., the boy I was going to introduce Anna to, had died of blood poisoning. They had taken him to the hospital a few days before to treat him, but he had died, nonetheless. They had kept the news quiet, hoping for a better outcome.

When Nick told me about the poor Coolidge boy, I burst into

tears. He sat down on the davenport next to me and patted my shoulder. "There now, Princess. I've never known you to take on so at the death of a child. When little Franklin expired, you expressed relief and said that Eleanor would be able to watch after her great numbers of children. Tears?"

They kept coming and coming and would not stop. I would take a deep breath to inhale, to stop the tears, but that did no good. It was as if something uncontrollable inside of me kept causing the tears. "I have to get to Grace and tell her of my sorrow. I was just going to have him meet Anna . . ."

Nick shrugged. "They have an older son, too."

I hit his shoulder and he jumped back, laughing a bit, and it was a little like the old times between us.

Still, I went to bed early that night, and as I fell asleep, I thought that I needed to speak with a doctor myself because my breasts hurt. I had heard of other women having such a symptom and leading to very sad outcomes. A doctor would be hard to come by because it was summer in the capital city, but still, because it was me, I might manage to pull it off.

The doctor came in the late afternoon the next day, and I explained to him. "I've never had this part"—I pointed to the front of me—"feel so tender before. I'm hoping there is no mass growing in there."

"Do you remember the last time that you had your monthly visit?"

I scrunched up my face. "No. I'm forty years old. Those things have come and gone all my life with no great regularity. I've never felt a need to keep track. Now, I just assume all the coming and going means that it will finally just go away."

The doctor regarded me with a strange look on his face. "I see. Undress, and put on your dressing gown and we'll have a look."

"I'm just talking about my front," I insisted as he walked out of the room.

"Yes, of course, Mrs. Longworth. I'm just doing my due diligence."

"I'm not real estate, you know," I yelled after him. He just chuckled.

Which I did not like. I may not have had as large a front as other women, but it was an area that my Borah enjoyed.

I did as the doctor told me to do and he inspected me quite thoroughly. Too thoroughly, to be quite honest. As if I were an automobile. When he finished, he told me to fasten up my dressing gown and said I could sit up.

"Congratulations, Mrs. Longworth. You're going to be a mother."

"A mother?" That word, so strange to hear, was not affiliated with me. And now it was according to this doctor.

"Yes. I would say around Valentine's Day."

"You cannot be serious. That's the worst day in my life."

"The day for lovers?"

"My mother died on that day." As well as my father's care and regard. "On the same day my grandmother died."

A baby? A baby was bad enough, but on Valentine's Day?

This god of Portia's had a terrible sense of humor indeed.

Alice

1924–1925

My Borah was, as one can imagine, thrilled. But still, as he knew and as I knew, everyone in the capital city and on Capitol Hill would not be so understanding. I never knew a woman of my age to be in the position of becoming a first-time mother, and everyone knew that my marriage with Nick had long been one of convenience.

Even Nick.

On one relatively rare occasion we happened to be at our house at the same time for dinner, I just went ahead and broke the news to him. There was no easy way to say such a thing. I mean, my usually sylphlike figure was already rounding.

"I'm going to have a baby."

Nick dropped his fork. I suppose it could have been worse.

"It's supposed to come sometime around mid-February."

"Frederick Gillett is going to announce he's running for Senate."

Both announcements were equally cataclysmic, but I knew what he meant by his announcement.

"Is he stepping down?"

"He's considering it. It won't be an easy race."

"You'll be Speaker of the House if he does."

"Exactly."

We ate in silence. Breaking the silence, I said, "Well, then my timing is quite poor."

He crossed his utensils on his plate and wiped off his mustache. "Actually, wife. It couldn't be better. Such a thing happening will immediately gain me votes in the coalition and more sympathy. After almost twenty years, you've finally done it."

I looked around our ornate dining room. "It'll change things around here."

"For the better, I daresay."

He stood and came down to my end of the table and patted my shoulder as if he were one of my brothers. "I'm just sorry that your father wasn't here to see it."

Actually, I was somewhat glad he wasn't. I just nodded. He went on. "So I'm allowed to spread the word?"

"Yes. You are." My appearance would do enough spreading of news in time.

He bent down to kiss me on the cheek, something he hadn't done in years, and went out to his event, whistling.

It was all less difficult than I thought.

There was one more person who I thought might take a little heart at the news. The next morning, I got myself dressed and ready to visit the White House. I knew the doorman, who, when he saw me approaching, shook his head. "It's not a good day, Mrs. Longworth."

I nodded. "I'll still go up. It won't be a minute. It might be a better day after I speak with her."

The black mourning crêpes hung around the White House in a sign of sorrow for their dearly departed. I went straight to the family quarters, and no one stopped me, since they knew I had been there several times before. The president himself was just coming out of his wife's door and put a finger to his lips. Poor Calvin looked as if he were taking the worst of it. He still was running his campaign for his own term and dealing with this tragedy. I leaned in and told him my news, and something lit up in his eyes. Without saying a word, as he was known to do, he spread his hands out, moved out of my way, and I went in to where the First Lady rested on a chaise lounge.

"Oh, Alice. I have so much to do and no will at all to do it." Her hands grasped at her beautiful dressing gown and I sat down next to her.

"Mrs. Coolidge. I'm going to have a baby."

She sat straight up. "What did you say, Mrs. Longworth?"

"I'm going to have a baby."

She embraced me, something we rarely did, and hugged me tightly, not wanting to let go. She did eventually. "You must let me throw you a party here. So many people will want to come and say congratulations to you, thinking that this happy event would never happen." Her mien of sorrow disappeared and she began to ready herself for the day.

My task was complete.

I was amused later to learn that Mrs. Coolidge was talking about my news at a reception and said, "I wonder when the baby will come."

"Sometime in February." The president put in and for once, his much more outgoing wife was shocked that her husband, known as Silent Cal, had more information than she did about such an event!

"How did you know that, Calvin?"

"Why, she told me herself."

She gave me a bit of a scolding the next time I saw her, but she got a kick out of the story. So many in the capital were completely fascinated by my news that many betting pools developed over due date and gender.

The one person not so delighted was Mother. She knew that Nick wasn't the father, and she was not so welcoming to my special event as she might have been. Eleanor was no longer living in Washington, but she wrote to express her excitement.

With so much investment in my child, I did not want to give birth in Washington, DC, so late in January 1925, I hired a special train car to take me to Chicago for the birth. Another one of my well-connected friends, Ruth, who was a senator's daughter, accompanied me to Chicago so that I wouldn't be alone. Neither Nick nor my Borah could take time away from the people's business to come with me, something that I understood. Ruth had several children of her own, anyway, and could spare the time, so, even though the winter weather was bitterly cold, we passed the days awaiting the birth in deep discussions and reading books. Of course, I wrote to my Borah. He developed a code so that anyone who intercepted our correspondence would not understand what was going on, but I did. His hellos conveyed the sentiment that he loved me, and for the first time during the entire travail, I felt a warm blanket of love surrounded me.

I would be fine. Even though I was frightened.

Ruth continued to reassure me. "So many things have changed since you were born. The care is much better and we're here in Chicago with a great many specialists to take care of your old lady birth."

She was just the right person for me to have around and kept my mind from dwelling too much on improbable sorrow. Still, another person that I turned to, via my correspondence, was Portia. Her words of comfort when she had visited helped me. Also, she was the one person who knew why I would be afraid and having weathered birth three times, was a light and uplift to me.

I would take out her letters from time to time and allow her words of reassurance to surround me. I read them aloud to the baby who was growing larger by the day and kept up movement inside of me.

Even though you don't believe in the God that I do, you have to know that the people who love you never completely disappear from us. My father's spirit accompanies me all the time and you must know that your father's does as well. As a matter of fact, I know that

*President Roosevelt could probably never imagine such
an adventure as childbirth. Even though our poor dear
mothers had the hardest of times, they are both guard-
ians to women such as yourself, a woman who is about
to endure the most worthwhile of travails. Please know I
hold you close in my heart and you have all of my good
thoughts coming to you and the babe.*

Even though the doctor had said it, I thought maybe my baby
would come on my birthday. After all, it was another presidential
birthday, Abraham Lincoln's, as well, but no. The baby showed her
own independent spirit and came on Valentine's Day, of course. I
knew if my baby arrived on that day that my child would be a girl.
Only a girl of mine would be that spirited. So now I was forced to
think of the day of horror in a new way.

Nick came out to Chicago right away after he received the telegram that the baby had come. By the time he had gotten there, I
had named her already. I thought of a name, a name that somewhat
echoed that of my dear friend of many years. "Meet Paulina," I greeted
Nick when he emerged in the doorway of the private hospital room
that had been assigned to me. The baby happened to be there, after
she was just fed, before they were taking her back to the nursery. I laid
her in the crib and Nick came in and held up a hand, looking down
at the baby.

"She's amazing. What a well-formed child." He reached right into
her crib and held her up, close to his chest, as if he were an old pro
at what he was doing. He looked extremely comfortable in holding
her, even as I was not.

"I suppose your mother knows." I surely didn't bother to tell her.

"I've told all the Longworths. Now they just have to know her
name. I'll telegraph that to them as well."

"We don't have to take her to Ohio, do we?" I was dreading that.

They knew full well that this was not Nick's baby and I didn't want to have to hear anything about that from them.

"Of course not." Nick kissed the baby on the forehead and put her back into her crib, so that they could wheel her away. "This is our baby, Alice. Not theirs."

I turned to him and peered at him. There was only one thing that I could say at this, his most embracing, loving, warm response to the situation. "Thank you, Nick."

He sat down next to the bed and covered my hand with his. "Alice. I want to say something to you."

I waited, wanting to hear his words.

"Thank you. For such a beautiful child."

"That's what you want to say to me?"

He nodded and, in spite of myself, more tears came. Darn this baby business.

"I'm sorry." I apologized for the tears and my weepiness, all due to Paulina's arrival. This was not like me at all, but I realized my apology would come across different. Instead, he just squeezed my hand.

"Have any of your history books ever told you that a Speaker of the House had a baby while in office?"

"I haven't looked that up."

"This Speaker will."

He kept his word. When we all returned to Washington, DC, we were the little Longworth family and formed a tightly knit unit.

Borah did not come by immediately, but when he did, he remarked on how beautiful Paulina was and told me the joke going around town was that I was going to name her "Aurora Borah Alice or Deborah." As in "De Borah" or "of Borah." We had a good laugh at that one. Our last laughs.

A distance developed between us with Paulina's birth that did not dissolve. Borah had been the love of my life, but now he was the father of my child, and he had no more use for me. This change didn't mean he had any use for anything or anyone else, it was just we were no longer alone in the world. The dynamics had shifted.

One afternoon, the nurse had put Paulina down for her nap, when the maid announced that company had come. "Mrs. William Borah," she said in all seriousness. If anyone knew who Paulina's father was, it was my maid.

I came into the hallway and there was Little Mamie, gesturing to a pile of gifts that hovered at the inside of the door. "I hope you don't mind me dropping in. It's Tuesday and I wouldn't have called otherwise."

"No. I don't mind."

"I just wanted to say congratulations. And bring the baby some gifts. Things she'll need." She stepped forward. There was something in her eyes that I wasn't expecting from her.

Joy.

"I've heard she's beautiful."

"She just went down for a nap, but only just. Come this way." I led the way up the stairs to the nursery, which was at the opposite end of the house, where Paulina and her nurse would be undisturbed.

We entered, and her nurse, a young Irishwoman, turned around and faced me with a scowl, but I ignored her. At that point, Paulina was small enough to fit in a bassinet and I parted the little curtains around her so that Mamie could see her.

She took in a sharp breath. "Oh, Alice. She's perfectly lovely." She turned her round face to me and she was weeping openly. "You must be so proud of her."

Her tears surprised me, but so did her visit and need to see the baby. "Nick is, certainly. I've never seen a man go so completely wild over a baby."

Bringing a handkerchief out of her reticule, she wiped her face. "That's so good to hear. I'm glad to hear her father loves her." She sniffed. "And that she's welcome here."

I nodded. "She is. There is no worry of that."

She turned to me, her eyes intent on mine. "She's welcome in our home. Always. I hope you know that, Mrs. Longworth." She nodded at me too. "Please bring her to visit. Whenever you like."

It was not like me, but this baby made me do things I normally would not have. I reached over and grasped her hand and squeezed it.

In answer.

Alice

1928

In the fall of 1928, Paulina was three and went to the House daily with her father. Her nanny would go, too, and take her away when she became short or impossible to deal with, but she always brought her back to Nick for lunch and was in the car to pick him up for dinner when they returned back to our home.

His close relationship with Paulina was too much for me. How could Nick have such love for someone not even his own biological child? Borah's attitude toward her made much more sense to me. He only saw her when Mamie came for her from time to time, if Nick were out, or out of town. When she didn't, then the Coolidges would send a driver for her to visit at the White House. I never minded that, though, because I knew Grace never had a little girl to spoil and my Paulina was a healing balm to the great loss of her son. On the fringes of her day, when my daughter woke, and when she had to go to bed, I got to be her mother. Honestly, those times were enough for me.

In the fall, however, the Washington Conservatory of Music was having a concert. My dear friend Portia was bringing one of her choirs to Washington, DC, and I would be able to go and hear that marvelous music that she had introduced to me in New England all those years ago. How proud I was of her as she circulated that music instead of the other tunes that I'd wanted her to play. More than twenty years had gone by in our friendship, but I was ever grateful for her patience as time and good sense caught up with me.

The concert was on a Sunday afternoon, so on Sunday evening, I brought Portia and Fannie back to my home for dinner. Since Nick was there, Paulina was there and when she saw them and I introduced them as my friends, her eyes went wide. Fannie, bless her, made quick friends with Paulina and she, in turn, was enamored of Fannie, who was quite the little mother to her. Bless Fannie. When I was that age, I had no patience for children, but she showed her several games and sang songs to her.

Once we were finished with a dessert of sponge cake, Portia and I went to the parlor while Nick retired to another part of the house, and we watched our daughters play. "They might get to be good friends as we are," I said to Portia, and she turned to face me.

"Maybe. But things will be different for Fannie than for your Paulina. Very different."

"What do you mean?"

She turned her lovely brown face to me and I could see that her eyelids blinked in a rapid way. "I'm going to leave him. Sid."

I put a hand to my mouth. "You are? Why?"

"It's too much. He's never liked Fannie. Once, he . . ." She turned away and looked at our daughters playing on the piano in the corner. "He hit her. I think that he caused her mind some injury."

A father? Hit his daughter? I scarce could imagine such a thing, after having been ignored by my own for so long.

Portia reached for my hand. "It's the way he looks at her sometimes. The way that he used to look at me. I'm afraid to leave her alone with him. Before we left for our trip, he made a big fuss about how some of the men in the choir would seek to have their way with her behind my back. I told him that I would keep very close tabs on her the entire time, but that was of no comfort to him. We had a huge argument."

Now the tears were flowing down her face. "I packed us a little extra and when the choir returns tomorrow, we are going on the train to Tuskegee."

"Why would you return there? Both your father and stepmother are dead. Your brothers don't live there anymore."

Portia bowed her head. "I don't know. I don't know where else to go. Our Fairmount Heights house here is rented to others. Tuskegee is home. I'm hoping I can get some teaching or directing work there if I throw myself on Dr. Moton's mercy. There is a school there for Fannie as well, where she might be able to become a teacher." She wiped her face with a handkerchief.

"All that work that you've done in Dallas." I tried to imagine having to pick up and go elsewhere, as I had to when we were banished to Ohio. Never. Again.

"He's gone crazy, doing less architecture, and instead writing some crazy newspaper about how Black men have been wronged. People in Dallas just look at him as if he's fresh from the loony bin. Then he accuses them of trying to destroy him. Other Black people." She shook her head, and her wavy hair, which was still long, shook too. "I just cannot be with him anymore."

"I'm so sorry to hear this. It won't be easy being a divorced woman in society."

Her hand slipped away from mine. "I'm not in society, Alice. That won't be a problem for me. I just need to make sure that Fannie finishes her schooling and she finds a good man to take care of her."

I nodded. I hoped the same for Paulina, even if that were years in the future.

"Why not come back to Washington, DC?"

"Maybe I will. One day. But for now"—she sniffed into her handkerchief—"it's too painful. Too much of a reminder when everything was new and fresh and possible."

"I see. But you know that you are always welcome, right?"

She tipped her head to the side and smiled. "I do. And I appreciate that so much. Thank you."

Now I was the one who took her hand and squeezed it. "We

motherless children must stick together, Portia. For the sake of our daughters."

She turned around, smiling for the first time since she had come there, and we sat in the positions that our mothers never got to be in, watching our daughters, laughing and carefree, as Fannie played "Old McDonald" on the piano.

They had so much more than we did and I, for one, was happy about that.

Portia

1930

When I reached into my mailbox, I pulled out a letter with a Dallas stamp and Sid's handwriting on it.

Well, this was just about the last thing I wanted to see.

My life had been peaceful, teaching at Tuskegee; even though there were those who had arrived on campus who did not like the ways I approached the teaching of our songs, they remembered who I was and deferred accordingly. My father would have been proud of this Tuskegee, still in the mission of educating the people of our race for service, but also expanding to include educating those of the professional class. That's what he always wanted for our people, no matter what Dr. DuBois had suggested. My father wanted gradual development in our professional class, and I was happy that Dr. Moton had taken the reins up to make that happen.

Margaret had passed on to join Father in 1925, leaving me truly alone with the new Tuskegee, but since my brothers had shown no inclination to taking up my father's work, I was determined to be the Washington on campus to attract the much-needed funds and attention to keep my father's work and dream alive.

But now, here was Sid, beckoning me to Dallas, a life I had left behind when I took Fannie and walked out back in 1928, when life was good.

Now, here he came, wishing to pull me back into his life just as I had sent Fannie on to school and I was free.

*These economic times have been hard on my newspaper.
I know you left because of Fannie and that was right for
you to do so. Maybe you can return to Texas and we
can live together to save on expenses. I hope you come
so we can be a family again.*

Typical Sid, to ignore that I had my work, and my school, to keep
me afloat. Still, our school Easter break was coming up. Fannie had
indicated that she wished to take her vacation with a friend, so it
freed me up to visit Sid. We were no longer a couple, but I needed
him to understand. Yes, our last bird had left the nest, but there
would be no reconciliation.

I MADE MY way to Dallas after the students had been released on their
vacations. Usually in such a circumstance, I would hire a hack or take
the streetcar to the address Sid had written from on the envelope. The
country's economic circumstances had taken a nose dive and some had
returned to wagons and mules for transportation. But when I disem-
barked from the train, obtained my bag, and made my way through
the station, I was surprised to see him there in the colored hallway.

"Sid, what are you doing here?"

Something of the polish had been knocked from him. He wore
overalls, not a suit, and the hat he took from his head was beaten
and weathered. The hair, usually slicked back and pomaded into
submission, looked dry and brittle. *Oh my.* "Portia. So glad to see
you. Let me take your grip."

How do you greet someone for whom you bore three children?
Someone who had made it his business to apply damage to your
body, your mind, your spirit, trying to ensure that you would not
or could not continue? I didn't know, so I just put the grip down
and he picked it up, so that I didn't have to touch him.

"You look really good, Portia. So glad to see you."

I said nothing. My unflattering assessment of his appearance would not have benefited anyone. I smiled a little thinking of the way my friend Mrs. Alice Longworth had twisted the old saying "If you can't say something nice, don't say anything at all" into "If you can't say something nice, come and sit by me." Bless her, I couldn't do it.

"You must be glad to see me, too, since you're smiling."

I stopped in that instant. He stopped, too. "What do you want from me? What?"

"I don't understand, Portia." His voice lowered and his face shifted, looking extremely pitiful to all who passed us.

I knew his tricks and his hangdog look. "What are you hoping to accomplish by having me come here?"

"Not a thing. Or maybe . . . I just thought, we could go back to us. You know, the way we were before the children, now they are all gone. We could be you and me, together."

My mind went back to that extraordinarily brief window before Willie had come and there was nothing great, good, or golden about it. "You mean when we were first in the unfinished Fairmount Heights house and I froze my behind off because it was November and there was no heat? That time?"

He shook his head. "That's not what I meant."

"Then what? Explain it to me."

"Why do you have to speak to me like this? Here? All in the street?"

"Because I'm not going anywhere where I would have to be alone with you. Where you can work your trickery, use kind words or a smooth way of speaking to get me to change my mind. I gave up an entire concert career for you. I had three of your children. I maintained your home for years, cooking, cleaning, working to help you to your architecture career, which you abandoned. Then you betrayed me by hurting my daughter, our only daughter. I don't even know why I'm here. I'm finished with it and with you."

Saying the words, it was true. I knew why I was there. I knew what to do. I had to finish what I had wanted to do two years ago. Our people had an old saying about how Negroes couldn't or wouldn't go to the courthouse if they didn't have to. The saying came about because of the time, bother, and expense of bringing white people and the government into the business of Negroes. I would make Sid see that just because I had not gone to a courthouse before or yet didn't mean that I was not willing to go.

Off to my left, there was an old man waiting with his mule and wagon—clearly a hirable hack. I took my grip from Sid and walked toward it, as if I had an appointment. Maybe I did.

"Where are you going, Portia?" Sid followed me.

The man driving the mule and wagon saw me approach, jumped down from his high sitting position, and moved to take the grip from my hand. He put it in the back, and greeting me cheerfully, handed me up to the high wagon platform to sit. He came around the other side, clambered up, and sat next to me, saying, "Where to, miss?"

"The Dallas County Courthouse." I made my voice sound out loud above the echoing clip-clops of the mule moving forward so that Sid could hear me.

I had driven behind many a mule in my life, but this mule started off faster than I thought, as if she understood I had a mission.

Sid came in behind the wagon and then moved around the side, trying to stop the mule from riding off, but he was not fast enough. Thankful for a moving mule, I left him in the street, shouting at me to come back to him.

The driver started humming a song, one of our songs, and I recognized the tune. It was one of those songs that had multiple meanings, because our ancestors would use it to help them plot their escape from bondage. He hummed, but I sang, in my ever-questionable alto, sing-shouting the words, with joy and pride thrumming through my veins:

Good news, chariot's coming
Good news, chariot's coming
Good news, chariot's coming
And I don't want it to leave me behind!

The driver joined in, and bless her, the mule clip-clopped me all the way to the Dallas County Courthouse, to my divorce papers and my freedom.

Leaving Sidney Pittman behind.

Author's Note

We are in a time of racial turmoil. Previously, people made pointed efforts to try to override the turmoil by making more social connections across racial lines. I think specifically of the late 1950s and early 1960s, when, due to the influence of the civil rights movements, the most segregated parts of United States society, schools and churches, spent a lot more time and effort in coming together to find common ground. My grandmother, who was a church worker, actually moved her church membership to a predominantly white Presbyterian church in Pittsburgh. That decision resulted in my growing up as a Black member of such a church without having much conscious thought about friendships between the races. I saw evidence of that all the time as I grew up.

However, as time went on, these conscious efforts to socially mix were withdrawn, and now we find ourselves back to our communities. This is borne out by the results of a 2015 Pew study where 81 percent of whites report they have no friends of a different race or ethnicity and 70 percent of Black people have no friends of a different ethnicity or race.

So it's very interesting to see that three historical fiction novels released within the past year have focused on famous interracial friendships. Two of them were cowritten by authors of different races. My effort, written solely by me, is the one that comes earliest, at the dawn of the twentieth century, at a time when interracial friendship seemed unimaginable. I guess that's why there was such a furor when, in 1901, newly sworn-in president Theodore Roosevelt thought to invite Booker T. Washington over for dinner without realizing that the country would explode at such a gesture. Some choose to look at the differences between these two men: one a son of great wealth and privilege and the other a formerly enslaved man who had endured great deprivation. However, I like to imagine these two statesmen commiserating at that dinner about what they had in common: the horrifying deaths of their young spouses, their great public successes at an early age, and their empathy with each other about the fates of their indulged eldest children, teenage daughters Alice and Portia, who were driving them both crazy, albeit for different reasons.

Since Alice and Portia were two young women of different races, their engagements with each other were not public and remain unknown to scholars. Indeed, the majority of the many biographies and historical fiction novels about the irrepressible Alice never mention Portia's name. A lot of my historical fiction novel is a reconstruction of my imaginings with the three texts that do make mention of the friendship: Stacy Cordery's biography of Alice Longworth, Roy Hill's biography of Portia Pittman, and Portia Washington Pittman's obituary published in the *Washington Post* in 1978.

Altogether, no more than a page exists that gives pointed reference to their relationship with each other. So it was up to me, a historical fiction author, to construct a narrative of what a secret interracial friendship might have looked like over the years. The fact that it was secret and unacknowledged for so long remains reflective of the state of interracial friendship in this country. My hopes are that in reading a reconstruction of their relationship, more of us might make the effort to understand what we have in common instead of keeping our relentless focus on how we differ. The details of a president's daughter's life are much better documented than that of a Black woman born in the Jim Crow South, even though Booker T. Washington was the most famous Black man of his day. I had to take some license with various dates and times.

I moved around Portia's break during her year at Wellesley so that she could come in contact with Sid Pittman at Tuskegee in late 1901. She later went back to Bradford College and graduated from there. There is no record of where Portia may have performed in Germany, so I placed her recital concert in Berlin at the Konzerthaus.

In spite of what Alice thought of the Longworths and Ohio, the family was an interesting one that deserves a historical fiction novel of its own. A lot of Nicholas Longworth's activities did not have to be created, and his philandering was an open secret in Washington, DC. I created the circumstances of how Nick and Alice almost miss the boat on what James Bradley called "the imperial cruise" in his book of the same name.

When the women's right to vote was commemorated upon its centenary in 2020, there was a lot of discussion about the women's suffrage march that took place on the eve of Woodrow Wilson's inauguration. Black women registered with the march but were coolly received by organizers Alice Paul and Lucy Burns. Some were even asked to march in the back, but many women, including Ida Wells-Barnett and Mary Church Terrell, marched with their state delegations. It's unclear if Portia Pittman, saddled with three young children at that time, would have marched, but for me, it was the perfect opportunity for the two to come together, so I had her join her friend Alice Longworth in the place were Portia would have marched, in the teachers' unit. Alice Longworth is known to have participated in the march.

Dr. Halle Tanner Dillon Johnson was, I imagine, an important role model for Portia growing up. A young widow who went back to medical school at the Women's Medical College in Philadelphia,

Dr. Johnson was hired by Booker T. Washington as a much-needed physician on Tuskegee's campus. She ultimately married a fellow instructor but, sadly, died in 1901 in childbirth. I imagine that the death of her childhood doctor from a cause similar to her mother's weighed heavily on Portia's mind when she met Alice, someone else who lost her mother from the consequences of childbirth.

I sent Willie Pittman to Howard a few years early to give Portia and Alice a chance to see each other in Washington, DC. He was ultimately a graduate of that proud HBCU (Historically Black Colleges and Universities), instead of Tuskegee, something I've always thought was very interesting.

William S. Pittman was the first Black graduate at the Drexel Institute of Art, Science, and Industry. They have a graduation ceremony for Black students named after him to this day. A few of the buildings he designed are still in existence in Dallas and Washington, DC, but the house he built for Portia and his family is not.

Portia was pregnant with Willie and not Booker when she had her recital in Washington, DC. She began her teaching career in 1925, and I also moved Portia's choral triumph a few years forward. Her triumph happened in 1927.

Portia Pittman appears twice in the 1930 census. When I saw the first listing, she was in Dallas, living with Sid. I screamed, but as it turns out, she is also listed as a conductor of the choir at Tuskegee. I think Sid, not believing that she would be brave enough to leave him, must have registered her as living with him in Dallas, as his "wife," when she had left him years before that. The subsequent census records of 1940 and 1950 show the Pittmans as divorced. Portia did indeed go to the courthouse to obtain her legal liberation, at a time when Black people, because of the expense and trouble, might not have bothered.

Some of the many texts I used to research
the lives of these fascinating women:

Nicholas Longworth by Donald C. Bacon and Anthony M. Champagne

The Imperial Cruise by James Bradley

The Roosevelt Women by Betty Boyd Caroli

Alice by Stacy A. Cordery

Guest of Honor by Deborah Davis

The Making of Nicholas Longworth by Clara Longworth de Chambrun

Booker T. Washington, volumes I and II, by Louis R. Harlan

Booker T's Child by Roy L. Hill

Theodore Roosevelt trilogy by Edmund Morris

Hissing Cousins by Marc Peyser and Timothy Dwyer

Crowded Hours by Alice Roosevelt Longworth

Mrs. L by Alice Roosevelt Longworth and Michael Teague

Booker T. Washington by Emmett Scott

Portia by Ruth Ann Stewart

A few interesting websites:

Women's suffrage march: https://www.nps.gov/articles/woman
    -suffrage-procession1913.htm

Portia Pittman biography: https://www.tshaonline.org/handbook
    /entries/pittman-portia-marshall-washington

William Sidney Pittman article: https://www.dmagazine.com
    /publications/d-ceo/2020/december/early-influences-william
    -sidney-pittman-was-a-pioneer-for-black-architects/

Acknowledgments

I'm always grateful to my agent, Emily Sylvan Kim, and my editor, Tessa Woodward. I needed some extra time to finish this one due to the loss of my sister, and they gave it to me. I appreciate the support.

Authors of historical fiction often have a difficult time with copy editors, but I do appreciate the efforts of the copy editor on this book, Laurie McGee. Thank you.

I'm so thankful for the words of encouragement and gestures of support for my work from my cousin, Maria Searcy. Thank you, cousin!

I'm also grateful for the support of my aunt and uncle, Jean and Johnnie Comer. It's been a hard road over these past few years, but I'm glad that you are in my corner. Thank you.

Thank you to the readers—all of those who have continued to support, uplift, and spread this different view of history in this tumultuous time. Thank you so much for opening your hearts and minds to seeing the lives of those whose historical viewpoint has been silenced. Please know I will never take your support for granted.

About the Author

PIPER HUGULEY is the author of *By Her Own Design* as well as the Home to Milford College and the Migrations of the Heart series. She is a multiple-time Golden Heart finalist. Piper blogs about the history behind her novels on her website, piperhuguley.com. She lives in Atlanta, Georgia, with her husband and son.

DISCOVER MORE BY
PIPER HUGULEY

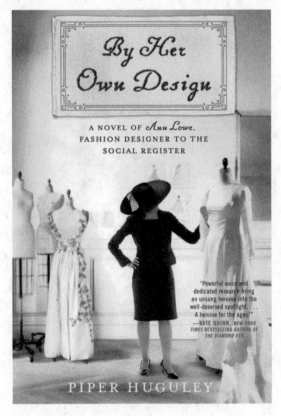

BY HER OWN DESIGN

The incredible untold story of how Ann Lowe, a Black woman and granddaughter of slaves, rose above personal struggles and racial prejudice to design and create one of America's most famous wedding dresses of all time for Jackie Kennedy.